# A DRAGON IN THE ASHES

### BOOK 3 OF
### IN THE DEN OF THE ENGLISH LION

## BY NEAL ROBERTS

**FREE DOWNLOAD**

Sign up for Neal's newsletter (bitly.com/FreeHistorical)
or visit www.authornealroberts.com and journey for free to
England's shores in 1558 with young Menachem in the exclusive
series prequel scene, *Escape.*

# ACKNOWLEDGMENTS

First and foremost, to my good friend and correspondent Brenda James, who alone deciphered the code in the dedication to Shakespeare's sonnets and who, together with William Rubinstein, began the long and arduous—but fascinating—task of introducing the true bard to the world. To a new friend and foremost investigator of the true bard, Dr. John Casson, co-author of the compelling new book *Sir Henry Neville Was Shakespeare: The Evidence.*

I'd also like to extend my heartfelt thanks to my treasured wife Myra, to Gigi, to the ever supportive and lovely Jennifer Nagler, Uncle Jack, the Donovans, Good Cousin Barbara (think screenplay), Nadine Rabinowitz (who first brought Mrs. James's work to my attention), Mom and her friend George, my wife's mother Lily, and all the other relatives and friends who've lent their time, and their moral and literary advice and support to this project. To Dr. Jeffrey Laitman for his advice concerning the many physical problems suffered by little people; any mistakes are solely my own.

To my editor, Martin Jones, I extend my sincerest thanks. To my ever-faithful reader and proofreader Laurel Busch. To my publicist Samantha Williams of Aurora Publicity, for her continuing Herculean efforts in dragging the recalcitrant niche of historical fiction into the 21st century, and to her associate, the world's most patient up-and-coming cover designer, Melody Barber.

Finally, many thanks to my good friend, the talented photographer Jeffrey Loeser, who took the photo appearing on the back cover of this book, and in so doing accomplished the extraordinary task of making me look presentable.

*To Myra, Adam, Gigi, Mom,*
*the rest of my extended family, and*
*Hicksville Comets '68 – '71*

# PRINCIPAL PERSONS OF THE STORY

ELIZABETH, BY THE GRACE OF GOD, QUEEN OF ENGLAND,
FRANCE, AND IRELAND

NOAH AMES, barrister, advisor to HM

MARIE AMES, his wife by remarriage

JESSICA, LADY BURLINGTON, his daughter

JONATHAN HAWKING, BARON SAINT IVES, his
son-in-law

ARTHUR ARDEN, barrister, his friend

ANDRES SALAZAR, barrister, his friend

YETTA, his friend and benefactor

ESTHER, his cousin

NAOMI ENGLISH, his mother

DAVID ENGLISH, his father

SIR HENRY NEVILLE, HM Ambassador to
France

DAVID "CHEERFUL" KILLIGREW, his wife's
nephew

GARDNER, Senior Yeoman of the Guard

FRANCIS, Yeoman of the Guard

CHESTER, Jailer of Cambridge Castle

GASTON DORSAY, resident of Drury House

FRENCHWOMAN, his common-law wife

CLAUDE "MONK" DORSAY, his servant

PAOLO NEREZZA, his friend, resident of
Drury House

BARNABY BELL, Steward of Burghley House

FRIDESWIDE BELL, his wife

BARBARA BELL, his daughter

THOMAS, LORD GREY

CHARLES PERCY, knight

JOSCELINE PERCY, knight, his brother

## The Cecil Faction

ROBERT CECIL, LORD KEEPER OF THE PRIVY
SEAL, Secretary of State

WALTER RALEIGH, knight, Captain of the
Yeoman Warders

## The Essex Faction

ROBERT DEVEREUX, EARL OF ESSEX

GELLY MEYRICK, his principal attendant

NICHOLAS SKERES, his servant

ROBERT POLEY, his servant

HENRY CUFFE, his secretary

HENRY WRIOTHESELEY, EARL OF
SOUTHAMPTON, friend to the Earl of
Essex

CUTHBERT BENNETT, barrister

TOBIAS BENNETT, barrister, his identical
twin

# PROLOGUE

**AS NAOMI THE** milkmaid finishes her morning delivery to the queen's town home and turns to go, she finds her way blocked by a platoon of soldiers carrying a terrified old woman securely bound to a makeshift ladder of twine and kindling. The woman is so near to her that Naomi can see she's praying intensely, despite the jostling.

The soldiers reach the woodpile assembled in the town square and clumsily insert the ladder's feet into two post holes, bringing the ladder and the old woman erect with a jolt. An eager crowd gathers under the lowering sky, evidently enthralled by the prospect of watching this old woman shriek, die, and burn to ash.

Naomi fervently hopes that this does not mark a resumption of the burning of Jews, that barbaric practice long prohibited by Good King Sigismund the Old. She shudders to contemplate the possibility that, unbeknownst to her, the king may have died, leaving her and all the other Jews of her village unshielded from the Inquisition. She takes a cautious step toward the woman to discern whether she's praying in Latin or Hebrew, but cannot hear her words.

Naomi turns around and spies Queen Bona standing on her ceremonial balcony, wringing her hands. Beside her stands a man cloaked in official-looking robes, his complexion dark like a Spaniard's. By his serene expression, he is accustomed to such horrid "acts of faith," as the Christians call them.

She curtsies, catching the queen's eye, but instead of her customary reward of a reginal smile, she receives a glimpse into the soul of a woman consumed by remorse for an atrocity about to be committed in her name.

The pretty milkmaid is horrified to see that she has also caught the unwelcome eye of someone else on the balcony: the queen's youngest attendant, a tall, swarthy, sharp-eyed youth about her own age. He gazes at her, evidently oblivious to the queen and the Spanish ambassador beside him, and uncaring of the atrocity taking place in the square. Although he cannot help but realize that Naomi has caught him looking, the lout lacks the grace to turn away. Instead, his gaze becomes a leer, a sickening mixture of desire and contempt that makes Naomi's skin crawl. She shivers and turns away.

A handsome young Jew approaches her from a distance. Although it takes her an extra moment, as his expression is unusually grave, she recognizes him as David from the village.

He sidles up to her. "You appear to have caught the eye of the queen's boy." He's chosen to speak in English, evidently to avoid being understood by the surrounding rabble. As David's family, like Naomi's, was deported from England, their families continue to speak English in their homes.

"What do you know of the queen's boy?" Naomi asks.

"He's a sly little shit, from what I've heard." David points with his chin to the woman about to die. "Do you know *this* poor soul, my beauty?"

"No," she replies, ignoring his ill-timed flirtation.

"Her name is Katarzyna Weiglowa."

"A Jew?" she asks.

He shrugs. "It depends upon whom you ask. She was born a papist, and professes to be one still. But, if you'd ever spoken with her, as I have, you'd know that her beliefs are quite the same as ours. She denies the papist doctrines of the trinity of God and the divinity of Jesus."

"But she's never converted?"

"No. Instead, she's foolishly insisted on promoting her beliefs to other papists, a crime known as 'Judaizing.'" David shakes his head. "Our rabbi would never help her to convert. You know what rabbis do when a gentile asks to convert, don't you?"

"No."

"They slam the door, literally. Makes sense, too. We Jews are left alone only because we *don't* try to persuade others of our faith. If we were seen to proselytize as gentiles do, we'd be wiped out without a second thought."

Naomi shivers to think how susceptible her people are to the vagaries of public sentiment.

The crowd murmurs louder as a long, somber train of chanting priests emerges from the church and begins its doleful, inexorable procession toward its victim. The priest at the forefront is dark and unfamiliar, vaguely resembling the man on the queen's balcony.

"I don't believe I've seen that priest before," says Naomi.

"And let's hope we never see him again," David replies. "He's an Inquisitor … from Spain. Here to purify the faith."

She frowns. "I've never taken Queen Bona for a religious fanatic."

David shakes his head. "She has no say in the matter. This poor wretch has been condemned as an apostate by the Archbishop of Krakow."

The Inquisitor stops the train near enough to be heard by the victim and the crowd, but far enough to avoid being scorched by the coming pyre. "Do you, Katarzyna Weiglowa," he shouts, "believe in God's only Son, our Lord Jesus Christ?"

The old woman stops her praying long enough to respond. "God had neither wife nor son, nor does He need this, for only mortals need sons. We are His children … and all who walk in His ways are His children."

The Inquisitor ignores the reply, and demands again, "Do you, Katarzyna Weiglowa, believe in God's only Son, our Lord Jesus Christ?"

A bolt of lightning splits the sky, and thunder rumbles across the square. Naomi expects that the threat of a dousing rain will cause the Inquisitor to hasten completion of his heavenly task, dependent as it is upon the earthly expedient of a dry woodpile.

Naomi is unnerved to find that she's now become the object of the serene gaze of the old woman about to die. "God had neither wife nor son …" pronounces the old woman, repeating her previous response.

But Naomi finds she can no longer hear the woman's words. Instead, she hears her *thoughts*, as though the woman has taken up residence inside her head.

"Leave this kingdom with your husband and never return, or *he* will kill you," pleads the old woman urgently. "Keep your child safe, my beauty! *Go now!*"

*He?* Jolted by the old woman's incursion into the innermost precincts of her mind, Naomi assures herself that she has nothing to fear. She must have *imagined* the old woman's voice. At the very least, she must have *misunderstood* it. Naomi is but eleven years old, after all, and unwed. Although she's daydreamed about marrying David (and has caught him secretly admiring her more than once), they're little more than children. And at present she has no child to keep safe.

She recalls her mother saying that those about to die are given the gift of prophecy, and her eyes go wide. She recoils, and steps back hard into David.

"What's wrong?" he asks, lifting her weight off his toes.

"She … she *spoke* to me," Naomi replies fearfully.

David regards her skeptically. "She was speaking to everyone, Naomi. She was just *looking* at you."

"No, David. She spoke to *me* … in … in my mind." She's flustered by David's incomprehension. "Oh, let's get away from here!" She turns on her heel and flees the impending horror, plowing her way through the crowd just as the first twigs burst into flames behind her. She shoves her way past a rowdy group of young men, and drops her milk pail. Though it clatters to the ground, she fails to notice.

So many urgent questions race through her mind. But one thing she feels no doubt about is just whom the old woman meant by "he," the one who would kill her and her future husband. She glances up at the balcony where the hideous queen's boy continues to leer at her, and lunges away in a stumbling run.

David picks up the pail and runs after her, amazed.

Though the rains of heaven arrive too late to save the old woman from immolation, they rapidly disperse the crowd. The blackened corpse hisses and steams in the sudden downpour.

As Queen Bona's attention is too fixed on the horror to notice the rain, the Spaniard unctuously interrupts her dark reverie. "Shall we leave the balcony and go inside, Your Highness?"

She allows the boy attendant to lead her by the hand to the parlor, where she assumes the seat that customarily serves as a substitute for her throne. She whispers something in his ear. He nods respectfully, disappears from view, and soon returns with a scroll bound by a simple blue ribbon. She accepts it and places it on a table beside her. The Spaniard bows respectfully.

After a thoughtful silence, the queen addresses him with conviction. "That is the last barbarous act of faith that will take place in this realm, Master Ambassador, unless His Holiness himself comes from Rome to officiate. Upon your return to Spain, please advise King Charles that no Inquisitors, Spanish or otherwise, will again be permitted to perform such acts in Poland."

"I am your obedient servant, madam, and shall pass your wishes along to His Highness."

The queen nods. "Now that this ... business is out of the way, we can address the Spanish Crown's request that I lend the money needed to purchase a parcel of my local property."

The ambassador bows and draws a sealed scroll in a red ribbon from his robe. "I thank you for broaching the subject, madam. King Charles has instructed me to assure you that I am his plenipotentiary for purposes of negotiating and sealing the bargain." He hands her the scroll, which she opens and reads. "As you can see," he says before she's finished, "I've been given final say in negotiating terms on His Highness's behalf."

She nods. "The paper is in order, Master Ambassador." She hands him back the scroll, and opens the one brought to her by the boy. "But I doubt there will be further negotiation." She points to some writing on the paper. "As you can see, King Charles and I have already agreed upon the size and location of the property, as well as its price."

The ambassador reads the writing indicated by Queen Bona, and nods in agreement. She returns the scroll to the boy, who rolls it up and ties the blue ribbon around it.

"Your Highness," says the ambassador, "I am led to understand that the property is presently occupied by a village of ..." his mouth purses in genteel disgust, "... *Jews*. Is this so, madam?"

Queen Bona sighs. "King Charles and I have already agreed that management of the property will remain subject to my sole discretion." She sees that her answer has not satisfied the ambassador. "The Jews are tenants only," she assures him. "They pay their way, and I have no intention of evicting them so long as they continue to do so."

The ambassador smiles unctuously. "Then I assume Your Highness will have the necessary deed drawn up?"

She raises an eyebrow. "The deed and *mortgage,* you mean."

"*Mortgage*, madam? Surely the Holy Roman Emperor is as good as his word?"

She smiles. "Of course he is. Yet, it never hurts to have these things in writing."

"His Highness has forbidden me," says the ambassador, "to execute any loan document that will be recorded in a public place." As the queen regards him askance, he buttresses his point. "It would be imprudent to inform all the world of business affairs between crowned heads. I hope you will agree."

She weighs his words. "I will keep the mortgage in my personal possession, and produce it only if Spain defaults in payment, or His Highness passes away. Please advise His Highness that, although I trust him implicitly to refrain from trying to sell the property unburdened by my mortgage, I have no such assurance that his eventual successor will feel so bound."

The ambassador persists. "But King Charles's heir apparent is *Prince Philip*! Although Philip is yet but a boy, his cleverness and handsome figure are already renowned throughout Europe. And, of course, he has very great expectations, madam, *ample* for this purpose. I expect Your Highness will have no problem in obtaining repayment should King Charles ... no longer rule. Please, madam, let us dispense with this commoner's notion of a … *mortgage*." He pronounces this last word with practiced contempt.

She equivocates, then decides on a middle ground. "I will produce the mortgage only if Spain defaults in payment, or if both His Highness *and* Prince Philip have passed away. Would that be satisfactory?"

The ambassador makes a show of equivocating.

She frowns. "Take it or leave it," she says in a grave monotone.

The ambassador bows again. "Very well, madam. You drive a hard bargain. But we shall take it."

She finds something about the ambassador's concern to be unsettling. Why should King Charles care if the mortgage is publicly recorded and available for public perusal? It occurs to her only in passing that, according to the bargain she has just struck, the king and his successor are assured that there will be only one record of the mortgage's existence … and it will be stowed in her closet.

"Very well," says the queen, "I shall have the papers drawn." She turns to the swarthy boy. "Show the ambassador to the door."

The ambassador bows, and follows the boy through several hallways and down a staircase to the street level. Before the boy opens the door, the ambassador glances about. When he's confirmed they are alone, he hands the boy a bag of gold coins and addresses him in quiet, familiar fashion.

"The Holy Roman Emperor, King Charles, instructs you, once the mortgage is signed, to report its location to me, and *only* me. Each time it is moved, you are to tell me precisely where it is located."

The boy bows silently and remains in that position until the ambassador places his hands on his shoulders and recites the expected blessing.

The ambassador brings the boy's chin up and looks him straight in the eye. "You are truly one of the faithful. And, as I've promised you," he says, "His Holiness of Rome shall surely learn of your good works, and you shall have his blessings, as well."

The boy nods and, without a word or change of expression, lets the ambassador out, discreetly pockets the pouch, and returns to his duties.

# CHAPTER 1

TOWER OF LONDON
MID-JUNE 1600

**IN A LARGE KITCHEN** housed in a cottage on the Tower grounds, Noah Ames sips a pint of ale at a rustic dining board commonly used by members of the Tower staff and their visitors. Also at table are Senior Yeoman Gardner and his assistant Francis.

Kitchen servants scurry about the ovens and cabinets, preparing late-afternoon coffee to take place at the royal residence across the courtyard. Two wheeled tables are being laden with confections, biscuits, and coffee. One is already half-filled with a fine assortment of pastries that fills the whole kitchen with a heavenly aroma.

Those at table have already begun their first course oblivious to the bustle around them when Andres Salazar, a young barrister and longtime friend of Noah from Gray's Inn, leads a fresh breeze through the front door.

"Welcome, my young friend!" says Noah, rising.

Andres acknowledges the greeting with a jovial bow and closes the door behind him, stopping the breeze that followed him in. "Good evening, gentlemen." He glances about. "But where is Francis Bacon?"

Noah replies. "I believe Francis is taking his coffee in the royal residence ... with the important people. But won't you join us chickens? We'll be enjoying the same fare—just a few minutes earlier." As an afterthought, Noah turns apologetically to Goodwife Barry, who is head of the kitchen, and adds, "except for desserts and coffee, which shall be served only *after* Her Majesty and her guests have quite finished."

Goodwife Barry curtsies her approval.

Andres removes his cap and hangs it from a peg by the door. "Don't mind if I do," he mutters with a smile, pouring himself a full cup of ale. "It's nearly dark outside. Excepting Francis Bacon, is our party complete?"

"We still await my new son-in-law, Lord Saint Ives," replies Noah, "who advised me he might be detained at Westminster. He's expected at any moment, but insisted we begin in his absence."

"How thoughtful of his lordship!" replies Andres sardonically, no doubt recalling those days, mere months ago, when Lord Saint Ives was "Master Hawking," just another barrister residing at Gray's. He arches an eyebrow. "And Smythe?"

Goodman Gardner smiles reassuringly. "The Queen's taster is always nearby with an appetite, master. Never you worry." It's one of Gardner's many jobs to ensure that no food or drink can enter the royal residence without first being sampled by Smythe.

"Andres," says Noah, "I was just regaling the assembled with a few memories of the 'Night of Errors' at Gray's Inn. I believe it was the twenty-eighth of December 1594. Is that not correct?"

Andres sighs. "People never seem to tire of hearing about that botched performance of *The Comedy of Errors*. Still, I suppose it's noteworthy, as Shakespeare wrote it to be debuted on that occasion."

Gardner scratches his head. "I remember that night, hearin' all the rumors of the uproar at Gray's Inn." He cocks his head curiously. "But wasn't Shakespeare ten miles away, at Greenwich Palace?" He knits his brow as though searching his memory. "He was performin' for the Queen with the Lord Chamberlain's Men." He nods with certainty. "Yeh, I saw 'im there."

Noah replies. "Yes, he was with his troupe that night, Goodman Gardner. You have quite the memory!"

Gardner preens at the compliment and cocks his head. "Don't it seem strange to you two gentlemen that Master Shakespeare would plan on missin' a debut of his own play?"

Noah shrugs. "Such are the demands of the player's trade, I suppose. Anyhow, Andres, I was explaining how the *dramatis personae* called for two sets of young, male identical twins."

Andres smiles with chagrin. "Hard to come by, those are."

"Aren't they, though?" muses Noah. "Yes, and none was available for that performance. In fact, the supposed identical twins looked nothing alike. Now, perhaps some of you already know this, but the Master of the Revels has no jurisdiction to oversee performances at Gray's Inn, which are considered 'private.' So, the Inn elects one of its members as 'monarch' to oversee the performance. The 'monarch' is supposed to refrain from strong drink throughout the evening, so that he may remedy any infractions."

"That's always been hopeless," Andres chimes in. "No one's sober there during Christmas revels."

Noah nods. "True. And the rules say that the 'monarch' may not be denied access to any place on the grounds. That night, true to form, he got rip-roaring drunk." He strives in vain to recall something. "What name did the monarch rule by that night, Andres? Do you recall?"

Andres puts down his flagon, smiling ear to ear. "Queen Henry!" he blurts out, to general mirth. "And, like Henri the Third of France, by then deceased, he attired himself in women's clothing … which I'm quite sure is condemned as abomination somewhere in the Bible."

Noah nods again. "As 'Queen Henry' was blind drunk, and subject to no restraint, he stumbled onto the stage late in the performance, just at the point where two of the twins realize that their faces are identical. And—while the twins spoke to each other in tones of wonderment—'Queen Henry' staggered between them and began chatting with them, heedless of the audience."

Already smiling, Francis asks: "What'd he say?"

Andres struggles to recall. "It was hard to make out his precise words, as they were slurred and the collar of his royal 'frock' had ridden up over his mouth, but he said something like this." He imitates a drunkard's speech. "'Are you two blokes supposed to resemble one another?' As these were not lines from the play, the players didn't answer, of course. 'Because,' says Queen Henry, 'you look like different species of animal!' The players stood there stunned, but the audience laughed, apparently thinking it part of the performance, until—" He suppresses a laugh.

"Until what, Master Salazar?" asks Francis.

"Until Queen Henry passed out cold onstage, and pissed himself." This sets the table on a roar. Andres waits for it to die down. "Before he could be carted away, he'd left a puddle for everyone else to slip on, which they ended up doing, of course."

Smythe the taster enters and leans heavily up against a stove, looking stout, but quite pale.

Gardner sees him first. "Feeling better, Smythe?"

"Truth be told, Goodman Gardner, I've felt better. This bellyache's been with me two full days now. I think I been eatin' too much o' that rich food. Oh, the *sacrifices* I make for queen and country!" This is met by groans, and hoots of derision. Smythe replies indignantly. "Oh? Would any o' *you* gentlemen like to take me place as Queen's taster?"

Noah answers. "No, thank you, Goodman Smythe. Our positions are quite precarious enough as it is. None of us would wish to assume yours, as well."

"Thought not," sniffs Smythe. He surveys one of the wheeled carts, carefully selects two biscuits, sticks them both in his mouth, and fills a china cup from an urn of fresh coffee, artfully lifting the cup and saucer from the loaded cart just as it's being rolled away. The cart clatters out through the servant's entrance toward the royal residence, and the door closes behind it, once again cutting off the fresh wind. Smythe sulks and holds his aching belly, but dutifully munches Her Majesty's biscuits.

The front door swings open again. Jonathan Hawking cuts a fine figure in black as he strides in and firmly snaps the door shut behind him. The assembled rise, and he waves them back to their seats, clearly mindful that, although he's just been created Baron Saint Ives, he learned the practice of law right beside Andres at Gray's Inn.

"Good e'en, m'lord," says Noah. "How is my lovely daughter, Lady Saint Ives?"

As Jonathan prepares to respond with a quip, suddenly his face grows unaccountably stern. "What's that *odor?*" he demands of no one in particular. His eyes dart about suspiciously, but he stands stock still, as if listening for a sound just beneath audibility.

Goodwife Barry wipes her hands on her apron with a look of concern. "*What* odor, Master Hawking? Is it unpleasant? Her Majesty would be most cross—"

Jonathan silences her with a raised hand. "Are there ... *almonds* in the food?" he demands.

She gives the question a moment's thought, and shakes her head. "No almonds." She smiles knowingly. "But there's *hazelnut* in the coffee. You're prob'ly just nosin' *that*, m'lord."

Jonathan shakes his head emphatically and his eyes sharpen. He sniffs about suspiciously, heedless that he has not so much as acknowledged his fellows.

For a moment, time seems to grind to a halt, and nothing is heard but the sound of water boiling in a pot on the stove.

The silence is broken by a deafening clatter, as Smythe, looking confused, drops his cup and saucer to the floor, and steadies himself woozily against the stove.

Gardner shoots to his feet, inadvertently upsetting the table.

Everyone else is immobilized by shock, except Jonathan, who runs to the remaining coffee urn and removes the lid. He lowers his face gingerly toward the steaming brew, and stands erect, shouting in alarm.

"*Where is the Queen?*"

"*What is it?*" says Gardner.

"The coffee!" shouts Jonathan. "It's been *poisoned!*"

Smythe seems unable to steady himself any longer, and collapses backwards in a heap, taking with him cutlery and plates that clatter and shatter on the stone floor. His unseeing eyes stare at the ceiling, wide with fear. He stops moving.

Goodwife Barry raises her hands to her face and cries out in dismay. Each member of the kitchen staff drops whatever he's holding, as though it were contaminated.

Francis, first to regain his wits, springs into action. With Noah and Jonathan hard on his heels, he races to the door by which the dessert cart passed moments earlier on its way to the royal residence. Smashing through the door, Francis inadvertently shoulders its full weight, ripping it off its hinges, knocking it flat to the hard ground, and injuring himself in the process. He falls onto his back and writhes, his eyes bulging in agony, gasping for air, clutching his broken shoulder with his opposite hand.

Noah and Jonathan take the lead. As neither knows the staff's customary route from the kitchen to the royal residence, they take the shortest way they know, which requires them to climb an exterior flight of stairs, run the full length of a corridor, and descend again to the ground floor. Noah prays that the reason no one is behind them is that the others have taken a more direct route.

They bound up the stairs two at a time, and sprint along the upstairs hallway shouting: "Majesty! Majesty!"

Hurtling down the final flight of stairs, they shout louder, but their pleas are ever more despairing. At last, Noah swings open the door and charges through the doorway, where he halts.

Fine guests mill about serenely in their light summer clothing. No one has yet taken a seat. Noah's eye quickly traverses the crowded room to the Queen, who stands at the far end of the long central table, her face turned toward Francis Bacon, with whom she appears deep in conversation. From her profile, Noah can see that she holds a coffee cup and saucer, and is raising the poisoned cup to her lips.

"*Majesty, do not drink!*" cries Noah.

But, at the same moment, Jonathan shouts different words to the same end, and the result is incomprehensible.

The Queen seems instinctively to prepare to take a small sip before turning toward the noise. Seeing this, Noah hurls himself across the table, sending plates and cutlery crashing to the floor, his momentum proving sufficient to take him only halfway to the opposite side. As he slides to a halt in the very middle of the table, the crowd gasps at his splayed form. Although he could not have reached the Queen in time to prevent her taking a sip, the resulting disturbance has succeeded in gaining her immediate attention.

Queen Elizabeth lowers the cup from her lips, places it carefully onto the saucer, then turns toward Noah in utter shock, her mouth slightly ajar, her eyes agog at this tumultuous interruption by a seasoned barrister and a baron.

The crowd observes Noah silently as he crawls the remainder of the way across the table toward the Queen, lowers himself off the side, and kneels before her like a supplicant with his palms upturned.

The Queen looks down at her long-time counsel, whose face is now flushed and bathed in sweat, and whose robes are torn and lie askew on his frame. Noah returns her gaze and speaks as calmly as he can. "Majesty, would you be so kind as to favor me with your cup and saucer … if you please?"

As the Queen's eyes move from Noah to Jonathan and back again, she evidently realizes that she's very likely been saved from an agonizing death by poisoning. She nods, but before attending to the cup and saucer, she smooths Noah's hair as well as can be done without a comb and replies, equally calmly.

"*Certainly,* Serjeant Ames. Please sit down in this chair, if you would." Without taking his eyes from the cup and saucer for a moment, Noah drops woozily into the proffered chair.

The Queen places her poisoned cup in its saucer on the table before him. "Serjeant Ames, you seem to have impaled your shoulder on a *fourchette.*" With every eye in the room on the Queen, she deftly tugs the fork out of Noah's shoulder and stanches the wound with a clean white serviette. Two ladies swoon, only to be caught by their husbands. The Queen takes Noah's other hand, places it firmly over the serviette, which is beginning to turn red with blood, and presses tightly. She leans into him and whispers privately. "Sit quietly, and hold that to the wound until the surgeon arrives."

Behind the Queen, a door flings open. Gardner and Andres forge through, followed by six burly guardsmen, their sharp weapons clanking as they enter. Quickly sizing up the situation, Gardner shouts. "Yeomen! Form a perimeter about Her Majesty, Lord Robert, and Master Bacon! All others, stand aside and *do not eat or drink* on peril of your lives!"

Goodman Gardner and Andres bow to the Queen. The visitors timidly step forward and place their cutlery and china among the demolished table settings, then step backward and bow low.

Noah, though swooning, stands and grabs Gardner by the shoulder. "You have to—" The world starts to go white. Gardner hugs him with one arm to prevent a fall. Noah takes a deep breath, and the color tentatively returns to the world. "The odor is still strong," whispers Noah. "Get her out of the room. As long as it can be smelled, it's *poisoning* her."

Gardner's eyes go wide, and he nods. "Your Majesty, Lord Robert, Master Bacon, and the other ladies and gentlemen, please follow me out this door at once. Baron Saint Ives, if you would, and Master Salazar, please assist Serjeant Ames." He steadies Noah on his feet, releases him cautiously, and turns away.

But before Jonathan and Andres can reach Noah, the world goes white, then black.

# CHAPTER 2

**WHEN NOAH REGAINS** his senses, his shoulder aches. He finds himself lying in bed in a small, dimly lit room he's never seen before. Through the small window, he can see daylight fading, and he wonders how long he's been asleep.

In the corner opposite his bed, two men confer in quiet, serious tones. He's unable to identify either man, as the one nearer him has his back turned, blocking the other man's face from view.

As though sensing Noah's stirring, the man facing him peers around his friend. It's Jonathan. "Well, Sir Walter, it seems Father has returned to us, at last." As far as Noah can recall, this is the first time Jonathan has referred to him as "Father," but he supposes it's appropriate.

The one with his back to Noah turns, as well. It's Sir Walter Raleigh, Captain of the Yeomen of the Guard. "Gave us a bit of a fright there, Serjeant, till the surgeon came to stitch you up. He said you were in shock, but that fortunately you suffered no major injury or blood loss. Before you ask, Her Majesty is well, if a bit shaken. The Warders have escorted her to Nonsuch Palace."

For the first time since awakening, Noah risks taking a full breath. Except for a little twinge, all seems well. "Was anyone injured?"

"Other than yourself and the unfortunate Smythe, only Francis," replies Raleigh. "And he's in far worse shape than you are. His shoulder's been badly twisted. The surgeon forced the bones back into place and tied him into some contraption where he'll need to remain for some time."

"Where is he?" asks Noah. "For that matter, where am I?"

"You're both still at the Tower. He's in the Warder's quarters. You, fortunate fellow, are in the royal residence. This room is sometimes used as an infirmary for guests who are injured or take sick. Now, if you gentlemen can spare me, I've been summoned by Sir Robert."

"*Sir* Robert?" says Jonathan. "Is Sir Robert not now Lord Keeper of the Privy Seal?"

Sir Walter smiles. "That he is," he replies, "but he allows his oldest, most weak-minded friends to persist in calling him 'Sir Robert' in private." He winks at Noah, who smiles in return. Sir Walter bows and goes.

Jonathan draws a chair up to the head of the bed. "Seems only yesterday that I was the wounded one. Were you simply too envious of all the attention?"

Noah replies tongue in cheek. "Look where it got *you*."

Jonathan smiles. "Yes, a barony and the love of my life, to boot."

"How long have I been here?" asks Noah.

"Overnight," says Jonathan. "We might have awakened you last night, but you looked so peaceful, we couldn't bring ourselves to do it. Surgeon said you can attend to your business whenever you wish, so long as you don't carry anything about. How are you feeling?"

"Not too bad. Has Marie been informed?"

"Yes. We sent Andres to her about an hour after the incident, as soon as we learned you'd be all right. He sent us back a note saying she seems to be taking it all in stride. She's quite proud of you."

"And Lady Jessica?"

"She was with your wife when the news reached her. Evidently, Jessica was considerably more shaken. She sent a note saying she'll be here before nightfall."

As if on cue, Jessica's excited young voice rings out in the hallway. She races into the little room, and Noah's heart soars to look upon her. "Oh, Daddy!" she cries, descending upon him with hugs, as though her father were a soldier mortally wounded in the field.

"Mind the shoulder!" cautions Jonathan.

"There, there!" says Noah, patting his daughter lightly on the back. "Nary a scratch, my dear. You needn't concern yourself."

"Now that I see you," she says, "I am much assured. But … who did this? Who would try to poison Her Majesty?" She turns to her husband.

Jonathan shrugs. "That's what Sir Walter and I have been trying to figure out," says Jonathan. "So far, no luck."

Noah sighs. "There are so few with reason to oppose Her Majesty, yet so many do." He turns to Jonathan with sudden purpose. "Where is the earl?"

Jonathan arches an eyebrow. "Essex? He's still in the custody of the Lord Keeper of the *Great* Seal, out of contact with the rest of the world—but for his creditors, who persistently seek to meet with him."

"And Southampton?"

"Still at liberty, I fear, at Drury House. He's been receiving visitors from abroad. Supporters of Essex, no doubt."

Suspicion shoots up Noah's spine. He sits up.

"Daddy," protests Jessica, "you must not exert yourself."

"Nonsense, my dear," he says. "The surgeon gave me a clean bill of health. Is that not correct, m'lord?"

Jonathan smirks at this new form of address. "Correct, Father."

Raleigh returns wearing a grave expression. "Good evening, Lady Jessica. Serjeant Ames, you've been summoned by Sir Robert. He wishes to see you now … alone."

As Noah approaches the open door to Sir Robert's chamber, shouting breaks out inside. There are several voices, but Sir Robert's is loudest. Evidently, some unseen persons are being dressed down rather harshly. A guard, upon seeing Noah approach, discreetly closes the heavy door to the chamber and takes up a position outside it. Silence prevails.

"Please take a seat, Serjeant," says the guard, nodding toward a group of four chairs to his left. "Lord Robert will be with you shortly."

Noah is disturbed to find that one of the chairs is occupied by the ever stylish Earl of Southampton, Essex's dearest friend and most fervent admirer. Noah bows to him politely and assumes the seat farthest away.

But Southampton rises, takes the seat nearest him and addresses him amiably, as though he were rather a confidant than an adversary. "Do you suppose *you'd* be better off under the Infanta of Spain?"

Noah is caught off guard as much by the earl's newfound geniality as by his evident lack of concern over the late attempt upon the Queen's life. He turns to Southampton and regards him quizzically. "M'lord?"

Southampton snorts skeptically at Noah's puzzlement. "Can there be any doubt that, if the Infanta were to become Queen of England, she would re-import the Inquisition? Things would be very unpleasant for those of your tribe, I'd imagine. She's a papist, after all, like her deceased father King Philip, long may he burn."

After a long silence, Noah replies with barely suppressed exasperation. "As Her Majesty's subjects are forbidden to discuss the Succession, that cannot be your lordship's intention. It is true that the prospect of serving a papist monarch is daunting to one of my tribe. But, is not King James of Scotland likewise a papist?"

Southampton shakes his head. "One of a different stripe, I assure you, who'd look far more favorably than the Infanta would upon Lord Essex—*and* his adherents. You might consider improving your own lot by joining us. Besides, what makes you think those two are the only alternatives? His lordship of Essex is Church of England." He arches an eyebrow.

Noah can scarcely believe what he's hearing. "The latest time his lordship suffered me in his presence," says Noah gravely, "he was incensed with me. I cannot imagine he would frown upon me less than a papist would."

Southampton waves away the thought. "Oh, he's had plenty of time to get over that, and his friends have pointed out that his fury at you was ... entirely misdirected."

The door to Sir Robert's chamber swings open, and three functionaries, red-faced and chastened, emerge and stride away without so much as a glance at Southampton or Noah.

Sir Robert calls from inside the chamber. "Who's left?"

"Lord Southampton and Serjeant Ames, sir," the guard replies.

After a moment's hesitation, a slightly calmer Sir Robert says, "Admit them together, please."

As Southampton rises from his chair, he whispers to Noah, "Think on it."

But the only things Noah can think on are his dismal prospects if Her Majesty were to pass, regardless who might assume the Throne.

The guard admits them to Sir Robert's chamber, backs into the hallway, and closes the door, leaving Noah alone with Southampton and the diminutive Sir Robert.

"Be seated," says Sir Robert peremptorily as he remains standing.

Though Noah and Southampton are seated, Sir Robert's face is little more than a foot higher than theirs as he strolls to the window and gazes out at the darkening sky, deep in thought. Noah cannot help but wonder what hardships Sir Robert has suffered his whole life by his diminutive stature and hunched back, and how much worse those hardships must be for someone of similar disfigurement occupying a lower rung on the social ladder.

"Serjeant Ames," says Sir Robert at last, "did you know that I am a principal proponent of the Spanish Infanta's succession to the Throne of England?"

While the sheer impertinence of Southampton's earlier inquiry caused Noah to suspect he'd been tossed into Bedlam Asylum, now he's *sure* of it. What the devil is everyone *talking* about? He rises indignantly. "That is the first I've heard of such a thing, Lord Robert."

Sir Robert turns to him serenely. "Oh, do sit down, Serjeant. It's the first *I've* heard of it, too." As Noah resumes his seat confused, Sir Robert turns angrily on Southampton. "It is, however, all the buzz about Drury House, where m'lord of Southampton presides. Is that not right, m'lord?"

Southampton smiles airily. "'Tis true I'm residing at Drury House, Lord Robert, but not *presiding*."

"Oh, don't mince words with me, m'lord!" Sir Robert shoots back. "Have you not been putting it abroad that I am chief proponent of the Infanta's claim?"

"I?" says Southampton. "Not *I*. But some of your own friends, m'lord, say they've heard you discussing the Infanta's claim."

Sir Robert goes red in the face and turns away toward the window. "If I do so, m'lord, it is only to anticipate what will happen if one of these blasted attempts on Her Majesty's life should succeed! God forbid."

"God save the Queen," says Southampton insouciantly.

Sir Robert turns on him afresh. "From your lordship and Lord Essex! Word has reached me that his lordship's friends from the Continent are beginning to gather at Drury House. Is this not so?"

Southampton shrugs. "Why, I have no way of knowing *what* information has reached you, Lord Robert." Sir Robert stares him down so sternly that Southampton resumes without further prompting. "Well, they're not being *summoned*, if that's what you're implying. But, yes, several of Lord Essex's supporters have recently taken up residence at Drury House."

"I trust they all have proper traveling papers, m'lord," says Sir Robert pointedly.

Southampton shifts uncomfortably. "I expect they do."

"We'll see about that," says Sir Robert smartly, handing Southampton a quill, a sheet of paper, and a piece of blotting. "If you'd be so kind, m'lord, please list their full names and places of origin on this paper."

Southampton reluctantly accepts the quill, paper, and blotting. "May I ask, Lord Robert, what use will be made of this list?"

Sir Robert smiles impatiently. "Such use as I—or any other member of the Privy Council—shall deem fit."

As Southampton sulks and writes, the air in the silent room is thick with unspent anger. He finishes, blots the ink, and proffers the paper to Sir Robert, who makes no attempt to accept it. Instead he says, "Serjeant Ames, is this writing legible to you?"

Noah accepts the paper from Southampton. "Thank you, m'lord," he says. There are five names on the list, with their cities and countries of origin. "'*Tis*, Lord Robert. I can read all the words."

"Very well," says Sir Robert. "Serjeant Ames, please retain this paper. M'lord," he says, turning to Southampton, "may I call upon you again in the event your assistance is needed in aid of the Queen's protection?"

"Of course," Southampton replies, and rises to go.

Sir Robert says, "I truly hope you have matters at Drury House well in hand, m'lord. 'Twould be a pity for any of Lord Essex's friends to wind up in the Tower."

Southampton frowns, opens the door, and proudly struts past the guard, who leans into the chamber quizzically.

"It's all right, William," says Sir Robert. "His lordship is free to go. Please shut the door again."

As soon as the door snaps shut, Sir Robert mutters, "That smug, seditious *prig!*"

Noah allows a long time to pass before he speaks. "Why did you ask whether the earl's list was legible to *me*, Sir Robert?"

"I'm afraid the men gathering at Drury House are an unsavory lot," replies Sir Robert, "though you'd never know it by their pedigrees."

"Unsavory, in what sense?"

"The Privy Council believes them to be a growing and deliberate threat to Her Majesty. If rumor is to be believed, many are important men in this and other countries. If, as is commonly expected, Her Majesty soon sets Essex at liberty, the fear is that these newcomers will prod him to his worst yet."

Noah is perplexed. "His worst? You mean …?"

Sir Robert nods. "Why, insurrection! Who's to say they were not involved in yesterday's attempt on Her Majesty's life? I told the earl to hand the list to you, Serjeant, because this is vitally important, and requires someone of your diligence and discretion."

Noah adds what Sir Robert has omitted. "And someone known to be incapable of noble preferment."

Sir Robert nods equivocally. "Although you are somewhat less suspect because you're not Church of England, don't think for a moment that your motives are entirely above suspicion at Drury House. Some will suspect you *because* you're a Hebrew. Others because you have gentile friends capable of enjoying such preferment as would enable them to provide *you* with employment for quite a long time, regardless of your faith. But this is off the point."

For the first time in Noah's experience, Sir Robert beseeches him humbly, almost desperately, his eyes bloodshot, his face careworn. "I need you to investigate these people thoroughly—*especially* the foreigners. Most of them probably have valid passports, so their mere presence in England may not be felonious. But I suspect some of them have criminal—even violent—pasts in their home countries, and I need you to ferret them out quickly, before Essex regains his liberty," he purses his lips in a moue of distaste, "something Her Majesty is certain to grant him despite my considerable efforts to the contrary."

"And before there's another attempt upon Her Majesty's life," adds Noah.

"Amen," replies Sir Robert.

"I must observe," says Noah, "I find the proposition highly doubtful that the late attempt on Her Majesty's life was approved or desired by either Lord Essex or Lord Southampton. Lord Essex has been known for many years to curry favor with Her Majesty's cousin, King James of Scotland, who you and I both know to be Her Majesty's preferred successor. If Her Majesty lives out her normal term, their protector will likely become King of England. It is rather the *Infanta's* adherents who would seem suspect in any attempt upon the Queen."

"True," says Sir Robert. "So it seems to me, as well. But the maelstrom that swirls about an insubordinate person such as Lord Essex draws in *all* who seek to thrive on the chaos he fosters, though their desired result be at cross-purposes with his own. Back to matters at hand. Sir Walter has been instructed to place at your disposal all the resources of the Tower of London, except torture. But, Noah," he says confidentially, "if you deem it advisable to inflict torture in order to obtain vital information that may keep Her Majesty safe, come to me discreetly, and I will obtain consent of the Privy Council, so you'll need answer to no one for your actions."

"At least, to no one temporal," says Noah, his stomach turning at the prospect. "But let's hope it never comes to that."

"Better to torture the wicked," says Sir Robert, "than to lose Her Majesty to these bloody-minded foreigners."

"If I deem torture to be the only solution, Sir Robert, I shall let you know, though I cannot promise to participate."

Sir Robert sighs. "I wonder how my father would have handled this band of ruffians."

Noah can see he's in need of reassurance. "Though I confess that sometimes I'd give my right hand to have Lord Burghley back, Sir Robert, I have no doubt you'll do precisely as he would have done. Look on the bright side. Better for him that he's not required to police this monthly sedition."

Sir Robert shakes his head. "To Father, sedition was a *daily* occurrence. As bad as things may seem today, they were never much better."

Noah wonders whether that is literally true. "Not to change the subject, Sir Robert, but how could the Infanta have any claim to the English throne? As I understand it, while her father Philip was King of England, he ruled solely by right of his wife, Queen Mary. His only chance of begetting a king or queen of England was to sire a child by her, which he failed to do. And when Queen Mary passed, Philip's claim to the English Crown died with her. The Crown's subsequent descent to Queen Elizabeth, God save her, was through Mary and Elizabeth's common father, Henry the Eighth. Is that not right?"

"Quite right. The Infanta can make no claim through her father." Sir Robert smiles wistfully. "But, would it were not so, like most children the Infanta had *two* parents."

"She claims through her *mother*?" Noah asks incredulously. "How is that possible?"

Sir Robert sighs. "To show you her claim in detail, we'd have to go someplace *big*, like the room where Mountjoy showed us his maps. To make a long story short, however, the eldest daughter of our John of Gaunt married the King of Portugal. From her, there's a direct line of inheritance to the Infanta's mother, Elisabeth of Valois. After our former King Philip suffered the loss of Queen Mary, he *married* this Elisabeth of Valois, and she bore him a child, known as the Infanta."

Noah furrows his brow incredulously. "You're speaking of John of Gaunt, who was father to King Henry the Fourth? The John of Gaunt who died in ... was it 1399?"

"That's the only John of Gaunt there's ever been," replies Sir Robert with a shrug.

"Why, Sir Robert," says Noah incredulously, "the present year is *1600!*"

Sir Robert throws up his hands. "That's the problem with primogeniture when a line ends. We cannot look forward to find our Sovereign. Yet, a Sovereign we must have. So, we must look backward. And things get very messy back there. I mean, my God, we could end up re-fighting the Wars of the Roses. What's even more depressing: if the Infanta were to succeed Her Majesty, England might as well have *lost* its battle with the Spanish Armada, as the result would be the same: papist Spain rules over protestant England."

Noah says solemnly, "One would have thought King Philip's claim to have burned to ash by now."

Sir Robert arches an eyebrow. "Have you never seen a heedless servant burn his hand while sweeping yesterday's coals out of the fireplace?" he asks.

Unsure where Sir Robert is leading, Noah says, "Only once. It's a mistake he never repeated, so deeply humiliated was he by his failure to guard against the possibility of a live ember. He jokingly blamed it on some outward cause."

Sir Robert smiles, evidently approaching some didactic point. "Do you recall his remark?"

Noah strains to recall words uttered so long ago by a servant rubbing cold water on his hand. "He pointed into the fireplace and said—"

"'A dragon in the ashes,'" offers Sir Robert, completing Noah's thought.

"Just so," says Noah. "I suppose the phrase wasn't original to him."

"No, indeed," says Sir Robert. "It's been a commonplace at least since my father was a boy, may he rest in peace, and that's long ago." A faraway look descends upon him. "My father once observed: when a servant forgets the possibility that an ember may yet burn in the cool ashes, he risks no more than a singed hand. But when those advising a prince forget the possibility of a live ember, much more may be lost than a patch of skin."

"Once again we find ourselves ruled by the dead hand of the past," laments Noah. "A dragon in the ashes, indeed."

"The past is a ghost that haunts us every moment of our lives," replies Sir Robert. "The past is *never* past."

The sky grows dark and a blustery rain whips about so harshly that Noah decides to leave his favored horse Bucklebury in the Tower stables, rather than to expose him to the wild night. He hails one of the carriages lined up outside the Tower seeking for business.

As Noah closes the carriage door behind him, a small cowled figure that must have lain in wait approaches him rapidly enough to startle the horses. The silent figure hands him a sealed paper through the open window and disappears into the night.

Himself momentarily stunned, Noah wonders whether the figure's graceful movements were those of a swordsman, perhaps a dancer. No, he decides, in all likelihood they were those of a young woman. And in hindsight he finds something about them that's familiar, even comforting.

Noah instructs the driver to wait a moment, so he can read the paper by what little torchlight escapes the Tower portcullis behind him. The few words he manages to read in the failing light are alarming. His sick cousin Beth requests his presence immediately. All thought of hearth and home dispelled for the present, Noah directs the driver to Beth's home in Southwark.

# CHAPTER 3

**ON THIS UNUSUALLY COOL,** windy June night, embers float up from Southwark's chimney tops and whip into the air on the chilly breeze. It's one of those free winds that seems to draw things away, rather than thrust them forward.

Noah turns up his collar and steps down from the coach, shivering at the mere possibility that Beth's final vision of the earth might be this bleak city landscape. The rude wind slaps his face and steals his breath away. Burying his mouth in the crook of his arm, he turns into the wind to pay the fare. The coachman, his cowled face lowered to shield it from flying debris, extends his palm and grasps the coin, drawing it in for examination by his downcast eyes. A gust drowns out his muttered thanks.

As the coach clops away into the night, Noah is left with the desolate feeling that he's just paid his fare to Charon, ferryman of dead souls across the River Styx.

A sudden gust shoves him roughly into the sheltered vestibule outside Beth's house, and he knocks loudly on the heavy wooden door. When there's no response, he turns the knob and leans into it, stumbling into the dimly lit foyer. He shuts the door behind him.

As he's still dressed for an official visit to the Tower, he wears the silk robes of a Serjeant at Law, a member of the upper echelon of barristers and judges. His robes have been cleaned of blood by the Tower staff, and the rent made by the fourchette has been so thoroughly mended he can find no remaining evidence of it.

Outside, the wild wind roars. Inside, all is silence, without sign of a living soul.

As he hangs his cloak from a peg, he notices a lit taper at the foot of the stairs, presumably left for his use. He walks over to pick it up, his boot heels clacking on the stone floor, echoing against the foyer ceiling. By the taper's remaining length, he judges it's been burning for the better part of an hour. It nearly gutters out when he picks it up but, after a moment's hesitation, it springs back to life with a puff of greasy smoke.

On the stairs up to Beth's room, he detects a faint scent of urine, though it's obvious every effort has been made to keep the house as spotless as ever.

The upstairs hallway is equally bereft of life. The door to Beth's bedroom is closed. He spies a note on it in her familiar handwriting. It tells him to enter and awaken her. He places his hand on the knob, but hesitates.

Having last seen her two months ago, he needs to prepare himself for further deterioration in her condition. He takes a deep breath, turns the knob, and steps quietly into the small chamber, holding the taper aloft.

Beth lies asleep on her stately bed. He approaches the bedside. Although her former fleshiness has abandoned her, she seems free of pain, and her face is at peace. Her familiar Star of David silver pendant rests on the collar of her nightgown.

Poor Beth. She's always lacked the ethereal beauty that alighted like some heavenly gift upon her cousin Rachel, Noah's first wife, now long-deceased. Yet, as Beth has thinned, for the first time he detects a family resemblance between them.

As her eyes open and alight on Noah, they're momentarily illuminated by the most serene joy. But, just as quickly, they dim, and she resumes her customary pout of mild indignation.

"For a moment there," he says, "you almost seemed happy to see me."

She scoffs. "That's because, for a brief moment, you seemed almost happy to see *me*! Then, I realized what was actually making you smile."

"Whatever do you mean?"

She sits up in a huff. "Do you think I lack a looking glass, Serjeant High-and-Mighty? As I've grown thinner, I myself have begun to notice a resemblance to my sainted cousin Rachel."

Though Noah was called "cousin" by both Rachel and Beth, neither of them could find an ancestor in common with Noah without tracing back four generations. And, while the remoteness of their bloodlines made it acceptable for Rachel to marry with Noah, it also excited false hopes in Beth that Noah would be available to *her* once Rachel passed on.

Noah is flustered that she's read his mind, and so denies it. "I've no idea what you're talking about."

"Oh, don't waste your breath. You seek Rachel in the face of every woman you see. And it's only when you find some suggestion of her that you smile."

No one can cut him to the quick quite as efficiently as Beth.

"I suppose your current wife Marie knows that," says Beth. "She's certainly sharp enough." At least Beth has avoided the "shikse" epithet by which she usually refers to Marie. "And it's a good thing your daughter resembles her mother so closely, or you'd likely show no interest in her, either."

Noah scowls, but holds his tongue out of respect for Beth's condition.

"Oh, don't be angry with me," she says, softening. "I'm bitter only because I never learned to cast such a spell myself." She sighs and kneads her hands together. "I've had plenty of time to contemplate my shortcomings over the past weeks, you see."

Noah is disarmed by her honesty. "How are you feeling?" he asks.

"I came through surgery a week ago. The surgeon said I should be 'right as rain' in a few weeks."

Noah's eyebrows shoot up. "I'm most pleased to hear it."

"Yes. Now you shall have me about for years and years. How delighted you must be!"

He smirks. "I'll give you *this* much, Beth. You're a *tonic* for the 'high and mighty.' You're like the slave who rode in the parade chariot of the Roman conqueror, whispering 'All glory is fleeting.' How did your messenger know where to find me?"

"As soon as I heard an attempt had been made on the Queen's life at the Tower, I knew precisely where you'd be—even if you hadn't been there for the event. Your daughter sent me a note later, saying you'd be leaving the Tower at sunset."

"You're recovering," says Noah pointedly, "and yet you sent a girl to summon me urgently on this blustery night. Was it merely so you could subject me to verbal abuse?"

Beth stares at her toes morosely. "No. I suppose I've roughed you up in order to prepare you for the serious tale you must now hear."

"Something urgent?"

"No, no," she assures him, "nothing like that—although it's hard to tell *when* it's become important to know something." She points to a wooden chair. "It's fallen to me to see that you learn a secret that's been withheld from you for your whole life."

Noah's stomach churns with dread.

Beth continues. "Uncle Avram, who took you in when you were sent into England by your poor Polish relations, did not want you to hear it. *Ever.* But his wife Sarah thought better of it and, as she lay dying, she made her daughter Rachel promise to tell you at some later time. Many years after that, when it was clear that Rachel's time was coming, she passed the burden along to me and made me promise that, if ever *I* were expected to die, I would tell you, so that the truth would not die with me."

What's this? Something *Rachel* could not tell him? Even *after* promising her mother she would do so? He'd kept no secrets from her, and yet she'd withheld this one from him. How horrible must the tale then be?

"But you just said you're *not* dying," he protests. "Why are you telling me nonetheless?"

"Whether I'm dying or not remains to be seen," she says indignantly, as though Noah's relief is indecently premature. "But I wanted you to hear this from someone having personal knowledge of it, and that person *may* be dying shortly. When the physician was here yesterday, he didn't expect her to make it through the night, but before he left today, she'd rallied a bit. He said she may have a few weeks left, but no more. Besides," she hesitates, "it will relieve me of an awful burden that ought never to have been passed to me."

"But who is it who has such personal knowledge?" he asks.

Beth pulls her blanket off and begins to rise from her bed.

"No, Beth," he says, "please don't get up!" But she ignores his protest, picks up a candlestick, and takes a few hesitant steps toward the doorway and out into the dark hall. He throws his hands up in frustration. "Beth, I'm sure you're not ready to be up and about."

"Nonsense," says Beth. "It's not the first time I've been up." Indeed, she seems fairly steady on her feet as she leads him down the hall and opens another bedroom door quietly. On a cot in the corner a wizened old woman lies asleep facing the wall, curled up as tightly as a baby, with blankets pulled taut around her.

Beth turns to Noah. "If you really want to help, fetch me that chair." Noah places the simple wooden chair by the old woman's cot. "You know who this is?" she asks him.

He cocks his head, and walks over to the sleeping woman's bedside. As she's turned in her sleep, her face is partly visible. Her brow is coarsely wrinkled, and her ancient hair a stark white, providing no inkling of its former color.

"I've no idea," he says.

"Remember who brought you to England?"

"Yetta?" he whispers incredulously. "Is that *Yetta*?" The shriveled old countenance yields only the barest resemblance to the kind and simple woman who transported him safely from his parent's hut in Poland all the way to Avram's grocery booth at Southwark Market.

"'Tis she," Beth whispers and leans gently toward the old woman, nudging her shoulder. "Yetta," she says quietly.

Yetta stirs and blinks a few times before fully opening her beclouded eyes. "Yes, Beth," she says hoarsely, in a heavy Polish accent. Spying Noah in the candlelight, she says, "Dis is—?"

Beth smiles proudly. "This is Noah Ames. The Queen's own barrister."

"Noah Ames," Yetta intones with interest, and turns toward him. "What was wrong wid 'Menachem,' little grandpa?"

Noah cannot help but laugh at her recollection of the name she used for him when he was but a small boy. "Have you not heard, Yetta?" he asks. "I cannot be 'little grandpa' any longer, for Beth has dubbed me 'Serjeant High-and-Mighty.'"

Yetta arches a sparse gray eyebrow and smiles weakly. "You were 'little grandpa' long before Beth called you dat. So, tell me. Who named you 'Noah Ames'?"

Noah looks fondly into the old woman's eyes, and smiles to encounter once more that glint that signified her pleasure in puncturing every pompous balloon. "That name was given me by Her Majesty, Yetta. I assure you I had no choice in the matter."

Yetta smiles briefly, but her face quickly blanches and she's overcome by a fit of convulsive coughing. She points urgently to a cup of water on the nightstand. Noah gives her a sip and strokes her hair gently.

"Menachem," she says, feebly caressing his extended hand, "you always please da women. It vas *born* in you." Her face grows grave. "De Doctor says he doesn't know how much time I've got, so let me tell you da story that Beth wants you to hear."

Noah pulls up a chair of his own. "Your English is greatly improved, Babushka. Go ahead, I'm listening." "Babushka" was the word used in Poland for an old woman's head scarf or, fondly, for the old woman herself.

She regards him gravely. "Tell me vat you know of your parents' death."

So, *that's* what the secret is about. Though he'd silently deduced what happened to his parents even before arriving in England, he'd never sought confirmation of it and, with a single exception, he'd managed to escape hearing of it for forty years. The exception took place on the night Noah first encountered the young Queen Elizabeth, when Uncle Avram hesitantly alluded to his parents' death by fire. Even then, Noah couldn't be sure it was the truth, as Avram might have been lying to garner royal sympathy.

Noah shakes his head. He might have known that long-ago catastrophe would catch up to him eventually. What was Lord Burghley so fond of saying? The past is *never* past. "You told me that they died when their cart overturned in a storm," he says.

Yetta suppresses a cough and swallows hard, with evident discomfort. She sits up with effort. "I had to tell you dat when you were so small. It would have given you nightmares to know how dey really died. Menachem," she says hoarsely, "your parents—dey were *murdered*."

Noah sighs. "Yetta, I've always known that they were murdered."

Yetta seems shocked. "*Tsk, tsk*. Who told you? Avram? Sarah? Dat's a shame. Dey should never have told you."

"They're innocent, Yetta. They did not tell me."

"Then who told you?"

Noah kneads his cheeks with his hand, as he does when discussing painful things. "No one."

"No one?" she says. "*Someone* must have told you."

"It was a combination of things, Yetta."

"Vat tings?"

"Well," he says, "on the night we escaped, smoke filled the forest, though we'd lit no campfire, and there was black soot on the hands of the soldier that your friend Tomas killed to save us."

"Killed? My God, Menachem. Who told you Tomas killed him?" She turns excitedly to Beth. "I swear to *God* I never told him."

"Yetta," says Noah, as he strokes her hand. "No one had to tell me. I was there, remember?"

"*Dere*? No. You were tucked away under a big oilcloth. And Tomas took da soldier away from da cart before he—How did you even know the soldier vas dead?"

"He walked away from us with Tomas, and I never heard his voice again, nor the jangling of his weapons. And I heard his warhorse being led away, riderless."

"All dis you could tell under the oilcloth. You didn't peek?"

Noah shakes his head.

"Oh, but still," says Yetta skeptically, "even from all dis, you vouldn't know dat your parents were murdered. I always told you dat—"

"That my parents were killed when their cart overturned in a rainstorm. But I knew that *you* knew the truth, and were lying to save me from it."

Yetta brings her hands to her face. "How could *you* know dat I knew the truth?" she asks miserably.

"Because of the way you reacted when Tomas told you what had happened. You would have been sad if you'd heard that my parents were killed by an overturned cart. But instead you"—Noah chokes back the horror he felt at that time—"you *wailed*. Besides, if my parents had really died the way you told me, you would have brought me back to the village, as I had other relatives who could have taken me in. That's what removed all doubt in my mind. The only reason you wouldn't bring me back there was that the village was—"

"Gone," says Yetta, weeping. "Oh, God. Dey vere all gone. I lost many members of my family in dat same fire, Menachem."

"I knew them, Yetta. Remember?"

"I see now why your Queen values you so much, Menachem. You're so clever, just like your parents. Dey knew vat vas about to happen before it did."

Noah nods. "Which saved us both from the flames, didn't it?"

Yetta nods, her face ashen. "Yes, both of us. God bless Naomi. And David. God bless dem both." She wilts. "And all de others."

"Tell me, Yetta. Was this an uprising against the Jews?"

Yetta waggles her head equivocally. "It had *more* to do with paying da rent."

Noah feels Beth's hand tugging on his shoulder. "Come, Noah. Yetta is very tired, as you can see."

Noah agrees. "Well, Yetta, let me come back to you tomorrow evening, and you can continue the story. Would that be good?"

Yetta smiles at him. "It's been so long since anyone wanted to hear my stories. Dat would be … *very* good, Menachem. But ven you go tonight, for my sake, you must take someone vit you."

Noah cocks his head quizzically.

Yetta turns to Beth. "Beth, you must keep your side of da bargain."

Beth rises. "Of course, Yetta. She should be in the foyer by now."

Beth goes to the door and opens it. The small cowled figure must have been only a few feet away, as it takes but a moment to appear.

Although this *could* be the same girl who handed Noah Beth's note a short time ago, he cannot be certain, for whoever came to him at the

Tower wore a cowl and kept her face down, just as this girl does now. He still cannot make out her visage.

Yetta extends her palm, as though formally introducing the girl from her sickbed. "Menachem, dis is Esther." The faceless figure curtsies silently. "She is granddaughter of your mother's sister. She is very shy, but I have told her dat I vant you to look upon her face. And she has agreed." The girl makes no motion to stand up straight or reveal her face.

*What is this?* wonders Noah. *What could be so special about the girl that Yetta would insist upon watching me see her face as it is revealed, as though the girl were a painting?* From the corner of his eye, he sees that Beth is also watching expectantly.

Mustering his resolve, Noah goes to the stooping girl, draws her up to full height, and gently pushes the cowl back off her face. Although she's obviously uncomfortable being the object of such direct attention, she stands bravely erect, and lets his eyes have their fill.

She is stunningly beautiful, with auburn hair and crystal green eyes. But what could be so special about her face? She's but a young woman, after all. But, there is something … *something …*

As he gazes into those kind green eyes, it all comes back to him. Everything. His jaw drops. *Oh, God.*

He's looking at his mother's face.

And his dead mother is looking back at him. He gasps and stumbles backward a step, as though the girl were a ghost. All his vaunted rationality instantly drops away to nothing. All his learning, his maturity, his beautiful words, evaporate in an instant.

He's a six-year-old Polish-Jewish boy again, defenseless in a cold world. And his only beacon of light and warmth has now returned to him. His heart aches for their lost time together. He wants to hold her, to save her from the flames. As his legs threaten to buckle beneath him, he covers his face with his hands, and silently weeps.

Beth gasps at the intensity of his reaction and rushes to his side. "Noah, remember this is not your mother, but simply a young girl who resembles her." She turns to the girl. "Do not be frightened, Esther. Please wait in the foyer."

Noah looks up in time to see the girl draw the cowl back over her face and rush from the room.

Beth leads Noah to Yetta's bedside. "I am so sorry, Menachem," says the old woman. "I had no idea the effect on you vould be so … complete. Perhaps I should have warned you vat to expect." She strokes his cheek with her cold, rough hand and smiles weakly. "If ever you vish to see your *father's* face, little grandpa, you need look no further than da nearest glass." She coughs again. "I knew your mother well, and I swear on my soul Esther's face is identical. But her bearing is quite different from your mother's. Esther is shy. Your mother was … regal. Your father called her his 'secret veapon,' because there vas not a man in Europe who would decline to see him, so long as she vas by his side."

Noah does not reply, his emotions still in turmoil.

Yetta waits a moment for him to gather his thoughts. "I have a boon to ask of you," she says.

"Yes, Yetta. What is it?"

"I brought dis girl from Poland only a few weeks ago, just as I once brought you here. She has been living wit me ever since. She is so shy dat she cannot work outside the home. She says little, even to me. She has no relatives in England … except for *you*. I need you to accept her into your house … as a servant. As she no longer has a home to go to, I need you to bring her dere tonight. Beth has been kind enough to tend to me, but I can impose on her no further to take care of da girl."

"I will do better, Babushka," says Noah. "I will treat her as my own daughter."

Yetta beams at him. "That is what I hoped you would say, Menachem." Now she regards him dubiously. "Dere is one more thing you must know about her, little grandpa. She has a special gift, same as your mother."

Noah cocks his head. "What special gift, Yetta?" he asks.

Yetta seems uncertain that her words will be believed, but speaks right on. "As you vill see with your own eyes in time, Esther has the second sight. I tink it is why she's afraid to speak. She doesn't always know when she's seeing something dat other people *cannot* see, and dey sometimes look at her like she's a fool, or worse … a witch."

Though the rationalist in Noah summarily rejects the notion of second sight, there's something in Yetta's tone that tells him he would be a fool to ignore such information.

Yetta takes his hand. "Menachem, you come back tomorrow night and the night after. As long as it takes. I promise I won't … leave before you know everyting."

Beth leads Noah downstairs to the front door. "Will you have some spare time in the next week or so?" she asks.

Though Noah is overcome with long-repressed feelings, he turns to Beth impatiently. "What do *you* think, Beth? Someone just tried to murder the Queen. Everyone in a position of responsibility will be working 'round the clock to unravel this mystery and apprehend those responsible."

She arches an eyebrow. "And this includes you?"

"Of course," says Noah. "But I will make time whenever I can, to come and see Yetta. I owe her so much." He kisses Beth's forehead. "And thank you. I hope your recovery is rapid and complete."

As he walks out of the door with his arm around Esther, he glances back at Beth, who watches the girl with an evident combination of envy and resignation.

# CHAPTER 4

**NOAH AWAKENS THE NEXT MORNING** at the house in Holborn only to find his wife Marie sitting attentively at the foot of the bed.

"Is your shoulder feeling better?" she asks pointedly.

He rotates his arm before replying. "It still smarts, but it's feeling a bit better today. Thank you, dear." Her tone concerns him. "Have you been waiting for me to awaken?"

"I have."

He sits up. "What's the matter?"

She sighs audibly. "You know, Noah, a few weeks ago when you agreed to appear in court on Lord Essex's behalf—albeit merely 'formally,' I believe you said—it occurred to me that you sometimes behave ... unexpectedly."

Noah rubs his eyes. "I thought we'd been all through that. As I predicted, Essex remains in the Lord Keeper's custody, none the better for my appearance on his behalf."

"Yes," she replies wistfully. "But still I regarded it as strange, as you're well known to detest him, and as he was complicit in the death of my first husband, God rest his soul."

He agrees tentatively. "I suppose that might be regarded as strange, at least to someone unaware of my unique circumstances."

She nods. "And now there's this *new* thing."

"New thing, Marie?"

"I awoke early this morning to find a stunning young woman asleep in one of the children's rooms."

"Oh, that!" he exclaims, no longer groggy.

"Yes, that!" she replies sternly.

"That young woman comes from Poland," he explains, "and has

nowhere else to stay."

"Well, that explains it," says Marie sardonically. "How foolish of me."

"No, no, no. You don't understand."

"*Make* me understand," she says impatiently.

"She's a relative of mine who was recently brought to England by Yetta, the woman who brought me here these many years ago. I met her at Beth's home last evening. Yetta is failing, and asked me to give the girl a home."

Marie regards him askance. "You know, Noah, you can't just pick up young women and bring them into our home without talking to me first. She's not a stray cat." She raises her eyebrows, as though curious whether she's being understood. "You *do* see the difference, do you not?"

"*Of course* I see the difference! I had every intention of discussing her with you last night, but you were already asleep and I thought it unnecessary to wake you."

Marie nods indulgently. "I would have forgiven you," she assures him. "What's her name? And don't tell me 'Tabby,' or some such thing."

"*Tabby*," he replies sullenly. "Tabby the cat."

Marie rises indignantly. "You obviously regard my feelings in this matter as utterly trivial."

"No, Marie, I don't. I just don't understand why you're angry with me. The poor girl's name is 'Esther.' She has nowhere else to go. She's *painfully* bashful—"

"Not too bashful to elbow her way into your home!"

It finally dawns on Noah that Marie is jealous of his attention to the girl. He rises and approaches her gingerly. After some initial resistance, she allows him to embrace her. "There's no need for you to be suspicious of this girl, Marie, or of *me*, for that matter. She's younger than Jessica, for heaven's sake. She's also a cousin of mine, and her face is that of my deceased *mother*."

Marie looks at him, amazed. "This girl resembles your mother?"

"Spit and image," he assures her gravely. "When first I saw her face at Beth's, I wept like the six-year-old I was when last I saw my mother."

Marie looks into his face sympathetically. "Oh, you poor thing!" She relents. "Well, I suppose one more mouth to feed won't impose *such* a hardship."

"She was offered to us as a servant girl," says Noah, "which is how you may regard her, if you wish. I thought it more appropriate to treat her as another daughter, assuming we can bring her out of her shell."

Marie's eyes well up. "Our new daughter she shall be," she says. "Now, dress and come downstairs. Lady Jessica is here, and Lord Jonathan will be arriving shortly."

As Noah plods down the stairs to breakfast, there's a knock at the front door. He answers it. It's Jonathan, wearing an earnest expression.

"Have you eaten yet, Father?" asks Jonathan.

"No, but I was about to. Won't you join me?" He lets Jonathan in. "And please call me 'Noah' privately, if you would."

"Not with Lady Jessica about, sir. She has provided me with instruction in appropriate forms of address."

"Very well, then, when we're alone, just the two of us."

"That's a relief," says Jonathan, his eyes darting about for any sign of his wife. "And please call me Jonathan, when we're alone."

Noah nods, and together they enter the dining room, where Marie and Jessica are already seated at table, giving instructions to the servants.

"Gentlemen," says Marie, "how splendid to have you both to breakfast at the same time!"

Noah and Jonathan take seats across from one another.

"You seem like a man with an agenda for today," says Noah as he's served his favorite flapjacks.

"I thought we'd start out conferring with Sir Walter at the Tower," says Jonathan, spooning some chicken's eggs from a serving dish.

There's a knock at the door.

Jessica, who has evidently been advised of their new arrival's place in the family, rises and says to Marie quietly, "I'll get Esther to answer the door, Mother. Please, do not stir."

Noah looks to Jonathan, ignoring the interruption. "And after Sir Walter?"

"Well, since we'll be at the Tower, I'd thought we'd look in on Francis, to see about his shoulder injury."

Jessica reenters the dining room. Jonathan's eyes light up to see her accompanied by a most beautiful young woman who resembles Jessica closely enough to be her sister. He shoots to his feet, and Noah reluctantly follows his example.

Jessica shakes her head. "Please be seated, gentlemen. This is Cousin Esther. We're just passing through for now."

Noah and Jonathan remain standing to see who's at the door.

"Go ahead, Esther," says Jessica, encouraging the girl to open the door, and stepping away to watch.

Hesitantly, Esther puts her hand on the knob, turns it, and draws it slowly open, eyes downcast.

It's David Killigrew, that strapping blond specimen of Cornish youth. David accedes to Esther's mute invitation and steps into the foyer. He removes his hat and studies her face. Already he's smitten. He bows politely. "Good morning," he says. "David Killigrew, for Serjeant Ames."

Esther nods but does not otherwise react. She turns to go.

Before she can get far, David says, "And you are ...?"

The girl stops a moment, but then rushes away through the dining room and into her room, where she closes the door quickly and quietly.

"I'm sorry," says David, looking imploringly to Jessica. "Did I—?"

"Not at all," says Jessica. "That's Cousin Esther. She's new to the house, and very bashful. She'll grow accustomed to you in time."

"I certainly hope so," muses David. "Good morning, Lady Jessica."

Jessica silently takes him by the crook of his arm into the parlor where they'll be alone, stands him still, and takes a discerning step back, casting him a skeptical look.

"Why, David," she says, pointing to his chest, "it appears you have buttoned your doublet askew." She examines the placket more closely. "Yes, you have an extra button at the top and an extra button*hole* at the bottom on the other side."

She peremptorily unbuttons his doublet, straightens it, and begins buttoning it properly from the bottom up, talking all the while. "Did you dress in a rush this morning, David? I cannot imagine being so careless with an appearance as handsome as yours—unless you lack a looking glass." She raises a questioning eyebrow. "You *do* have a glass in your bedchamber at Uncle Henry's in Lothbury. Have you not, David?"

"I have, m'lady," he says warily.

"Did you not refer to your reflection this morning before leaving your bedchamber?" she asks, wide-eyed.

David turns beet red. "I did, madam."

She smiles wryly. "Then I surmise you have had occasion to see *Rosalind* this morning. Is that right, David?"

He stands mute with embarrassment, and wonders whether henceforth she intends to bring him up short every time she sees him.

Jessica smirks and smooths the placket. "Well, you should tell Rosalind that henceforth, when she's taken something apart and then reassembled it, she ought to inspect her handiwork before letting it out of her sight."

David bows respectfully, wondering all the while whether he'll ever become quite the man Lady Jessica hopes him to be, taking a woman quite as seriously as she demands. To David at the moment, women seem the most delightful of playthings. Yet, he is aware that at some point in their lives they tend to become rather peremptory, as Lady Jessica has evidently become. (Actually, he has no basis on which to conclude that she was *ever* much different than she is now.) And then, at some point, they become downright dowdy ... and dreary. He shudders to think of it, and hopes that for him, at least, a woman shall ever remain a plaything.

Jessica leads David into the dining room, where he bows to Marie and takes a seat next to Jonathan.

"Marie, my dear, when will the younger children be coming home?" asks Noah.

"Within the week," she replies. "But we'll still have an extra room for Esther until Stephen returns from Sir Henry's embassage in Paris."

"And when he returns?" asks Noah.

"We can move Esther into one of the maidservant's chambers ... temporarily, of course."

David chimes in. "With Sir Henry away, there are several vacant rooms at Lothbury." The dining room is silent as he spoons a few eggs onto his plate. He looks up to see everyone in the room regarding him as though he's lost his mind. He blushes. "I meant only—well, I'm not *alone* there. There are servants all over the place. I mean ..."

Marie comes to his rescue. "That's very thoughtful of you, David. Lady Jessica has made a similar offer, but Serjeant Ames and I deem it best to keep Esther by our side until she feels comfortable visiting family and close friends."

"Of course, Mistress Ames," David replies. "Very prudent."

Jonathan leans into David.

"Nice try," he mutters.

David blushes again, while pretending not to have heard.

Noah rides into the Tower of London with Jonathan and David.

"I don't remember security at the Tower being quite as tight as it is this morning," remarks Jonathan.

"Still," says David, "even with all the checkpoints, there don't seem to be many Yeomen of the Guard here."

Raleigh strides up to them, evidently having heard their discussion. "That's because most Warders go where Her Majesty goes."

Noah raises an eyebrow. "Which is where, at the moment?"

"We're bound not to say and, besides that, she's being moved from time to time, at least until we can provide her with assurance that the immediate threat has passed." He bows to Jonathan. "M'lord. Gentlemen, won't you come into my office?"

They dismount, follow him in, and take whatever seats they can find.

Sir Walter plops himself behind a desk that seems somehow too small for him. It's not that he's tall or stout, but rather that his boundless energy is too great to be contained indoors. He smiles broadly. "Serjeant Ames, Sir Robert has informed me that you are charged with investigating the vermin beginning to swarm at Drury House."

Noah arches an eyebrow. "I trust those were not his exact words. Some such men could be entirely innocent."

Sir Walter shakes his head. "No, they can't. Perhaps they've committed no treason yet. Perhaps they'll even decline to do so when the time comes. But, no matter how naive, none of them is truly 'innocent,' which would imply they don't *know* of the danger Essex poses to the Crown." He shakes his head. "At the very least, they know they're tickling the dragon's tail. I'd think it best we show them the devil they'll need to pay for their little whiff of danger."

"Perhaps," says Noah, "but that's not in my commission. It's my responsibility to find out whether any of them participated in the latest attempt on Her Majesty's life, or knew of it in advance."

Sir Walter smirks. "Plenty of ways to find that out here at the Tower. Why not just arrest the whole lot of them?"

"On what charge, Sir Walter?" says Noah impatiently.

Raleigh shrugs. "Suspicion of high treason?"

Noah frowns. "Some of these Essex supporters are well-heeled enough to retain counsel, who would require us to make a showing of probable cause before a magistrate. Perhaps something a little more subtle," he suggests. "Perhaps we could interview them each separately. I want to find out their professed reasons for congregating at Drury House, which may allow us to head off later problems. In my experience, if you want to know what someone intends, it's best to learn how he thinks."

"So, what are you going to do?"

"I need to speak with them somewhere neutral and familiar to them, somewhere they'll be off-guard."

"Isn't Drury House within sight of your home on High Holborn?" asks Sir Walter.

"Very nearly," replies Noah.

Sir Walter laughs aloud. "Perhaps you should interview them in your wife's parlor!"

"While the last thing I'd want them to know is where I live, unfortunately, Southampton already *does* know. He's been there once. Still, I wouldn't want even his lordship in my wife's parlor under present circumstances," says Noah. "Regardless of where the Drury House denizens are interviewed, Southampton will know immediately that I'm there to keep track of him and his merry band."

"How will he know that?" asks Raleigh.

"Sir Robert instructed Southampton to make a list of current residents at Drury House and hand it to me."

"That seems uncharacteristically foolish of Sir Robert," says Raleigh.

Noah shakes his head. "Sir Robert is no more foolish than was his father before him, who was no fool at all. He knows that Southampton hopes to turn me to their side by promising me continued security after … the Succession. Sir Robert wishes me to cultivate Southampton's vain hope, which I have every intention of doing." He returns to the present question. "I *had* considered hiring rooms at nearby Gray's Inn, but Essex's men would not feel at ease there. However"—he pauses—"they do *drink* publicly."

Sir Walter's interest is piqued. "And?"

"Well, there are a few inns and taverns in the vicinity. Some have private dining rooms that could be used for interviews."

Jonathan points out, "Some have overnight rooms for transients, too. You could take a room for a few days, assuming you want them to know where to find you."

Noah turns to Jonathan. "Where would you suggest? I wouldn't feel comfortable at Mountjoy's Inn. It reminds me too much of its late resident Doctor Lopez. I think of that poor soul every time I pass it."

"I'll tell you which inn my old master Graves would have suggested," says Jonathan.

"Which is that?"

"Saracen's Head Inn, Newgate. It's right on Snow Hill, next to the chapel. Very close to Drury House. I'd be surprised if Southampton's friends don't already frequent the place."

"Is that the one with the hideous sign?"

"The very one," says Jonathan with a smirk. "I expect Saracens don't actually look as ferocious as the one depicted on the sign, but such depictions are effective in keeping the general population in fear of them."

"Well, I suppose the Saracen's Head is as good as any," says Noah with resolution. "Get us a private dining room. I can't see spending the night there, however. Not with my own home so nearby."

"Perhaps not," says Raleigh, "but it might be a good idea to have some muscle staying there to back you up, just in case things get out of hand. I'd suggest Francis but, as you know, he's out of commission for the time being."

"Yes, we'll go and see him after our discussion. How about Yeoman Gardner?" suggests Noah.

Raleigh looks at him askance. "Bit old for that sort of thing, no?" He hesitates. "How about … me?"

"Now you're talking," says Noah, "although I doubt it will be necessary for you to stay overnight."

Francis is a disturbing sight lying abed in a makeshift infirmary in the Warder's quarters. His damaged arm and shoulder are suspended by a rope and pulley tied around the "tester," the elevated section of the bed that rests on the four bedposts. He's lying in an awkward position in obvious pain, his face white and sweaty, his eyes bloodshot and ringed in red and black.

"So, my friend," says Raleigh jauntily, "I see they've got you suspended from the yardarm. How are you feeling today?"

Francis's voice is hoarse and his expression weary. "About how you'd expect after bein' tied to a yardarm all night, suh. I can't get no sleep at all. But the surgeon says this odd contraption oughta help, so I'd best give it a fair go."

"Good man," replies Raleigh.

"At least I'm a damn sight better off than the Queen's taster, old Smythe. Physician tells me he's in Abraham's bosom and no mistake." He looks up at Raleigh. "Is that right?"

Raleigh nods morosely. "The poor fellow never moved again. God rest his soul."

With some discomfort, Francis turns his face toward Noah. "Serjeant, I heard you'll be headin' up the investigation of the attempted murder o' the Queen." He hesitates, his face suddenly stern. "I got a nice repayment to make to whoever done it, so please don't let me down, suh."

"We'll get our man, Francis," replies Noah, "or die trying."

After supper that night, Noah returns to Beth's home in Southwark. He sits on a chair beside Beth's, and together they listen to more of Yetta's tale.

Even in the low candlelight of the sickroom, Noah can see that Yetta has rallied a bit, as though the prospect of unburdening herself of her present tale is sufficient inducement to keep her alive.

"In our little Jewish village in Poland," Yetta begins, "your father David England made a good living as a tailor."

Noah interjects. "But I thought the Jews in Poland didn't use family names."

"Ah," says Yetta, rolling her eyes, "look who knows so much! For your information, David belonged to one of two families in da village dat came from England. It's true ve didn't use family names, but ve did sometimes call each other by da place we came from. Both David's and your mother's family vere called 'England.' But they vere not related to each other. Now, if I may go on, Master *Chuchem*?"

Noah looks at her blankly.

She scowls. "You know this word *chuchem*, little grandpa?"

To Noah, the word sounds as though she's clearing her throat. "No, Yetta."

"It means 'wise,' but it can also mean *too* wise." She looks to Beth for assistance. "Beth, what is the English for *chuchem*? You know vat I mean."

Beth replies. "I'm sorry, Yetta, but I don't speak Polish or Yiddish.

You may recall that I was born here in England. We spoke only English in my parents' home."

Yetta nods, embarrassed that she's forgotten this bit of family history. "And dey vere right, your parents, to forget de old tongue right away, so you young people vould never be tempted to go back."

Beth corrects her gently. "My parents spoke Spanish, Yetta. They were never in Poland."

Yetta pretends to smack her forehead. "Of course, how could I forget? They were *sefardim*, Spanish Jews. Oy, I'm getting so *farmisht!*" She resumes her mental search for the English equivalent of *chuchem*, then settles on a word. "Wiseacre. You know dis word?"

Noah and Beth smile at each other. "Yes, we know 'wiseacre,'" says Noah.

Yetta smiles sagely. "As I said, your father David vas a tailor. But he vas also an apothecary. It vas in dat profession dat he earned da respect of all da villagers, as everybody knew dat apothecary takes much skill and learning. But, for all his success, David vas best known as da man who captured da heart of da most beautiful girl any villager had ever seen. Her name was Naomi. She had pale skin and dark red hair, like an Englishwoman, and green eyes that looked like emeralds in the sunshine. Do you remember your mother, Menachem?"

Noah dredges up the many times he has tried without success to conjure a clear image of his mother. Until seeing Esther last evening, all he could ever remember was the comforting feeling she'd given him that everything would be all right. Until, of course, it wasn't. And never would be again.

"Doesn't matter," says Yetta. "Ven Naomi grew up, she married David and bore him one child, who was named 'Menachem'—vatever the Queen of England would call him later." She waves away Noah's current name.

"The little Jewish village was built on land dat all da villagers thought was owned by Queen Bona Sforza. Queen Bona was beloved in da village, as she vas kind, and respected the religions of all her subjects. The villagers used to say her husband, King Sigismund de Old, vas da best royal friend the Jews ever had, while the *chuchem* would say he vas the *only* royal friend the Jews ever had. Vell, the villagers counted themselves blessed to be governed by such a man, and to have royal protection. Some villagers even called Queen Bona and her husband 'righteous gentiles.'

"Little Naomi vas a milkmaid. Every day she would deliver milk to the queen's house in Krakow. On special days, she would be met by da queen herself, who vould never fail to say how beautiful Naomi was, and ask about things in the Jewish village. She gave Naomi treats, maybe kosher, maybe *not*," she shrugs, "but who can judge? Anyway, Menachem, you don't seem to keep kosher. You don't even have a beard." She points to her own pate. "Or a *kippe*."

Noah smirks. "No, Yetta. I don't wear the required skullcap, nor do I decline treats offered by the Queen on grounds they might not be kosher. I hope you will forgive me."

Yetta grunts. "The villagers all thought that Queen Bona owned the land, because every year they vould send David and Naomi to pay her da rent."

"Why would they send my parents?" asks Noah.

"Because the queen knew and trusted your mother from ven she vas a little milkmaid. And nobody ever refused to meet with Naomi, she vas so beautiful, just like Esther. Also, the queen vould ask your father if he had a cure for whatever ills she might have, and he vould help her, if he could. He was always so worried she might get worse, and then they would blame da Jews for poisoning her, and ve vould have an uprising against da Jews.

"One day, Queen Bona told dem dat the land vas really owned by da King of Spain. Dis vas a terrible thing for da villagers, because Spain did not tolerate the Jews, and Spain also had the Inquisition that forced every Jew to choose between conversion and death.

"Every year, ven dey paid da village's rent, David and Naomi explained to Queen Bona dat da village needed protection from da barbarians, the Tatars, who would invade the town whenever they liked, and steal grain and animals. A few times, the Tatars raped women and killed men and children. Every year, Queen Bona vould listen to such atrocities, and vould promise to give da village better protection.

Most years, she seemed to do vatever vas in her power and, even in the leanest years, she made sure our protection was not made less.

"Ven David and Naomi vould go to Krakow to see Queen Bona, Naomi vould be admired by women and men, both. The women would admire her dignity—she walked like a queen—and her clothing. Most men would come to see her beauty. But a few of dem vould come to ogle, and tink of vays to take her for demselves. One of dose was a very young man. He worked for Bona Sforza. But more about him later.

"In 1548, King Sigismund de Old died. Although no villager had ever seen his face, they mourned his passing. His son became king, but all da Jews in Poland worried that he vould not protect dem as his father and mother did."

Yetta's energy is flagging.

"Babushka," says Beth, "you seem much better now. But maybe Noah can come back tomorrow to hear more. What did the physician tell you?"

"He said I could live another few months," says Yetta. As she smiles, the wrinkles on her face become more pronounced. She shrugs and waves her hand dismissively. "But vat does *he* know?"

Noah rises. "I'll come back tomorrow, Yetta, same time. But I should go now. I have some nasty people to meet with tomorrow."

# CHAPTER 5

**THE FOLLOWING AFTERNOON,** in a private dining room at the Saracen's Head, Noah and Raleigh review Southampton's short list of suspect Drury House residents.

Raleigh points to a name on the list. "Well, Lord Monteagle we know. He's certainly not foreign. He's young and a recusant papist, which renders him suspect in any imaginable plot against Her Majesty. He's often found in the company of two others on the list"—he runs his finger further down the paper—"namely, the young Percy brothers, Sir Charles and Sir Josceline. Sir Josceline's about the same age as Monteagle, Sir Charles a few years older and ought to have more sense."

Noah scowls. "Presumably, the Percys are Reformed Church of England, so what's *their* grievance with Her Majesty?"

"I doubt they have one. More likely they're just caught up in the glory of their 'great leader' Essex, and their own romanticized version of warfare. Utterly lacking in experience, those two. Certainly, no one who's seen the real thing could harbor any illusions about it."

"Do we know anyone who can tell us more about these two young men?"

"I suppose your good friend Sir Henry Neville might know something of them, as they're his kin. Their mother was a Neville," offers Raleigh, "Katherine, to be precise. May she rest in peace."

Noah shrugs. "I'll write to Sir Henry, but I doubt we'll be hearing back from him soon. He's in France somewhere, traipsing about after the French king. Besides, the Nevilles are too large a family for anyone to keep track of—even Sir Henry, although he seems to make the effort." He moves down Southampton's list. "What about the Frenchman? It says here, 'Dorsay and his servant.'"

"A gentleman of some sort. Perhaps Lord Saint Ives might strike up a conversation with him."

"Jonathan?" says Noah. "I suppose he might, though I'd rather keep him out of it entirely. Isn't there also an Italian on the list?"

Raleigh nods. "Last name on the list. Nerezza. An Italian by name, but a long-time courtier at Paris."

"How long at Paris?"

"He's been at the French court since shortly before Henri the Third took the throne."

"*Before?*" exclaims Noah. "That's a remarkable tenure. When did Henri's predecessor die? Who was it, King ... Charles?"

Raleigh smiles. "Not a bad recollection for someone who purports to care not a whit about foreign aristocracy. Yes, it was Charles the Ninth, and he died a raving lunatic a few years after (and some say *because* of) the Saint Bartholomew's Day Massacre of Huguenots in 1572."

"King Charles was a papist, was he not?" asks Noah.

"He was."

"Then why would he be overcome by guilt over a massacre of protestants?"

Raleigh smirks. "Well, I can only tell you from my own experience that the blood of the innocent leaves a blot on the butcher's soul, and King Charles had the blood of *ten thousand* protestants on his. That's an *ocean* of blood." He steps toward the open window and lights his pipe. "The irony is that he didn't order the massacre. But once it started, with the murder of the Huguenot Admiral Coligny, he lost control of the situation and publicly supported the mob. Statesmen *always* fear the mob, whatever they say."

"And *there's* the death of statesmanship," Noah laments. His mind returns to matters at hand. "Would you please have someone examine the Frenchman's traveling papers?"

"And the Italian's?"

"No. Leave the Italian to me for now. I want him to feel at ease. I'll interview him when the time is right."

Noah's young barrister friend Arthur Arden knocks lightly on the door and sticks his head inside. "Gentlemen, you have two visitors."

"My, but word gets around quickly!" says Sir Walter. "Who are they?"

"Two young knights surnamed 'Percy.'"

Sir Walter turns to Noah. "Should we admit them separately?"

Noah considers it, but shakes his head. "They're here voluntarily. Besides, each of them is bound to be a bit more loose-lipped in the presence of his brother."

Arthur disappears. In a moment, Noah can hear the approaching clop of three pair of boots on the wooden floor. The door swings open, and Arthur enters: "Serjeant Ames, Sir Walter Raleigh, permit me to introduce Sir Charles Percy and Sir Josceline Percy."

As the two young men enter, Noah remains seated behind the little bureau, while Sir Walter remains standing. "Master Arden, perhaps these knights have worked up a thirst. Gentlemen, may we offer you a pint?"

Sir Josceline looks toward his elder brother, who addresses Noah. "Is it customary for Her Majesty's officers to conduct official interviews over a pint of ale?"

Noah sits up. "I beg your pardon, Sir Charles. Have you received a summons to attend an interview here?" Sir Charles is momentarily non-plussed. "Because, if you have, please show it to me, as it would have been issued without my authority." He turns to Sir Walter, feigning indignation. "Sir Walter, have you been issuing summonses without my knowledge?"

"Certainly not, Serjeant," replies Sir Walter, feigning defensiveness. He turns toward the Percys. "Perhaps someone *else* has?"

Sir Charles clears his throat. "We have not been summoned."

Noah smiles. "Then this is not an official interview, which means that we're conversing in a tavern, where I believe it is customary to offer one's guests a spot of ale."

Sir Charles hesitates. "Will you two gentlemen be imbibing?"

"I see no harm in it," says Noah. "Sir Walter?"

Sir Walter shrugs. "I'm a bit thirsty, myself. Master Arden, please have the wench fetch us four pints."

Arthur smirks, obviously detecting Noah's clever ploy, and disappears down the hallway.

"So, gentlemen, what brings you to our private room?"

At last young Sir Josceline speaks. "We were told by Lord Southampton that you wished to interview everyone residing at Drury House." His elder brother glances at him with irritation. Evidently, the elder was supposed to do all the talking. "Was he mistaken?"

Noah equivocates. "Not mistaken, but a bit over-inclusive. We're interested in speaking with those from the Continent commonly believed to be supporters of Lord Essex."

"Why?" asks Sir Charles.

There's a knock at the door. Noah signals the wench to place two of the pints on a small table flanked by two chairs, and to hand the other two to Sir Walter and himself. "Please be seated, gentlemen." The Percys sit by the table.

Noah raises his glass. "God save the Queen!" he says cordially, and notes that the two brothers dart a glance at one another before joining in the toast.

"God save the Queen!" they intone with Sir Walter, and down half their pints.

Noah takes a long swig and can't help but notice how sweet ale can taste on a summer's day. "You ask why we wish to speak with Lord Essex's supporters residing at Drury House. Perhaps you've heard that an attempt was made on Her Majesty's life a couple of days ago. We wish to ensure that no one intending harm to Her Majesty conceals himself among those patriotic souls supporting the earl."

Sir Charles ventures. "It's difficult to see why any such person would lodge himself at Drury House, as Lord Essex and Lord Southampton are Her Majesty's most avid supporters."

"As is well known," Noah assures them, while believing quite the contrary. Although he's pleased that the atmosphere in the room is more cordial than when the Percys first entered, he struggles to conceal his dismay in finding that these young men are as deluded about Essex and Southampton as Sir Walter suspected. "Still," he says, "there are some *foreigners* at Drury House, which is a little disturbing. At least it seems that way to us, in our heightened state of alert."

Sir Josceline chimes in. "We arrived there with Lord Monteagle and don't even *know* the foreigners."

"Never been so much as introduced?" asks Raleigh, sipping his ale.

"Well," says Sir Charles, "they briefly introduced us to the French one, Dorsay—"

"And his servant?" asks Raleigh, always seeking for a criminal's possible confederates.

The two young knights look to each other and break into smiles. Sir Charles replies. "I take it you gentlemen have not had the pleasure of meeting Dorsay's servant?"

Noah and Raleigh shake their heads.

"An odd fellow," says Sir Charles, "as you'll see in time. We did not speak with him. But we were introduced to the old gentleman."

"The Italian?" asks Noah.

Both Percys seem confused by the question. "*Is* the old one Italian?" asks Sir Charles.

Noah pretends to look it up in his papers. "Lord Southampton indicated that he is from Italy. But he has spent a great deal of time at the French court. Perhaps you thought him French?"

"Well," replies Sir Charles, "he may be from Italy or France, I suppose, but he doesn't speak like any Italian or Frenchman *we've* ever encountered, and we've both toured the Continent, including Italy and France."

Before Noah can delve further into this curious question of nationality, a commotion suddenly erupts down the hall. Unless Noah's ears fail him, it's broken out in the main room of the tavern.

A man's stern voice rings down the hallway. "Where *are* they, young man?"

At the sound of the angry voice, the Percys sit up sharply, fear registering on their faces. Evidently, the voice is known to them, and a cause of some anxiety.

Raleigh stands at attention. "Whoa!" he says, as though trying to rein in a runaway horse. He looks to the Percys. "Is that Lord Grey?"

They both nod, wide-eyed with fear. Down the hall, there's an excited reply in what sounds like Arden's voice.

"Give me your pints, quick!" says Noah in a hushed tone. They all yield up their glasses. Noah puts them out the open window, lowers them as far to the ground as he's able, and tosses them gently in different directions to avoid their colliding with one another.

"Let me by!" says Lord Grey, now directly outside the door.

Seeing Sir Walter's hand on the hilt of his sword, Noah restrains him and waves everyone back to his place. "Do not draw!" he commands them in an excited whisper.

Lord Grey bursts through the door, sword drawn, with Arthur in his wake. Arthur bows apologetically to Noah. "Serjeant Ames, Lord Thomas Grey wishes to speak with you ... and evidently will not be denied." Arthur leaves in a huff.

"M'lord?" says Noah, as casually as possible.

"Are you Serjeant Ames?" Grey demands, receiving a nod in reply. "And are you not the Queen's Jew?"

It takes every ounce of restraint for Noah to resist the overwhelming impulse to rise and hold forth in his courtroom voice. But that would be imprudent. He sighs instead. "You make it sound as though Her Majesty maintains a menagerie where she keeps one adherent to each faith, m'lord. I assure you she does not." Grey clearly recognizes this as deliberate insolence, but it's Noah's intention to draw his ire away from the young Percys. "To respond to your query, m'lord, I *am* a Jew, and one of the Queen's men."

Grey huffs loudly. "And yet here you sit, carousing with these two treacherous pups."

"Good e'en, Lord Grey," interjects Sir Walter equably.

Grey becalms himself to greet his old companion at arms. "Sir Walter," he mutters and nods, but then raises his voice to Noah once again. "Were you not sharing a pint with these two ... these two ... *ingrates?* It smacks of a *brewery* in here."

Noah folds his hands in front of him. "This is an *alehouse,* m'lord. Its odor should not be surprising."

"And do you conduct the Queen's business in such a place?"

"Not without interruption by your lordship, evidently. Heads of state have stayed at this inn, m'lord," says Noah with exasperation. "Sir Charles and Sir Josceline have come to see me about a matter touching upon the Queen's safety, and your barging in here has assured that the Queen's business shall *not* be advanced today. Now, m'lord," says Noah in a deep and impatient voice, "kindly put up your sword."

Lord Grey looks skeptically at the Percys. "And what if *they* draw, two against one?"

Raleigh stirs. "If I may, Serjeant Ames?"

Noah nods his assent.

"M'lord," says Raleigh, placing his hand over his heart, "if either of them draws once you have put up your sword, *neither* shall leave this room alive." The Percys wince, their fate now in the hands of a man who's sworn to kill them if they so much as touch their weapons—and who could do it, too.

Faced with such an assurance, Lord Grey at last shows the good sense to sheathe his sword.

"Sir Charles, Sir Josceline," says Noah without taking his eyes off Lord Grey, "please leave us now, and let us convene at another time of mutual convenience."

The Percys stand and cautiously sidle past the glowering Lord Grey, who never takes his eyes off them. Sir Josceline nods his silent thanks to Noah and closes the door behind him, leaving Lord Grey alone to face Noah and Sir Walter. Grey blushes.

"You wish to speak with me, m'lord?" says Noah.

"Do you know who those two are, Serjeant?" he asks, pointing to the door.

"I do, m'lord. Were they not who they are, I would not be wasting the Queen's resources on speaking with them in this blasted tavern. It has occurred to you, has it not, that your lordship is not the only subject wishing to prevent Her Majesty's enemies from assembling for treasonable purposes?" Noah folds his hands and rests his chin on them.

Lord Grey stands his ground. "Those two are Southampton's friends, Serjeant, and so Essex's. I accompanied Essex and Southampton on the Islands Voyage and—of late—to Ireland, where Southampton demanded ... *demanded*, mark you ... that I swear allegiance solely to

Essex, to the exclusion of Her Majesty's other counselors, such as Robert Cecil."

"So I have been informed, m'lord," says Noah, "and I have also been informed that you, as a true and valiant subject, vehemently declined to take any such oath—notwithstanding that you had no choice but to complete the Irish adventure under Lord Essex's command. That must have taken tremendous dedication and courage on your part, m'lord, and everyone admires you on that account." Noah's voice gradually becomes more stern. "On more than one occasion, Sir Walter and I have ourselves commended you to Her Majesty to prevent your lordship from being committed to the Fleet Prison on grounds of brawling, as you have repeatedly taken your feud with Southampton to the streets of London, in disobedience of an order delivered to both you and Lord Southampton by Her Majesty *personally*."

Grey persists in defending himself, however weakly. "I cannot be called to answer for *Southampton's* misconduct, Serjeant."

"M'lord," says Noah, raising a skeptical eyebrow, "are you suggesting that the Earl of Southampton has commenced a brawl with your lordship?"

"Do you doubt it?"

Noah cannot help but smirk at such a blatantly evasive reply. "If your lordship will not deign to tell me it's so, then I have no reason to *believe* it, have I? Without such an assurance from m'lord, I can rely only upon what little I see with mine own eyes." He shifts in his chair, as though to inquire into a related matter. "Incidentally, is it your view that your lordship's drawing your sword today was *provoked* by the Percys … who were chatting peaceably with us when you barged in?" Noah is pleased to see that the wind has at last left Lord Grey's sails. "Lord Grey," he resumes, "Her Majesty knows you to be a good friend to the Crown, but she is exasperated by your insistence on demonstrating your loyalty by *brawling* with her other subjects. A man of your blood and experience surely understands that the peace you break *belongs* to the Crown."

Lord Grey is at last chagrined. "I do understand, Serjeant. And I will thank you to refrain from informing Her Majesty of this … unfortunate interruption."

"That I *cannot* promise, m'lord."

Grey's eyes meet Noah's indignantly.

Noah shakes his head in exasperation. "While I will do my best to keep confidential any information you may provide privately, m'lord, please understand that Her Majesty looks to me to report to her all matters of interest of which I become aware. When you insist upon carrying your feuds into public places, such as this tavern, Her Majesty learns of it eventually and, if she were to learn that I witnessed such conduct without informing her, she'd regard me as presumptuous, perhaps even *disloyal*. And I shall *never* give her cause to doubt my loyalty ... *ever*. Not for any man.

"As today's interruption was only momentary, I shall minimize its importance. But please understand," says Noah pointing toward the door, "that I may never have another opportunity to question those two upstarts while they're off-guard, and responsibility for that lost opportunity rests solely with your lordship's intemperate conduct."

Lord Grey shifts his gaze to Sir Walter, who half-smiles in return, as if to say, *you asked for it.*

Lord Grey nods. "Good day, Serjeant. Sir Walter."

Noah rises and bows. "Good day, m'lord," he says. Sir Walter nods his farewell to Lord Grey, who turns and goes, closing the door quietly behind.

Noah resumes his seat. A full minute passes in silence.

"A real hotspur, that one," says Sir Walter, at last. "But I'd rather have him on Her Majesty's side than Essex's."

"I fully expect he'll be with us, should the time come," replies Noah, "even if we have to spring him from Fleet Prison to join us."

Sir Walter scratches his head. "But why did you put the pints out of the window?"

"Because Lord Grey wished to find us 'fraternizing with the enemy,' and I was determined to provide him with no recountable basis for any such foolish accusation, should it behoove him to lodge one during one of his many fits of pique." He turns affably to Sir Walter. "Would you care to join Mistress Ames, Master Arden, and me for an early supper at

Holborn, Sir Walter?"

"That's very considerate of you, Noah, but I have an appointment early this evening."

"As do I," says Noah pensively.

"Oh?"

"Dying relative, I'm afraid."

# CHAPTER 6

**NOAH AWAITS THE RESUMPTION** of Yetta's tale seated in the same chair as last night, but tonight Esther sits beside him. Noah can see sympathetic tears welling up in Esther's eyes, for Yetta's looking much weaker. This evening has grown warm, and the room stuffy, although Yetta seems neither to know nor care.

"You're sure you're feeling up to this, Yetta?" asks Beth.

"Yes, dear." Yetta is ashen, but persistent. "You're good to me, but I'm very tired, and I vant to finish dis story before it's too late." She smiles and her face takes on a wistful, almost melancholy expression. "No one ever really finishes a story. Every story is written by de Almighty, and it has no beginning and no end unless He vants it to. So, dis story, like all de others told by old babushkas like me, is really just da *middle* of a story. Da beginnings we never knew, and de endings we never live to learn." She sighs. "Still, let me finish telling my part.

"About eight years after da king died, Bona Sforza, who vas now queen mother, left Poland and went back to her family's home in Bari, Italy, more than a *thousand* miles away. After dat, da Jewish village vas told to pay its rent to a local man." She shrugs. "He vas honest, as far as ve could tell, but he could do nothing to protect us from the Tatars. When the Tatars found out dat some Jews have money, but no protection, dey forced us to pay dem every year to stay away. In a few years, ve had barely enough left to pay da rent.

"By 1558, things got so bad dat da villagers sent David and Naomi to make da long trip to Bari to meet with Bona Sforza and beg her to give us more protection from da Tatars. She still owned many lands in Poland, but she vas no longer queen and had no power dere as queen mother." She shrugs. "Your father once told me dat Bona vas a good woman who did a bad thing."

"What bad thing?"

Yetta sighs, as though this is something painful to tell. "Ven your parents were quite young, Queen Bona was persuaded by her closest counselor to allow de execution of an old woman for heresy. The voman was a Christian, but her beliefs vere different from the Roman Church. Her ideas vere Hebrew. Vell, da queen went along with her counselor's advice, but she regretted it to her dying day.

"Many years later, ve found out that her trusted counselor was da one who had ordered the poisoning of da queen consort, who vas Bona Sforza's daughter-in-law."

"Who was this disloyal counselor?" asks Noah.

Yetta's mouth purses bitterly. "Pappacoda." As was common in the old country, she pretends to spit over her left shoulder after saying a name of the wicked. "May his name be forgotten!" Weak as she is, her body grows tense. Beth draws a blanket up to her shoulders.

"He did all this himself?" asks Noah incredulously.

"No," replies Yetta. "Dere vas a young man who did dis, who vas once a houseboy for Queen Bona."

"What was his name?" asks Noah.

Yetta collects herself. "I never learned his real name. But, if you'll lean close to me, I'll whisper to you vat people used to call him. I do not vish for Esther to hear it."

Noah rises and places his ear right to Yetta's mouth.

She whispers, perhaps a bit more loudly than she intended. "Ciemnoci." To Noah, it sounds like *Chemnochee*.

Noah's eyes go wide, and he resumes his seat, nodding. He remembers the name, or something like it, from long, long ago.

Yetta pretends to spit over her shoulder and resumes her tale. "He vas da one who vanted your mother da most. I remember how he ogled her. You could almost see his evil mind at vork as he plotted to get her for himself. I even saw him speak vit her once or twice. He tried so hard to make her believe he was her friend. Ah, but *she* knew." She taps her temple to show how intelligent Noah's mother was. "*She* knew vat he vas." She sighs. "I suppose he knew he could never win her. So, he put her to death vit everyone else."

Yetta's words have reawakened long-sleeping memories buried deep in Noah's mind. "That's the name that Tomas said to the bad soldier."

Yetta draws a deep, hoarse breath, sits up, and regards Noah as though he's some sort of prodigy. She puts her palm to her cheek, and says to Beth, "Look how he remembers! So long ago, and he remembers every vord."

Beth comforts her.

"Menachem," says Yetta, "your father vas a very important man. He brought your mother to talk with Bona Sforza in Milan. Bona Sforza invited them in and heard vat dey had to say. We know now dat, just after that meeting, Pappacoda poisoned her.

"Some months later, vile your parents vere returning to the village, they heard dat Pappacoda had sent his man ahead to do mischief to the villagers. Your parents never had a chance to tell me whether dey recognized the man on their vay home.

"As you know, Pappacoda had ordered his man to force all da Jews into da synagogue, and burn dem. But he'd ordered dem to vait for your parents to return, vich gave you and me just enough time to escape.

"Once your parents came back, they vere pushed into the synagogue by … the nameless one … and vere burned along with the Torah scrolls, and vith all the villagers inside." She weeps, and wags her aged finger at Noah. "And dis vas *not* an uprising of fearful *goyim* against da Jews. It was *murder*, plain and simple! Pappacoda"—Yetta feigns spitting again—"vanted the land clear of all tenants. Since the tenants vere all Jews, it vas cheapest to burn dem, and make it look like a general uprising against Jews, so some local idiots could be blamed."

"Why would Pappacoda murder Bona Sforza?" asks Beth.

"He vanted her to sign over her lands."

"To him?"

Yetta shakes her head. "Dat's vat most people thought, but I don't think so."

"What do *you* think?" asks Noah.

Yetta weighs her words. "Your mother wrote a letter to my cousin Tanya; it arrived just before your parents vere expected to arrive at da village. The letter told Tanya that I should take you away from the village right away. But it said something else, too. It said that your father had found out Pappacoda was being paid by King Philip of Spain, who owed Bona Sforza a lot of money. Your father believed dat the Spanish king wanted the lands he bought from Bona Sforza to be made free and clear of da mortgage, so he ordered Pappacoda to get her signature on a Satisfaction of the mortgage and den … to kill her, and den clear the land of unwanted tenants, like da Jews.

"When drugs did not persuade her to sign, Pappacoda twisted her arm and *forced* her to sign, then finished her off with poison." Yetta's breathing is becoming labored. "Anyway. It doesn't matter now. Pappacoda is dead." She looks up. "Thanks be to God!"

"Pappacoda did all this by himself?" asks Noah.

Yetta squeezes her eyes shut and shakes her head. "No, he vas too old. He had his young man do all of his dirty work. It was the young one who used to work for Queen Bona, who poisoned the queen consort, and later Bona Sforza herself—and set fire to the synagogue."

She chokes and weeps, despite Beth's attempt to comfort her. "Only you and I survived." Her face blanches, and tears flow freely down her cheeks. She coughs, and struggles to breathe.

Noah gently strokes Yetta's forehead. "Thank you, Babushka. I know so much more now," he assures her. Though she's too weak to speak, she smiles wanly, her face ashen once again.

Noah wonders if she'll survive the night.

Next morning, under a sky that threatens to open up with the rains of heaven at any time, Noah mounts Bucklebury and clops off to Sir Walter's office at the Tower. As there's no one in the immediate vicinity, he ties off Bucklebury and knocks on the office door, which has been left ajar.

"Sir Walter?" he calls. No answer. Finding the office vacant, he enters and takes a seat. As he's eager to return to his private room at the Saracen's Head, time passes slowly. His mind wanders to Yetta's face as he left her last evening. Her gray visage, drawn tautly over its flaccid supporting muscles, resembled a death mask entirely too closely for his liking. He considers writing Beth a note to inquire after Yetta, but thinks better of it. Perhaps he'll visit them both unannounced, as Southwark is not far from the Tower.

Outside in the distance Sir Walter shouts, apparently addressing some underling. "Where should you search!" he says derisively. "*Everywhere!* A scullion does not simply disappear." He strides into his office alone and seems momentarily alarmed to find it occupied. When he realizes his visitor is Noah, however, he greets him heartily. "To what do I owe this unannounced visit?"

"I wanted to see the progress you were making into that perennial question: *How did the intended assassin gain entry to the Tower?*"

Sir Walter plops down into his too-small chair, looking chagrined. "Not much progress, I'm afraid. We have determined that the poison was dropped into the bowl, not baked into the coffee beans."

"What's your basis for that conclusion?" asks Noah.

"Several things. First, the beans had none of the foul odor detected by Lord Saint Ives. Second, Her Majesty's chief cook, Goodwife Barry, said that—without hurt—she'd personally ground the coffee beans that wound up in the poisoned bowl, and that those beans had gone into dozens of people's coffee for more than a week without ill effect."

"Have you spoken to those who drank coffee made from other beans in the sack?"

"Not only have I," says Sir Walter, "but *you* have, too. In fact, you're talking to one right now."

"You?"

"The same, and to me we may add every Yeoman Warder on the grounds."

Noah protests. "But they drank the coffee that was in the sack *prior* to the attempt on Her Majesty. What's happened to the coffee sack since then?"

"We removed it from Her Majesty's kitchen permanently," says Sir Walter, smiling craftily. "And put it to good use here in the Yeoman's mess. Been using it for days. There's nothing wrong with it, I assure you. Would you like some?"

Noah regards Sir Walter with amazement, and rolls his eyes. "I'm so pleased you find this amusing, Sir Walter. Have you checked all the other food?"

"Yes. There was no sign of tampering with any of it. And, to varying degrees, it's all remained in use since the attempt on Her Majesty. It appears we're dealing with a single, well-targeted attempt."

"So, how did he get into the Tower grounds?"

"Not a clue. As yet."

"What is it I heard you shouting just before you came back into your office?" asks Noah.

"Oh, that! We can't find the cook's assistant who was at work on the evening of the attempt, one 'Sally Firth.' I think she may have had something going on with Francis of the shattered shoulder. She failed to show up at her job the day after the attempt, and I was telling my subordinates where to seek her out."

"'Everywhere' is a bit broad, no?"

"I meant everywhere on the grounds. They know that. If they un-cover nothing, of course, we'll search her dwelling place off the Tower grounds. If we turn up no one, then she may be the culprit."

Noah is skeptical. "A cook's assistant? She'd have a devil of a time finding work after trying to poison her employer." He considers the situation and draws a likelier conclusion. "If you can't find her, she's likely fallen victim to the same culprit."

A breathless voice comes from outside. "We may have found some-thing, suh," says a Yeoman Warder, catching his breath as he appears in the doorway.

Sir Walter sits up. "May have? *May* have found something?"

"There's a body in a barrel of malmsey wine, suh. It's small. As soon as we spotted it, I ran down here to tell you, as per your orders, suh."

"Quite right," says Sir Walter. "Take us there at once. Serjeant Ames, would you care to come along?"

Noah jumps to his feet and steps alongside Sir Walter. "Drowning in a barrel of malmsey wine," he says, "was the technique used by Richard the Third to dispose of his elder brother, the Duke of Clarence, in clearing his way to the Throne." Sir Walter barely acknowledges this bit of erudition, leaving Noah feeling a bit foolish. What could be further from a duke than a scullery maid?

They climb a flight of exterior stone stairs and enter through a door leading to servants' quarters. The door to the room adjacent to the wenches' dormitory is marked "Special Victuals," and it's wide open.

Sir Walter explains to Noah. "The more valuable edibles that might be pilfered are stored right next to the wenches' dormitory, so that any thief would be immediately apprehended by other members of the staff."

In one corner of the room is a barrel of malmsey wine with its top removed. Jutting up out of the barrel are two smallish feet. One bears a woman's slipper and the other no shoe at all. Sir Walter wordlessly appoints two of the Yeoman Warders to extract the corpse.

Spreading an oilcloth on the floor, they hoist the body out of the barrel. The spill of malmsey wine onto the oilcloth sounds like a downpour of sudden rain on a slate roof. Despite the Warders' best efforts to handle the body with care, it thumps face down onto the oilcloth. They reverently turn it over.

Sir Walter requires only a glance to recognize the face. "That's Sally." He turns away in anger, composes himself, and turns back to the Warders, whose arms are covered in dark amber wine. "Is there anything else in the barrel?"

With a look of combined apprehension and disgust, one of the Warders fishes around in the barrel, but comes up empty. "Nothin', suh."

Sir Walter nods gravely. "No one is to tell Francis," he instructs them. "I'll tell him myself. Is that clear?"

The Warders shoot to attention. "Yes, suh," they reply.

"You may go. Wash your shirts straight away."

"Aye, suh."

In a moment, Sir Walter and Noah are the room's sole living occupants.

"Francis will be crushed," observes Noah.

Sir Walter shakes his head. "Worse than crushed. He'll be mad with fury. One can't see it from his everyday demeanor, but he has a violent

temper. And he's strong as an ox. Once he knows Sally's been murdered, it will take everything we have to keep him strapped into that
blasted contraption, or even in the Tower."

"Tell the Warder's surgeon to administer some laudanum before
you break the news," suggests Noah.

Sir Walter nods. "That might help ... briefly."

"Meanwhile, Sir Walter, please check every room in the Tower for
possible tampering before this evening. Perhaps it will provide information about the killer of this poor girl."

# CHAPTER 7

**THAT AFTERNOON,** Noah trudges dourly into his private room at the Saracen's Head, having left Raleigh at the Tower to investigate the murder of the kitchen wench.

As neither Sir Walter nor Arthur was at liberty to accompany him this afternoon, Noah is very much on his own. To enliven his solitude, he leaves the door ajar, admitting pleasant sounds of distant conversation and clinking glasses.

He fervently hopes that today will bring no repetition of yesterday's incident between Lord Grey and the Percys that threatened to break out into earnest swordplay in these cramped quarters. More for good measure than for any practical purpose, he taps Uncle Avram's dagger, which he keeps hidden beneath his robes. He opens the curtain behind him to admit more light for reading on this overcast day, sits down, and opens the folio before him.

As he's about to begin, he's startled by what appears to be a human face gazing up at him expectantly, directly across his desk. Noah gasps, and jerks back into his chair.

Although the face belongs to someone the height of a boy of perhaps nine years, it's definitely not that of a child, but rather of a young man whose face and head are entirely too large for his body. By contrast, his arms and hands appear small and smooth, like those of an infant. The hair is brown, as are the eyes.

It quickly dawns on Noah that he's looking into the face of a dwarf. He's never met one before, although Sir Robert exhibits a few of their traits. The few dwarfs he's seen on the street were only passing by, and they'd disappeared into traffic before he could observe them long enough to be sure that's what they were.

The face now observing Noah is proud and defiant, no doubt in reaction to a lifetime of watching every new acquaintance struggle to classify its wearer in the catalog of men. It's the countenance of someone consigned to a difficult life, in part by his diminutive stature, to be sure, but far more by his stature's uncomfortable effect on the viewer. To Noah, this fellow is due some respect for having to fight a battle every day that's been forever spared to other men.

The dwarf appears to wear a military uniform, complete with short sword and scabbard, though of which nation's army Noah cannot guess. It appears rather to have been pieced together from the uniforms of sundry European powers. The cap is a sky-blue tricorn with a long white feather jutting straight up from its rear like a cornstalk. The dark blue jacket (with shiny white buttons) is fitted to the fellow's form as neatly as possible, given the unusual contours of his body.

Dwarfism appears to be but one of this young man's ailments. His skin is drawn, his face emaciated, with pockets where his cheeks should be. For another, his left arm is suspended in a sling, its hand puffy, suggesting that it might be more wilted than convalescent.

The dwarf, as though to dispel the impression of physical infirmity fostered by his left arm, shoots his right up in sharp military salute. "Good morning, sir," he says in a French-accented voice sounding partly strangled in the back of the throat, no doubt another symptom of his condition. "Have I ze pleasure of making ze acquaintance of Monsieur Serjeant Emms?"

As everything about this young man's appearance is calculated to ensure that he'll not be trifled with as a monster of nature, Noah resolves to treat him precisely as he would a similarly dressed man of average height. He glowers at the dwarf, whose posture stiffens in response.

"Who wants to know?" asks Noah pointedly.

"*Pardonnez-moi, monsieur.* I am desolate to have astonished you. As ze door was open, I took ze liberty to enter without knocking. My name, *monsieur*—at least ze name by which I am generally known—is 'Monk.' I attend upon a most extraordinary gentleman of France who goes by ze name of 'Monsieur Gaston Dorsay.' I come to you also at ze request of his good friend, Monsieur Paolo Nerezza."

Noah nods reservedly, recognizing the names from Southampton's list of Essex's foreign supporters who've taken up residence at Drury House. "In that case, sir," confirms Noah, "I am indeed Serjeant Ames." He leans back into his chair, observing the dwarf impassively.

The little soldier nods. "Ah! I have guessed most fortunately. My master and Monsieur Nerezza have heard zat you would like to speak wiss zem. Would you wish to see zem *ensemble*? I mean, 'togezza,' as you English say?"

Noah considers the offer. "Perhaps it would be better if I were to meet them separately, Monsieur ... Monk." As the dwarf scowls to hear this form of address, Noah hastens to add humbly: "Unless you have attained some rank, sir, which I, being a mere civilian, have failed to recognize by your uniform ... for which, of course, I apologize."

"No, no," replies the dwarf, blushing. "'Monk' is not my surname, nor is it truly my name at all. Zat is simply what people call me who know me well."

Noah nods indulgently. "May I have the privilege of calling you 'Monk,' as well?"

The dwarf smiles at the prospect of respectful familiarity. "It would please me greatly, Monsieur Serjeant."

"Ah, but in England we use 'Serjeant' as a substitute for 'Master,' so I myself am simply 'Serjeant Ames.'"

"Very well, Serjeant Emms. We have come to an amicable understanding on zees point. Now, to return to ze matter at hand. Which of zees gentlemen would you care to speak wiss first?" The dwarf looks to Noah hopefully, apparently wishing for him to say the name of one such gentleman, and not the other, although it's impossible to tell which name Monk is hoping for.

"Monsieur Nerezza, I should think?" conjectures Noah.

A dark cloud passes over Monk's face and he blushes again. "I see," he says.

In light of Monk's obvious discomfort, Noah adds: "Unless that is not your preference, Monk."

The dwarf brightens to hear Noah say his name. "Not at all. Shall I go and fetch ze gentleman now?"

Noah bows. "If you would be so kind … assuming the gentleman is agreeable."

"He is here at ze tavern. I shall bring him to you at once." Monk bows and goes out through the open doorway.

A few moments later, Noah hears a ruckus. "Away, runt! Half-pint varlet!" shouts a gruff voice.

Monk's voice replies, although too softly for the words to be made out.

"Very well, then, take me to him, and then retreat to your accustomed mouse hole." This must be the voice of Nerezza for, just as the Percy brothers observed, the accent is neither Italian nor French, but sounds rather to have originated somewhere in the huge undifferentiated land mass known to Noah as Eastern Europe. The shifting names and borders of countries in that region have no hold on Noah's mind.

Monk re-enters red-faced and stiff, followed by a thin, sharp-eyed old man in black robes whose countenance relaxes only as he spies Noah—or rather as he spies Noah spying *him*. The old man bows. "Serjeant Ames, I expect?" he says.

Noah bows and smiles. "Indeed, I am, sir."

Monk turns to the old man and stands on tiptoe to whisper but the old man, instead of bending down to hear, turns on him with a stern fury, standing up straight and delivering a boot to his buttocks, with a kick hard enough to shove the dwarf a few feet. "I've told you *numerous* times not to interrupt your betters when they're speaking. Now, get *out*! And don't let me catch you stuffing your fat little face with eat or drink." He looks to Noah exasperated, and turns to Monk again. "Return to Drury House at once!"

Obviously humiliated, barely maintaining an outward composure, Monk turns to Noah and bows. His subsequent bow to the old man is met with a threatening open hand. In the face of this rejection, Monk departs with as much dignity as anyone could under the circumstances, closing the door quietly behind.

Although Noah maintains his professional demeanor, he would like nothing more than to kick this old man in the arse and throw *him* out.

Instead, he raises an eyebrow. "Is this how we treat our friend's servant, sir?" he asks matter-of-factly.

The old man's eyes flash momentarily, then resume their less unpleasant aspect. "I apologize for this outburst, Serjeant. The boy is an unmitigated nuisance, marching about like a marionette. As you recognize, he is not *my* servant, but that of Monsieur Dorsay."

"Is Monk not a military man?" asks Noah. "I assumed he is, by his manner of dress."

"*Pshaw!*" says the old man with undisguised contempt. "Which self-respecting army would have him? He is too small to march or fight. But he *eats* great quantities, I can tell you, like a little *horse.*"

While Noah is tempted to change the subject, he finds himself too sorely offended by the old man's treatment of his friend's servant. "Judging by his face, he appears rather to be famished," Noah points out.

The old man shrugs. "I expect you would not know this, Master Jew, but Our Lord provided us with no special guidance for the treatment of dwarfs."

Noah regards the old man dubiously. "Does not the Bible say, 'As you have done to the least among you, so have you done to me'?"

The old man raises an eyebrow, evidently pleased to see that the heathen before him has some knowledge of the New Testament. "Matthew 25:40! So, it's true, as they say, the devil *can* cite scripture to his purpose."

Noah shakes his head pleasantly. "*Am* I the devil, sir?"

The old man shrugs and smiles. "Some would think so. I'm sure you have heard the phrase, 'Jew devil.' But, I hasten to add that I do not believe a Jew to be a devil ... necessarily."

"So, like the ancient playwright, you count nothing human alien to you. How ecumenical of you, sir!" says Noah with false bonhomie. "In that case, won't you take a seat and tell me something of your past?"

The old man smiles. "Permit me to introduce myself. I am Paolo Nerezza." He hesitates as he studies Noah's face dubiously. "You have an interesting aura, Serjeant Ames. That you have an aura at all is another reason that I, unlike many of the True Faith, believe that Jews have souls." Evidently, the man has a mystical bent.

Noah observes him skeptically; argumentation seems pointless. "I expect, sir, that you are a papist?"

"Of course," says Nerezza, continuing to study the area around Noah's face. "It is the one true religion. All others are founded upon erroneous premises. Tell me, have you ever seen me before?"

Noah studies the old man's wizened face for some sign of familiarity. "I do not believe so, sir. What makes you ask?"

The old man cocks his head. "You have been to Paris, perhaps?"

"I have been to Paris once, but lo these many years ago. Why do you ask?"

"What was the year in which you visited?"

"Well, let's see. I was twenty-seven years old, so I suppose that would be … 1578."

"No earlier than that?" asks Nerezza. When Noah shakes his head, Nerezza regards him dubiously. "Longer ago, I would have guessed," he mutters. "And you were admitted to the presence of King Henri the Third?"

Noah shakes his head. "No, never had I the honor of meeting King Henri of France, but—"

Nerezza finishes his sentence. "You met King Henri of Navarre. Correct?"

Noah smiles curiously. "I did, sir, but he is Henri the *Fourth*. You asked about Henri the *Third*, did you not?"

Nerezza smiles sagely, as someone confident of having superior knowledge. "Henri of Navarre was Henri the Third of Navarre before he assumed the French throne and became Henri the Fourth of *France*."

Noah is impressed, vaguely recalling that he himself had found the dual reckoning confusing. "He was indeed, Master Nerezza. But why do you ask whether I've been to Paris?"

"Because I expect that's where I saw you," says the old man, "or at least your aura. What was your business there?"

"I was on European tour with Master Henry Neville, now 'Sir Henry.' He is in France at present, as Her Majesty's ambassador. And now you have me on the hip, sir, as you know something of my past while I know nothing of yours."

The old man chortles. "I remember your aura. Your face may have changed, but your aura? Never. Never throughout the whole of one's life. Perhaps you and I are in some sort of spiritual grouping of which we are unaware."

Noah shrugs, repulsed by the notion that, if there are indeed spiritual groupings, his spirit would belong to the same one as this stonyhearted old man.

The old man continues. "I will be pleased to tell you of my past. It is ... more *varied* than interesting, I should think. But, tell me first, have you any children?"

"I have a daughter: Lady Saint Ives, formerly Lady Burlington."

Nerezza gasps. "I have seen the lady, sir. She is most beautiful. Exquisite. This is your daughter? A Jewess?"

"She converted long ago to reformed Church of England."

Nerezza still seems puzzled. "Curious. She is not of the True Faith, and yet incomparably beautiful. Well, I suppose her acceptance of Jesus as her Savior has gentled her condition."

Noah allows some of his irritation to show. "She was just as beautiful prior to her conversion, Monsieur Nerezza. And her mother was equally beautiful, though she remained a Jew all her life."

Nerezza bows gravely in his seat. "Then I conclude your wife has passed away. I extend my most sincere condolences." He smiles contemplatively. "They say that a child's beauty is a reflection of the father's soul."

"I take that as a compliment. Have *you* any children, *monsieur*?" Noah has come to expect that, if he's going to glean any information from this man, he'll need to demand reciprocal answers.

Nerezza frowns. "I have not had the pleasure of children. But I tip my hat to you, sir, as you surely have a remarkable soul. While it is troubling to know that it shall remain in peril until your conversion to the True Faith"—he speaks of Noah's conversion as an inevitability— "you will make a very promising convert."

"And conversion would assure me a favorable fate?" Noah asks doubtfully.

Nerezza shrugs. "Your *eternal* fate, yes." But he shakes his head and purses his lips as though tasting something bitter. "Not your *worldly* fate, however, to be sure. That is governed, as are all of our worldly fates, by the *Rota Fortunae.* You have heard of this?"

"The Wheel of Fortune?" asks Noah. Although the Wheel is a familiar trope—a favorite of Sir Henry Neville's—Noah wishes to hear Nerezza's view of it. "I've heard of it. It is a card in the Tarot deck, as I recall, but perhaps you can say more."

Nerezza smiles, as though given a welcome opportunity to expound upon a favored subject. "As the Wheel is generally depicted, four human figures are placed on it, at even intervals. The Wheel rotates in clockwise manner. On the left side of the Wheel is the young man, labeled Regnabo, which means 'I shall reign.' He represents a man in his youth, when he has the world to gain and nothing to lose. At the top is Regno, which means 'I reign.' Naturally, he wears a crown, as the formerly young man has now come into his fortune, and feels it is his place to remain on his throne indefinitely. But, alas, he cannot reign forever. When he reaches the right side of the Wheel, he has become Regnavi, which means 'I have reigned.'

"And ultimately he is transformed into the lowly figure at the base of the Wheel, the most miserable of all, Sum Sine Regno, which means 'I am without kingdom.' This is the point to which all men must come in the temporal world, for we all are subject to the turning of the Wheel—even your Queen Elizabeth." At this point, he mumbles something under his breath in a foreign tongue; the only word Noah can make out is *puta*, meaning "whore," a filthy word used by papists to refer to Her Majesty. "Even she will lose her kingdom."

Noah is amazed to observe how the old man uses every explanation as an opportunity to provoke the listener. Noah's patience is exhausted, and his aversion to this man has taken on a permanence in his heart. He raises an eyebrow and picks up a pen, as though to jot down Nerezza's answer to his next question. "And have you come to London to assist Lord Essex in ensuring that Her Majesty will soon become Sum Sine Regno, and lose her kingdom?"

But Nerezza merely chuckles at the accusation. "Lord Essex has no designs on this kingdom, at least none that I know of, and neither do I. No, it is the action of the Wheel itself that will bring your Queen low. I was simply explaining that, at every point in a person's life, he—or she—occupies a point *somewhere* on the Wheel. There is no person, no king, no queen who is immune to its motion. Each of us merely sits at a certain point at a given time." The old man sits back, touched with melancholy. "The tragedy of the Wheel is that it turns in only one direction, and each of us ends up ... at the bottom."

Noah lets his impatience show. "Come now, sir. After all, the Wheel is merely a trope—a metaphor. Perhaps you will agree that it would garner us little to spend the afternoon discussing it. You were about to tell me of your past, which I find more interesting. How did you come to know King Henri de Navarre?"

"Shall we begin my history so recently? For I knew his predecessor, as well. In fact, I knew his *predecessor's* predecessor."

Noah can hear a long tale coming on, but decides to let Nerezza tell his story at his own pace. "Begin wherever you feel appropriate but, first, please tell me where you are from originally."

"I am Lithuanian by birth, an apothecary by trade, but that ancient part of my life, even what little I can recall, would be of no interest to you. When I was young, the King of France was Charles the Ninth. He was a member of the Valua family. At the time of which I speak, King Charles was only twenty-two years old. *Henri* Valua was the king's younger brother, and so never expected to become King of France.

"But the Valua family held large territorial claims in other parts of Europe, including my home country of Lithuania. I came to the attention of Henri Valua while visiting Paris in 1572."

Noah sits up and takes notice. "Around the time of the massacre of Huguenots?"

Nerezza seems irritated by the interruption. "Shortly before that terrible time, yes. When the king of Lithuania died, the throne became vacant for a time. Ultimately, it was decided by election that Henri Valua would occupy it."

This is all news to Noah. "So, Henri Valua was King of Lithuania before ascending the throne of France?"

"Yes." Nerezza chuckles darkly. "There is a whole *world* on the Continent about which you English care to know very little. King Charles, though himself a member of the True Church, attempted to appease the protestant Huguenots, going so far as to order his sister to marry the protestant Henri of Navarre. After the wedding, however, the people resisted, and slaughtered the Huguenot protestants in the streets." To Noah's horror, the old man's memory seems to linger fondly on the atrocity. "King Charles knew that he would be overthrown by the people if he appeared to oppose the massacre, so he went along, after it had already spread and taken on a life of its own.

"Meanwhile, the king's younger brother Henri had left France to take up residence in his new kingdom of Lithuania. It is perhaps an irony that, shortly after I met Henri, I became his Lithuanian subject, though both he and I were yet living in France. During Henri's absence, King Charles was so overcome by guilt about supporting the massacre that he lost his mind, and eventually died of consumption.

"Charles died without heir. As Henri's true heart was in France, he resigned the Lithuanian throne and returned to rule France. Unfortunately, Henri, like his elder brother, was both childless and inclined to indulge the protestant heresy—for political reasons—very much against the popular will. At that time, it was expected Charles would be followed on the French throne by the Infanta of Spain, daughter of Philip the Second, a devout member of the True Faith. But, alas, it was not to be.

"Instead, Henri the Third ruled France. After fifteen years on the throne, he was murdered for his pains. As there was a religious war throughout France, and the protestant Henri of Navarre proved unable to take Paris by force, he converted to the True Faith and became Henri the Fourth of France."

"Yes," says Noah. "I recall the new King Henri being quoted as saying, 'Paris is worth a mass.'"

Nerezza sneers contemptuously. "That phrase seems to comprise the sum of English knowledge about the terrible religious wars suffered by France. So, with the death of the papist Henri the Third, we French are now ruled by Henri the Fourth, who fought the True Church for as long as he could (even allying himself with your Queen Elizabeth for a time), but then joined the True Faith in order to become king. You might say it was his attempt to suspend or reverse the motion of the Wheel."

Noah turns and peers through the window contemplatively. The day seems darker than ever, but the cleansing rains have failed to appear. He spies something curious by a corner of the inn not visible to Nerezza.

Monk evidently declined to return to Drury House as he was ordered, having been sidetracked into a game of fetch-the-stick by an emaciated three-legged retriever. Monk throws the stick, and the dog hops along in its crippled gait, mouths it, hobbles back, and drops it at the feet of its diminutive companion, who waits with a treat extended on the open palm of his wounded left hand, which Noah is pleased to see is not in fact wilted. Noah cannot see which treat Monk is offering; it's small—possibly just some oats scooped out of a saddlebag—but the dog seems well pleased by it.

While there's something heartening about seeing two such outcasts enjoying each other's company, Noah lacks the peace of mind to appreciate it fully just now. In fact, the happier the dwarf seems, the more pitiable also, as it's surely unfair for someone of good heart to be trapped in the company of a curmudgeon such as this Nerezza.

Nearly forgetting what he was about to say, Noah turns back to the old man and observes: "It's almost as though there was a guiding hand ensuring that, one way or another, France would remain papist."

Nerezza regards him askance at first. "Almost," he ultimately agrees.

There's a knock at the door, and it's opened a crack from outside. The head of a full-grown man pops in. "*Pardonnez-moi*," he says somberly, "Serjeant Emms, permit me to introduce myself briefly. I am Gaston Dorsay. I wish to know if you have completed your interview with Monsieur Nerezza." He enters and bows perfunctorily. "Monsieur Nerezza and I have an appointment elsewhere just now."

Nerezza looks at the clock. "*Saint Hilaire!*" he exclaims. "Gaston, you are quite correct." He rises. "Serjeant Ames," he says, bowing, "I must beg your forgiveness. May we continue another time?"

Noah rises. "Certainly, gentlemen! Monsieur Dorsay, I hope you will come and speak with me at your earliest convenience."

Dorsay eyes him suspiciously while holding the door open for Nerezza. "Perhaps in a few days' time," he replies with obvious reluctance.

As Nerezza passes through the doorway, Noah hears Dorsay whisper something to him in French. Although Noah's French is far from perfect, he understands enough to conclude that Nerezza has been admonished with words meaning: "You need not humiliate him that way. He's not an animal," evidently referring to Monk. Their voices and footsteps die away down the hall.

Noah looks at the clock and ties off his portfolio in preparing to leave. He takes it under his arm, and locks the door from the outside.

Before leaving the Tower this morning, Noah had asked for a private meeting with Sir Walter, and now has less than a half hour to get there. As he walks down the hall and traverses the nearly vacant dining room, he spies two figures in a far corner crouched together in a posture that can only be described as conspiratorial.

It's Sir Gelly Meyrick and Nicholas Skeres. Although Noah's history with both is long and combative, at this moment he feels he has earned some of their good will, as quite recently he saved their lives and their freedom by concealing their role in a misbegotten plot to smuggle a military map out of the country. Unbidden, Noah approaches their table.

In a move evidently intended to be unseen, Sir Gelly kicks Skeres under the table to shut his mouth. He rises with a smile and bows. "Good afternoon, Serjeant Ames. Nick," he says to Skeres, "get up and greet our old friend."

Skeres forces a half-smile, rises, and bows.

Noah takes a long look at them both and can barely keep from laughing, their demeanor is so comically guilty. "It was not my intention to interrupt a discussion of importance," says Noah.

"'Course not," says Meyrick. "We're just plannin' a brief respite outta town."

"Oh," says Noah, "where are you bound for?"

Meyrick's eyes momentarily dart toward Skeres and return to Noah.

"Up about Cambridge ... for a week's holiday."

Noah bows. "And well deserved, I'm sure," he replies blankly.

"And yerself, Serjeant Ames?" says Sir Gelly politely. "How are you farin'?"

"Oh, the Crown never sleeps, Sir Gelly," says Noah wearily, "and sometimes *I* don't, either. I must be going now. Gentlemen," he says, excusing himself.

As Noah turns to walk away, he hears Skeres admonish Meyrick in a whisper. "What'd you go and tell him *that* for?"

Noah smiles privately at the incompetence of these two boobs, and tucks away in his memory a reminder to investigate precisely where they're going, and why.

# CHAPTER 8

**NOAH ENTERS THE TOWER GROUNDS** through the portcullis. As he emerges from the inner gate, he's surprised to find Sir Walter and a young Warder waiting for him across the courtyard. As it's summer, and a few hours of daylight remain, Noah finds it especially curious that Sir Walter holds a burning torch in his hand.

After Noah trots over to this small welcoming party, Sir Walter takes Bucklebury's reins and turns them over to the Warder.

"I would have found you, Sir Walter," says Noah. "There was no need for you to await me."

"Come, Noah," says Sir Walter earnestly, walking off toward an exterior flight of stairs. "I've something to show you."

Noah jumps down from Bucklebury and follows. "Care to tell me what we're to see?" he asks, but Sir Walter ignores his inquiry, evidently lost in thought.

They enter a stone building and climb three flights of stairs to a dark and oppressively warm attic hallway with spider webs in every corner, where the ceilings are too low for them to stand erect. As the attic's frame is comprised of dry unfinished wood, it's redolent of sawdust.

Sir Walter lowers the torch and bends forward to escort Noah down the hall. He stops and points to an open door. "When the Warders came up here earlier," he says, "they found this door closed and locked."

Noah tries to scratch his head, but his hand bumps the ceiling. "Well, if the room was locked, why did they even think to check inside?"

"Because, quoting you, I told them to leave no stone unturned."

Sir Walter walks through the doorway and beckons Noah into a cramped attic room containing two nondescript trunks, such as one might use to transport clothing during travel. They're unopened. What little air there is in the tiny room is even warmer and more stagnant than that in the hallway.

"Wait! Don't step there," says Sir Walter, warding Noah away from a place hard by the nearest chest. He lowers the torch further, and points to the floor. "The Warders were careful not to enter this room. Yet, see the dust?"

Noah leans so low that his nose nearly touches the floor. "Yes, the dust appears to have been disturbed here," he muses. He looks about the floor nearby. "There are bootprints." He turns to Sir Walter. "How long have these trunks been here?"

"By their dusty condition," says Sir Walter, "some years. It would help to know what's inside them."

"Are they locked?" asks Noah.

"I doubt it," replies Raleigh. "They appear to be commonplace traveler's trunks. Ordinarily, any locks would be visible on the outside. As you can see, however … no locks."

Noah observes, "Whoever left these here was no doubt relying on the lock on that door," he says, indicating the open door.

Raleigh nods. "Which might have proved adequate if the intruder hadn't a key."

"*Had* he a key?"

Raleigh nods. "There's no sign of forced entry. So, he, she … or *they* must have had one."

"I'm fairly certain it was the last," surmises Noah, "for there are prints here made by more than one boot. Look!"

Raleigh leans forward and squints. "Yes, you're right."

"Why haven't you opened the trunks?"

Sir Walter seems apprehensive. "This Tower was constructed centuries ago, Noah. There's no telling *what* the trunks might contain." There's something disturbingly apologetic in his tone.

"Well, we shan't find out without opening them," Noah replies.

"But," says Raleigh hesitantly, "should we disturb them without obtaining permission first?"

"Permission. From whom?"

"Richard the Third, for one," offers Sir Walter.

Perplexed at Sir Walter's reticence, Noah studies his earnest and sweaty face in the torchlight, recalling Lord Burghley's old-standing shibboleth: The past is never past. "You think these trunks might contain the Princes in the Tower?"

The Princes in the Tower, as they are universally known, disappeared shortly before the crowning of King Richard the Third, and have never been seen since. As one such prince was himself about to be crowned King Edward the Fifth (thus snuffing out Richard's regal ambitions), common speculation has always been that the princes were put to death on orders of Richard, and their bodies hidden in some remote corner of the Tower.

Although Raleigh is not wont to be frightened by old stories, Noah spies real reluctance in his eyes. He shakes his head and mutters, "Rubbish!"

"And if we look inside, and it turns out to be they?"

Noah turns impatiently to Sir Walter. "Then *I'll* answer for it, for heaven's sake. Sir Walter, it's nearly the seventeenth century. If those boys were murdered, it would have happened in ... 1483."

"Still—"

Noah shakes his head in disbelief. "If it turns out these trunks contain their remains, we'll discreetly double-lock the room and inform Her Majesty privately."

"Not Sir Robert?"

"At this point, it's Tudor family business. If Her Majesty wants Sir Robert to know, she'll tell him." Noah can feel the discovery of the recent boot prints spurring him to immediate action. "But these trunks *don't* contain their remains," he says confidently.

"I suppose you're right, if only as a matter of probabilities," says Sir Walter.

"No, Sir Walter, that's not it. You're an experienced warrior, but you haven't the mind of a cold-blooded murderer. If the princes *were* murdered here on King Richard's orders, their bodies would have been disposed of far, far away, probably burned. But even if the bodies *had* remained on the Tower grounds, they would have been buried deep underground or sealed off by masonry somewhere.

"To store them in a dry attic room such as this with a flimsy door would have both ensured preservation of the clearest evidence of the dastardly deed *and* enhanced the likelihood of eventual detection. Why would a king do that? Besides, the dust would be thicker. These trunks can't have been left here more than twenty or thirty years ago." Noah's back is beginning to ache from crouching, and sweat runs down his face. "Have we learned all there is to learn from the trodden dust?"

"I expect so," Sir Walter replies.

"Then we have no choice but to trample it. Please bring the torch closer."

Noah opens the first trunk, which creaks as though annoyed by the disturbance. It contains sundry items: some dishes, a cloak, a candlestick, but nothing that seems particularly important. To Noah, the contents seem to consist of last-minute personal items, such as might be tossed in a trunk during a rushed evacuation.

He flips open the second trunk, which contains a few similar items, but also contains a separate compartment stuffed with papers set neatly on edge.

"No princes," says Noah, arching an eyebrow toward Sir Walter. "But papers!"

Running his fingers over the papers, Noah sees that, every few inches, a tab juts up from a divider, each with a year neatly printed on it. Nearest him is the earliest year: 1570. Moving his fingers toward the back of the trunk, the next tab says 1571.

But the next says *1574.* After that, there's a tab for every subsequent year through 1580.

"What happened to 1572 and 1573?" asks Raleigh.

"Good question," says Noah. "Perhaps determining what these papers are will help us to answer it."

Noah removes the first sheet from the compartment. It appears to be an item of correspondence from Paris, dated May 12, 1570. As the Continent did not adopt the Gregorian calendar until 1582, the date would have been the same in England.

The hand is unfamiliar, but the signature at the foot purports to be that of one "Fra. Walsingham." And the greeting is to "Lord Burghley, William Cecil," Sir Robert's deceased father, who was then England's Secretary of State.

Raleigh, who's been reading over Noah's shoulder, observes: "It's addressed to Burghley, but that's *not* Walsingham's handwriting."

"No, indeed," replies Noah. "I became quite familiar with Walsingham's handwriting during the Lopez case, years ago."

"Could it be a forgery?" asks Raleigh.

Noah shakes his head. "Far more likely it's a scrivener's copy. Though we can't be sure at the moment, it appears that our intruders removed copies of all correspondence for 1572 and '73."

"Now, why would they do that?" asks Raleigh. "Well," he volunteers an answer to his own question, "I suppose they might have wanted simply to see what the letters said."

"That would still leave unanswered what they thought they might find there." Noah shakes his head. "No. If that's all they wanted, there would have been no need to remove them from this place. If they'd broken in just to *read* the letters, they'd have put them back, with no one the wiser. No. It was important for them to ensure that we do *not* see what the letters said."

"But, why those years, especially?" asks Raleigh.

Noah strokes his chin. "As we discussed the other day, 1572 was the year of the Huguenot massacre at Paris and its immediate aftermath. You said the massacre began with the murder of Admiral Coligny. How was he killed?"

"Shot on the street from a first storey window, evidently," replies Sir Walter.

"By whom?"

"Well, the Duke of Guise was blamed for it, and he was likely behind it, as he blamed the admiral for his brother's murder. But the actual killer?" Sir Walter shrugs. "It was rumored to be Lord Maurevert, but to my knowledge, no one really knows, at least no Englishman. What difference does it make?"

"Possibly none," Noah replies, but then he thinks back on the long history of the French wars between papists and protestants, and the smug satisfaction taken by Nerezza in the papists' victory. "But you're certain the admiral's murder took place in 1572?"

"Oh, quite."

"And it took place in Paris?"

Raleigh observes Noah curiously. "Yes, why?"

Noah chortles. "Then there's *one* Englishman who bloody well knew who killed the admiral." He smacks the front of the chest with his open hand. "Walsingham was Her Majesty's ambassador to France at that time, and I'll warrant he was in Paris when the admiral was murdered."

Raleigh exhales with a contemplative whoosh, and nods. "Oh, yes, that's certain. Walsingham barely escaped with his life. For five days, the English embassy was surrounded by stone-throwing papist mobs, while bootless Huguenots banged the door, seeking sanctuary. Until order was restored, no one at the embassy slept." Sir Walter mops his brow. "Walsingham himself was quite shaken ... and Walsingham was hard to shake."

Noah nods, causing the sweat to drip into his eyes, stinging them. "Lord Burghley was Secretary of State, and may already have been appointed Lord Treasurer. And evidently Walsingham was corresponding with him."

"Doubtless," observes Raleigh. "Walsingham might *also* have been corresponding with Her Majesty, but he would have sent the important intelligence to Burghley."

"Are the *originals* of the purloined letters extant?" asks Noah.

"I've no idea," says Sir Walter, "but Sir Robert would know for certain. And he'd know of any other copies. Burghley was his father, after all."

Noah wipes the sweat off his face with a handkerchief. "Where's Sir Robert?"

"Here at the Tower."

"Let's go and see him at once," says Noah.

"Shall we put the papers back as we found them?"

Noah nods excitedly. "Quickly! And double-lock the door on the way out!"

As a sweaty Noah and Sir Walter approach Sir Robert's chamber, the doorkeeper swiftly admits them.

"Gentlemen," says Sir Robert, seated behind his bureau, "what can I do for you? William tells me you are quite exercised. I was hoping it would be good news, but your frowning seems to say the contrary."

Raleigh begins. "My men have been searching the Tower for any sign of tampering performed by whoever murdered the serving wench—"

Sir Robert interrupts. "Have you yet determined whether the serving wench was murdered by the same person who tried to murder Her Majesty?"

"No," says Sir Walter.

Sir Robert nods. "Or whether the wench was murdered—and the Queen very nearly so—during the same intrusion into the Tower?"

Sir Walter is chagrined. "No, Sir Robert, although that has been our assumption."

"If your assumption is wrong," says Sir Robert, "then we may yet be infiltrated by hostile persons unknown, or we may be dealing with an intruder who has found a way to come and go as he pleases."

Noah replies. "We won't be able to tell for certain until we find out who did it. We have come upon a potentially important clue, however."

Sir Robert sits back. "Proceed."

Sir Walter resumes. "The Yeoman Warders discovered that someone, or perhaps more than one person, removed certain old records stored in an attic in the Tower's northwestern quadrant."

"How recently were they removed?"

Noah volunteers. "The dust around the trunks holding the papers appears to have been trodden quite recently, no earlier than the past few weeks."

"I see," replies Sir Robert. "But why would you assume that a theft of old records has anything to do with the recent attempt upon Her Majesty's life?"

"We've made no assumption on that score," says Raleigh. "It's what we're investigating."

"Which records are missing?" asks Sir Robert.

Noah replies. "Scrivener's copies of Secretary Walsingham's correspondence with Lord Burghley. The missing letters appear to be those during the years 1572 and 1573."

Sir Robert stares blankly at his desktop as though searching his memory. "Those would include letters written during, and just after, the Huguenot massacre at Paris."

"Yes," says Noah, "and, as it happens, at least one of the foreign visitors we're investigating at Drury House was in Paris at that time. We expect the letters may have been removed because they might have provided us with information needed to identify whoever was behind the recent attempt on Her Majesty's life. It may even be one of the foreigners who's already taken up residence at Drury House." Noah equivocates. "Or, perhaps, someone whose arrival is imminent."

Sir Robert appears perplexed. "But it would have made sense for them to suppress the correspondence *only* if they knew that it contained something compromising to them, no?"

Noah shakes his head. "Not necessarily. It would have been enough if they *suspected* that Walsingham had collected compromising information and sent it on to your father."

"But they would have had to know that the records were there beforehand," says Sir Robert, "and where to find them."

"Yes," says Sir Walter. "And, as there was nothing at the scene suggesting that the lock on the door had been forced, they must have had a key."

"I see," says Sir Robert contemplatively. "Well, gentlemen, I'm sorry to inform you that those were the only copies remaining in my father's possession at the time of his death."

"Does anyone else have copies?" asks Noah.

Sir Robert speculates aloud. "Walsingham would have kept copies in the ordinary course, certainly of the *official* letters sent during his embassage, which didn't end until some months after the massacre. No one admits to knowing where *those* copies are, but the betting is that Essex has them. He was Secretary Walsingham's son-in-law when

Walsingham died, after all. As to where he'd store them? If you were to ask me, I'd speculate they're somewhere on the top storey of either Essex House or Drury House—if they yet survive."

"Essex House is a mere stone's throw from Drury House," says Noah rising, "where our suspects are staying. And their host, the Earl of Southampton, could readily have gained access to Walsingham's copies at either such location. If they were at Essex House, he could have obtained them by Lady Essex's leave, which would surely have been granted. If at Drury House, he would have required no permission other than his own."

Sir Robert and Sir Walter exchange a glance and await Noah's next thought with interest.

"Suppose," says Noah contemplatively, "just *suppose* ... that those who invaded the Tower were Southampton's guests, and that he'd allowed them to review copies of Walsingham's correspondence. And suppose that such correspondence referred to evidence inculpating them in some past wrongdoing, perhaps even the Huguenot massacre."

Sir Walter shakes his head. "Wouldn't they simply have destroyed the copies?"

Sir Robert corrects him. "No. First of all, they would have had no need to destroy *Essex's* copies, as they'd have been confident that neither he nor Southampton would ever turn them over to us. Besides, if Southampton's guests had destroyed the copies, then Southampton would have learned of it and might have been rather peeved by their destruction. Or perhaps they didn't want Southampton to learn of their past guilt at all."

"That's right," says Noah. "And the culprits would quickly have realized (much as we did) that they were not viewing the only copies in existence. The possibility that other copies might be discovered would eat away at them as a mortal threat." He turns to Sir Robert. "So they purloined the Tower copies."

Sir Walter regards Noah skeptically. "But that's just so much surmise."

Noah nods tentatively. "And, if accurate, it would be truly ironic, as we'd never have discovered the Tower copies missing if the varlets had simply *left them alone*. It's only their breaking in that led us to the discovery in the first place."

"Doesn't that make our whole theory rather implausible?" asks Sir Robert.

Noah shakes his head. "Guilt oft gives rise to an obsessive fear of being caught. Think of Shakespeare's Richard the Third, whose fear for his own safety only *increased* the further he hacked his way through his rivals for the Crown. Now, how might we *test* our hypothesis?"

"We could break in to Essex House or Drury House and search for the copies," suggests Sir Walter as though he'd relish the opportunity. Spying Noah's distaste, he adds, "… or perhaps obtain a warrant."

Noah shakes his head. "Employing either such technique would signal to the adversaries that we're onto them. At that point, they could scatter, and we'd never bring them to justice. Besides, as Sir Robert just suggested, it's nothing more than surmise to say that the copies were there or *anywhere* in Essex's custody. No magistrate would issue a warrant on that basis. We couldn't even bear our burden to show that *those* copies were evidence of a crime. After all, *they're* not the ones that were purloined."

Sir Robert smirks. "Never worry about the warrant. We have enough judicial connections to obtain that. But you're quite right that, once the adversaries realize we know the Tower copies are missing, they'll know that *we* suspect the records to be important. They'd destroy them or move them, and escape on the four winds."

"If I may ask," says Noah, "Sir Robert, are the *originals* extant?"

Sir Robert exhales loudly. "Well, yes, but they're far away from here, I'm afraid."

Sir Walter is not prepared to let the matter rest. "How far?"

"The originals in Walsingham's own hand would be at Burghley House," replies Sir Robert despondently, "which passed from my father to my elder brother Thomas together with the barony."

"Where's Burghley House?" asks Noah.

Sir Walter says glumly, "It's more than a hundred miles from here, almost due north. To Cambridge, and then nearly as far again."

"Cambridge?" mutters Noah, his mind working. "Who just spoke to me of Cambridge?"

Sir Walter resumes. "Still, I suppose we could travel there to examine the letters. But it would take some days to get there and back, even by fast horse. And if we were to go ourselves or send a detachment of Yeoman Warders, it would surely draw attention, forewarning our adversaries."

Sir Robert shakes his head. "On those grounds alone, neither you nor Serjeant Ames could go. Nor could a large contingent of Warders." He leans forward and places his chin on his folded hands. "Besides, we can't even be certain the letters are of any importance."

Noah now recalls where he heard talk of Cambridge. "I think we can, Sir Robert. Unless I'm mistaken, at least two of Essex's attendants are being dispatched to Burghley House to take hold of the originals, possibly even to destroy them."

"*What?*" say Sir Robert and Sir Walter at the same time.

"On my way here," explains Noah, "I ran into Sir Gelly Meyrick and Nicholas Skeres at the Saracen's Head. Sir Gelly blurted out that the two were planning a trip to Cambridge. And I believe it to be true, as Skeres was visibly annoyed at Meyrick for telling me so. I suspect, however, that they're going not only to Cambridge, but, as Sir Walter just suggested, 'nearly as far again.'" He glances at the shocked faces of Sir Robert and Sir Walter. "Of course, if I'm mistaken or if it was a clever ruse of theirs …" He allows his voice to trail off.

"I've known Meyrick for years," Raleigh says with disgust. "He's incapable of anything clever."

Sir Robert leans forward. "Does either of you have in mind a small group we might dispatch, who might be nimble enough to overtake Meyrick and Skeres and prevent the theft of the letters? They would need to be capable of fighting it out in a pinch, but would also need to be men of learning and discretion, capable of understanding the import of the letters they're going there to protect (should they be fortunate enough to have the opportunity to identify and remove them), and capable of keeping their mouths shut about what they find." He rests his chin upon his folded hands once again, and looks to Noah.

Aping Sir Robert's posture, Sir Walter puts an elbow on his knee and rests his chin upon it, likewise looking expectantly at Noah.

Noah is exasperated. "Are you referring to the barristers who recently aided the Crown in preventing the smuggling of one of Lord Mountjoy's battle maps out of the country?"

"Well—" begins Sir Robert.

"Gentlemen," interrupts Noah, "those men are barristers by profession! They have only just returned to the bar after that ordeal, and they have numerous cases before the Crown's courts. The judges cannot be expected to relieve them of their responsibilities in the conduct of active cases."

Sir Robert replies calmly. "Serjeant, you're thinking now like a lawyer or a judge, not as one of Her Majesty's trusted advisors. It is the Crown that appoints those judges of whom you speak. As far as adjournments and such, they'll bloody well do what we *tell* them. Count on it."

"But the barristers will lose their clientele," replies Noah, only a little mollified.

"Do you really think," asks Sir Robert, "that a litigant will abandon counsel of such importance to the Crown as to be conscripted by royal commission to aid in Her Majesty's defense?" Noah makes no reply. "A barrister lacking any skill *whatever* could make a good living from such a reputation. Besides, the Exchequer will pay them commensurately for their time."

As Sir Robert has mollified enough of Noah's concerns about Arthur and Andres, he leaves them aside. "But what of David Killigrew?"

Sir Robert shakes his head impatiently. "Oxford—and half the damsels in Oxfordshire—will have to make do for one more term without him. The Exchequer will pay for his next term. Besides, as you well know, Master Cheerful would be outraged to be left out of this affair."

Noah gulps, turning the topic to someone of another character altogether. "And Lord Saint Ives? Will he be commissioned, as well?"

Sir Robert and Sir Walter look skeptically at one other.

With a mystified expression, Sir Robert asks, "Is his lordship still taking private cases?"

"I'm uncertain," says Noah, "but he's a barrister, and at liberty to do so."

Sir Robert regards him askance. "He's a *nobleman*, Serjeant Ames—with, incidentally, a fine endowment. As such, he is expected to come to Her Majesty's aid at a moment's notice. Why would *he* require a commission?"

Noah looks pleadingly to Sir Walter, whose face reddens as he bursts into laughter. "Serjeant Ames wants his lordship to be commissioned by the Crown," says Sir Walter pedantically, "so that Lady Jessica will not blame her father for bringing her new husband into this perilous affair."

Sir Robert laughs into his sleeve. "Very well. Lord Saint Ives will be commissioned, as well. The scrivener surely has his work cut out for him tonight. Serjeant Ames, I expect you shall be occupied here at the Tower for some time, sending out all the commissions you have requested." He turns suddenly serious. "Sir Walter, send two or three of your best men along with the barristers. Just be careful that no one knows which duty they've been impressed into. And I don't want this detachment gathering here at the Tower, on the off-chance there's a spy among us. Serjeant Ames, muster the troops at your home in Holborn tomorrow morning. Write to them tonight, instructing them to travel to you secretly at first light, singly, and fully armed, and to avoid being seen by anyone at Drury House or the Saracen's Head. Sir Walter, please meet them there and dispatch them with an appropriate plan. Now, if that will be all—"

# CHAPTER 9

**AS ESTHER PREPARES** to leave the grocer's in Holborn at dusk, the skies suddenly darken to a slate gray and let loose a persistent pelting rain. She opens the grocer's door a crack and finds the street as dark as night and strangely devoid of traffic, a desolate expanse of wet cobblestones. Peering nervously across, she scans the doorways and the alleyways between buildings.

It's been a few days since an unknown woman in threadbare foreign clothing approached and tried to speak with her, making the hairs on the back of her neck stand on end. On that occasion, Esther escaped by scurrying away with the superior quickness of youth, which she could very likely do again should the need arise, judging by the woman's advancing years. Still, Esther fervently hopes never to see—or even *think* of her again.

The woman seemed forlorn, pitiable perhaps but, even in that brief encounter, there was a whiff of something wicked about her. Although the eyes—always touted as windows to the soul—revealed no evil intentions, yet the woman seemed at war within herself, as though burdened by knowledge that her reduced state was the result of her own folly in allying herself with the wickedness of others. And she seemed tragically aware of an aura of untrustworthiness that clung to her like wet leaves and needed to be overcome with every new acquaintance. Whatever it was that had made the woman miserable had evidently led her to this peculiar pass, where it had somehow become important for her to accost a young woman like Esther in the street for reasons one could not guess.

Through the crack in the doorway, Esther peers left, the way she came. The Ames residence is so nearby that even in the gloaming she can discern the few steps leading up to the front door, yet in this downpour she expects her outer garments to be thoroughly rain-drenched by the time she gets there.

In the Ames's front window, a single candle burns. A half-hour ago, their cook realized that the few parsnips remaining in the kitchen had turned black, and asked Esther, the newest member of the household, to make a "quick run" to fetch replacements, as the pot was near boiling. No doubt Cook, in a moment of regret, placed the candle in the window to remind Esther she's being looked out for.

Well, at least Esther has shown the foresight to bring a bonnet of oilcloth, essential on an occasion as damp as this. She pulls the bonnet over her hair, reaches into the little sackcloth bag she brought with her to cover the parsnips as best she can, and steps down to the cobblestone street.

Instantly, she feels the spray of the rain as it splashes about her feet. Countless drops strike her bonnet and drum in her ears, while those striking the cobblestones hiss all around her. As she takes a few steps toward her new home, she hears a different kind of hissing directly across the street and glances toward the sound.

It's that woman again, now wearing a rain bonnet not unlike hers, waving to her demurely while obviously preoccupied by the rain spraying all about her feet. Almost inaudibly, the woman mutters something in a foreign tongue, while drawing a cloth from her pocket and dabbing her ankles with it.

This second appearance could not be more unwelcome. Esther is convinced that nothing this woman has to say could be good, and that it certainly would not be worth standing about in the rain to hear. She doubles her speed once more to escape being accosted.

"Tsk, tsk!" clucks the woman, as she realizes Esther is determined to avoid her once again.

Esther turns to see that the woman has also picked up her pace, but not enough to intercept her before she reaches the Ames residence.

"Alors!" mutters the woman, barely audible over the tumult of the rain. This is the first time Esther has heard her voice. "Pardonnez-moi, ma jeune fille," she calls with a beseeching note in her voice, then with evident exasperation, *"Ach, qu'est-ce que tu crains?"*

Although the woman's voice is more pleading than threatening, Esther has suffered all too many upsetting confrontations with kind-seeming strangers in her young life, and has no intention of undergoing another on this miserable evening. What legitimate business could this woman *possibly* have with someone like her, who's been in England less than a month and resided in High Holborn less than a week? Esther stretches her youthful gait for additional speed, leaving the woman well behind.

Esther reaches the Ames's door out of breath, and turns back to see that the woman has doggedly halved the distance between them. As she opens the Ames's door, she hears the woman's voice cut through the din of the rain once more. *"Je suis sa femme!"*

Esther slams the door behind her and enters the dark and quiet foyer. She hears an exasperated *"ach!"* outside. Heart pounding, she peeks out through a pane in the doorframe and spies the woman turning back the way she came, thoroughly drenched by now, but still stopping every few steps to wipe the rain from her ankles.

"May I help you with your wet things?" comes the gentle voice of a young man, frightening Esther out of her wits. She gasps and turns, instinctively backing up against the door, but before she can draw her concealed dagger, she realizes it's David Killigrew, Serjeant Ames's handsome young friend. His long blond hair is dry, from which she surmises that he arrived before the rain came, but he's dressed in riding clothes, as though prepared for a long trip out of doors. In his hand is an opened letter, which he places down on a small table in the vestibule. "I'm sorry to have startled you."

Though she's never spoken in his presence until this moment, she feels impelled to say something.

As the girl has bolted into the house in such a rush, David is certain she's failed to notice him at the other end of the dark foyer. She's out of breath, as though she's been chased along the rainy street and only just made it to safety. She peers out through the window a long moment, apparently until she's satisfied she's shaken her pursuer.

The girl is known to be so skittish, he's unsure what to do. If he withdraws from the foyer now, she'll hear him go. On the other hand, if he simply stands there mute, she'll be startled when she inevitably turns toward him.

"May I help you with your wet things?" he asks quietly, afraid that to speak more emphatically might cause her to bolt away like a deer in the park. "I'm sorry if I startled you." He's never heard her voice before, and longs to hear it now. He wonders whether it could possibly match the extraordinary beauty of her face and form.

Once she composes herself, she seems momentarily lost in thought, as though pondering how her voice will be greeted. "I was followed here ... by a strange woman," she says slowly and deliberately in a throaty, barely accented voice that makes her seem a gypsy from some mysterious part of the world where women speak out of a deeper register of their vocal range. Combined with her facial beauty and natural reticence, her voice instantly renders her most intriguing.

"Did she threaten you?" he asks.

"I do not know. She spoke in French, I think, but I do not *know* French."

"Come in and dry off, then," he says amiably. "I saw the candlelight in the kitchen and came to the back door. Cook let me in. I'm waiting for Serjeant Ames." He smiles pleasantly, but she still seems unsure of herself ... or perhaps of him.

Just then, the aproned cook turns into the foyer, wooden spoon in hand. "Oh, there you are, Esther," she says in a voice loud enough to break the intimacy. "I'm so sorry I sent you out. I'd no *idea* such a storm was comin'," she says, smiling apologetically to *David* of all people, "or I woulda gone meself. You won't mention this to the Ameses I hope, suh." Taking the grocery bag from Esther's hand, the cook seems suddenly aware that she's intruded upon a quiet moment. "I'll light a few tapers by the fireplace in the parlor," she says, "so it's not so gloomy when Serjeant Ames gets home. Mistress Ames is upstairs, buried in her business papers. Why don't you two dry off in the salon? It's been so damp in the house, I lit a small fire there."

David is surprised and happy to see Esther accept the suggestion and lead him into the small parlor on street level, seating him in an upholstered chair by the fire. Esther warms her hands and tosses in a fagot before choosing a wooden chair for herself, setting it where they can talk without being overheard. She graces the spindly chair with such delicacy that it neither creaks nor groans under her weight.

She speaks again in her throaty whisper. "Serjeant Ames is a great man. Is this not so?"

David smiles to think of Noah being the object of such adulation. "Yes, I suppose he is. I've known him a long time, and seen him come through the fire several times."

She furrows her brow and points to the fireplace. "Fire?" she asks.

He laughs aloud. "Not *real* fire ... although he's come perilously close to *gunfire* a few times. He's always come out of it, though, more highly regarded than ever."

"Oh," she says. "*Poetry* fire. Not real fire."

He takes a moment to discern her meaning. "*Metaphorical* fire, we would say at university. A metaphor is often used in poetry, I suppose, so one *might* call it poetic fire."

She arches an eyebrow. "*You* are at university?"

"Yes," he replies, "the same one Serjeant Ames attended."

Esther nods, impressed.

"Why do you ask?" he says, glancing at his equestrian clothing which, he has to acknowledge, does make him seem more wayfarer than pupil. "Do I not impress you as a university man?"

Taking a metal poker, she delicately nudges the wood she just put in, which smokes as though reluctant to burn. "I thought you were a ... *soldier*. Is that the right word?" He smiles fondly. "You look like ... Viking, maybe." She blushes but doesn't turn away. Indeed, she seems to be enjoying his company.

"Well," he says, "they say that, on this island, if one has blond hair and blue eyes, there's a fair chance he has some Viking blood in his veins. And Vikings *were* great lovers of the sea, as are my people in Cornwall."

"It is pretty in Cornwall?" she asks.

Now she's touched on a topic dear to his heart. What to tell this lovely foreigner of Cornwall? He sighs. "Well, it's just the most beautiful place in the world. Not that I've seen every other place in the world, mind you. But the bright sun there lights up the most beautiful meadows. Do you know there are plants there that will grow nowhere else in Britain? And we have beautiful sandy beaches and the loveliest ports. It seems nothing bad could ever happen there."

Jessica's voice chimes in from the hallway. "Master Cheerful, Lord Saint Ives might not share your vision of Cornwall as a place of such benignity."

David shoots to his feet as Jessica enters. "Why, Lady Jessica, what an unexpected privilege! When did you arrive?" Esther rises and curtsies silently.

Jessica nods in Esther's direction, and returns her attention to David. "I arrived just a few moments ago. Cook told me to tread lightly, so as not to interrupt your discussion. But, you know *me*. I couldn't restrain myself for long." She turns to Esther. "Good e'en, dear. I trust this rascal has not abused your ears in any way?"

Esther smiles. "Not at all, m'lady. Master Cheerful was just telling me that he is a Viking from Cornwall who lives in a meadow of sand."

David's jaw drops to hear himself so badly misquoted, believing he must have credited Esther's English much too highly on the basis of scant evidence.

Esther bursts into laughter to see his expression, and David realizes he's been had.

She places one hand over her mouth and blushes, evidently misinterpreting his bemused expression as signifying that he's taken offense. The other hand she places on his chest. "Oh, I am so sorry, Master Cheerful. I speak silliness sometimes." Her throaty laughter has the oddest effect on him. Even though he's her object of fun, he finds it delightful.

He takes her hand in his own and bows gracefully. "Your laughter is a rare music, Esther, and I'm most pleased to be its cause."

David feels Jessica tugging him backward into the hallway by his shirt. *Here she goes again.*

Jessica whispers pointedly, "How are things with the fair *Rosalind*, Master Killigrew?"

He looks at his feet. "I'm afraid things are not going well between us, m'lady."

"Oh?"

"Rosalind wrote me after I had not called on her for a few days," he replies. "She said that, henceforth, I'd better make up my mind as to my intentions before calling on a lady."

"Imagine!" she says. "Incidentally, Lady Sheffield, who lives a few houses away from here, was quite distressed earlier."

"Oh?" says David as innocently as he can.

"Yes," says Jessica. "Evidently, her pretty young spice maid disappeared without excuse today for more than an hour."

"You don't say," says David earnestly.

"Oh, but I *do*. You wouldn't know anything about that, would you, Master Killigrew?"

"Surely not, madam," he lies.

Jessica stands on tiptoe and pulls a piece of straw from David's hair that evidently escaped his notice when he glanced in the looking glass upon his arrival here. It was likely concealed by his hair, which is of nearly the same color.

Jessica studies the straw intently. "You haven't been lying about in the stables, *have* you, Master Killigrew?"

"No, madam," he assures her.

Jessica leans in, and sniffs him lightly. "Are you quite certain?" she asks.

"*Quite* certain, m'lady," he replies. "If I smack of the horse, I must apologize, but I … I rode rather hard to get here."

She regards him indulgently. "Tell me, Master Killigrew, does your horse smell like … cinnamon?"

David blushes a bright red. "No, madam."

"Well, *you* do," she whispers sternly, one eyebrow raised. She looks up at him with a wry expression. "I can't *imagine* why Rosalind is doubtful of your intentions," she says sardonically. "By the by, what *were* your intentions?"

David shuffles his feet. "I can't say that I had *formed* any real intentions."

She arches an eyebrow. "How old are you, David? Twenty-one? Twenty-two?"

"I've nineteen years, m'lady."

She looks upon him fondly. "Well, I expect you're a bit young to form serious intentions regarding a girl. But you must take heed that you are an exceptionally appealing young fellow, David. Where you go, a lady's heart is sure to follow. And her parents are sure to know it, as I expect Rosalind's were."

"Do you suppose they had a hand in her writing the letter?" asks David.

"Did it seem like her voice when you read it?"

"No, not really," says David.

"I expect her parents composed it, and made her copy it in her own hand."

"So," says David, "I expect that her parents do not much like me."

Jessica shakes her head. "You should rather expect that Rosalind liked you *too* much for her parents' purposes. But that leads me to my real question." Apparently no longer concerned about being overheard, she speaks in normal tones. "What are you doing here?"

Now it's David's turn to blush. "I'm sorry if I've offended, madam. I was having what I thought was a pleasant conversation with your cousin."

She scowls at him. "Give me some credit, David. That's not what I meant, although it might be prudent for you to restrain your adulation." She smiles. "Give the girl some breathing room."

"Was it that obvious?" he asks.

She brushes some imaginary lint off his jacket. "Yes, but there's nothing wrong with that. I'm pleased she's coming out of her shell." She turns serious again. "What I meant to ask you was why you have come to *my father's house*."

"Why, he *sent* for me," replies David. "Evidently, there's a bit of hugger-mugger afoot. Your father has sent Queen's commissions out to those who've been called upon to put things right."

"*Things?* Has this anything to do with the recent attempt upon the Queen?" asks Jessica.

David regards her sympathetically, as he's been forbidden to discuss the matter with anyone other than those enlisted. "I'm sure I can't say."

"Aha!" she says, folding her arms. "Would *Jonathan* be a recipient of one such commission?"

David observes that Lady Jessica has never been wont to let one gracefully avoid answering a question. "Lord Saint Ives may be called upon at a moment's notice, m'lady, even without a commission. It's an obligation of nobility."

The voice of Noah Ames booms from the kitchen. "It's called 'noblesse oblige,' m'lady. Comes with the barony." Noah strides into the hallway with Sir Walter Raleigh right behind, both still dripping from their ride from the Tower. Noah places a kiss on his daughter's cheek, which she accepts with a certain skepticism.

Noah tugs David back into the parlor. Without a word, Raleigh pulls the mesh aside from the fireplace, tosses in several pieces of wood, and he and Noah warm their reddened hands by the fire.

Noah returns to Jessica in the hallway, where she awaits him with her arms folded, tapping her foot. "We *all* serve the Crown, m'lady," Noah says privately, "each of us with a role to play." He leans in close to her and mutters, "Be grateful for yours."

"Lorenzo was never so called upon, Father," she protests.

"Your first husband Lord Burlington was no swashbuckler," he observes.

"Oh," she says, "but I suppose Jonathan *is?*"

Noah arches an eyebrow. "He fought for—and *saved*—your life, my dear. I should think there'd be little question remaining on that score."

"So, it was *your* idea to enlist Jonathan in this … this"—she points with her chin to Sir Walter and David—"whatever *this* is?"

"It was not my idea. For *that* you may thank Lord Robert Cecil."

"But you said nothing to discourage it?"

"'Twas he who ordered the commission, m'lady. Once that was done, there was nothing left to say."

Jessica whispers, "Does it not trouble you, Serjeant, that the father of your future grandchild is being sent into harm's way?"

Noah looks skeptically at her face and takes a step backward to observe her shape. Although she holds her hands meaningfully on either side of her belly, she shows no swelling or other sign of being with child.

"Are you …?"

"Possibly," she says indignantly.

He softens considerably. "Well, if you are, my dear, I'm ineffably happy for you … and me." He smiles upon her. "But there's nothing to be done about this present business." He takes her by the hand. "So, go home. Be with your husband now, for he's expected here early in the morning." He leans in and kisses her forehead gently. "I'll be sure he's returned to you none the worse for wear." She regards him skeptically.

At that moment, Marie enters the hallway, having just descended from her bureau upstairs. She glances disapprovingly into the salon and observes dourly, "I spend a few hours attending to business affairs, only to find fighting men a-mustering in my parlor. I take it this betokens some assignment from the Crown?" Before Noah can reply, she asks, "Lady Jessica, where is your cousin?"

Jessica looks into the parlor and purses her lips impatiently. "She must have gone to help Cook when Father and Sir Walter arrived." She steps off, as with a purpose.

Marie regards Noah with a hint of exasperation. "I'm not going to ask into particulars of this assignment, Noah. I have too much experience to think I'd get a straight answer. Just tell me: shall you be going with them?"

"No, Marie. I shall remain behind with Sir Walter."

"But," she says, full of concern, "you're not sending Cheerful on his own, are you?"

"Hardly. He'll be accompanied by a good friend. And they'll soon be followed by others."

"Who's going with Cheerful?"

A whoosh of air rushes through the hallway, followed by the sound of an outer door closing hard in the kitchen.

"I expect *that's* Andres now."

Once Jessica has left for home to share the evening with her husband, the others sit down for supper, and everyone joins in the pleasantries, except for Esther, who has returned to her previous taciturnity. After the meal, Marie retires, and Esther helps the servants clean up.

Noah and Sir Walter share a brandy in the upstairs parlor awaiting David and Andres, who have been summoned to receive their orders.

The moon shines brightly through the windows. A few wispy clouds pass by from time to time.

"Well, it's clearing nicely," observes Noah. "At least they'll have light to travel by. What do you suppose they'll find when they arrive at Burghley House?"

Sir Walter shrugs. "I suppose it depends upon whether they arrive before our friends from Cornwall."

Noah snorts. "Meyrick and Skeres have about as much to do with Cornwall as I with the moon. Suppose our men *do* arrive there before Meyrick and Skeres. How can they hold them off until the cavalry arrives?"

"Oh, they're resourceful young men," says Sir Walter in a reassuring tone. "I expect they shan't run out of good ideas."

In a moment, David and Andres appear together, looking more than a little apprehensive. They enter, plop down on the floor, and wait to be spoken to.

"Gentlemen," says Sir Walter at long last, "we'd offer you brandy, but you won't have time to sleep it off. I want you on the road together two hours before daylight. That gives you barely five hours' sleep. Fortunately, if the weather holds, you'll have a fair amount of light before sunrise.

"Your orders are to report first to what's called 'Cambridge Castle.' It's used as a jail now. The jailer is called 'Chester,' or at least he was when last I visited that ruin. He's a stalwart fellow, and craftier than he looks. He won't know you're coming, so give him this paper," he says, tossing a sealed paper to Andres. "He'll give you two post horses to ride the rest of the way to Burghley House and back. Your own horses will be reasonably well tended until your return."

"Why do you call the castle a 'ruin'?" asks David.

Raleigh sighs. "Because there once *was* an important castle there, built by William the Conqueror, and much fought over in the barony wars. What they now call the 'castle' is little more than the gatehouse of the old castle, and a few tumbledown stones resting on an adjacent mound, mournfully marking where the keep once stood." He takes another sip of brandy, as though the neglect of this historic place is somehow a personal indignity. *"Sic transit gloria mundi.* 'Thus passes the glory of the world,' or at least of our sacred English history. And even the gatehouse has fallen into disrepair." He laughs darkly. "Leave it to us English to come up with new ways to neglect our patrimony. The jail's roof leaks, but don't worry. The stable where they'll keep your horses is still dry, though it's the only part that is. At least, it was when last I saw it."

"What happened to the rest of the castle?" asks Andres.

"Yes," adds David. "Weren't they all stone in those days?"

Sir Walter takes a sip. "The stones of the castle were donated by English kings and queens for the construction of King's College and other buildings at the university. Queen Mary donated some of its stones for the construction of a private residence ... although none of you Oxford types would find that interesting. Anyway, once you're on the road and the sun's up, you're to ride hard all the way there, which will take you a couple of days. Then, take the post horses to Burghley House. We have reason to believe that a party of several Essex support-ers left London today for Burghley House. How many, we don't know, but there are at least two, and neither is known for his horsemanship, so we expect you'll arrive first."

"Who are the two we suspect will be traveling there?" asks Andres.

Noah interjects with a note of distaste. "Sir Gelly Meyrick and Nich-olas Skeres."

"Thomas, Lord Burghley and his family are here in London," says Sir Walter, drawing a paper from his pocket and proffering it to Andres. "He gave me this note for you to hand to his steward in charge of Burghley House, whose name is Barnaby Bell. That should be easy enough to remember. He'll give you the run of the place, which should enable you to find and remove the letters, or to defend the place till your reinforcements arrive, led by your old friend Jonathan, Lord Saint Ives. His party will be leaving here late tomorrow morning, but they won't cover ground as fast as you two, and they'll be a good eight hours behind, in any event."

"Is there some barrier around Burghley House, natural or man-made, to help us defend it?"

"I suppose, if you call a sheep-dip a natural barrier," Sir Walter says ironically. He shakes his head again. "But there's no wall around the place. It's in a meadow. Very lovely," he hesitates, "... in peacetime, anyway."

"Well, how the devil are we to defend it?" asks Andres.

Sir Walter smiles in the candlelight. "You needn't defend it. If you arrive first and remove the papers to us, what they're looking for will already be gone. If they arrive before you do, they'll be cantering back to London with the papers. In that case, as well, you won't need to defend Burghley House, as you'll be in pursuit of the papers."

"What if they catch us while we're there?"

Sir Walter is unimpressed by the possibility. "That would require a very precise coincidence, I must say. But if it were to fall out that way, you'd have several advantages. First, you have *two* kinds of surprise. They don't know you're going to be there. And, which is more, they don't even know anyone suspects what they're doing. Second, you should have at least a few hours to locate the documents they seek, and to conceal them or otherwise put them out of reach. Third, you'll have plenty of muskets and pistols from Lord Burghley's armory, and you'll be inside a big stone house with a hundred windows providing varied vantage points for shooting, while your adversaries will be standing out in an open field with no armor, no wall to hide behind, and nothing but their dicks in their hands." He equivocates. "*Pistols*, perhaps." He takes another sip. "With all those advantages, if you can't think of something, you should consider retiring to the clergy—if even *they'll* have you."

"Do you have any questions about the documents you're to bring back here?" asks Noah.

Andres shakes his head. "Walsingham-Burghley correspondence, 1572 through 1573," says Andres. "That's pretty clear, assuming we can find it."

Sir Walter sits up. "Oh, and just in case they've got there before you and removed the papers, you must take the papers back—by any means necessary."

David sits up. "You mean …"

"Kill them, if you must," replies Sir Walter without hesitation. "Remember the bastards who sent them for these papers are suspected of an attempt on the Queen's life that very nearly succeeded. If you kill them, you'll probably be saving them the terrors of Tyburn. If you must chase or confront them, first try to get word to Lord Saint Ives about where you are and where you're heading. He can't help you if he can't *find* you." Sir Walter rises and stretches. "Now, if that will be all, I wish you both the best of good fortune. Please refrain from getting your heads blown off." He turns to Noah. "I'll be turning in now, Serjeant Ames, and suggest you do the same."

Noah nods. "Shortly, Sir Walter. I'll remain here for a moment before retiring, but don't let me keep you. Good night, boys."

Noah sits alone a while, staring into the fire, musing what it might mean to become a grandfather. It's certainly a role he's never seen himself in, as his life has always seemed to rest precariously on a knife's point and he never expected to live as long as he already has.

As his eyes begin to close involuntarily, he jars himself awake, considering whether to douse the fire or let it burn out. Economy dictates that he douse it and preserve the wood, but his mind wanders back to something Sir Robert said: "A dragon in the ashes." If he lets it burn out, by morning there will be no live embers. If he douses it, it's more likely some ember will remain alight to scorch the servants' hands. As he mulls over what seems a fairly inconsequential decision, Esther lightly pads in wearing slippers, takes a seat by his, and regards him expectantly.

"Good evening, dear Esther," he says, stroking her hair as he once had his daughter's. "To what do I owe this visit?"

"I wish to speak with you, sir."

"It would be my pleasure, dear. Lady Jessica proudly informed me that you happily participated in a conversation with Master Cheerful today."

"Yes. It is Master Cheerful I wished to ask you about," she says with a hint of sadness. He waits for her to continue. "He will be going into danger tomorrow?"

Noah assumes that she has grown fond of David, as everyone seems to do, but as young women seem to do rather immediately and wholeheartedly. "He will be accompanying Andres on horseback before sunrise. Once he arrives at his destination, he'll be in moderate danger for a few days, after which he'll return to London ... and you."

She frets and, in the firelight, he can see tears welling up.

"Esther," he says, "England is not a perfect place. Sometimes young men of breeding need to show their mettle by risking all in a noble cause." He's not surprised to find her unsatisfied by this reply, so he takes another tack. "David is an excellent horseman, an excellent swordsman, and the Queen favors him greatly. He shall be all right. You'll see."

She gulps and tries to smile, but apparently cannot do so. She rises, bows, and leaves.

A few moments later, Noah rises, fixes the fireplace mesh firmly in place and decides to let the blasted fire burn itself out. No call for any dragons just now.

# CHAPTER 10

**NOAH'S BEEN ASLEEP** no more than a few hours when he's stirred by the deliberate movement of two heavy-booted young men downstairs. While he would ordinarily rise to make sure who they are, the house is so quiet that he readily recognizes the hushed voices of Cheerful and Andres preparing to leave for Burghley House. Against his better intentions, he falls back to sleep.

It seems only a few minutes later when he's again awakened, this time by a quiet but heated discussion between Jonathan and Jessica downstairs. The only other sound is that of Marie's contented breathing beside him. Spying the first gray of dawn seeping through the window, he decides to rise and prepare for the other men-at-arms who will be arriving in a short while.

Donning his Serjeant's silks, Noah creeps to the bedroom door and opens it quietly. He closes it behind him with his eyes down as he listens intently. The discussion downstairs, though no less heated, seems to have retired to somewhere deeper in the recesses of the house, probably the kitchen.

As Noah has forgotten that he assigned the other bedroom on this floor to serve as Raleigh's sleeping quarters, he's momentarily startled to find Sir Walter waiting silently before the closed door across the dark hallway, arms folded. As on every other morning, Raleigh wears that infuriating grin that makes it seem he's been up for hours, patiently waiting for all the others to sate their infantile need for sleep and shake off the incomprehensible stupor that follows.

"Quite a row going on down there," whispers Sir Walter.

"What about?" whispers Noah. The rise of the distant voices in the kitchen is almost loud enough to drown out his whisper.

"Your daughter wants to know why Lord Saint Ives has been selected for this service."

"I thought that was it, as soon as I heard her voice. She shouldn't have followed him here." He shakes his head sadly. "I confess I was never able to take her to task once she lost her mother." He looks imploringly to Sir Walter. "Anything you can do?"

Sir Walter gives it a moment's thought and nods. "Leave it to me," he says reassuringly and quietly descends the stairs.

Noah follows him into the kitchen, where Jessica leans reproachfully into the much taller Jonathan. Although she's obviously in one of her more petulant moods, upon seeing Sir Walter and her father enter, she backs off and casts her eyes down.

While Sir Walter's first words should properly be directed to Jonathan, instead he addresses Jessica, in a small but obvious breach of protocol.

"What seems to be the problem, m'lady?" asks Sir Walter.

Jessica's eyes go momentarily wide, as she realizes that Sir Walter has slighted Jonathan by addressing her first. Just as Sir Walter intended, she has quickly taken the point that it is *she* who first diminished her husband's stature, presuming to interfere with his performance of his duties to the Crown.

At that moment, the venerable Yeoman Gardner enters through the mudroom door. As he sees that he has walked into a tense moment, he stands silently aside and casts his eyes down.

Jessica clears her throat and speaks without looking up from the floor. "Sir Walter, I am concerned that his lordship is being called to duty that could just as readily be performed by any one of a number of men of lesser station."

Sir Walter nods indulgently. "Has your ladyship anyone to offer the Crown as a substitute for my lord?"

Noah goes to Jessica and lends support by placing his hand firmly on her shoulder.

Jonathan appears about to speak, but before he does, he spies Noah shaking his head firmly from a place where Jessica cannot see. Jonathan takes this as his cue to say nothing.

At last Jessica looks up at Sir Walter. "As a substitute, you mean one of my servants?" she asks shakily.

"Well," says Sir Walter, "it would have to be someone of equivalent skills in leadership, such as intelligence, knowledge of the law, and firearms, to name a few. Has my lady any such manservant to offer as a substitute for this duty?"

Jessica's face reddens. "Do you mean to say that this duty shall require a man of *all* such skills, Sir Walter?"

"*All*, madam," he says, bowing.

To Sir Walter's plain surprise, still Lady Jessica does not relent.

"There must be someone else who can do it," she insists. "Do you disregard my wishes simply because I am a woman, Sir Walter?"

Sir Walter's eyebrows shoot up innocently. "M'lady, every order I carry out comes from a woman. And Lord Saint Ives's orders come from the very *same* woman. We are as bees in a hive, madam. We have many females, but only one queen."

While Jessica obviously credits the metaphor, she gives no sign of relenting.

"Sir Walter," says Noah, "will you be so kind as to inform her ladyship what action you must take if his lordship does not serve, and yet no suitable man is offered in his stead?"

Sir Walter looks to Jonathan for leave to answer Noah's question. Jonathan sighs and nods his assent.

Sir Walter replies reluctantly. "In that case, your ladyship, I would be duty-bound to instruct Yeoman Gardner there to escort Lord Saint Ives to the Tower and place him in the stockade, there to remain until he can be charged with insubordination, desertion, and in an appropriate case … high treason."

Jessica draws in a deep breath and composes herself. Apparently realizing at last that the matter is out of her hands, she says, "That will not be necessary, Sir Walter."

She turns to her husband and curtsies. "Godspeed, m'lord," she says, and turns to go.

But Jonathan cannot bring himself to allow her to leave without a word from him. "M'lady," he says, extending his hand to her, "please rest assured that I shall return to you as soon as I may, and all in one piece."

Jessica hesitates and nods dutifully to her husband. Everyone bows low to her, none lower than Sir Walter. By contrast, Jessica raises her head high and lifts her skirts from the floor. She traverses the room and walks out the front door with great dignity. Silence reigns as her footman opens the carriage door, closes it firmly behind her, and guides the carriage away.

"So proud," says Noah, shaking his head contemplatively. "So much like her sainted mother."

"Thank you, Sir Walter," says Jonathan. "I don't know what to do when she gets like that. Fortunately, she rarely does, except in matters of my personal safety."

Sir Walter smiles. "Give me an army of men with such spirit, and we'll mow down the Irish rebels in a few weeks."

Jonathan turns to another subject. "I must confess to both of you gentlemen that I was dismayed to hear you'd sent Cheerful to accompany Andres Salazar as the vanguard to Burghley House."

Noah arches an eyebrow. "And why is that?"

"He's a bit young for such service, don't you think?" replies Jonathan.

Noah laughs. "No younger than you were when you pointed an unloaded gun at Gelly Meyrick's head and threatened to blow it off."

Jonathan is shamefaced. "That was most rash on my part," he confesses.

"But effective," says Noah.

Sir Walter regards Jonathan skeptically. "I've had younger men die in my arms on a battlefield. Your Master Killigrew is quite old enough to take care of himself. And he's a natural horseman ... and swordsman. He'll be fine, as will your lordship."

"Amen," says Noah.

Arthur Arden enters through the back door, just as the first rays of sunlight break over the horizon. "Did I miss anything?" he asks.

"Nothing of consequence," replies Sir Walter. "Let me walk you through your written orders. Pay especial attention to the places where you may expect to receive messages from your vanguard. We all hope there'll be no trouble, but if there's to be any, that'll be where you first see sign of it, and you'll need to know what to do." He hands written orders to both Jonathan and Arthur. "Have my four Yeoman Warders arrived at Serjeant Ames's stables?" he asks Arthur.

"They have, sir," says Arthur, "precisely as ordered."

"Yeoman Gardner," says Sir Walter, beckoning.

"Sir?" replies the grizzled captain as he approaches.

"As Francis is still unwell, send the most senior man in the stables back to the Tower to take charge. I'm sending you personally along with Lord Saint Ives and Master Arden." He smiles at Noah. "Can't have anything untoward befall his lordship." He mutters under his breath. "And I bloody well don't wish to answer for it."

As Sir Gelly's traveling party clops northward on their first day's travel, Saint Mary's Church at Harlow comes into view, at last. Though they've gone but half the distance he'd hoped (one-quarter of the way to Burghley House), they got so late a start that he'd had to accede to his companions' desire to stop for the night. He turns his head to take in the rest of their ragtag party.

Before leaving London, Sir Gelly and Nicholas Skeres reluctantly agreed to bring along the notorious drunkard Robert Poley who, truth be told, hasn't slowed them down yet. Poley, they knew, was a dubious choice for any task. While he'd rarely provide any dependable service, they knew that bringing him along would impose upon the whole party the inevitable hazards presented by a drunkard either keenly hunting for drink or slothful for having found it. But he'd begged so earnestly for the work (as he'd had no steady source of money since Lord Essex had been locked up months before), they brought him along for the extra pair of hands.

They'd also been compelled by their current employers to bring along the dwarfish soldier "Monk." Though they'd also brought along his pony, Monk preferred to share Skeres' saddle, and now clings to his back, sound asleep.

"There's the church," says Sir Gelly to Skeres. "You're certain your friend's inn is nearby?"

"Quite," mutters Skeres.

As they leave the road, Skeres mutters, "Dunno why we're travelin' so late, anyhow. It's nearly pitch dark, and *this* little bugger's been droolin' on me shirt for the past hour. He can ride his pony tomorrow. That's why we brought it along, ain't it?"

"Dunno," says Meyrick, "seems a pleasant enough chap to me. A life spent bein' the size of a young boy can't be an easy one. No hope of growin' to full size, no man inclined to take him seriously."

Skeres smiles knowingly.

"No, nor woman, neither," says Meyrick, "though by yer smilin' ye seem to say so."

Skeres snickers. "One can always have a woman for pay."

Poley yawns. "It'll be nice to settle into a pint and a nice warm bed."

"Yeh," replies Skeres impatiently, "well, ye better make it *one* pint, as we ain't got time to sober you up, come mornin'."

"What's the rush?" asks Poley. "They've already got both copies of the letters. Don't see why they need the originals, anyhow."

Sir Gelly glances contemptuously at Poley. "We've been through all this, Robert. If the Warders notice the Tower copies are missin', they're sure to look for the original letters at Burghley House, by which time we better be good and gone with the originals in our saddlebags."

"But Bob's got a point," says Skeres. "What're the odds the Warders'll even look inside the room in the Tower where the letters was stored? Dorsay said it looked like nobody'd been in there for ages."

"What's the matter, Nick?" replies Sir Gelly. "Not payin' ye enough?"

"That ain't it, and you know it," says Skeres. "It's that we don't even know if Essex wants us freelancin' like this. If you, me, or Bob here get caught, it'll fall right back on Essex, and he don't need no more troubles at the moment. I've a plan to get us out of the rest of this task, if I can find the men I've in mind in Duxworth. And whoever *this* little bugger's workin' for," he says, pointing his chin at Monk, "probably wouldn't be too 'appy to have 'im in the Clink, neither."

"A man's gotta eat," pouts Poley. "Essex has got 'imself locked up for—we don't know *how* long—and we're out 'ere fendin' for ourselves. It's only been a coupla weeks since the Queen's Jew had us all trussed and ready for the hangman."

Sir Gelly's losing patience with his companions. "Quit yer belly-achin', the two o' ye. If we'd been caught by anybuddy but Serjeant Ames, we'd be in the Tower by now, waitin' to have our guts sprayed all over Tyburn to fatten up the kites," he says, referring to the infamous place of punishment for high treason and the resident hawks that relish the bloody executions.

Skeres scoffs. "Yeah, well, if y'ask me, the Jew got us off to suit 'is own purposes. He's got no love for the likes of us."

"True enough," says Poley. "Is that the inn up there?" he asks, pointing to light in a nearby window.

"Damned if it ain't," replies Skeres.

Sir Gelly finds the inn more to his liking than he expected. The food's good and the lodgings clean. But there's only one vacancy, so the four of them will have to pile into one room.

The innkeeper escorts them down the hall by candlelight. He's a grizzled, paunchy old fellow—a reformed thief whose every other word now extols the virtues of wife, kith, and hearth. "No, I mean it," he says to Skeres as he unlocks the door to their room. "Dunno why I carried on in the trade so long. Never 'ad much to show for it. 'Course, not every cadger's lucky enough to get catched by a wealthy widda like my Patience."

Skeres prods him good-naturedly. "She'd have to be Patience *itself* to put up with the likes o' you. Yer snorin' *alone* would put any other woman outta sorts."

"Very like," says the innkeeper thoughtfully. He smiles. "'Course, it don't 'urt that she's hard o' hearin'."

The innkeeper laughs aloud. Though he's clearly tempted to retaliate in kind for his old friend's friendly jibe, a piteous glance at Skeres' deeply scarred complexion evidently changes his mind, brushing away any thought of an insult. "Well, 'ere y'are, boys. It ain't much, but it'll keep ye safe and dry fer the night."

Skeres pays the innkeeper and has a private word with him in the hallway before entering the room, by which time Monk has already fallen asleep face down in the middle of the single bed, leaving the three other travelers to draw lots for the two spaces on the double bed beside it. One of them will have to sleep on the floor.

"Tell ye what," says Skeres, pointing to a part of the room piled with extra blankets, "if Bob's willin' to sleep in that corner, I say he's good for one more pint before retirin'. What d'ye say, Bob?"

Poley gives it some thought. "Two pints," he counters, "and *you're* buyin'." Poley deftly catches Skeres's coin and heads down the hallway to the taproom.

Skeres silently observes Monk in the candlelit room, shaking his head disapprovingly. Before Sir Gelly can ask why, he sees that Monk's face is buried in a drool-stained shred of old blanket he's evidently brought with him as a sleeping aid.

"Who *is* this little blighter, anyhow?" asks Skeres. "We runnin' a nursery?"

Sir Gelly plops onto the double bed and pulls off his boots. "What difference does it make?" he replies. "This little trip'll be over soon, and ye need never see him again."

Skeres merely shrugs and collapses on the remaining spot on the double bed. In a moment, they're both asleep.

Unbeknownst to Cheerful and Andres, although they've been on the road a day less than Sir Gelly and his men, they're nearer Cambridge by fifteen miles. There was only minimal conversation on their way to slow them down, as a disagreement arose between them shortly after sunrise. Now, after a long day's ride, they stable their horses and bed down at the Crown Inn at Puckeridge.

David lies awake staring at the dark ceiling, when he hears Andres toss and turn in the dark, as though he's about to resume their earlier conversation.

"So, *why* do you think Esther would rebuff my advances?" asks Andres. "Is it because I'm Portuguese?"

"No," says David. "That's not it."

"Because," Andres continues, as though his previous question had been entirely rhetorical and David's response superfluous, "Lady Burlington's mother was Spanish. That means that Lady Burlington and possibly Esther herself are half so."

"Well, racially," says David, "Serjeant Ames's mother was *Hebrew*, wasn't she? As is Lady Burlington. Esther must be, too."

"So, then, you think it's because I'm a Christian?"

"No. More likely, it's that you're merely a barrister," says David, as though it should have been obvious all along.

"What's wrong with being a barrister?" demands Andres.

"Nothing … by itself."

"It *is* a learned profession, you know, not some common trade," sniffs Andres.

David props himself up onto one elbow. "If you must know, I think your chances are small solely because you're not a gentleman by birth."

Andres props himself up on an elbow to face David in the dark. "Ah, then you believe Esther wishes to marry into the aristocracy."

"Not necessarily, although Jonathan has told me such was the aspiration of Esther's cousin, Lady Burlington. And Lady Burlington *did* marry nobility … twice, as you know, hard as it is to believe that Jonathan has become nobility."

Andres sighs. "I suppose anyone as beautiful as Lady Jessica has her choice of husbands," he sighs, and collapses back on his pillow. "And Esther looks as though she's Lady Burlington's *sister*."

"It's true. They resemble one another closely," replies David wistfully. A quiet moment passes in the dark, after which he muses, "How do you suppose Serjeant Ames comes to be related to two such beautiful women?"

After a moment's silence, Andres ventures. "Well, I suppose Serjeant Ames himself might be regarded by many women as having a pleasing face."

"You think so?" asks David.

"Surely," says Andres. "We can't see it because we're men," he observes confidently.

"I do expect Esther would like to marry into a family of some name," says David.

"Oh, such as *your* family, the Killigrews?" says Andres. "You know, you're not particularly well known outside of Cornwall."

"*My* family? This has nothing to do with me!"

"Doesn't it, though?" asks Andres pointedly. "I think you fancy Esther for yourself."

"Don't be ridiculous," says David. His thoughts hark back to Lady Jessica's admonition to avoid making advances on any more young ladies until he's decided what he wants from them. "Andres, if you wish to pursue Esther, be my guest. Just don't say I didn't warn you." He settles back down onto his pillow, turns his head away, and begins to wonder whether Andres is completely wrong about his motives.

And with that, weariness overtakes them, and they sleep.

# CHAPTER 11

**THE NEXT DAY** is warm and overcast. Marie's house in Holborn is quiet. No men-at-arms tramp through the place; there are no heavy-footed comings and goings as there were yesterday.

Sir Walter tosses a jangling keyring onto the blotter on Noah's desk.

"You're certain that's all of them?" asks Noah.

"As certain as I can be," offers Sir Walter, plopping himself down in an upholstered chair. "Since I took over at the Tower, those are the only three keys that might have been used to gain access to the room holding Walsingham's correspondence."

"When did you take over?" asks Noah.

"I was appointed in 1586 and served until 1592, when John Best took over. Then I was reappointed two years ago."

"So you have no knowledge of the Tower between 1592 and 1597?" asks Noah.

Sir Walter regards him askance, as though unsure whether he's being toyed with. "Well, I saw it from *confinement* for a bit of that period, if that's what you mean."

Noah's face reddens. "Oh, I'm so sorry, Sir Walter. Was there some incident …?"

Sir Walter laughs aloud to find Noah chagrined. "The Queen discovered that I'd wed one of her ladies-in-waiting without royal consent. Honestly, Noah, you must be the only person in the land who doesn't know. Bess Throckmorton was the lady in question, and we've been happily married ever since, thank you."

"Now I vaguely recall," says Noah. "But, preoccupied as I was with the Lopez case at that time, I never learned why Her Majesty was so upset as to toss both you and your lady love into the Tower."

"Yes, that was 1592, a fateful year for both you and me. Bess and I were taken to the Tower in June of that year," says Sir Walter. "I was released to fetch Her Majesty a prize on the high seas in high summer, but poor Bess remained there until the end of December."

"August was when you brought back the merchantman—the *Madre de Dios* wasn't it?"

"Ah, I see you remember *that* much. It was the *Madre de Deus*. It was Portuguese, not Spanish."

"Fetched the Queen a tidy sum, as I recall," says Noah.

"It would have been an *unimaginable* sum," says Sir Walter, "but we made the mistake of docking at my home port of Dartmouth, in Devon. Thieves carried off much of the loot, but Her Majesty still wound up with booty worth 140,000 pounds." Sir Walter smiles again. "And I got my Bessie back. Worth every penny!"

"But still, Her Majesty made you wait some additional months to resume your wedded bliss."

"How can I describe how angry she was?" He searches the ceiling for the right word. "'Furious?' No. 'Apoplectic?' No. There are no words. She said it was because Bess was one of her wards, but I doubt that was her reason."

"Then, why, do you suppose?" asks Noah.

"Her Majesty was jealous. She'd shown me every favor, and I suppose that in exchange I was expected to remain forever grateful, forever available for her amusement, and forever *unmarried*, which I found especially unfair. The Privy Council would never have allowed Her Majesty to marry me, of course."

"Oh?"

Raleigh scoffs. "For one thing, I was an Englishman, and they'd been trying to marry her off to one Frenchman or another for years. For the good of the realm, you see."

"I see. Well, I suppose you learned little of the Tower while in confinement."

"You'd be surprised what you can learn about a place, even without the run of it. The place runs like a clock. Everything is done at precisely the same time every day. Anything that upsets the routine gets immediate attention."

"It must have been dismaying to live in the shadow of the gallows," says Noah, shivering despite the warm day.

Sir Walter nods wistfully. "For some, I suppose. But Bess and I always knew that Her Majesty, God save her, was never bloodthirsty like her father. She *was* intent on frightening the wits out of those who displeased her, though. Still is." He sighs. "You know, I've always been fascinated by the Tower's antiquity. I'm sure you've heard the old saw that it was built by Julius Caesar."

"I have," replies Noah, "but I doubt it."

"As do I," says Sir Walter. "The White Tower is the oldest part of the place, and shows no signs of Ancient Rome, nor of having been built before the Conqueror arrived in 1066. Think of all the monarchs who've occupied it since then; some great," he laughs, "most mediocre."

"And don't forget the wicked," says Noah.

Sir Walter nods. "I don't suppose it would be impolitic of me to place King Philip of Spain in that category."

Something in Raleigh's musings about the age of the Tower strikes a note in Noah's mind as being relevant to their discussion of the keys, but it quickly fades.

Noah picks up the keys that Sir Walter tossed on his desk. "Two of these are identical. Why are there fewer teeth on the third?"

"We call that a quadrant key," says Sir Walter, "what's sometimes called a 'skeleton key.' It will unlock not only the room where Walsingham's old correspondence is stored, but all the surrounding rooms in the quadrant, as well. Very handy."

"I suppose the point of having a key that will unlock only the *one* room is to ensure that the bearer will enter that room only, while keeping him out of the neighboring rooms."

"Precisely."

"But why would a key with *fewer* teeth unlock *more* locks?" asks Noah.

"Well, that's a mystery of the locksmith's trade, isn't it? I'm no expert, but I'll tell you how it was explained to me. Imagine you've mistakenly inserted the wrong key into a lock. You try to unlock it by turning the key, but there's a plate in the lock that won't allow the wrong key to turn it. That's because the plate has been designed with obstructive areas, called 'wards,' that are not cut away. The wrong key won't turn because the key has one or more teeth that butt up against the wards."

Noah scratches his head. "So, in a way, the teeth on the key, besides enabling it to work on the right lock, also prevent it from working on the wrong lock."

"Precisely," says Sir Walter. "As a general matter, the fewer teeth on the key, the more locks it will open."

"But surely," says Noah, "there are brigands and thieves who discovered that long ago and would love to copy the skeleton key."

"No doubt," says Sir Walter. "For them, the trick is to figure out which teeth can safely be omitted, but to accomplish that efficiently they need to possess the skeleton key, and we're careful to deny them access to that. In the Tower, there are only three copies of each skeleton key, each copy remaining at all times on the person of a most trusted man."

Noah conjectures. "They would be you, Gardner, and … Francis?"

Sir Walter nods. "The one in your hand belongs to Francis. I took it from him before he was placed in that horrible traction device."

"How is he coming along?" asks Noah.

Sir Walter's expression becomes suddenly grave. "Bodily, he's improving. But his spirits seem to have been quite dashed by the death of the kitchen girl."

Noah nods dourly. "Injuries to the soul can take a long time to heal."

As they contemplate Francis's troubles, there's no sound but the distant clinking of plates in the kitchen. The front door opens, and Lady Jessica's distinctive voice can soon be heard chatting with Cook.

"Anyway," asks Noah, "do you suppose that whoever broke in to steal Walsingham's correspondence had a copy of the skeleton key?"

Raleigh shrugs. "Either that, or a copy of the key that fitted only that lock. No way of knowing."

"Have any of the keys gone missing over the past few months—

even for a moment?"

Sir Walter shakes his head. "None."

"Then how did the varlets gain entrance to the Tower?"

"*I* know a secret entrance," says Jessica, whose sudden appearance in the parlor startles them both.

Sir Walter shoots to his feet. "Lady Saint Ives," he says, bowing, "to what do we owe this most welcome visitation?"

Lady Jessica smirks. "You may rest easy, Sir Walter. I do not hold you responsible for my husband's enlistment in this affair."

Noah raises an eyebrow. "So, I suppose *I'm* the culprit, in your estimation?"

Jessica sighs. "Oh, I suppose not. Her Majesty has a new toy in the form of Lord Saint Ives, and wishes to try it out."

Noah nods skeptically, not quite sure he's off the hook. "You were saying something about a secret entrance to the Tower?"

Sir Walter asks, "Through the outside stables?"

Lady Jessica smiles. "Oh, so you know of it," she says. "I was admitted that way some weeks ago, to see Her Majesty."

Sir Walter's face reddens, and he shakes his head in exasperation.

Noah cocks his head. "Something wrong, Sir Walter?"

"I've told them a dozen times that no one is to use it, nor even *know* of it," comes the bitter reply. "You see all those high walls about the Tower? One means of breach, such as that door, makes a mockery of the whole battlement!" He paces impatiently. "To bring a noblewoman in that way ... it's unseemly." He turns to Jessica. "I'll wager no one even asked you to keep it secret, did they, m'lady?"

Lady Jessica obviously wishes to avoid getting anyone into hot water. "Francis did mention that it was secret and that it was used only sparingly."

"How wide is the passageway?" asks Noah.

Sir Walter replies. "It was designed so that armed men would have to enter single file, and slowly, but if the door is left unattended, we might as well nail a public notice to the door inviting one and all."

"Is that the only secret passage into the Tower?" asks Noah.

Sir Walter sits back down in the upholstered chair and exhales deeply. "There may be others. There are secret passageways in and out of every castle, to allow the residents to escape in the event it becomes indefensible. I expect you know that, Serjeant Ames." He sighs. "And the Tower was built by an invading conqueror, which means he had much to fear from his neighbors, many of whom were displaced nobility. The conquering royals would have needed several avenues of possible escape in case rebels broke in—to avoid being slaughtered on a killing ground."

Noah is reminded of that fateful night at the Tower long ago, when Her Majesty suddenly appeared in an outbuilding, leaving her many attendants none the wiser. Trapdoors and secret passageways are evidently not the mere product of the playwright's febrile imagination. "I'd warrant some passageways are known only to the royals," he muses, "and that their secrets are passed down orally from generation to generation."

"Very like," says Sir Walter. "The passageway mentioned by Lady Jessica is the only one I'm sure of."

Jessica recalls her latest trip to the Tower. "Francis mentioned to me that it had been used by our late beloved King Henry the Eighth. I suppose he had it built."

"I doubt it," says Sir Walter. "I expect it was built long before. But I, too, have heard that it was used extensively by King Henry in comings and goings on his many trysts." He blushes and bows to Jessica. "I do apologize for my loose talk, m'lady."

Jessica smirks. "One would have to be prim indeed not to know that Her Majesty's father had six wives, and that such an achievement would have been unattainable without considerable dalliance."

Sir Walter bows to her worldliness.

Esther appears at the doorway, looking agitated, an open letter dangling from her hand.

"What's wrong, dear Esther?" asks Noah, hoping that her glum visage does not betoken some ill news of her new friend, Cheerful.

"I have received a letter from Beth, sir. She asks us to come to her," Esther replies in her dusky voice, near tears. "It's Yetta. She's dying."

# CHAPTER 12

**NOAH CHOOSES A CLOSED CARRIAGE** to bring Esther to Beth's home in Southwark, and closes the coach's curtains to allow her to weep without fear of prying eyes. Marie's footman guides the horses skillfully through the streets of London.

Esther crouches over a moist handkerchief, as she's done all the while, and it's not till they reach London Bridge that she stops weeping long enough to converse.

"There was a woman in the street the other day," she begins hoarsely, "when it rained. She wanted to talk with me, but I could think of no good reason she'd want to talk, so I ran away into your house."

"Was she harsh with you?" Noah asks, as beggars have been known to become aggressive when they're desperate, and many are just now.

"I felt sorry for her," she says, "but I was also afraid."

"Did she say anything to you?"

Esther sighs. "She tried to, but I could barely hear her over the noise of the rainstorm. And I was running away."

"What did she say?"

"I don't know," says Esther. "I think it was in French, which I do not understand."

"Can you remember any of her words?"

"*Famm*, I think," ventures Esther. "Yes, *famm*. What does it mean?"

"Did she say '*j'ai faim*'?" he asks, pleased to distract her from her morbid thoughts, even if only momentarily.

"Maybe. Something like that. What does it mean?"

Noah shrugs. "It means, 'I'm hungry.'"

To his dismay, this sets Esther to weeping again. "Oh," she cries, "I should have given her some money. She was dressed in worn foreign clothes, but she did not look to be very poor or hungry." She fusses with a dry corner of the handkerchief. "When I saw this woman, it reminded me that Yetta had traveled thousands of miles to bring me here. Who knows how many times she was left with no choice but to beg a stranger for money, just to eat and to feed me! And they *must* have given her something, or we would have starved to death." She sobs. "And yet I turned this woman away with nothing."

Noah places his arm around her. "Esther," he says comfortingly, "that was not Yetta, but another woman about whom we know nothing. And, from what you tell me, she was not destitute, nor about to starve to death. Look." He reaches into his purse and draws out a coin. "The next time you see her, give her this." While Esther studies the unfamiliar coin, Noah wonders how many forms of currency she's seen in her young life while traveling through so many countries as a refugee. "It's tuppence, dear," he says. "Enough to get her a good hot meal. There, there." He takes a fresh handkerchief from his pocket and wipes away her tears.

She looks up at him with her large eyes; they're still a beautiful green, despite being bloodshot from the flood of tears they've endured. *She's still a child*, he thinks. She's had a hard life. But she's still a child.

"Yetta has been so good to me," she says tearfully.

Noah nods. "She has been a blessing to me, as well. I would be neither alive nor in England if it weren't for her goodness and determination. We both owe her so very much." He chokes back a tear of his own.

In a short while, the coach pulls up in front of the house, and Noah leads Esther down the coach's steps to the street. He notices in passing how much her posture has improved since she's become a part of his household. Not regal yet, but confident, at least. He dispatches the footman to water the horses and return in an hour. Noah watches the carriage clop away in the warm evening.

Although Esther is eager to see Yetta, Noah dreads going inside for fear of what they'll find upstairs.

Beth greets them in solemn silence and leads them up the stairs to Yetta's room, where she stops before opening the door. She draws Noah aside.

"I'm not sure you've arrived in time," Beth says with concern, "but Yetta's been half in dream for some hours, saying the same thing over and over: '*She* wants me to tell Noah something. *She* will not be denied.'" Beth looks up at him. "Noah, I have no idea whom she means by *she*."

Noah finds the news a little unsettling and would like to consider it for a moment, but Beth waits only long enough for him to acknowledge what she's said before opening the door to the little room.

The curtains have all been drawn to keep it as dark as possible. Only the dullest gray light seeps around the curtains, barely enough to obviate the need for a taper.

"She likes it dark," Beth says apologetically. "The light hurts her eyes."

Seeing that Esther has placed herself at the foot of Yetta's bed, Noah approaches the bedside. He solemnly observes Yetta's wizened gray face, expecting these to be her last few minutes of breath. Though her chest rises and falls, her breaths come further and further apart.

Noah notices a whitish film forming on Yetta's upper lip. He squints and leans closer in the dim light to see what it is. He reaches his hand out gently and touches it with his finger.

It's *frost*. And he's amazed to observe that he can now *see* each of her shallow breaths, as though she were not lying in a bedroom on a summer's day at all, but rather on an icy lake in midwinter. Suddenly, he realizes that he can see the vapor of his own breaths, as well. And that the room has instantly become frigid.

He glances up at Esther, whose breath is also crystalline. She shivers. From her fearful expression, Noah can see that she suspects something momentous is about to happen.

"Good lord," mutters Beth, chafing her hands. "I must set a fire." A moment later she adds with a note of confusion, "But it's … it's summertime."

During the next few moments, so many things happen that it will later seem as though time itself must have slowed down to accommodate them.

The room begins to move. Not in any particular direction that Noah can discern, but it's moving nonetheless. Noah looks up at the curtained windows. The gray light formerly seeping around the edges of the curtains has been replaced by an eerie glow coming from a different direction, lending a bluish cast to the room. He briefly considers opening a curtain to see what's happened to the overcast day, but something tells him that he's not *supposed* to see what's out there now, and that, whatever it is, it's not an overcast day in Southwark.

He turns about to see Beth chafing her shoulders, shivering with cold, confusion on her face. She looks about the room—a room, he thinks, she must have seen ten thousand times—and asks him fearfully: "Noah, where are we now?"

He's suddenly overcome by the unmistakable scent of cloves. Although always a favorite of his, it quickly becomes overpowering, so intense that he can barely breathe.

The door to the hallway slams shut behind him, and he turns toward it. Unbidden, Esther moves in front of it, and turns toward the center of the room with a dagger in her hand that must have been concealed in her gown. She stares at something .... or someone ... that isn't there, as though facing an invisible predator of some sort, the same height as Esther herself.

Her countenance fearful and threatening, Esther assumes a feral crouch. In a foreign tongue, she mutters a command to her invisible adversary. Evidently unsatisfied with the reaction, she repeats it. To Noah, her commands sound like they're spoken in Polish, which he does not understand.

Taking a hesitant step forward, Esther holds the point of her dagger to the fore, in a pose that brings to mind a poor gypsy woman protecting her child. She thrusts it threateningly toward her invisible adversary and growls, "I will tell him. Now, step away from him. I don't care. Now! Step away!"

The room seems to settle back on its foundation with a shudder. From the depths below comes a low boom like an earthquake, shaking the house. The sickly blue glow creeping around the curtains yields to the former gray of an overcast day. The scent of cloves fades into memory.

The day's warmth returns to the room in a rush, and for a moment Noah gasps for air like a man who's been fished from the sea. Yetta, whose still form has remained motionless and silent until now, breathes her last with a single long exhalation.

At last, she is at rest.

Esther looks to Noah in confusion and horror, as though she's just awakened from a nightmare. Her hand opens and the dagger clatters to the floor. Her eyes roll up into her head. Noah rushes to her aid and catches her in his arms just in time to keep her from striking the floor.

Beth goes to the door that slammed on its own mere moments before and, after the barest hesitation, steels herself, swings it open, and charges through the doorway.

"Bring her in here," she says, crossing the hallway and opening the door to a room with a single bed. Noah places the unconscious girl gently down on it. Beth adjusts her hair into some semblance of form.

Noah is relieved to see that Esther's breathing is strong.

Noticing his concern, Beth assures him, "She is protected by her youth. She'll be fine."

Noah turns to Beth. His voice croaks. "Could you …. see what Esther was seeing?"

Beth half-smiles. "I saw nothing."

"Nor I," he replies, amazed.

"But I could hazard a guess," says Beth.

Noah regards Beth expectantly.

She sighs, as though confident she won't be believed.

"A ghost," she says matter-of-factly.

Noah glowers. "Oh, please, Beth. Do we believe in such things now?"

Beth shakes her head just the way Marie does when he's being "dense."

"We believe in that which we sense, don't we?" she asks.

He turns back to Esther, who's slowly begun to stir.

"I suppose we do," he replies.

"I sensed *someone*," says Beth over his shoulder. "Didn't you?"

Noah lovingly runs his hand along Esther's cheek. It amazes him how quickly this girl has assumed a place in his heart alongside his true daughter. His mind slowly returns to Beth's question. Come to think on it, he *had* sensed a presence. But it was rather comforting, not frightening, as Esther took it to be.

Esther opens her eyes and smiles. Noah kisses her forehead.

"It's so good to have you back, child," he says.

"Where have I been?" she asks.

"That's a good question, Esther," he replies hesitantly. "I had the distinct feeling we did go somewhere, all of us together."

"But where?" asks Esther.

"Have you no recollection?" he asks.

She sits up with a start, eyes wide. "That woman! She was ... she was ... suddenly *standing* there! It was so cold." She looks to Noah. "She was *pleading* with you. Did you not hear?"

"I heard ... nothing," says Noah, feeling chagrined, as though his failure to see or hear the ghost is somehow a sign of moral failing.

"Nor did I," says Beth, gently pushing her way past Noah to Esther's bedside. "Esther, did you get a good look at the woman?"

Esther nods, wide-eyed, her eyes darting from Noah to Beth and back again. "She was very beautiful. She spoke to me in English ... quite refined."

Noah can barely contain himself. "Did she resemble ... *you*, Esther?" he asks, wondering if it was an apparition of his departed mother.

Before Esther can even respond, Beth snorts derisively at the question.

"No, sir," replies Esther. "Well, maybe a little bit, but ..."

Beth interrupts her halting reply. "She looked a great deal more like someone *else* we know. Did she not?"

Esther nods sheepishly.

Beth places her hand reassuringly upon Esther's. "Did she resemble ... Lady Jessica?"

Esther nods. "Yes, very *much* so." Suddenly realizing the implication of what she's said, she blurts out: "Oh, but Lady Jessica is alive and well, while this woman was …"

"Dead?" asks Beth.

"Yes … dead," Esther replies, rubbing her hands. A look of horror crosses her face. "Oh, my God! A dead woman was talking to me."

Beth continues. "Did the ghost look just a tiny bit like … me?"

Esther studies Beth's face. At first, she shakes her head, but then she cocks it skeptically. "Just a bit, but …" Her voice falters.

Beth smiles bitterly. "But prettier. More feminine."

Esther evidently cannot bring herself to answer. But it's clear to Noah that Beth's remark was not a question, but rather an exasperated observation.

Beth rises and turns to Noah impatiently. "You *still* don't know who it was, Noah? Even though she wore oil of clove, your favorite scent in the whole world? The scent she always wore because it acted upon you like catmint?" Her face reddens with humiliation, and she covers it with her hands. "My God, even in death … she upstages me."

Noah rises and approaches Esther with tears in his eyes. "Esther, that was an apparition"—he gulps, overcome with emotion—"of my beloved first wife." He sighs. "Oh, I loved her as I loved the whole world, and the world beyond this." Esther regards him with a look of pity. "She was Lady Jessica's mother, and Beth's cousin. Her name"—he almost weeps to say it—"was Rachel."

There is a war inside him now between the rationalist, to whom this visitation was nothing more than a fleeting apparition, and the man who needs with all his heart to believe that Rachel exists for him still. It grieves him that, in some form, she was here but a moment ago, yet he was unable to see or hear her. Why would she appear only to Esther, who's too young to have known her in life?

"May she rest in peace," he says at last.

Esther regards him sympathetically. "She is *not* at peace now," she says.

He turns to her with concern. "What did she say?"

"When she knew you couldn't see or hear her, she turned to me and refused to go until I agreed to pass along her message."

"What was it?"

"It was: 'Noah, run ... from ... the dark.'"

A short while later, Noah sits in Beth's salon, his hands folded in his lap, waiting for Beth to return after closing the curtains so Esther can nap. There was something distracted about Esther's aspect following her bout with the supernatural that, Beth was sure, could be cured only by sleep, and he could not disagree.

His mind is all at sixes and sevens, as so many things remain to be done to assure the Queen's safety. Yet he's enervated, sapped of all energy and desire. He looks down at his hands and feels hopelessly detached from them. He wonders idly whether they would move if he wanted them to.

As his thoughts to turn to Yetta herself, he's dismayed to realize that he knows almost nothing of her now-ended life, having never once thought to inquire after her. To the child he once was, she was simply a woman who was called upon from time to time to transport Jews secretly from places of great jeopardy to places out of harm's way, almost as though she were a member of a different race whose assigned lot in life was to perform such selfless deeds. He's embarrassed to realize that his own debt to her shall remain forever unpaid. How could he have been so selfish for so long?

Did Yetta ever marry or have children of her own? If she did, have any of her children survived her? Where would they be? How could they possibly be found? Did she have any property to leave to them, and where would it be?

Perhaps all domestic and familial comforts were denied her by the exigencies of her chosen occupation. And was it *truly* chosen? How did she fall into it? Why did she persist in it?

To Noah, certainly, Yetta's occupation seems to have been nearly thankless. He himself never thanked her adequately. He cannot imagine himself performing her job. What was she paid? It had never even occurred to him that she must have been paid *somehow*; otherwise, she could not have lived so long or continued in her chosen path.

And, as Esther observed a short while ago, Yetta spent her whole life in harm's way. What abuses had she suffered for the sake of her young wards, so they could thrive in their new homes while she once again slunk away into danger and darkness to help the next child in need? What compromises, what concessions must she have made to keep body and soul together, not only her own, but those of her young charges? What brutal insults, mental and physical, must she have suffered during her many long journeys? How many a night had she passed in the firm belief that it would be her last, whether by starvation, untended illness, or violence?

Knowing so little and being guilty of such ingratitude, he finds it only fitting that he can glean little from her life. The most he can learn from her is to do as she did; to persist against all obstacles—to put one foot in front of the other until there are no more steps available.

In a moment, the heavy shuffling of Beth's slippered feet approaches. She enters the salon looking disquieted.

"Well?" she says to him expectantly.

It seems almost too much effort to respond to such a general question, so he musters the least energy necessary. "Well ... *what?*" he replies in kind, unwilling to put more effort into his answer than she did into her question.

"Are you going to run?" she asks.

He cocks his head impatiently. "Run to where, Beth? Where should I run?"

She shrugs. "*Away*, perhaps?"

He considers the suggestion. "Away? Away from what? The *dark?* Be the earnest adult I know you to be. In what way is darkness a threat to me? Indeed, sometimes I feel it's my only friend."

Her expression turns bitter. "Who are *you* to feel that way, you most ungrateful man? You have a loving wife and daughter, a beautiful home, a high position, friends who risk their very *lives* on your say-so. And if worse comes to worst, you have *me*." She turns away. "Am I nothing?"

Noah summons the strength to rise and put his hands on her shoulders. "Of course you're not, Beth. You're a dear, dear friend and kinsman." He turns away. "And of course I do have other friends, and all those other things you remind me of. I suppose the only thing I lack is … Rachel."

Beth turns on him. "You need look no further than this empty house to remind you that others have it worse than you. *Far* worse." With an obvious effort, she changes the subject. "I was hoping you would know what Rachel meant," she says, chafing her hands from the memory of the ghostly chill, though the salon is comfortably warm.

"Can we be sure it was she?" he asks. "Suppose it was just an apparition sent to trick me."

She looks at him askance. "Demons don't tell you to beware, Noah. They try to put you *off* your guard."

Noah takes a seat on a sofa. "The Queen is in great danger. Her enemies are gathering. A dozen men have been sent on a mission at my suggestion. Shall I run? Has my *home* suddenly become a danger to me? Shall I take up lodgings elsewhere?" he asks. "And where might I run that does not grow dark at day's end? *Nowhere*. I'm afraid this exhortation from beyond is a bit short in specifics, as it has provided me with absolutely no idea where the danger lies." He sighs. "Indeed—and I suspect this is so—the danger may lie *everywhere*, in which case, what's the point in running? And whom should I bring with me? Marie? Esther? *You, Beth?* Sir Walter? No one?"

"Then why do you suppose she made her appearance?"

"You knew Rachel as well as I, Beth. She was known for her purity of heart, less for diligence of thought."

"But what was she trying to tell you?"

He sighs. "Only the most important thing in the world, I suppose." He looks up at her. "That she loves me still. Indeed, she could have brought me no more comforting message." Beth's expression shows that she feels cast aside once again, but before she can reply, he continues. "Just yesterday, Jessica made a similar demonstration for her new husband's sake. She tried to dissuade him from going into harm's way on the Crown's instruction. What was she trying to tell him? That she believed *she'd* suddenly become expert in Crown affairs? Of course not! She was expressing her love for her husband. And, as welcome as such expressions are, they're hardly prescriptive. She might as well have kissed him on the cheek and said, 'Take care.'"

"So, what are you going to do?" asks Beth.

"I'm going to *take care.*" He shakes off this draining sadness, and turns indignantly. "But why would she deliver her message to Esther, and not to me?"

Beth shrugs, and says, "There must be a reason."

# CHAPTER 13

**DAVID SHIELDS HIS EYES** from the late afternoon sun and peers up the hill at a partial battlement standing next to a mound of earth of about the same height with a few scattered stones at its base.

"That's a castle?" he asks incredulously, stroking his mount's withers. "Are you certain? Because these horses are bone weary, and it would be a shame to climb all the way up there only be told we're in the wrong place."

"It's just as Sir Walter described it," says Andres, shrugging. He adds dubiously, "He said it serves as a jail now."

David shakes his head. "Doesn't *look* like a jail. Doesn't look like much of *anything*, for that matter."

They dismount, and lead their horses up the hill. Reaching the top, David turns and peers out over the town, finding it quite beautiful, a collection of ancient buildings and little shops surrounded by verdant hills.

"Well," he says, "at least it's got a beautiful view of the university. Who would dismantle an ancient castle?"

"From what little I've heard," says Andres, "the kings ordered it done to ensure that no peer of the Crown could occupy it and resist the king's forces. A similar fate befell many of the inland castles."

David smirks. "If the king wants you arrested, then arrested you shall be."

Andres nods in agreement. "And without much ado."

David looks again at their dilapidated stopping point. "And now it's just an eyesore. You think they really have post horses in there for us?"

"Let's go and see the gatekeeper. If Sir Walter's memory holds true and things haven't changed too much, his name is Chester."

On the other side of the little gatehouse, they find an opening that's too small to allow them to lead their mounts inside. They tie off the horses and take a few steps into the opening. It's quite dark, almost cavernous.

Their horses' chuffing outside echoes off the damp stones. The only other sound is the wind wafting over the hilltop. David is about to shout for attention when Andres holds out a hand to stop him.

"Did you hear that?" whispers Andres cautiously.

David listens intently. All he can hear is the wind. But soon there's another sound, a low rhythmic growling coming from inside. "A *bear,* perhaps?"

The two travelers cock their pistols and creep forward in the darkness.

After a few paces, in the dim light there appears an array of empty wine bottles on the earthen floor, a few standing upright, most tumbled over onto their sides. Amongst the bottles is a small desk occupied by a sleeping man in a black gown, his face resting on the desk, eyes shut. Beneath the man's mouth, the blotter boasts a large dark stain which must once have been an impressive puddle of drool.

"You suppose he's dead?" whispers Andres.

As though in reply, the man lets out a snort followed by a deep, throaty snore.

"Well, there's your *bear,* anyway," says David.

Andres points to a mortar cap resting on the desk. "A *matriculated* one, evidently. One of Cambridge's finest ursine scholars, no doubt."

David pokes about the desktop to see if it holds a clue to the man's identity.

"Is there a name tag or something there … on the gown, perhaps?" asks Andres.

David shakes his head. "Nothing," he whispers. He leans in toward the sleeping man. "Chester?" he ventures quietly. He leans toward the man's ear and repeats himself, a bit louder this time. "Chester?" He rolls his eyes in exasperation and shouts. *"Chester!"*

Failing to rouse the man, David kicks the chair's leg, garnering no reaction. "Chester, you drunken sot!" Still nothing. He grabs the man's hair and lifts up his face. At last, one bloodshot eye opens a slit, only to close again immediately.

None too carefully, David lowers the man's head back onto the blotter with a light thump. He shakes his own head in exasperation. "They're not going to have post horses for us here, and I'll be damned if I'll leave *my* horse here for so much as a day. Let's go!" He takes a step toward the horses.

From deep inside the gatehouse, a man's small voice echoes off the wet stones.

"Wait!" says Andres. "Did you hear someone back there?"

"How's that *our* affair?" asks David.

"Well, if that voice comes from *this* man's prisoner," Andres says, pointing to the drunk, "he could well be dying of thirst or hunger, don't you think? This fellow's in no condition to see to his *own* necessities, let alone a prisoner's."

"I suppose," admits David, and pouts. "Oh, all right," he says reluctantly, "let's go and see."

They venture further into the dark jail, guns drawn and cocked.

The first thing they pass is a stall obviously designed to house post horses, as it contains a long hitching post anchored firmly to the earthen floor. A few bridles hang from the wall, and one dusty, decrepit saddle rests on the floor amidst a stack of straw. The stall is otherwise vacant. By the absence of any stench of dung, it appears to have fallen into disuse years ago.

"So much for fresh horses," says David.

"Over 'ere, kind suh," comes the voice again, followed by a half-hearted clanging of pewter against prison bars.

They follow the sound. Inside one of the jail's scant four cells stands a thin, middle-aged man with matted hair, leaning up against the bars, reaching his hand out to the two travelers.

"Do a good Christian turn, kind suhs," he pleads. "Lemme out."

"Who are you?" asks Andres.

"I'm Chestuh, suh." When they don't respond, he averts his eyes and confesses with chagrin, "I'm the jailer."

David snickers. "Then who's that drunken sot up there?"

"That's my prisoner, suh," says Chester ingenuously.

Perhaps it's due to the past two days' hard ride, but Andres and David cannot help but laugh.

Andres glances at Chester, who's red-faced and evidently feeling rather foolish. "Well," says Andres, by way of excusing himself for laughing, "you can see how implausible that sounds to us, can't you?"

"Aye, suh," he replies. "I s'pose it would seem that way to somebody in yaw position. But, as for me, I'd much appreciate it if you'd take the keychain from that fella up front and ... let me outta here."

"Perhaps," replies Andres, "but—given your present circumstances—we'll need some proof that you are indeed who you claim to be."

The jailer scratches his head. "I don't rightly know how I could do that from in here, suh. Papers are all in my desk up front, y'see, and I'm not even sure if anythin' up there would satisfy you gentlemen."

An idea occurs to David. "Well, then," he says, "perhaps you might identify a famous military man who's passed through here during your long tenure."

The man plops down onto the little bunk in his cell, thinking hard. "Well ... in all the years I been here, suh, I don't suppose more than one's come through. That was Sir Walter Raleigh, and that was some, oh, ten ... fifteen years ago. Is that who ye mean?"

Andres nods and strides off to get the keys.

David looks askance at Chester. "I don't suppose you have the post horses we were told to expect, *do* you?"

Chester shakes his head dolefully. "No, suh. Been *years* since they trusted us with post horses. The university men kept borrowin' 'em at night, without permission. And it's just been me holdin' the fort, if you take my meanin'."

David's heart goes out to the jailer as he imagines the tribulations suffered by an aging officer left alone to the thankless task of controlling a town full of rowdy, transient young men. Andres returns and unlocks the cell.

Chester pauses before crossing the threshold and bows low. "Thank you, gentlemen. If ye'll folla me to my desk, I'll show ye my commission before I give a thrashin' to that young fella."

As they approach the desk, even in the dim light it becomes increasingly obvious that the drunken man no longer occupies his former chair.

Chester races all about the desk trying to catch him hiding in the shadows, but comes up empty-handed. Plainly befuddled, he leans on the desk a moment, then turns toward the gatehouse entrance. Without another word, he darts outside to the rear of the gatehouse with Andres and David right behind.

The jailer stops abruptly at the edge of the hillside in an agitated state, peering down in the direction of the university. Halfway down the hill, the newly reinvigorated scholar is afoot, alternately stumbling and sprinting away, his right hand firmly atop his mortar cap to keep it from flying off, his gown flapping in the wind.

"Come back here, you drunken lout!" Chester shouts, and bolts down the hill in pursuit of the fleeing student, leaving the two travelers alone with no fresh horses and no provisions—without even so much as advice about lodgings for the approaching night.

"Well, *this* worked out well," mutters Andres. "Thank you, Sir Walter."

As the two travelers carry water to their horses from a stream flowing past the gatehouse, they wonder aloud how best to proceed.

"I suppose," offers David, "we could wander about the streets of Cambridge in search of an inn."

Andres shakes his head. "That wouldn't do. If Meyrick is among the opposing party and they happen to march into town, he'd recognize me and the jig would be up. If there are enough of them, they could capture us. If Sir Walter were to hear we took such a risk for a good night's sleep, he'd surely have us flogged, or worse."

David has to agree. "Even if they weren't to take us, they could steal a march on us and get to Burghley House before we do. That would make things difficult indeed. I suppose Meyrick might remember my face from St. Ives. So, even if you were to remain up here, we could still be caught out. I suppose we *could* wait until cover of darkness and seek shelter at one of the churches."

An unexpected man's voice says: "And why would you need to do that, masters?" It's Chester, cresting the hillside, looking a bit winded, but cordial enough.

David notices that he's alone. "We weren't expecting to see you again, Goodman Jailer. Where's your ... scholarly quarry?"

"He had too much of a lead, suh, but he'll be back. He'll need *this* soon enough," replies Chester, holding up a mortar cap. "Besides, I know his name."

"How'd you learn that?" asks David.

Chester points to what, at this distance, looks like an inkstain on the cap's inner lining. "It's inked in right here."

David laughs.

Andres is not so amused. "Goodman Jailer," he says formally, "we are in need of your good and prompt counsel. We're here on a Crown affair and need food, rest, and fast horses."

Chester thinks for a moment and smiles. "Plenty of those in Cambridge, suh—I mean, food and fast horses. Plenty of inns for good rest, too, *and* a good pint." Seeing how Andres glowers up at him, he hastily adds, "I mean, *if* you was to have the time and inclination, suh."

Andres half-smiles. "I suppose we've plenty of inclination, and thirst to match, but we've little time, as we need to set out early."

David turns to Andres, pointing down to a spot on the road a half-mile to the south. "We have even less time than you think, Andres. Look!"

In the fading light Andres squints toward the place indicated by David. There in the distance is what could, at first blush, pass for a ragtag band of minstrels being led by a boy wearing a fanciful multi-colored military uniform, seated proudly atop a white pony. Behind him ride five men dressed variously in doublets and other ordinary street clothing. While they might include Meyrick, Skeres, and their drunken friend Poley, Andres can't be certain at this distance. Bringing up the rear are two big black horses drawing a wagon of some heft, judging by its stiff movement. Out the back of the wagon juts a vaguely cylindrical structure covered in blankets and rags.

Before speaking, Andres draws both of his companions back off the edge of the hill, putting the gatehouse between them and the company on the road. "Was that a boy on a pony leading them?" he asks.

David and Chester look at each other and shrug.

"Think they saw us?" Andres asks anxiously.

"How would *I* know?" replies David.

Chester clears his throat. "Pardon the interruption, gentlemen, but if yaw worryin' about whether those men down there could recognize you … they couldn't."

David regards him askance. "How can you be certain?"

"Look where the sun is, behind ye," says Chester. "Been down on that road many times meself this time o' day. Even if they spotted ye, ye'd appear no more than shadow figures. And if they 'ave spotted ye already, they saw *three* men, includin' meself, o' course. What's more, from their position, yer horses are hidden behind the gatehouse. Those men can't see 'em. So, if they was on the lookout for two horsemen, they'd 'ave no clue it was you up here." He shrugs. "Could be anybuddy."

David smiles. "You seem a useful fellow, Chester. Something tells me you didn't learn to observe details in this way by serving as Cambridge jailer."

"No, suh," says Chester humbly, suddenly wistful. "Been in the wars. That was *years* ago, 'course." He bows respectfully. "Mind my askin' how you two gentlemen earn yer daily bread?"

David looks to Andres before answering. Andres nods approvingly.

"Master Arden here is a barrister at Queen's Bench."

Chester looks impressed and bows. He turns to David. "And *you,* suh?"

"I'm matriculated at Oxford." David extends his right hand. "My name's David Killigrew. Friends call me 'Cheerful.'"

Chester shoots a skeptical glance, first at David, then Andres. "Are you two gentlemen plannin' on fightin' that crew down there?"

Andres replies. "We're hoping we won't need to, but," he sighs, "there may be no alternative."

"Alone? Just the two o' ye?"

"As I say, we may have no choice."

"With your permission," says Chester, "I mean to take one more glimpse at those men. It'll take just a moment. You two gentlemen, stay here outta sight." He returns in a moment, looking somewhat dismayed.

"Something wrong, Chester?"

"Mebbe, suh."

"Why? What did you see?" asks David.

"D'ye see that wagon bein' drawn by those two husky horses?"

Andres nods. "The one covered in old laundry?"

"Ay, suh," says Chester dismally. "They could coat it in *pitch* if they like, but I'd still know what it was."

"And what is it?" asks David, with trepidation.

"It's a falconet. An old one, by the looks of it, but it's about the same vintage as yer obedient servant. I seen 'em plenty."

"What's a falconet?" asks Andres.

Chester's eyebrows shoot up in surprise at the question. "Why, it's a *cannon*, suh." Andres stares at him, slack-jawed.

A moment later, Andres nearly jumps out of his skin. "God's blood! A cannon!" he shouts. "Why the devil would they need a cannon to steal a few papers from a private residence?"

David places his hands on Andres's shoulder to calm him down. "No call for choleric words, old man!" he says. He draws Andres out of Chester's hearing and lowers his voice. "Leaving aside your ill-considered choice to let fly with blasphemy in front of a fellow we barely know, you seem to have forgotten that our mission is secret ... or at least it *was!*"

"I expect he heard much worse during his service in the wars," says Andres excitedly. "Don't you see the likelihood that this thing will get out of hand? Facing down a bloody cannon is a bit more than Sir Walter expected of us, don't you think? I mean, how can we do that without a cannon of our own? All we've got is two dull swords, two pistols, and a pair of horses too tired to shit!"

"Well," says David. "We've got more than that, haven't we? We've the law on our side. We could enlist the local constable."

"It's a *secret*, remember?"

David nods. Andres is quite right, of course. But David is confident Sir Walter will understand that the introduction of an enemy cannon into the equation has changed the calculus somewhat. "We've got our wits, too, and a day or two to come up with a plan." He points his chin toward Chester. "Didn't Sir Walter praise this fellow for his loyalty and skill?"

"Who ... Chester?" Andres asks in subdued tones.

David nods.

Andres rolls his eyes, evidently about to lose his temper once again. "Need I remind you, Master Killigrew," he whispers in exasperation, "that, when we found Goodman Chester, he'd been locked in a jail cell by his own prisoner?"

David waves off the objection. "Sir Walter referred to Chester as a stalwart, or some such thing," he says. "Perhaps we should bring him along. We need someone to get us lodgings and food for tonight, anyway, don't we? You and I can't very well go canvassing the local inns ourselves. Not with *those* thugs looking for us."

Andres relents. "I know I'm going to regret this ... but call him over," he says.

David beckons to Chester, who comes quickly, his face full of curiosity.

"Chester," says David, "have you your commission?"

Chester searches his pockets. "I know I grabbed it from the desk before. Yes, here it is." He offers the yellowed paper to David.

Andres reaches for it instead, and unfolds it. His eyes go wide. "This says you're an honorary member of Her Majesty's forces for life, Chester. You must have performed some valiant deeds in battle."

Chester shuffles his feet humbly, evidently reluctant to talk about his wartime experience, a trait common among men who've distinguished themselves in military service. "I took some men with me behind enemy lines, and disabled a few artillery positions. Simple as that, suh. Fact is, I felt safer behind enemy lines than out in front of those fierce cannon."

David observes Chester with a newfound respect. "I'll warrant there was some hand-to-hand fighting back there, as well."

Chester is momentarily lost in reminiscence. "Aye, sir. It was bloody ghastly, but we had the edge ... on account o' surprise."

Andres folds the paper respectfully and hands it back to Chester. "Keep that safe. In the meantime, we'd like you to accompany us on our mission. We'll make sure your pay is equal to ours. If the Exchequer declines to pay, we'll pay you out of our own pockets. What do you say?"

Chester seems lost in thought. "I couldn't just abandon me post here, suh. I'd have to secure a replacement."

"Have you one at the ready?" asks Andres.

"I expect so, suh. He owns an inn down in the town. If everyone's healthy there, his wife can run it while he covers the jail. He's got two strapping young sons who can help, too."

"I suppose he has a stables?" asks Andres.

"'Course he does, suh. What's more, it's a *big* stables for that little inn."

Andres reaches into his purse and hands Chester several shillings. "Chester, we need you to secure a room there for all three of us, as well as stabling for our horses. Tell your friend and his wife to keep it to themselves that we'll be staying there. You should also tell him that he'll be on duty here at the jail beginning tomorrow morning, and he may need to go as long as ten days without relief. Between us, I doubt it'll be anywhere near that long. A couple of other things, too. We need to be certain those men who entered the city a short time ago won't be staying at the same inn. If possible, find out where they *are* staying, then return to us here. If you can grab any food for us on these errands, I assure you it would be much appreciated. We're famished."

David interjects. "One more thing, before you go," he says to Chester. "Here's another shilling. Take the jail's key to the blacksmith and order a copy made. Then, tell your replacement to fetch it from the smith and keep it in his boot. No more of this jailed-jailer nonsense."

Chester accepts the shilling with a smile. "Shoulda thought o' that years ago. Woulda saved me a lot o' trouble. Thank you, suh."

A couple of hours before dawn, Andres awakens with a start. He wonders whether he's overslept, as last night was the first time in a few days he'd gone to sleep with a full belly. But, no, there's no sign of daybreak through the open window.

The sound of Chester's soft snoring fills him with tranquility, and he's just about to doze off again when he realizes that the window was closed when he dropped off to sleep last evening. He opens his eye a slit. It's open now.

He sits up and leans over to the next bed, only to find just what he was expecting. David is gone, and so are his clothes and boots. Gone out of the window to explore, no doubt.

Just then, David's handsome face appears outside the window, illuminated only by a partial moon. "Good morning, sleepyhead," David whispers. "Get dressed. I've found us some fresh horses."

"Whose?" asks Andres, rubbing his eyes.

David smiles from ear to ear. "Theirs," he says.

"*Theirs?*" Andres echoes, still clearing the cobwebs from his mind.

David nods vigorously. "Theirs! They're sleeping at a nearby inn that had insufficient room in its stables, so they left Poley outdoors to guard some of the horses." He collapses in a silent fit of laughter. "Can you imagine that? *Poley?* I needn't tell you what condition he's in."

"Out to the world," ventures Andres, as he rouses Chester.

"Yes, but there's no telling how long he'll be that way, so you two had better hurry. Put your shoes on, and let's go. Don't stir the house. Step out this window. We'll leave our horses in the inn's stables until we can safely return to fetch them. *Come on!*"

Andres and a groggy Chester dress and climb out of the window, where David awaits them with Chester's horse. It has their saddlebags slung over its back. Slowly, they begin walking in the direction indicated by David.

"Did you write the note to Jonathan last night, and dispatch it to the checkpoint?" asks David.

"Aye," says Andres.

"Were you sure to mention that they have a cannon?"

Andres stops in his tracks. "No, David," he says caustically. "That *completely* slipped my mind. Thank heaven you're here to remind me!"

"Whew! Just checking, Master *Huffy*," says David.

"Where are the horses for you and me, might I ask?" whispers Andres.

"They're beauties. They're outside the stables of the inn where their party is staying, as I said."

"How far?"

"About an eighth of a mile," David assures him. "A mere jaunt," he says and hands Chester the horse's reins.

About halfway there, Andres says, "Their horses must have been working just as hard as ours, mustn't they?"

David shakes his head. "Not these two. They're big chargers. As you saw yesterday, they've been riderless while pulling the cannon. And, unless I'm sorely mistaken, they haven't dragged that blasted thing all the way from London. I expect it joined them somewhere nearby."

"How do you know the two you're scouting are the ones that towed the cannon?"

"See for yourself," he says, pointing up ahead.

In the open air of a grassy field next to a neighboring inn is the silhouette of a cannon with two horses still hitched to it, asleep on their feet.

As Andres takes a step toward unhitching them, David takes him by the shoulder and points to the pile of laundry draped over the cannon. Cradled in the pile is an insensate lump, known as Robert Poley.

Andres whispers impatiently to David. "He's sleeping on the cannon. We'll surely awaken him when we unhitch the horses."

David holds his finger up and whispers, "I've considered that possibility. That's where Chester's demanding role comes into play." He grabs a fagot off a nearby woodpile, and hands it to Chester. "You see that man?" he asks, indicating Poley.

Chester nods.

"If he moves," says David, "nay, if he so much as *snorts in his sleep*, hit him very hard in the head with this." He hands the fagot to Chester.

"Pardon me," whispers Chester hoarsely. "I'll defer to you two gentlemen on matters such as this, but ... isn't stealin' horses a violation of Her Majesty's laws?"

David nods sagely. "Ordinarily it would be, Chester. You're quite right. But, see, we are on a mission to save the Queen from a possible assassin. None other than Sir Walter Raleigh has told us that we may *kill* those buggers, if need be." Chester's eyes go wide. "I should think stealing a couple of their horses is therefore also permissible. Andres, what's that Latin phrase you barristers use for such an argument?"

Andres smiles despite himself. "*A fortiori*. The rule of interpretation is that the greater includes the lesser," he says, and then uses it in context: "If we can kill them, then, *a fortiori*, we can leave them alive but take their horses." He gives it some thought. "It will also have the salutary effect of slowing them down."

Evidently satisfied, Chester stealthily takes up a position beside the sleeping Poley, holding the fagot over his head as though wielding the Sword of Damocles. In a moment, unbeknownst to the oblivious Poley, the horses are unhitched.

Andres and David affix their saddlebags to their new horses, and the three jesters head north a full hour before sunrise.

"Hah!" says David. "Chester the jester!"

# CHAPTER 14

**JUST PAST SUNSET,** Noah sits in the candlelit parlor upstairs. Marie stands before him, hands on her hips.

"A *ghost?*" she asks with enough incredulity in her voice to make Noah regret coming home straightaway.

"Yes, dear," he replies. "That's what Esther told us. *I* did not see … the ghost. Nor did Beth, evidently."

"What did it look like?" she asks.

"Please summon Esther to tell you, dear. She saw it first-hand."

Marie nods firmly. "Wait here," she says, and goes to fetch Esther.

The fact of Yetta's death and its surrounding circumstances have weighed heavily on Noah's mind throughout the hours since the incident. All that time, his rational mind has been diligently beveling the sharp edges of memory, smearing pellucid images, doing everything possible to erode his confidence in what he saw and felt during those few alarming moments.

But now, with the sun setting and the radiant blue of the summer sky waning to black, it all seems plausible again, which he finds ironic, as darkness is precisely what Rachel came from the grave to warn him of. He hears the approaching footsteps of the two women along the hallway.

Esther follows Marie into the parlor, looking a bit uncertain, as though her position in the household somehow depends upon what happens now, which must be more frightening than ever for her, now that Yetta is no longer alive to help her find her way.

"Sit, child," Marie says equably.

Esther darts a glance at Noah, and chooses a backless bench where she can reliably see both their faces.

"Serjeant Ames has informed me," Marie begins, "that, just before Yetta's passing, a ghost appeared to you."

"Yes, madam," says Esther.

"What did it look like?"

Noah detects Esther's apprehension. She's evidently unsure whether he's told Marie who the ghost was. He can see all the questions in her face: *If not, why not? If so, why is Marie seeking my confirmation?*

Esther begins hesitantly. "The ghost was … Lady Jessica's mother."

Marie looks dubiously at Noah, and sits comfortingly by Esther's side, stroking her hand in her own. "But you are too young to have seen Lady Jessica's mother in life, dear. How could you know that's who the ghost was?"

"Miss Beth Fernandez asked me questions, and my answers told her who it was."

"What did Beth ask you?"

"She asked me who the ghost most looked like."

"And you told her …?"

"Lady Jessica, and also a tiny bit like Beth."

When Marie looks to Noah in evident confusion, he expects it's because she's never heard mention of any resemblance between the two cousins. "Beth has lost a great deal of her weight during convalescence," he volunteers, "so the family resemblance has become … detectable, though still quite attenuated."

"I suppose you have no likeness of Rachel," says Marie. "No drawings or paintings?"

Noah shakes his head emphatically.

Marie turns back to Esther. "And the ghost told you nothing?"

"Nothing, except what she was trying to tell Serjeant Ames."

"To be afraid of the dark?" asks Marie.

Esther nods. "She said, 'Noah, *run* from the dark,'" she says, correcting Marie's paraphrase, as only someone who heard the original warning could.

"And what language did the ghost speak?" asks Marie.

"First, I spoke to the ghost in Polish, but she didn't understand. Then she spoke to me in English."

"Very well, my dear," says Marie. "You may go, and thank you."

Esther rises hesitantly. The level of confusion evident on her face suggests she still hasn't the vaguest idea why she was summoned. She bows and returns to her duties downstairs, leaving Noah alone with Marie once more.

Marie's thoughts are unreadable. "Do you credit this ghost tale?" she asks.

If it weren't for the ghostly blue light in Yetta's room, the eerie feeling that the room was *moving*, and the arctic temperature, he would have replied with something skeptical or equivocal, just to put Marie's mind at ease. But Esther has now confirmed the truth of the story to Marie, and he can't allow Marie to wonder whether her new ward has gone mad, when she hasn't. Esther obviously saw *something*, whether Rachel herself or a mere apparition. And Noah knows perfectly well that she did.

"I *do* credit it," he says simply. "I've no doubt Esther is accurately reporting what she saw and heard."

"What do you suppose it signifies?" Marie asks.

He scratches his head. "When you and I had known each other but a few weeks, or even days, I had a dream in which the voices of the dead addressed me by my birth name of Menachem, told me I was in danger, and even then implored me to run."

After a respectful moment, Marie smiles. "I trust they weren't telling you to run from *me*."

He shakes his head emphatically. "At that time, I was indeed in danger. So were you. To run blindly, however, and to leave in danger those around me would have made me a lesser man. So, I declined to heed their advice. However, I *did* heed their warning. And it turned out they were quite right about the danger."

"Surely you'd disregarded dreams of that type before?" she asks.

He nods. "But none was quite that *real*, if you understand me. And there was something else."

"What?"

"You know the prayer book I keep with that candlestick I brought you?"

"The candlestick with the Hebrew writing on the bottom that told me you were a Jew?"

He smiles, remembering. "The very one. Well, when I awoke from the dream, I found the prayer book on the floor." He looks her straight in the eye. "When I'd gone to sleep, it had been safely stowed in a locked cabinet. When I awoke and picked it up from the floor, the lock on the cabinet showed no sign of forcible entry, and the key was still in my pocket. The book had simply ... *come out*. I took that as a sign."

Marie nods sympathetically. "I suppose I have no cause to be jealous of your first wife?" she ventures.

He regards her fondly. "Marie, if your first husband Stephen were to come back and warn you of true danger, I would shake his hand." He kisses her. "No, Marie. I loved her whilst she lived. But I love *you* now."

As Noah comes down to breakfast the next morning and takes his accustomed seat at the kitchen table, Esther enters the house through the kitchen door and removes her bonnet excitedly.

"Serjeant Ames!" she says, and hastens to his side. "I saw that woman again."

"The beggar woman in the rain?" he asks.

She nods excitedly. "Only this time, she did not see me." She leans into him. "She was meeting someone. A Frenchman. I heard her call out his name. 'Darcy' or 'Dorsey.'"

Noah's eyes go wide, for this could be the Frenchman he's investigating, the one whose servant is the little fellow called "Monk."

"Could his name be 'Dorsay'?" he asks, carefully emphasizing the second syllable.

Esther shrugs. "Could be," she says. "They were quite familiar with each other. So, it's all right, don't you see?"

Noah's beginning to think he's a bit slow this morning. "Please, sit, dear," he says, patting the seat of the chair next to him.

She hangs her bonnet on a peg over the fireplace, and takes the proffered seat, making a show of calming down.

"*What* is all right?" he asks.

"I was afraid she was starving, but I see now that she has a man to take care of her. So, I don't feel bad any longer."

"As I recall, you'd felt bad that you hadn't given her money for food."

"Yes."

"And now you don't. So, she *wasn't* hungry?"

"No. Now that I saw her in the sunlight, she seems perfectly well fed," replies Esther. "But she was still distressed. Even more so than last time."

"About what?" he asks.

"She was quite agitated," says Esther. "As you know, I don't speak French, so I couldn't understand her words. But she had the appearance of a woman desperately worried about someone."

"Not about herself?"

"No, someone she loves."

"How could you tell?"

She titters. "Like when I saw the ghost. More witchcraft, perhaps!"

Noah's eyes dart about to ensure no one's heard. "Esther! You must never joke aloud about such matters," he says gravely. "You must understand, dear. Many Christians take that sort of thing very seriously. They think it *is* witchcraft. And they *expect* it of a Jewess, which makes it that much more dangerous for you—indeed for all of us." Recalling yesterday's conversation in the carriage to Beth's house, he says, "It looks as though I may have inadvertently misled you, Esther."

She looks at him curiously.

"Is it possible," he asks, "that, during the rainstorm, instead of saying *j'ai faim*, the woman said, *je suis sa femme?*"

"It *could* be," she says uncertainly. "What would it mean?"

"It would mean that, instead of saying *I'm hungry,* she was saying *I'm his wife*. Did she appear to act as though Dorsay is her husband?"

Esther contemplates the question. "Well, they didn't kiss on the mouth, or touch each other in such manner as only a husband and wife might do. But they were quite familiar, and he was trying to comfort her. She was very upset."

He sighs. "Esther, I must take you into my confidence now. I wished to avoid doing so for a much longer time, but circumstances have forced my hand. You must not share with *anyone* what I'm about to tell you. Is that understood?"

She nods, smiling.

He puts on a somber expression to impress upon her the importance of secrecy. "These are matters concerning the Crown, so that repeating them could result in a charge of high treason ... and death. You understand, dear?"

She shifts uncomfortably in her chair. "Yes, Serjeant," she says solemnly, in a voice so husky he needs to suppress a laugh.

The poor child has shown not the least interest in learning why agents of the Crown seem to appear at the house at all hours, and now she has thrust upon her, willy-nilly, the burden of knowing such matters and keeping them secret.

"I am investigating the Frenchman Dorsay, and I expect he may be the same man you saw walking with the mysterious Frenchwoman. You must continue your practice of refusing to listen to her or speak with her. Same with him. No contact whatever. And you must mention them to no one but me." He appraises her expression, which shows her to be a bit awestruck by her new responsibility. "There," he says somberly, "that's not so bad, is it?"

"No," she says in a pout. "Not bad."

"Now if I'm not mistaken," he says jovially, "Mistress Ames is going to the dressmaker's today, and she's bringing along her beautiful new daughter for a fitting."

Esther's eyebrows rise inquiringly. "Who?" she asks.

"I mean *you*, Esther. *You're* her beautiful new daughter."

"Oooh!" she intones and turns to him. "I'm getting a new dress?"

"More than one, I should imagine," he says. "You can't be relegated to Lady Jessica's old hand-me-downs forever, you know. You have your *own* life to live."

Esther shoots to her feet so quickly she nearly overturns the table.

"I must prepare!"

Alone that afternoon in the private room at the Saracen's Head, Noah awaits the hour appointed for his first interview of the day.

He cannot help but wonder how his young friends are faring on their journey to the remote Burghley House, both the vanguard consisting of Andres and David, and the larger party, led by Jonathan, sent afterward to assure their success. As yet there is no news, but even the vanguard could not be expected to have arrived yet. It's simply too soon.

There's a polite knock at the door.

Expecting it will be Monk in his fantastical military uniform, Noah takes his accustomed seat behind the large desk.

"Come!"

The Frenchman Dorsay opens the door and peers around it before entering. "Ah, Serjeant Emms. I see you are arrived already. You are at liberty for me, yes?"

"I am, sir," says Noah. "Please have a seat. I was hoping you'd be introduced this afternoon by your servant Monk."

"Oh? He has impressed you favorably?" asks Dorsay. "I have dispatched him on an errand. He will return shortly." He takes a seat in a small chair halfway across the room, to Noah's left, so that his line of sight is diagonal to Noah's.

Noah sighs. Accepting the challenge, he declines to turn his head. Indicating the seat directly in front of the desk, Noah says, "Perhaps you would prefer *this* seat, sir," and leans back patiently in his chair, staring pleasantly at the vacant seat before him.

"If you prefer," says Dorsay, as though his choice of seat had been purely arbitrary. He rises and assumes the seat across from Noah, deftly turning his chair a few degrees off center before lowering his full weight into it.

*Could this man make it any more obvious that he's hiding something?* In keeping with good interrogator's form, Noah smiles. "I must observe," he says, "that your servant Monk shows great commitment to you, sir ... but also to your traveling companion Monsieur Nerezza, who treats him … rather less well."

Dorsay clears his throat. "Indeed, he does. I have spoken to Nerezza many times about his mistreatment of Monk, but it does no good. It infuriates him only."

"What is your relationship to Monk, if I may ask?"

Dorsay shrugs. "He is my servant, as you say."

"He is of no relation to you otherwise?"

"*Non.*"

"If you don't mind my asking," says Noah, "are you married, sir?"

The Frenchman's eyes show that he's considering how to answer. Given the simplicity of the question, Noah sees that he misjudged this man at their first meeting, when he assumed on the basis of nothing more than Dorsay's defense of his servant that he was in some way morally superior to Nerezza.

"Come, sir," says Noah impatiently. "It's a simple enough question."

As though the topic had come as something of a surprise, the Frenchman says, "Indeed it is. If you will permit me, sir … I was just wondering why you would ask it."

This man is becoming irksome. "May I remind you, Monsieur Dorsay, that you are here at the sufferance of Her Majesty Queen Elizabeth, who is under no obligation to let you remain in this kingdom. If you will not answer a few simple questions that no reasonable man would find overly intrusive, then it will be my recommendation that you be marched to the nearest port and returned to your own country directly."

Dorsay impassively brushes a piece of lint from his doublet, and says perfunctorily, "I am unmarried."

This is something of a surprise, given Esther's observation of the manner in which Dorsay behaved in the company of the Frenchwoman. Perhaps this *is* a different man, after all.

"I shall tell you my reason for asking, as you have now been kind enough to divulge to me your marital status. One of my local assistants has seen you in the company of a certain Frenchwoman."

Dorsay brings himself up in his chair as though insulted. "Have you set spies upon my personal quarters, sir?"

Noah must suppress a laugh at the ease with which this man has given up more information than requested. *So, she's been in his personal quarters!* "Only if you consider a public street to be a part of your personal quarters, sir. And I didn't send anyone to spy on you. The fellow merely passed you in the street."

"I don't know what woman you are referring to," comes the reply.

"I suppose it's of no importance," says Noah, making a show of recording the response in his liber. "What business brings you to England?"

"I am a man of leisure, Serjeant. I have seen some plays at your theaters in Southwark, as well as bear baiting. I also enjoy 'games of chance,' as you call them."

"Oh, come, sir. Seeing a play is something one does to busy himself while visiting a foreign city on *other* business, is it not?"

"Sometimes," confirms Dorsay, while offering nothing further. He shifts in his chair. "To be totally honest with you, sir, I am a man of some intrigue in affairs on the Continent of Europe."

"Were you invited to England by Lord Essex?"

Dorsay shakes his head. *"Non."*

"By Lord Southampton?"

"I will be completely open and honest. I was not invited by the earl, but I was encouraged to come here. He is a great admirer of dramatic plays, also, especially ze plays by Monsieur Guillaume Shakespeare, *non?"*

Noah nods impatiently. "And he invited you here to attend plays with him?"

Dorsay replies with a Gallic shrug, momentarily jutting out his chin and raising his shoulders.

Noah knows enough Frenchmen to recognize that this gesture is meant to impart nothing. He rises behind his desk. "And since we are, as you have now twice said, being totally open and honest with each other, I will tell you honestly that your answers to my simple questions have been completely unsatisfactory. I don't know for certain what the Privy Council will do with my recommendation, sir, but I strongly suggest you stay where I can find you. If I have to search for you, things will not go well … for you." He bows. "Good day, sir."

Dorsay makes a show of not caring. He rises, bows perfunctorily, and leaves, closing the door firmly behind.

Noah wonders what errand Monk's been sent on, and hopes it wasn't to fetch sensitive papers from Burghley House.

# CHAPTER 15

**NOAH RISES EARLY** in the dark, dons his robes, and goes quietly down to his study. He lights a taper and eagerly thumbs through the letters that were slipped under the door this morning. There's nothing but a few bills seeking payment for fodder for the horses, seeds for the garden. Nothing from Paris, though he's been hoping for a reply from Sir Henry providing information about the foreigners turning up at Drury House in support of Lord Essex.

Shortly after dawn, on the other side of the house, the kitchen door opens and closes, and the floor shudders slightly, as with the emplacement of something heavy. Noah taps Uncle Avram's dagger and strides to the kitchen, where he finds a traveler's trunk left askew across the doorway. Hearing someone moving down the hallway to young Stephen's room, he hastens there to ensure nothing is amiss.

At the opposite end of the hallway stands young Stephen himself, freshly returned from Paris. He's opened his bedroom door only to find Esther asleep in his bed. Stephen turns to Noah, eyes agog, and whispers wistfully. "My prayers have been answered."

Noah chuckles quietly. "Close the door," he whispers. "I'll explain."

But Stephen seems reluctant to dispel the fantasy of his newfound roommate, and takes one more peek. He turns back to Noah. "Can we keep her?" he asks hopefully, as though she were a puppy who followed him home.

"Yes, Stephen," replies Noah. "We'll keep her. Now close the door or you'll frighten her."

With one last, longing look, Stephen closes the door. He takes Noah's extended hand in his own. "It's good to see you, Serjeant Ames."

Noah draws him in for an affectionate embrace. "Welcome home.

It's so good to see you, too. We weren't expecting you until next week. How did you get away so soon?" He beckons Stephen toward the study. "Come and tell all." As soon as Stephen spots the softest chair in the room, he collapses into it, the weariness of the road etched about his eyes.

Noah remarks to himself that travel and fatigue have aged his stepson beyond his twenty-five years. But then again, he supposes, a young man is bound to appear older after a few sleepless nights, such as those encountered in travel from the Continent.

Stephen smiles wanly in the pale early light. "Sir Henry sent me home. He himself will return to England earlier than you might expect. Her Majesty has evidently taken pity on him and given him leave to return home for a while. As for his embassage, he's feeling it's hopeless, that he won't be able to secure repayment of Her Majesty's loan until King Henri's been relieved of the extraordinary cost of defending his country from the bloody Spanish."

"And how fares my old friend?"

Stephen's sigh is audible in the preternatural quiet of early morning. "Sir Henry spends a great deal of his time writing—correspondence, I suppose, although it's hard to imagine anyone having so many correspondents." He takes a long breath and arches an eyebrow. "Now tell me of the angel in my room."

"Her name is Esther," Noah replies. "She's a distant cousin of mine from Eastern Europe. She's nowhere else to go. The woman who escorted her to England (the same one who brought me here) passed away at the home of my Cousin Beth in Southwark. We would have moved Esther out of your room yesterday, of course, if we'd known you were arriving today."

"I wrote to Mother," says Stephen, "but I suppose I've outrun my letter." He snaps his fingers and reaches into his pocket. "Speaking of letters, I've one for you from Sir Henry." He hands it to Noah.

Marie enters the study in her dressing gown. "Stephen!" she exclaims. "Oh, my bouncing baby boy! I'm so pleased to lay eyes on you at last!" She falls on her eldest boy's neck, who rolls his eyes for Noah's amusement. "Why didn't you tell us you'd be home today?"

"I did write to you, Mother, but I appear to have arrived before my letter."

"Oh, never mind that," says Marie. "Come to the kitchen and we'll cook you up something. You must be starving!" She turns to Noah. "Serjeant Ames, come and join our happy reunion."

Noah holds up the letter from Sir Henry. "I'll be there anon, my dear. I plead affairs of state."

Marie purses her lips at him impatiently.

"Just a few minutes, dear," says Noah. "Don't let the poor lad wait for me. Get started with the food!"

Marie regards him skeptically, but moves off to the kitchen with young Stephen.

Noah slits open Sir Henry's letter, which begins with the customary familiarities, and the usual heartfelt regards to Lady Jessica and Mistress Ames. Near the end, at last it addresses matters much on Noah's mind.

> Your latest letter managed to jar loose a memory or two concerning the Frenchman about whom you inquired.
>
> I plainly recall Mister Secretary Walsingham mentioning that he suspected a certain "Dorsey" of nefarious involvement in several French catastrophes, including the Massacre of Huguenots, and also (unless memory fails me) the demise of the French King Charles the Ninth. I made a few discreet inquiries, in the course of which I discovered that Dorsey was a long-time friend of the scoundrel "le Loup," who you advise was recently slain by our Jonathan, now Lord Saint Ives.
>
> If the Dorsay of whom you inquire is the man I heard spoken of, best tell Raleigh to set a watch on him. You personally must steer clear of him, as he's a ruthless fanatic, hates protestants, and will harbor even less love for the Hebrew who serves them. Lord Saint Ives must also stay as far away from him as possible, as must Lady Jessica, who is commonly believed (here, at least) to have been present when le Loup was killed. If you deem it prudent to move them out of London to someplace as far as Windsor, send a note to our footman Walker at Lothbury. He's been authorized to close the Lothbury house and open a wing at Billingbear, should the need arise. Windsor ought to be far enough, so long as the newlyweds' whereabouts are kept secret.

In any event, don't believe a word your Dorsay says, and lock your doors at night.

As for the Italian you mention, I don't recognize the name from our mutual European tour, nor do I recall anyone fitting that description. He may simply be mistaken about recognizing your aura (a foolish figure, that). If not, he's probably remembering you from somewhere else, though where that might be I haven't a ghost of an idea.

As I'd imagine young Stephen has already told you, Her Majesty has consented to my return to England for both a respite and a badly needed replenishment of money for this embassage. The Exchequer is well behind in footing the Crown's share of the cost.

I have the greatest confidence in my secretary, Ralph Winwood, to conduct daily affairs in Paris during my absence, and expect to suffer no regrets on account of his work while I'm back at home. Look for me when least expected (but especially in early August).

Your Very Loving Friend,
Henry Neville

So, Walsingham suspected Dorsay of some misfeasance regarding the massacre. It appears certain that the Dorsay currently housed at Drury House is the same man, as he identified himself as a man of intrigue, whatever that might be. Still, Noah wonders what he can do with such knowledge. Much as he dislikes the Frenchman (for allowing his dwarfish servant to be mistreated, if nothing else), he'd need to know the *basis* for Walsingham's suspicions in order to proceed to an arrest.

It occurs to him that Walsingham himself may have had nothing but a vague suspicion, as he seems not to have informed on Dorsay to the French authorities, at least not in a manner resulting in arrest. Then again, perhaps Walsingham had solid evidence, but deemed it inimical to English interests to turn him in.

Noah laments that whatever information was available to Walsingham cannot be reconstructed after so many years, at least not without Walsingham's files and, if those exist, they're likely in the possession of his son-in-law, Lord Essex. At this point, it appears only a confession by the wrongdoer would suffice to support an arrest.

And what of the Italian, Nerezza? Sir Henry evidently has no recollection of the name or the man himself, and finds Nerezza's reference to an "aura" to be mere foolishness. But his letter goes on to observe that he has not a "ghost of an idea" where Nerezza might have seen Noah before. That's a strangely supernatural locution for Sir Henry to utilize, peculiarly disquieting so soon after Esther's encounter with the ghost at Yetta's deathbed.

When could the Italian have seen Noah, if not on the Continent? Has he been to England before? If so, he *might* have spotted Noah, who's been at court on and off for the past seven years.

And what of Sir Henry's admonition about the danger to Jonathan and Jessica? Jonathan is on his way to Burghley House and out of reach. In any event, he's surrounded and protected by men-at-arms.

But what of Jessica? She must be persuaded to move temporarily—but to where? To Henry's ancestral home in Windsor? Noah has no doubt that his headstrong daughter will refuse to be moved so far away from town, at least without a serious threat of plague. Besides, there will be virtually no one there, with Sir Henry and Lady Anne away in Paris. That decides him. Jessica will have to move in with him and Marie here in Holborn, at least until Jonathan returns.

But they're running short of rooms now that Esther has moved in, Stephen has returned, and Marie's younger children are expected to return soon from their visit to relatives in Surrey.

Noah rather welcomes the feeling of being crowded by his family at a time like this. He feels the urge to draw them all in and keep them safely with him, enfold them in his robes in a sense, but protected by … what? Uncle Avram's dagger? He shakes his head at the foolish run of his idle thoughts.

As he prepares to join Marie and Stephen for breakfast, his mind is boggled by what seem to be limitless sources of peril, and he can't help but wonder whether his practical position has been improved even slightly by the information contained in Sir Henry's letter.

Andres, David, and their new recruit Chester canter northward. Their destination comes into view at last. It's a large, isolated Italianate manor house of white stone, with a cupola atop every turret, making it look rather antique, but in a cheerful way.

"That's Burghley House?" asks Chester. "Why, it looks like a king's castle!"

"To be specific," says Andres, "it resembles Richmond Palace."

David slows down to take in the view, and the others follow suit, making it possible to hold a normal conversation. "It really *does* look like Richmond, doesn't it?" he remarks.

"Shouldn't be surprising," Andres assures him, "as it's *fashioned* after Richmond. Lord Burghley was ever solicitous of the Queen's approval, and she's always been known to favor Richmond."

"Can't say's I ever saw Richmond Palace," says Chester. "*This* is a beautiful place, though."

"*So* beautiful," says Andres with trepidation, "that Sir Walter will hang us if we let it come to harm."

"As by cannonfire," adds David, drawing to a stop and glancing about suspiciously. The others stop and regard him curiously. "What if they're already here?" he asks. "What if they have someone watching us right now?"

"Doubtful," says Andres, "but I suppose we should take precautions."

Chester nods. "Words o' wisdom. It'd be smart if only one of us knocked at the door." His eyes search the vicinity. "Maybe the other two of us hide in the woods where we can see the door, and wait for the all-clear signal."

While David pounds on the elegant wrought iron gate guarding the grand entrance to Burghley House, he glances up at the three storeys above ground level that loom over this section of this house. At the center of each is a large set of windows having an unobstructed view of the copse where Andres and Chester have attempted to conceal themselves and their horses.

They've agreed that, if David finds anything amiss at the door, he'll proffer some excuse allowing him to consult with the other two before entering. If nothing's amiss, he'll accept the invitation to enter, and the other two will remain in the woods awaiting the signal to come ahead. If David fails to signal them in a half-hour, they'll move to extricate him.

He also can't help but glance over his shoulder for any sign of Meyrick's party. Though he expects they're at least a half-day behind, it's possible they've sent a scout ahead to clear their way.

A door concealed behind the gate opens. Some unseen person cautiously traverses the darkened doorway and peeps at him through a gap in the wrought iron.

"Who's calling?" comes the voice of a mature man who sounds educated and local.

"My name's David Killigrew, here on Her Majesty's service." He peeks through the gap, but the man on the other side is a full step back of the gate, well concealed in shadow.

"Queen's business?" comes the voice again. "What sort of errand?"

"Before I can disclose that," says David, betraying the slightest impatience, "I need to know whom I'm speaking to."

"Well," says the man inside, "my name's Barnaby Bell, for what good that'll do ye."

David smirks. "Would it ring true, Master Bell, to say you are steward at Burghley House?"

"*Does Master Bell ring true?*" says the man indignantly. "Now you tell *me*, Master Cavalier, how it comes about that a Cornishman feels free to play so nicely with a venerable name of the north."

David laughs, as he's gotten as good as he's given. "We Cornish would much rather share a pint of ale with such men than play with their names."

"So I've heard of Cornishmen," says the man behind the gate, accepting David's friendly words with good cheer. "And you've a fair chance at that, if you'll tell me your business first."

"I have a note here from the master of Burghley House for his steward, Master Bell. It must be given to no other. Are you said steward, sir?"

"No other," says Master Bell. "Let's see it, and perhaps I can let you in."

David slips the note through the gap, and feels it snatched smartly away. He waits while the paper is read.

"Ah," says Bell, "why didn't you say you were traveling secretly, and in a rush, Master Killigrew? Go back to your two friends—who look downright foolish standing there with their horses behind a couple of bushes, pretending to be invisible—and bring your horses 'round back to the stables where they can't be seen. I'll let you in, and your friends can wait back there until you and I have sorted this out."

David turns about to observe Andres and Chester. He laughs silently. In truth, they do look rather daft standing out there, visible from the gate and, no doubt, from every one of the thirty or so windows in the front of the house. "But how can I be sure," asks David, "that you're not already under some compulsion by our adversaries, Master Bell?"

A thoughtful silence gives way to Bell's voice. "Because if anyone had come to this gate seeking entry by force, Master Killigrew, there'd be a big pool of blood right where you're standing, as I would have blown his head off with the very pistol I now have trained on you."

"What a cautious and persuasive fellow you are, Master Bell!" David instinctively likes this fellow, who's mostly business but has enough humanity to make him personable. "We'll be around back in a moment."

David is pleased to find he's not misjudged Steward Bell, who is a pleasant middle-aged gentleman, well educated and well spoken. On first sight, David finds his coloring darker than one would expect in the North of England, perhaps Spanish or partly so, his silvered beard lending him an air of maturity and authority.

At the conclusion of their brief interview, Bell folds his master's note and puts it in his pocket. "Well, the note's in my master's hand; that's certain. And he instructs me to give you and your companion Master

Salazar the run of the place, as well as any assistance you might need. But before I invite your friends in from the stables, I have one question."

"What's that?" asks David, eager to begin preparing for their adversaries' arrival.

"Who's the other fellow with Master Salazar?"

"The other fellow?" asks David, as he's momentarily forgotten they've accumulated an extra man.

Bell nods. "My master's note tells me to expect only two of you."

"A reasonable question, Master Bell. The third man's name is Chester. He's the jailer at Cambridge Castle."

The steward seems to search his memory for a moment, then scoffs. "Cambridge Castle, indeed! You mean that little *jakes* up on the hill?"

David smirks and lowers his voice. "I see you have been there," he says. "You might wish to keep such phrases out of the conversation, as Chester's been in charge there many years and takes his job rather seriously, though the scholars at the university persist in making light of it. He comes highly recommended by Sir Walter Raleigh."

Bell shrugs. "Well, if Sir Walter vouches for him, I suppose he's all right. Now," he says, "what kind of assistance can I offer you? We've no menservants here now, unfortunately. Even the gardener left a few weeks ago on holiday. Seems to think his plantings are perfectly capable of growing in his absence for a few weeks."

"Is there no one else here to help us?"

"Well, there's my wife and daughter. Bring in your two friends, and I'll introduce everyone."

In a moment, the three travelers have assembled in the kitchen, awaiting introduction to Master Bell's ladies.

Master Bell enters first, leading in an attractive blonde woman his own age, who curtsies silently. "This is my wife, Frideswide. Best cook this side of the silver sea, as you'll come to know, depending upon how long you remain here."

Evidently recognizing the wife's Christian name, Andres begins to hold forth. "The name Frideswide is well known about Oxford, where I attended, and where David attends now. If I'm not mistaken, Saint Frideswide built a church there ..." His voice trails off as Master Bell's daughter enters.

David guesses she's about his own age of nineteen, and has evidently been doing some form of manual labor, as her long black hair is unbound and has fallen about her slender shoulders. Even her modest frock cannot conceal her shapeliness. Her face is comely, her complexion fair like her mother's, but her eyes sharp and black, like a moor's. David glances at her father and finds a striking resemblance about the eyes.

Andres has suddenly lost his voice, too smitten to speak, his mouth agape at the sight of the girl.

Evidently accustomed to his daughter's garnering such admiration from young men, Master Bell graciously ignores Andres's momentary loss of the power of speech. "This is our daughter Barbara," he says proudly, and turns to her. "What have you been doing, dear? Arranging old documents again?"

Barbara smiles and nods, plainly enjoying her effect on Andres, perhaps even reciprocating it in a modest way.

David is surprised and delighted that the girl is both literate and familiar with documents stored in the house. "Would Miss Barbara happen to know the storage place of correspondence between the deceased William, Lord Burghley and Secretary Walsingham during the years of our Lord 1572 and 1573?"

Barbara curtsies and looks to her father for permission to disclose such information to these newcomers. When he nods his approval, she says, "I have a general understanding of the location of those documents. That is, I believe I can narrow it down to three large rooms on the second storey."

"Three large rooms?" Chagrined, David turns to Andres. "Master Salazar, it appears you have your work cut out for you. Better get to it." Andres nods silently and begins to follow Barbara out of the kitchen.

"We wouldn't want to disappoint Serjeant Ames," says David. As Andres steps over the saddle to the hallway, David wickedly adds, "Nor his young *niece*." This latest emendation induces a momentary hitch in Andres's stride.

But Andres wisely declines the opportunity to face his tormentor, and follows the girl up the stairs.

# CHAPTER 16

**IT'S A SULTRY AFTERNOON** by the time Sir Walter visits Noah's private room at the Saracen's Head.

"Any interesting interviews lately?" asks Sir Walter.

"Not really," says Noah, "as we've confined ourselves to the foreigners who've taken up residence at Drury House. I've heard reports that more Englishmen are arriving all the time. I wonder whether they portend Essex's release."

Raleigh nods. "There are rumors of such, but they've come to naught so far."

"Who are the new English residents? Do you know?"

"I've heard of a few that might be of interest," says Raleigh, "but they're unlikely to have been involved in the late attempt on the Queen."

"Such as?" asks Noah.

"Well, Sir Christopher Blount has appeared a few times."

"Essex's stepfather?"

"The same," Sir Walter assures him. "Sir Ferdinando Gorges. Sir Charles Danvers. They're all associated with Essex in some way, but that hardly makes them regicides."

"Any luck finding out how the intruders got the keys to the Tower room?"

"None."

Noah sighs. "Then, I suppose our best hope is that the jesters bring us correspondence condemning Dorsay. Any other news from the Tower?"

Raleigh shakes his head, but then equivocates. "There is one thing that's a bit disturbing. The surgeon says Warder Francis will soon be out of that horrible contraption he's been suspended in."

"So soon?"

Sir Walter nods with a grave expression.

"Why's that disturbing?" asks Noah.

There's a faraway look on Sir Walter's face as he strokes his beard. "When I told him that the kitchen wench Sally had been murdered, just as I expected he roared like an agonized beast and struggled to break loose from traction. It must have hurt like the very devil, but the pain only incensed him more. I'm concerned that once he's ambulatory he might attempt to mete out some punishment without ..." His voice trails off as he looks to Noah with concern.

Noah nods. "Without adhering to the niceties of law?"

Sir Walter nods. "Or any niceties at all, for that matter."

"Have you considered confining him to the Tower?"

"I have. Enforcing such an order should be a simple matter in light of the protocol we've temporarily instituted for everyone entering or leaving the Tower. Without my signature, *nobody* leaves."

"Then what's the problem?" asks Noah.

"Warder Francis has been trained as Gardner's eventual replacement. That means he knows more ways in and out of the Tower than anyone except Her Majesty—even a few unknown to *me*." Raleigh rises and shakes off his concern. "I'm heading back there now. Let me know if anything interesting transpires here."

"Before you go—" Noah begins, but thinks better of it.

Raleigh waits indulgently. "Yes?"

Noah reconsiders whether it's worthwhile to involve Sir Walter in what is, essentially, family business. "I don't want to burden you."

"Well, you've piqued my interest," says Sir Walter. "What is it?"

"Lady Jessica has declined my invitation to move into Marie's house in Holborn until this matter's been resolved."

"I'm not surprised," says Sir Walter.

Noah *is* surprised. "Well ... *you've* spent the night there. Did you have some problem?"

"Not in the least," says Sir Walter, "but where's she supposed to sleep, for heaven's sake? On the couch? The room I slept in is now occupied by Mistress Ames's young daughter. And her younger boy's already sharing a room with Stephen. And Esther's in the other room. Isn't that right?"

"I suppose my daughter finds the accommodations at our humble home beneath her station," Noah says sadly.

"Nonsense!" protests Sir Walter. "Do you even have a bed for her?"

"Well, how am I to protect her?" says Noah, exasperated.

"Please take no offense, Noah, but *you* can't protect her anyway, except to lock your doors at night. And I strongly doubt she's in peril simply over being nearby when le Loup was killed." Sir Walter arches an eyebrow. "More than likely, if she's in any peril at all, it's because she could be used as a means to get to *you*."

"That's an uncomfortable thought," says Noah. "Could you assign someone to look in on her? She's staying in town, but she's alone."

Raleigh shrugs. "I could send someone around once a day, but I can't assign her a continuous guard. Costs a bloody fortune. Unless you can prevail upon Her Majesty to allow her to stay at the Tower."

"Let me think about it, Sir Walter. I'll speak with Lady Jessica again."

As Noah gazes out of the window watching Sir Walter depart on horseback, a nervous figure near the inn's entrance catches his eye. It's a man, pacing as though unable to decide whether to enter. Unless Noah's mistaken, he's seen this man in the company of Henry Savile, Noah's old master, which suggests that, like Savile, the man serves as a secretary to the Earl of Essex.

As the summer heat seems to have dissuaded any visitors from coming 'round, Noah folds up his portfolio and prepares to depart. Just as he's about to walk out, however, the nervous fellow appears at his door, perspiring, his face flushed.

"Pardon me, sir," says the fellow, his eyes darting about as though concerned that he might be seen. "Are you Serjeant Ames?"

"I am, sir. Please come in," says Noah, resuming his seat in an attempt to put his nervous visitor at ease. "Feel free to close the door behind you."

The man does so, and turns back to Noah, his eyes darting from chair to chair, as though much depends upon his choice of seat, or perhaps his choice whether to sit at all.

"And you are ...?" says Noah indulgently.

The man's eyebrows shoot up, as though he had no idea he'd be asked such a personal question. "Um," he begins tentatively, "I am Henry Cuffe, a secretary to Lord Essex—although I hasten to add that my being here has nothing to do with Lord Essex." He shakes his head emphatically.

"Of course," says Noah. "Ah, yes. I believe I've seen you in the company of my old master, Savile."

"Indeed? Well, yes. That stands to reason."

Noah waits for him to say something more. And waits. This fellow seems to have little in the way of social grace. A philosopher, perhaps. "Did you stop by simply to introduce yourself? If so, I'm *very* pleased to make—"

"Oh, no, no, no!" Cuffe exclaims in the practiced manner of a pedant. He lifts both hands above his head, palms forward in gentle protest. His gesticulation dislodges a letter from his pocket, and he watches in horror as it wafts from his robe to the floor. He accidentally steps on it, impressing a dusty bootprint, then quickly snatches it up, apparently to prevent Noah from getting a good look at the address. "I came by today," says Cuffe, "to ask you if you've heard from Henry."

"Savile?" asks Noah.

"Oh, no," says Cuffe. "*Sir* Henry. Sir Henry *Neville*. I beg your pardon, of course. They're both named Henry, aren't they?"

"Yes," says Noah genially, "as are you." He smiles and nods, wondering whether his correspondence with Sir Henry is a matter fit for conversation with others. "Sir Henry and I correspond occasionally," he admits, seeing no possible hazard in revealing that much, "although it has been difficult lately—with his moving embassage in France, you see. Why? Do you need something from him?"

Cuffe scowls and shakes his head. "Oh, no, no, no," he says again with the same gesticulation, but a bit more restrained than before, lest the letter fall again. A darkness seems to come over Cuffe, who leans in confidentially. "While I hope that Sir Henry finds things comfortable upon his return, one hears his name spoken at court so often that I wonder whether his reputation has not been harmed by his lack of success in his present embassage."

Noah finds such talk distressing. "Is it supposed at court that some-one else could have done better?" he asks.

Cuffe sighs. "There are so many jackals," he says, deep in thought, but in a moment waves away the thought. "Sir Henry's reputation is certainly sound with the earl my master and all his retinue." He leans in again. "Actually there *is* something I'd care to discuss with Sir Henry. You see, he has a copy of a manuscript for a book I've written, and—"

"Oh?" interrupts Noah, who finds he's perversely enjoying keeping this fellow off balance. "Not the *only* copy, I hope."

"Oh, no, no, no." Noah suppresses a laugh at the rapid way in which Cuffe habitually says *oh, no, no, no,* when a single *no* would do just as well. Cuffe continues. "It's just that I was very skittish about asking him to review it. He's *such* a great man, of course."

Noah nods, a little confused at the fellow's unbounded adoration for Sir Henry, although he's encountered it in others. "He *is* a great man, it's true. And a good and loving friend. Tell me, what is the matter?"

"Between who?" Cuffe asks ingenuously, as though Noah's asked about some point of dispute.

"I mean the matter of the *book* you've written."

"Oh, of course!" says Cuffe, a bit befuddled. "Why, it's entitled—at least I *think* it will be entitled—whenever it's published, of course—I mean, *if* it's ever published—" He blushes, and his face is such utter confusion, it's all Noah can do to keep from bursting out in laughter. "What was I about to say?" asks Cuffe. "By the mass, I was about to say something. Where did I leave off?"

Noah suppresses a laugh. "I believe you were about to tell me the present title of your manuscript, a copy of which you lent to Sir Henry Neville."

"Oh, yes," says Cuffe, chagrined. "It's called *The Differences of the Ages of Man's Life,* and so on. The title goes on for a while. Well," he says, evidently bringing the interview to a close, "it's been a pleasure to meet you, Serjeant Ames."

Noah rises and bows in place. "The pleasure has been all mine, Master Cuffe," he says, pleased that the fellow never asked him when Henry is returning. "And if I do write to Sir Henry, I shall be sure to mention your interest in his review of your manuscript."

"Oh, no, sir. Please make no mention of it. It can readily await Sir Henry's return to England." Cuffe leans in confidentially. "In fact, I would much appreciate it if you were to avoid mentioning my little visit today ... to anyone."

"Of course, Master Cuffe," replies Noah reassuringly.

The fellow bows and sticks his head out of the doorway, checking both ways before leaving.

Noah has no idea why maintaining the secrecy of such an innocuous meeting could possibly be of concern to anyone.

But he's fairly certain that the letter Cuffe dropped was addressed to Sir Henry Neville.

Barnaby Bell is proudly showing David the exquisite ground floor of Burghley House when there's a shout from upstairs.

"David!" calls Andres urgently.

David and the steward look to each other and together race up the stairs to the second storey, where Andres waits to escort them down the hall. After passing several closed doors, they reach the door of the corner room, which is likewise closed.

Andres says to David gravely, "Are you ready?"

"For what?" asks David.

Instead of replying, Andres swings the door open wide.

David finds himself looking down a narrow corridor flanked by two long rows of storage chests stacked shoulder high.

At the opposite end of the makeshift corridor, the steward's daughter stands atop a stepstool, pen and paper in hand, carefully sorting

through the contents of the topmost chest, oblivious to the men at the
door. She wears a protective smock jotted with numerous smears of ink,
presumably made by her own pen as she's made her way through the
papers taking copious notes.

As David is about to speak, Andres says, "Wait!" He leads them back
into the hallway to the next door. "Come here." He swings it open on a
roomful of stacked chests much like that in the first room. Once again
David begins to speak, but once again Andres cuts him off, admonishing
him to wait.

Andres crosses the hall and opens the door to yet a *third* room,
which differs from the first two only in being so jammed with chests
that there was evidently no room to leave a corridor. The chests are not
even neatly stacked. A few are open, and a few stand precariously on
their ends.

Seeing David speechless, Andres asks humorously, "You had a question?"

Dismayed, David turns to the steward. "How much of this material
has been catalogued?"

"Honestly, I don't know," the steward replies, leading them back to
the corner room where his daughter is hard at work. "Barbara," he says,
"how many of these chests have you catalogued?"

David would love to hear that she's working on the last few, but he
harbors no real hope of that. For one thing, the disorganized chests in
the third room gave every appearance of having been undisturbed since
they were delivered, whenever that was.

Barbara looks up from her work, evidently having just noticed her
father. Her brow furrows. She purses her lips at the interruption, wipes
the pen on her smock, and steps down from the ladder, gravely
regarding the stack of four chests she's been working on.

Barbara points to the bottom chest in the stack. "I started there."
She points to the open top chest that she's been going through since her
father and David came upstairs. "That's as far as I've got."

David and Andres look to the steward impatiently, but Master Bell
merely shrugs. "We've only been here a few weeks, gentlemen.
Organizing these papers is a Herculean task that our family was

certainly *not* retained to perform. Thomas, Lord Burghley invited Barbara to try her hand at it as a mere afterthought, as she expressed an interest. He seemed to think that her cataloguing might lighten the load for an archivist hired to put things in proper order. There's never seemed much urgency to the task—until now. Barbara had hoped to get a fair way through these papers next winter."

"Next *winter*?" says David. "We have only a few hours to find these letters. Perhaps not even that!" When the steward looks at him with dismay, he offers some slight reassurance. "With luck, we'll have until morning."

"Barbara," says Andres, "have you thought of looking in each trunk at the first few papers to come to hand, so you can form some understanding of what else is likely to be found in it?"

The girl shakes her head. "I thought of doing it that way, but I'm afraid these heavy chests quite wore me out. I could barely lift those in the stack I've gone through."

Andres turns to David. "I think that's what we have to do. I suppose we might make a few wrong guesses in the process, but the only alternative is for us to cart away all these chests before *they* get here." He shakes his head. "But we don't have the horses to do that."

"Nor the time, nor the men," says David anxiously. "It would take a dozen men and as many horses to get all these trunks away by morning. No, we'll have to play for time, and prepare to defend this place ourselves in the event they catch on."

"*Defend* it?" exclaims Andres. "They have—"

"I *know* what they have," interrupts David, to avoid alarming the steward and his family. "We'll just have to outwit them."

The steward glowers at them. "Gentlemen, just whom are we speaking of, and *what* do they have?"

"A few ruffians," replies Andres. "But they have a—" he glances back at the girl, then leans in toward the steward to whisper his thought almost inaudibly—"a cannon."

"A *cannon*?" cries Barbara, who's evidently overheard. "What are they going to do? Blow the house down … like the wolf in the adage?"

The steward puts his arm around his daughter's shoulder. "There,

there, dear. I'm sure it won't come to that. We'll simply have to find the letters these two gentlemen were sent to fetch."

Barbara petulantly stamps her foot. "And if they do, Father, and then those ruffians come—with their cannon—and find the letters gone, do you suppose they'll just ride off without a word?"

David looks to Andres, who returns his gaze. In their determination to get the letters first, they haven't given a moment's thought to the fate of the steward and his family should they *succeed*, thus leaving their adversaries incensed with frustration.

And should they fail and the *ruffians* take the letters, it would be even more unlikely that those at Burghley House would be left in peace.

Andres sees that David shares his sense of resignation. He turns to the girl, and speaks for them both. "Looks like we'll be staying here until reinforcements arrive. We'll protect you ... or die trying."

Hearing this, at first Barbara rushes forward as though to hug Andres, but then turns aside and places her head on her father's shoulder instead. David suppresses a laugh, as Andres's beet-red face comically underscores his unworldliness.

"But let's make sure it doesn't come to that," says David. "By your leave, Master Bell, may I suggest the following? Master Salazar and Miss Bell must *find those letters* while you and I—and Chester—come up with some ruse to gain more time."

# CHAPTER 17

**THE NEXT MORNING,** after dozing for only a few hours on a couch in the rear of the first storey, David is awakened by a man's shout coming from the other side of house.

"They've got a blasted cannon, all right!" It's the voice of Barnaby Bell.

Before David can reorient himself or consider what danger he's in, the first thought to come to mind is that the night was too blasted short. The second is: *Where the devil are Jon Hawking and our reinforcements?* Expelling both useless thoughts from his mind, he trots to the parlor, where Bell looks out through the front window.

"How many are there?" asks David, entering the parlor.

"Looks like three," Bell replies, looking over his shoulder at David. "Two big ones and one little one in a strange-looking uniform."

David steps over to the steward and stands beside him, gazing out of the window. In a sparse copse of trees a few hundred yards away stand three unmounted men holding their horses' reins, engaged in intense discussion. Immediately behind them is a cannon drawn by two moderate-sized horses that seem to have been worn out by their burden.

"Any chance they're your reinforcements?" asks Master Bell hopefully.

"Afraid not," says David. "Those are the ruffians. And that's not all of them. I'd expect at least three more. We saw six lodging together at Cambridge. That little one puzzles me."

"I suppose we could have got lucky and the other three split off."

David contemplates the possibility and shrugs. "I suppose so, but that would be quite a change of luck in our favor."

The steward turns to David with a puzzled expression. "Why does everybody think they can't be seen in that copse?" he asks.

"That's where my two friends concealed themselves yesterday, isn't it?" asks David. The steward nods. David shakes his head at their own ineptitude.

"It's a convenient hiding place," reasons Bell, "except you can see them from here, plain as day."

"Where's Chester?" asks David.

"I encountered him going out on foot before dawn," says Bell. "He said he'd scout the vicinity. Hasn't been seen since."

"Have you got any reports from Andres and Barbara?"

The steward shakes his head. "The missus and I've been checking in on them once in a while. Last I checked, they'd fallen asleep where they sat amidst the papers. Haven't heard from them for a couple hours," he says pointing his chin at a soft chair in the corner, "though I caught a nap over there, so there's been nobody for them to report to."

David climbs the back stairs and turns down the hallway to the room where he left Andres and Barbara searching for Walsingham's letters. Hoping they've made it through the whole panoply at least once, David opens the door to the third room where chests lay scattered the previous evening. The room is quite stuffy, and he wonders why it never occurred to either Andres or Barbara to open a window and admit a merciful breeze.

David is somewhat heartened, as it appears as though every chest has now been opened. A few pages at the front of each chest stand on end, their precarious posture secured by the weight of surrounding papers.

Andres lies sleeping, his exhausted face resting uncomfortably across the contents of the last chest to be opened. On the floor next to him lie the papers on which they'd been taking notes. Barbara is curled up asleep on the floor at the opposite end of the room, her long smock carefully positioned to preserve her modesty.

David examines their notes himself, if only to afford them a few more minutes of sleep. He finds that Andres has drawn virtually the same diagrams he would have done under the circumstances.

They consist of three pages, each bearing a rough drawing of one of the three rooms. Each stack has been assigned its own letter of the alphabet. Once the letters of the alphabet were exhausted, the next stack was assigned the letters *AA*, the next *AB*, and so on. The rough notes accompanying each drawing refer to a given chest by the column's assigned letter, together with a numeral providing the chest's vertical position in the stack, with the numeral *1* designating those resting on the floor.

The chart of the room in which Andres and Barbara have fallen asleep is by far the most complex, because of the random placement of chests. But the notes are no less meticulous.

Some notations bear a crude asterisk, others a cross, evidently indicating some special characteristic, but the papers bear no legend defining those symbols. A very few chests bear both an asterisk *and* a cross. As David contemplates what the symbols might indicate, there's a pounding downstairs at the front door, and his heart flies up into his mouth. He reluctantly gives Andres a light shove. "Company's arrived," he says.

Andres raises his head groggily, his cheek deeply creased by the papers where his face lay. Opening his eyes, he sees it's David and says: "How many?"

"So far, it looks like three," says David. "No sign of Meyrick, Skeres, or Poley ... yet."

"Shouldn't you be answering the gate?" asks Andres.

"We've decided to ignore the first knock entirely," says David, "so you two must keep away from the windows, and don't light any fires. The first phase of our plan is to pretend there's no one at home."

Andres regards him askance. "Oh, that must have taken *hours* to come up with," he says testily. "What's the second phase? Take to the cellar and pretend we're barrels of ale?"

"We're not past the *first* phase yet," says David, ignoring the jibe, "but it can't be carried on too long, as they're sure to break into the manor if they become confident no one's here. And may I remind you that wasting their time is to *our* advantage?"

"Only if Jonathan shows up in time," Andres says grimly. "The intruders. They've got the"—he casts a guarded glance toward Barbara—"flibbertigibbet?"

"The *cannon*?" says David unashamedly. "Yes. Why the cipher word, Andres? She already knows they've got one."

Andres casts a fond look at his sleeping companion. "She's a bit nervous."

"Despite your manly assurances?" David asks jocularly. "I'm sure Esther would have been *entirely* reassured."

Andres regards him with irritation. "David, you're a few years younger than I."

David detects a lecture coming on and rolls his eyes, but decides it's best to listen.

"The time will come," says Andres, "when you realize that the life you've made for yourself is entirely lacking in what you need most—I mean the love of a good woman, and a family of your own—and every fiber of your being will impel you to find the right woman—urgently."

David does his best to look receptive.

Andres continues. "When that happens, your younger friends will think themselves quite clever to berate you for earnestly seeking a wife. And you'll be sorely tempted to strike them in the mouth."

David arches an eyebrow and draws back a step, just in case this is leading to fisticuffs.

Andres smiles. "But you won't do it."

"And why not, Father?" asks David warily.

Andres sighs. "Because you'll remember that *I* didn't do it to *you*. Now, if you'd be so kind as to stop deriding me for such things, we'll get on better." Andres has been so direct and sincere that David regrets his teasing, and resolves to make amends.

David looks over at Barbara, who hasn't moved. Unless he's sorely mistaken, though, she's awake and skillfully keeping her eyes closed, no doubt so she can hear the rest of the conversation. "And you think this Barbara person might be the right one for you?" he asks. "More so even than Esther?"

Andres sighs. "She's delightfully clever and highly literate. I must congratulate Master Barnaby for schooling her so thoroughly. She's worked with me tirelessly on this thankless task, and has remained pleasant and engaging without fail. Add to that her sheer comeliness. With all that to commend her, I'd be a fool not to think so. Don't you agree?"

Feeling, in light of their incipient peril, that he's played Cupid long enough, David points to one of Andres's papers. "What do these markings mean?" he asks.

"An asterisk means that the first pages in the chest included correspondence of Lord Burghley."

"And the cross?" asks David.

"It means the first pages in the chest bore dates from the pertinent years, those directly following the massacre of the Huguenots. After Barbara dropped off to sleep, I finished opening the last few chests."

"So, those with both the asterisk and the cross seem most promising?" asks David.

"Yes, and she was beginning to go through them when she dropped off to sleep. And I was about to turn to them when her restful breathing quite subdued my good intentions."

David smirks. "As a young woman's restful breathing is wont to do."

"Good morning," says Barbara, popping her head up over a few boxes, her hair tousled and unbound, a raven lock falling seductively over her cheek. "What are you two gentlemen discussing?"

There's another pounding at the gate.

David rises and bows. "That's my cue," he says, and flies down the back stairs to speak with Barnaby Bell.

"As Mistress Bell was forbidden to make a fire or be seen in the kitchen, she went back to bed," says Bell, "but she's up now, in case of ... visitors."

"Any movement since our visitors' second knocking?" says David.

"I saw the little fellow return to his friends. It's just a guess, but I suppose they'll wait a few minutes, and send him back alone one last time to confirm that the house is yet unoccupied."

"Let's hope you're right, or they'll be clambering through the ground-level windows any moment now."

A door in the back of the house shuts quietly. David and Bell go wide-eyed and freeze in place. A moment later they're relieved to see Chester amble in.

"Got any food?" asks Chester dourly.

Bell leads them to the kitchen by a circuitous route, to avoid being seen through the windows. On the table in a small windowless room off the kitchen is half a loaf of bread, a cup of butter, and a tin pitcher of water.

Chester cuts the bread and slathers on the butter, as he prepares to tell them what he's found.

"I take it you've seen the three out front?" he asks. "With the falconet?" He takes a big bite of the buttered bread, and his face is overcome with satisfaction. "I've been starvin' all mornin'."

David nods. "We've been watching them the past few minutes."

"Well," says Chester as he eats, "that's all there is, for now at least. I been watchin' 'em since dawn and there's been nobuddy else. And they haven't dispatched anyone, which—if they had—might have meant they were maintainin' contact with another group nearby." He takes another big bite of bread, finds a clean wooden cup, and pours himself some water from the tin.

"I suppose," says David, "it's still *possible* that there are others on the way."

Chester moves his head equivocally from side to side. "Not *impossible*, but unlikely, and gettin' more unlikely every minute that passes without 'em showin' up." He shakes his head. "I think your other three birds 'ave flown." He stops for a moment and searches his memory. "Didn't you say they told your master they were goin' on holiday?"

David nods. "Yes, but we've all assumed that was just to throw him off the trail."

Chester shrugs. "May have been, at first. But mebbe they couldn't stand that little Frenchman," he smirks, "railin' on about the importance of honor all the time."

"Honor?" asks David incredulously. "And you got close enough to hear?"

"Aye," says Chester. "I learned the terrain well enough yesterday to sneak up on 'em, which I did—soon as I was sure there warn't nobody else out there."

"Did you catch any of their names?"

"The little one's 'Monk.' Ever heard of 'im?"

David shakes his head. "And the other two?"

"'Bennett.' Unless I'm mistaken, the little one called 'em *both* by that name. Brothers, I guess. They look alike. It's possible he was callin' only *one* of 'em Bennett but, in that case, he never said the other one's name, leastways so's I could hear."

David's mind runs through Andres's tales of derring-do. "I believe Master Salazar once knew two brothers named Bennett, who fought alongside him in aid of the Queen's men years ago. Were they *twins*, these Bennetts that you saw?"

Chester shrugs. "As I said, they look alike," he replies, "but I can't be sure."

There's a new pounding on the gate, the most determined yet. David hopes they haven't overplayed their hand and that it's still the small one seeking admittance.

David and Barnaby exchange a serious glance.

"There's the summons," says Bell. "The curtain rises."

David turns to Chester. "Take care not to be seen from the windows. Look out of the window upstairs. If those two out in the copse have disappeared, come and tell me right away. I need to know they're not right here at the gate. If they're still out there at the copse, best go to the armory on the second storey. Ready a few muskets and pistols, and wait. Stop on the way and remind Andres and Barbara they must keep dead silent and out of sight. It must appear there's no one in this house but Barnaby and Mistress Bell. Go, go!"

Chester salutes informally and trots up the back stairs.

David and Barnaby go to the grand entrance, David removing two loaded pistols from their leather cases and standing aside, out of sight of the doorway.

With a deep breath, Barnaby opens the door and steps halfway to the gate, leaving him in shadow and invisible to the visitor, just as he'd done with David the day before.

David peeks around the door. Apparently, the only person at the gate is the little one that Chester called "Monk." He wonders where the Bennetts are.

"Who's calling?" asks the steward in his most formal and demanding voice.

"My name is Monk," says the dwarf with a heavy French accent.

"And what is your business here, sir?" asks Barnaby.

"I am a student at university, sir, and I have been told this is ze only place where I may read some … historical documents."

After a brief pause, Bell says, "This is not a university library, sir, but rather the private residence of Lord Burghley. May I ask what university you attend?"

"Certainly, sir. The Collège de Sorbonne."

"Is that a college at Cambridge University? For I've never heard of it before."

"You have never heard of ze Sorbonne, *monsieur*?" asks Monk incredulously.

"I have not. Where is it?"

"It is in Paris, sir." There's some slight exasperation in Monk's voice, as he evidently was not expecting quite this level of ignorance.

"Is that in France?" asks the steward.

David nearly laughs aloud. But Bell is right. This little Frenchman has no idea whether a steward of a great house in the North of England would know anything about Paris or its colleges.

Monk sighs audibly. "Yes, sir. It is in France, I assure you."

"Where in England were you staying before you came here?" Bell asks.

"*Londre*," says Monk. "I come here from London. I have come to examine certain letters written by Mister Francis Walsingham to Lord Burghley," says Monk, sounding the "g" in Burghley.

Bell replies. "But Lord Burghley does not allow anyone to read his correspondence. Besides, sir, Mister Walsingham is long dead, and Lord

Thomas much younger. I would expect that they never had much cause to correspond with each other." When this is met with profound silence, Barnaby adds, "Perhaps you might visit Mister *Walsingham's* daughter."

"And where does that lady live?" asks Monk. David is shocked to hear equivocation in Monk's voice, as though he might actually take advice to seek the papers elsewhere.

"I expect she is married to the Earl of Essex," says Bell, "who currently abides, if I'm not mistaken, in the house of the Lord Keeper of the Great Seal ... also in London."

"Lord Burghley. He is not dead?"

"Why, perish the thought, sir! My master is alive and well, and temporarily residing in the City of London. So, you see, it is impossible for me to obtain the necessary permission to allow you to enter Burghley House."

Monk examines a paper he has removed from a pocket in his uniform. "William, Lord Burghley," he says. "He is not dead?"

"Oh, *William*, Lord Burghley," says Bell. "He was *father* to the present Lord Burghley. I regret to say that Lord William has indeed passed ... and so no longer conducts correspondence."

David winces. If that last doesn't tell Monk that Bell is having him on, he wonders what would.

Bell tries to resume the conversation before the vacuousness of his latest declaration can sink in. "Did you say, Master Monk, that you wish to see certain correspondence between *William*, Lord Burghley and Sir Francis Walsingham?"

"Yes," says Monk, sounding exasperated. "Yes, yes."

"Ah, then I have good news for you, sir."

"Oh?"

"Yes," replies Bell, and then waits, dragging the matter out just as agreed.

"And what is your good news?" asks Monk impatiently.

"There are complete copies of all such correspondence available for examination at the Tower of London. *Er*, that's also in London, sir. I regret that you've come all this way only to learn that, sir."

David snickers silently. This is a clever mode of attack. For, having come from London and having now been referred to the Tower, how can Monk object to seeking out the papers there? If he now admits he already *knows* the copy was at the Tower, then it shows him to have been lying to the steward about his need to seek out the papers here at Burghley House. On the other hand, if Monk *denies* having prior knowledge of the copies at the Tower, then he can offer no justification for refusing to seek them out there. And he absolutely *cannot* admit without revealing guilty knowledge that he knows there were copies at the Tower, but that they've disappeared, which would raise the steward's hackles and ensure that Monk would never be granted admittance to Burghley House.

Realizing his conundrum, Monk pleads for mercy. "I beg of you, sir. I have come so far to see zese documents, and it has cost me so much of your English pounds, that I will look foolish to tell my college than I have spent all their money unnecessarily, as I did not need to leave London. They will say that I have spent their money on a personal sojourn, and expel me. I must see zese papers while I am here! I have barely enough money to bring me back to Paris."

Monk seems to be imploring now, but David suspects that if he's turned away, he will see no choice but break into the manor house, which will certainly lead to a bloody confrontation.

"Well, sir," says Bell according to plan, "those papers have not been catalogued here at Burghley House, and we have no way of finding them."

"But, *monsieur*, if you will show me to ze room where such records are kept, I shall find zem myself."

The steward rejects such a notion out of hand. "*Tsk, tsk, tsk*. This I cannot allow under any circumstances, sir. I hope you will understand. But I cannot allow a complete stranger to rifle through Lord Burghley's papers. I would have to call the official curator to identify these papers first, and he does not dwell here. If you write down which papers you need, I can send someone for the curator."

"How soon can he come, sir?" asks Monk.

"Well," says Bell, scratching his head, "if we send someone tonight to fetch him, and if he's at his home, then I suppose he might arrive as early as noon tomorrow."

Monk bows to the gate. "If you will provide me with directions to his residence, sir, I shall save you ze trouble and bring him here before then." Evidently perceiving Bell's reluctance, Monk adds, "I will see that he is well compensated."

"But where would you obtain the monies to pay him, sir, as you have barely enough to return to Paris?"

David smiles. Bell would make a good lawyer, as he just caught Monk in an outright lie.

"Very well," says Monk. "Please send for your curator. When he arrives, I shall write down which documents I seek to examine."

"I'll send someone out for him in a short while, sir. Please return here tomorrow at noon."

Monk nods thoughtfully. "But permit me to ask you a question, sir."

"Certainly."

"How many people occupy this manor house as we speak?"

Bell realizes that, as he's promised to dispatch someone to fetch the curator, and it's obviously not to be his wife, then there must be at least three people in the house, which is one more than the agreed story. "We are three, sir," he says, at last, and glances back toward David.

"You, and who else?" asks Monk.

"I don't suppose that's any of your affair, sir ... but my wife and a stableman."

"So you will send your stableman?"

David considers Monk's possible motives in posing that question. Could he simply be testing the steward's veracity? Or is he assessing the likely resistance to be encountered in subduing the house's occupants, should he break into the manor house before noon tomorrow?

"Yes, sir," replies Bell. "I am not permitted to go, and I certainly won't be sending my wife."

"And where were you when I first knocked on your gate, that you did not hear me?"

This question was entirely unanticipated. Bell looks back toward David beseechingly, and throws his hands in the air, as if to say, "well?"

David points down. Although it takes a moment for Bell to catch on, he replies as intended. "If you knocked earlier, sir, we didn't hear you.

We were in the cellar ... brewing ale."

"With your wife and stableman?" comes Monk's dubious reply.

Bell glances heavenward. "Yes, it's a big job brewing for a household as large as this one, sir. Sorry for the delay."

Monk toes the gravel under his feet, as though mulling over the steward's veracity.

"Return here tomorrow at noon," says Bell. He turns about and re-enters the house, closing the door behind him. David uncocks his pistols.

Bell turns to him apprehensively. "I think he's on to us. If he's not already, he will be, once he's given it some thought."

David nods distractedly. "You've given us an opportunity to send someone out of the house on horseback. Let's see if Andres and Barbara have found the documents."

"*Eh*," says Bell, stopping awkwardly, "before we go to see them again, might I ask if you're ... familiar with Master Salazar? I mean, on a friendly basis?"

David is somewhat surprised by the peculiar timing of this line of questioning, but he supposes it's only right for the old fellow to seek some assurance that his daughter isn't spending hour after hour with a man of ill character. "I am, sir. He has been my friend for many years."

"Is he ... the sort of man you would have ... spending time ..." Bell's voice trails off.

"With my daughter?" asks David.

Bell equivocates. "Well, as you appear too young a gentleman to have a daughter, I was going to say your sister."

David smiles inside. "You have a very comely daughter, Master Bell, as you know." Bell bows curtly. "I would be inclined to trust Master Salazar with her far more than I would the next fellow. While I would never counsel you to take your eyes off any man who fancies her, I can tell you from my own knowledge that his intentions for Barbara would please any father I know."

Bell breathes a visible sigh of relief. "Thank you, Master Killigrew."

David bows. As he walks beside Bell, he blushes to think that Andres could not in good conscience have offered the same assurances about him.

# CHAPTER 18

**"THE BENNETTS!"** exclaims Andres, taking a momentary break from his document search. "We lost track of them *years* ago. Last I heard, they'd set up practice in Cheltenham, although I'm not sure how a barrister earns a living up there." He regards David dubiously. "Doesn't sound right. Is Chester certain he heard correctly?"

"Shall I fetch him?" asks David.

"No," says Andres. "There's no point. We'll have to deal with them the same way, whether they're the Bennetts from Gray's Inn or not. Whoever they are, at the moment they're attempting to frustrate the Crown's investigation of an attempt to assassinate the Queen, and by doing so they've placed themselves in extreme peril."

"Did they ever discuss their politics with you?"

"Nary a word," says Andres, "although they were true zealots when it came to protecting Serjeant Ames from Essex's men." He shakes his head sadly. "It would be a shame if they've become admirers of Lord Essex, although he has many, chief among whom is Lord Mountjoy."

"Essex's replacement in Ireland?"

Andres nods thoughtfully. "The Bennetts never had occasion to meet *you* back in their Gray's Inn days, did they?"

"No. Even if they had, I was eleven years old, so I doubt they'd recognize me."

"Well, they'd certainly recognize *me*," says Andres, "so any plans that involve their seeing me will need to be changed."

David looks about the room, where Barbara works diligently, unperturbed by their conversation. "How's the search going?"

Andres squeezes his strained eyes shut and rubs them, accentuating the pronounced black bags beneath them. "So far, it's unrewarding work."

"We told Monk we're sending for the courier," says David, "so we now have an opportunity to get someone out of the house on horseback—with the papers stuffed in his saddlebag."

Andres sighs wistfully. "No papers yet. I'll let you know as soon as we've found them."

"I'll take over here for a few hours," says David. "You and Barbara get some food and a few hours' sleep."

"It goes much quicker when you have someone to work with," Arthur advises him. "One of you can read while the other makes notes. Perhaps Barnaby can help you?"

David shakes his head. "He refuses to leave the ground level. He's discreetly patrolling the windows with a musket, to make sure they're not breached."

"*Mistress* Bell, perhaps?"

As Barbara is within hearing and thoroughly occupied in reading documents, David silently mouths: *"She can't read."*

"No need to whisper," says Barbara without looking up. "I know my dear mother's illiterate. Literacy wasn't expected of girls in her day."

Andres turns to her. "I swear, darling Barbara, you have the ears of a *cat*." She makes no reply and continues reading.

David rolls his eyes and silently japes: *"Darling!"*

Barbara chimes in. "So Master Salazar addressed me as 'darling,' Master Killigrew. What of it?"

David turns to her defensively. "You couldn't have heard that. I didn't even *say* it!"

"I didn't have to *hear* it to know you *said* it," she scoffs. "Why don't you ask Goodman Chester to assist you? As he's a jailer, *he* must be literate." She snorts derisively. "Even if his jail *is* a piss-pot."

"I'll go fetch him," says David, feeling rather deflated. "You two can hand off your research to us for the remainder of the afternoon."

Late that night, David and Chester are interrupted in their long trudge through Burghley's papers by the return of Andres and Barbara, who appear ready to take over the work after a hot meal and a long sleep. While Andres converses with David, Barbara has already quietly picked up where Chester left off.

"Just so we don't duplicate work," says Andres, "you and Chester have read every document in the chests you've marked as *done*?"

David is so weary, he can barely nod. "Every blessed one of them," he says. "I figure, between you and Barbara working the past day and a half, and Chester and me working all afternoon and evening, we've gone through roughly two thirds of the whole batch."

Andres regards him despondently. "Are you thinking what I'm thinking?"

David rubs his eyes. "You mean, that the papers are not here?"

Andres nods.

David shakes his head. "I've been considering that possibility since before we arrived, but it's become my firm belief that they *are* here."

"Based on what?" asks Andres.

"Based on the observed fact that every other blasted piece of paper from Burghley's public life *is* here." He observes the stacks with grudging admiration, like a warrior observing an adversary who's withstood his best blows. "I found a receipt in there, given Burghley by a foundling's home for a contribution of ten pounds, for heaven's sake. The man never threw anything away. It's certain he wouldn't have destroyed anything as important as original correspondence with Francis Walsingham. No," he shakes his head, "as he deemed the letters worthy of copying, he'd certainly deem the originals worthy of retention." He sighs, and looks Andres in the eye with grim determination. "Those bastard papers are in here. We just haven't found them."

"*Oh, yes, we have!*" exclaims Barbara, excitedly drawing a sheaf of papers out of one of the remaining chests. She places the quill between her lips, holds the papers over her head and begins dancing a rhythmic and energetic Scottish jig.

"Oh, thank God!" says Andres, throwing his hands up.

To David's amazement, Barbara continues her quiet dance. He's unsure whether it's because she's wearing only slippers that she makes no noise. Then he remembers that the Scots don't deem the thumping of heavy shoes a necessary part of the entertainment, relying instead on the visual appeal of the dancer's graceful movement.

As David smiles and claps, he glances sidelong at Andres, only to find him utterly rapt in the girl's smile and movement.

A thought occurs to David that there's no such thing as love at first sight, but instead a long-awaited matching of a new face to an ancient dream. It's not the girl who holds his friend in thrall, but rather a dream that nature planted long ago, of an ideal girl lacking only a face. And now imperious nature has chosen—just at this moment—to impress the face of *this* girl onto Andres's dream. Perhaps, he speculates, when a young man finds the face that fits this dream of nature (a dream he foolishly fancies his own) comes the tipping point, that moment when he willingly surrenders the joys of freedom and the easy camaraderie of men to become a husband, or "wer to a wife," as old Killigrew was wont to say back in Cornwall.

David finds it eerie, and more than a bit unnerving, to contemplate that nature has implanted just such a dream in his *own* mind, and that, at some unguarded moment, this dream of nature will choose a girl for him. Esther's beautiful face comes to mind as though summoned by a sprite, and lingers there long enough to make him wonder whether that fateful moment has not already arrived, perhaps as he chatted with her in the Ames's parlor before departing for Burghley House. Was a spell cast on him then? And, if so, by whom? By nature … or by Esther herself? And perhaps a woman's fate is the same as a man's, but seen in a looking glass, with nature casting an uxorious spell on her at a time of, not her own, but *nature's* choosing.

"Clap in time, boys!" she commands as she whirls. "Timing is all," she says, with such appropriate timing that David fleetingly wonders whether she could have been reading his thoughts a moment earlier.

David and Andres clap lightly in time, unable to shake off the dread that their high-spiritedness might alert the intruders, or mask the breaking of a window presaging an invasion of the house. In another moment, Barbara bows to quiet accolades.

"Let's see what you found," says Andres, and Barbara hands him the sheaf of papers.

Andres thumbs through them, scanning them for dates, addressees, and signatures. He looks up. "These are the papers, all right. By sight, there appear to be several letters in the months following the massacre."

"Can we transcribe them all before dawn?" asks Andres, looking to Barbara for an answer.

She shakes her head. "Not completely and accurately, no."

"But," says David, "Andres and I can read them for the subject matter that Serjeant Ames is interested in, and prepare abstracts, so we'll retain the information for him, even if the intruders manage to steal the originals. Meanwhile, Barbara and Chester should put the chests back as they were prior to the search. When Andres and I are through, we'll hide the originals in a safe place, and hide the abstracts elsewhere."

Andres regards David solemnly. "You don't suppose we could dispatch Chester with them right away, just to get them out of their reach?"

"Now that we've done all the work for them?" David shakes his head. "All they'd have to do is waylay Chester in the dark, and they'd have won. And if we were to dispatch him before we've made our abstracts, then the information would be lost to us for all time."

"No. I suppose you're right," replies Andres somberly, and his eyes look far away. "Where the devil is Jonathan?"

Noah has had trouble sleeping these past few nights, but tonight is worst of all.

After trying for hours to sleep in his bed, he begins to suspect that his tossing and turning are disturbing Marie, so he pads off to his study. On the off-chance that his discomfort is caused by the damp chill in the air, he lights a small fire and plops down in the soft chair behind his desk.

The fire's warmth fails to dispel his unease. Hours pass before he dozes off into a recurring dream of Andres and Cheerful being pursued by a squadron of men sent to murder them and steal the papers they were sent to fetch.

He's awakened at some ungodly hour by soft movements in the room. It's Esther, who's wandered in as he slept. Plainly distraught, she sits before the fire chafing her hands, evidently unaware that she's awakened Noah.

"Esther, dear," he mutters, "what keeps you up at this hour?"

She regards him wearily. "I might ask the same of you," she replies in her dusky voice. "Oh, Serjeant Ames, I am very worried about your young friends, David and … and …"

"Andres," he suggests, privately observing that she can't be worried about them equally if she's unable to remember one of their names.

"Yes," says Esther, "I keep seeing David in my mind's eye. He is in danger."

"What sort of danger?" he asks.

"You must promise not to laugh at me."

Noah knits his brow and nods assent, as he's in no laughing mood.

She continues. "I see David challenged at sword," she continues, "by a tiny man—a dwarf."

While it has occurred to Noah in passing that Monk might be among those sent for Walsingham's correspondence, until this moment, he's given it no serious consideration. Those being sent appeared to include Meyrick and Skeres, and each of them alone was quite dangerous enough to cause him worry. Come to think on it, Monk hasn't been seen for *days*.

The youthful contours of Esther's face, illuminated by the red glow of the dying fire, already hint at the careworn woman she's bound to become someday. She's beautiful, but serious, and acutely aware, even in the flower of her youth, of the terrible loss that threatens us every moment of our lives.

Although for some time Noah has known Esther to be an unusual girl, it occurs to him that he may be underestimating her still. After all, she was not only *aware* that a spirit had appeared beside Yetta's deathbed, but she *saw* it as a specific person of flesh and blood, and thought it real enough to warrant drawing a blade against it.

It occurs to him that Esther has never seen Monk, nor has he mentioned Monk to her. Though reluctant to give credence to dreams and portents, he leans over his desk toward her. "What does he look like, this dwarf who threatens David?"

Esther glances at him sidelong, then back at the fire. "I can't see his face, but I can see into his heart. He is at war with himself. He respects David—even *admires* him—but *hates* him also, because David is ..." Her voice trails off, as though the search for words is simply too exhausting to be undertaken while in such turmoil.

"Because David is well formed?" suggests Noah.

Esther removes a handkerchief from her sleeve and quietly weeps. "Yes, but the dwarf hates *himself* for hating David, even more than he hates David."

Noah nods. "He's in torment."

Esther's eyes open wide. "Yes! That is the word! He is in *torment!* And I am afraid he will ... harm David."

As Esther's apprehension is so similar to his own, Noah struggles to find words that might comfort her. He decides commiseration is best. "How do you think *I* feel, Esther, who have sent the two of them off into danger to fetch me some papers?"

"Are you worried about them, too?"

"Not really," he says, his rational mind returning from its former torpor, "as I know them to be nimble young men. It's more that I'm unaccustomed to sending others into danger. Oh, I've encountered my share of danger, but I can bear it when it's directed at me alone. To send young men whom I love like sons into danger ... does not comport well with my constitution."

"They are 'nimble'?" she asks.

It takes a moment for Noah to realize that she's seeking reassurance about David's abilities. He's only too happy to oblige. "David is quite the swordsman, you know."

"He is?" she asks, obviously wanting more.

"Oh, certainly. A full-sized opponent would have little chance against him, let alone a dwarf. And, of course, he rides as no one else can."

Esther seems a bit relieved. "And his friend?"

"Andres has been with us through far tougher times than this. He also is well-trained at horse, and an excellent shot with pistol or musket. Most importantly, he's highly intelligent. Both of them are. I expect they're several steps ahead of their opponents, who are no doubt more in need of pity."

A twinge of apprehension strikes Noah from an unexpected point. While he feels no remorse for any injury sustained by Meyrick or Skeres, he suddenly realizes that he would deeply regret any serious harm coming to Monk. He silently berates himself. How foolish to be concerned about the welfare of an agent of the wicked! But what if Monk is not himself wicked, but has merely been trapped into aiding them?

Suddenly aware that Esther is watching him delve into his doubts, he offers her a broad smile. "Go to bed, dear, and rest easy. This shall all be over in a day or two, and our friends will be back here in good condition."

Esther rises, bows, and traipses off to bed, leaving Noah alone to dwell in his misery. A spiteful hint of daybreak appears at the study windows.

# Chapter 19

**IN THE EARLY MORNING STILLNESS,** the pounding on the gate rings out like a death knell. The steward, already washed and dressed, promptly opens the door and advances halfway to the gate. Outside is the same little soldier sent away the day before with the promise that a horseman would promptly be sent to fetch the curator.

"Good morning, sir," says the steward in kindly fashion. "Have you had your breakfast?"

The little man seems startled. "And good morning to you, sir. No, I have not eaten zis morning. Would you be so kind as to share your breakfast with me?"

"It would be my privilege, sir, I'm sure. If you would be so kind as to hang your weapons from that hook to your left, I would be pleased to admit you."

The little man suspiciously eyes a hook set directly into the stone facade, then gazes skeptically at the figure of the steward concealed in darkness behind the gate.

"I'm afraid," says the steward by way of encouragement, "that no weapons are permitted to enter Burghley House, *monsieur.*"

The soldier eyes the height and breadth of the manor house. "You do not suggest, sir, zat a great house such as this lacks an armory?"

"I suggest no such thing," the steward replies. "I simply insist, as I am required to do, that no weapons be brought into the house by ... outsiders."

The soldier removes a pistol from his pocket, hangs it on the hook, and turns to the gate to be admitted.

"*Eh*, the *sword*, as well, *monsieur*," says the steward apologetically.

Monk looks down at his chest, as though he'd forgot that he carried a sword. "But zis sword is merely ornamental, sir. And it is of some value to me, as it is an heirloom of my grandfather." He looks about the yard, as though for unsavory characters. "It may be stolen, if left unattended."

"Ah," says the steward courteously, "I see. Although I am authorized to make no exceptions in allowing weapons into the house, if you would slip it under the gate, I will hang it up inside the gate, and you may be confident that it will be untouched by anyone outside."

"But—" begins Monk, only to be cut off by the steward.

"As I mentioned, sir, there are only my wife, my daughter, and my humble self in the house." The anticipated question about the addition of Bell's daughter fails to materialize.

"*And* your stableman," corrects Monk.

"No, sir. He is not *in* the house, and he does not enter through this door. Surely, you cannot suspect that *I* would—"

"Of *course* not," says Monk, as he slips sword and scabbard under the gate.

The steward opens the gate and invites Monk in, being careful to place himself between Monk and his sword as he passes into the house.

"If you will walk this way," says the smiling steward, "I shall lead you to the servants' quarters off the kitchen. I warn you that the setting may be humble for your taste, but I promise that my wife's excellent cooking will be well worth the small indignity."

As Monk follows the steward to the rear of the house, his eye is caught by countless treasures beyond his experience, the furniture, paintings, frescoes, the gold plate and massive crystalline chandeliers.

"*Mon dieu,*" says Monk, "this house is fit for a king. Lord Burghley, he was ... highly placed, *non?*"

"His lordship came from quite humble surroundings," explains the steward, "but he became Lord High Treasurer for Her Majesty Queen Elizabeth, and served long in that position until his unfortunate death two years ago."

"And in all this time since his death," asks Monk skeptically, "no one has arranged his papers?"

"Here we are," says the steward as they arrive at the servant's kitchen, a simple affair of sturdy, unstained block furniture. "This is my wife and the light of my life."

The lady curtsies low, and Monk bows lower still, not to be outshone in humility. "Thank you, madam," he says. "I am humbled by your willingness to share your repast with a humble scholar such as myself."

"*Enchantée, monsieur,*" says the Englishwoman, pronouncing her French words so miserably that Monk considers instructing her, in friendly manner, by repeating what she's said in better accent. But he catches himself before doing so, realizing that it might be regarded as pedantic and discourteous.

Out of sight, upstairs in the first storey hallway, David watches Monk enter the house and gawp at the furnishings while he follows the steward to the back kitchen. When they're safely out of sight, he creeps into the upstairs parlor at the front of the house to check whether Monk's two friends and their cannon remain at the copse where they were "pretending to be invisible," in the steward's turn of phrase.

Keeping out of sight of anyone peering through the window, he peeks around the shutter, and is alarmed to find men, horses, and cannon all gone. He creeps down the hallway, and peers out the east window surreptitiously. At first he sees nothing, as the sun is low on the horizon and shines almost directly into his eyes. Then he sees them. The men have situated themselves and their cannon in another copse, closer to the house, and tied their five horses to various trees, leaving the cannon maneuverable by hand. One of them begins to look up, but David drops to his knees out of sight, hoping he was in time to escape detection.

It occurs to him that the men are quite close to the stables. What if Chester's not guarding the stables, as he ought to be? What mischief might they make there while their small compatriot is indoors being entertained by the staff?

Inside the stables, Chester sleeps soundly in the stableman's chair beside the entrance to the house. A distant banging at the front gate reminds him of his surroundings, but he promptly dozes off again.

A few minutes later, he's awakened again, this time by a creaking stable door. He sits up with a start, as the sound can't portend anything good. If the steward or one of his young companions wished to see him, they'd be entering the stables from the house. No, this creaking means someone is entering from outdoors, which almost certainly means it's the intruders.

Chester silently retreats behind a hay bale in a vacant stall, and crouches down to watch, his thumb caressing the hammer of his pistol, prepared to cock it at need.

The two full-sized intruders he scouted out the day before steal up and down the stables, while the small one is nowhere to be seen. Each horse they pass rustles slightly, until they reach the two stolen from them at the inn where Poley slept atop the cannon. The two stolen horses chuff and stamp as they're discovered by their previous owners.

One of the Bennetts, evidently satisfied that they're alone, whispers, "'sblood! Are you seeing what I'm seeing?"

"Aye. These two big black ones are *ours*! Look, Cuthbert! Here's the scar from that little nick he got on his haunch last month."

"Doesn't it strike you there's a surfeit of horses in here, Tobias?"

Tobias grunts. "If you ask me, they've got more people in the manor house than they let on."

"Pshaw!" mumbles Cuthbert. "I *told* you Serjeant Ames would have men here before we arrived."

Tobias scratches his head. "Cagey Jew. If they've been here all the while, why do you suppose they haven't left yet?"

"Maybe they were telling Monk the truth, and they haven't found the papers!"

"And I'll bet they didn't send anyone to fetch a curator yesterday, either, although we can't tell that for sure just from the number of horses remaining."

"I tend to agree with your assessment," says Cuthbert. "As I told this Monk fellow, I think they're just stalling."

"But, until which eventuality?" asks Tobias.

"How'd you mean?"

"I mean, are they stalling just to tire us out?"

Cuthbert grunts. "My guess is they're awaiting aid, though in what form I cannot guess."

"And what happened to their stableman?" asks Tobias. "There's nobody here watching the stables." He turns to his twin as though a brilliant idea has just come to him. "Maybe they sent *him* for the curator."

"There's no blessed *curator*, Tobias!" whispers Cuthbert in exasperation. "And *of course* they would have sent the stableman. The steward can't leave the place, and he's not going to send his wife."

"Well," replies Tobias indignantly, "if they didn't send the stableman to fetch the curator, then where is he?"

"We watched this bloody stable door all evening, and half the night," says Cuthbert. "Nobody went anywhere, at least not on horseback."

"Then, he's somewhere inside the house," says Tobias.

Cuthbert sniffs loudly. "Smell that?" he asks. "That little bugger Monk's feasting on breakfast in there, while we eat three-day-old bread in the woods." He glances at the doorway to the house. "Perhaps we might join him."

Chester puts his finger on the hammer in case these two decide to enter the house. He only wishes he had an additional pistol as, once he fires, he'll have no time to reload, and will have to hurl himself at the remaining twin.

"May I have the privilege of meeting your daughter?" asks Monk, stuffing himself with two more chicken's eggs and half a loaf of bread slathered with butter.

Bell and his wife look at each other. "I believe," says Barnaby, "she may be reading, sir."

"Is she, perhaps, looking for the papers I have come all this way to examine?"

"I expect she is, sir," says Barnaby, "as the curator was not at home, and she requested an opportunity to find them for you."

"Oh?" says Monk. "Could you bring me to her?"

"Why certainly, sir," says the steward, bowing pleasantly. "If you'll follow me." He walks in stately fashion to the stairs and they climb two flights of stairs, making small talk about the age of the manor house and the choice of its setting.

"Down this hall," says Barnaby. "The three rooms at the end."

When they reach the last room, Barnaby knocks perfunctorily and opens the door. At the end of the first row of chests sits Barbara, bent over the open top chest, poring through documents just as she was when David and Andres arrived, the room having been carefully restored to its original condition.

"Barbara," says Barnaby, "we have a visitor."

Barbara looks up, and is visibly surprised to find their visitor to be only a few feet tall. Her surprise clearly troubles the visitor, but it's too late to save his feelings. Instead, she climbs down from the ladder and curtsies.

"*Enchanté, mademoiselle,*" says Monk, obviously impressed by the girl's beauty. "Have you perhaps found the papers that I seek?"

Barbara gives him her most appealing smile. "I have tried, sir, but I'm afraid I've been unable to locate them in the few hours since you first arrived."

She reenacts Andres's gradual revelation of the numerous chests calculated to emphasize the quantity of paper needing to be searched, opening the door to each room in sequence. "As you can imagine, unless one were quite fortunate, it would take one person many weeks to find just the documents you seek."

"Ah, yes," says Monk, "I see your predicament." He turns on his heel and bows gallantly to the steward. "*Alors, monsieur,* I see that I have come all this way only to realize that, unfortunately, the papers I wish to examine have yet to be found." He smiles, as though chagrined. "I can say only that I have much appreciated your kindness in sharing your repast with me." He turns to Barbara. "Perhaps the lovely *mademoiselle* would be so kind as to escort me out?"

Barbara looks to her father for permission, who wavers a moment, and accedes at last. "We shall *both* accompany you to the gate, sir, and may I say that we have been pleased to make your acquaintance. Perhaps, if you will write in a year or so, the curator will have all these papers arranged, and we can accommodate your course of study. Who knows?" he says. "If his lordship consents, we might even have copies made and sent to you in France."

"That would be … most satisfactory, *monsieur*," says Monk. "Now, I shall take my leave of you. If you would show me the way out." He bows and extends his hand toward Barbara's. She blushes and places her hand in his. The steward follows them down the stairs to the front door.

As Andres peeks through the doorway of a bedroom on the first storey, he catches sight of Monk passing by on the way downstairs, hand-in-hand with an uncomfortable-looking Barbara. He turns back to David, who's lying across a well-made bed.

"That little bastard has her by the hand!" says Andres in an exclamatory whisper, evidently seething with jealousy.

David regards him skeptically. "Contain yourself, Master Salazar," he says sardonically. "He's four feet of solid man, it's true, but I still give you the edge."

Andres turns on him. "I'm glad you find it laughable, but what if he tries to kidnap her?"

"Then we'll kill him and take her back," snaps David, "but keep your blasted voice down, as it's unlikely he'll try any such thing. What good could he see in it?"

"I'm going to watch, to make sure he leaves without incident," Andres blurts outs, and runs entirely too fast through the doorway to the first storey landing.

The steward opens the front door and bows to his departing guest.

"We hope to see you again sometime," says the steward.

"Perhaps next year," says Monk. "I shall be sure to write. Perhaps I shall come in person, as I would not willingly miss the company of zis fair damsel." He kisses Barbara's hand.

Suddenly, a swarthy young man wearing a sword tumbles down the stairs and lands on his arse. From someone remaining unseen on the first storey comes the whispered exclamation, "Shit!"

# CHAPTER 20

**MONK'S EYES GO WIDE** and he grabs the girl, placing her between himself and the steward. Backing up through the doorway, he eases her slowly through the entryway and grabs the sword he surrendered upon entering. Keeping the girl in front of him, he bumps open the unlocked gate and gropes blindly for his pistol. Finding it on the hook where he left it, he draws the terrified girl outside.

The steward drops to his knees in horror, and pleads with Monk. "Please, sir, let my daughter go. She has done nothing but try to honor your request."

Monk is red-faced with anger. "Honor? You dare speak to me of honor, *monsieur*? When you have lied to me all along? Zere are more men in zis house than yourself and your stableman. At least two more! About what else have you also lied to me? You sent no one last evening for ze curator. No one has left zis house!"

"But, sir!" pleads the steward. "The papers are just as you have seen them. It would take many weeks to find anything there!"

Andres bursts out the front door, tugs Barbara away from Monk, and stands her aside. He unsheathes his sword and brandishes it at Monk.

Taken by surprise, Monk glances to his right, but his men are vanished. In the woods he sees only a few tied-off horses and an unattended cannon. "Idiots!" he shouts furiously, and draws a single-handed, straight-bladed sword in answer to Andres's challenge.

But out of nowhere appears a similar sword of greater length that smacks the point of Monk's sword to the ground.

"Go inside, you two!" shouts David as he intercedes between Monk and Andres.

"No!" shouts Andres. "*I* brought this on. It's my job to finish it!" Barbara looks on in horror.

David shoots a dirty look at Andres as he circles Monk and holds him at bay. "Take your lady love inside, Master Salazar," he says, adding drily, "you've accomplished quite enough."

Barbara pulls Andres into the house.

"So," says Monk to David, "you fancy yourself ze savior of your friends, sir, come to defeat the terrible intruder."

"Not really," replies David apathetically. "I've been watching you all along. You seem rather a gentleman, which only makes it more bothersome that I shall have to kill you."

Monk reacts with surprise. "Kill me, sir? I shall save you ze trouble by killing *you*, sir!" He thrusts the deadly point forward while continuing to circle.

Parrying Monk's first thrust, David observes that fighting a fellow this small is sure to pose something of a challenge. Although the proportional brevity of the dwarf's sword requires its user to make his thrusts longer and therefore slower, David will need to take especial care to protect his legs, requiring him to dip further to parry each thrust.

To David's dismay, out of the corner of his eye, he sees Monk's two companions appear by their horses. Fortunately, they're closely pursued by Chester, who's drawn his sword and swings it wildly, trying his best to ward the two men away from the cannon. In no time, the clank of steel from that quarter tells David that the two men have indeed drawn swords against Chester, who can't last long, two against one.

As though detecting David's momentary distraction, Monk thrusts again, but David's attention returns in time for him to knock it away and follow with a thrust of his own.

"I see you have some skill at this," says David, as they continue to circle. "Is that sword Spanish?"

"What makes you ask?" says Monk.

"The hilt is cupped," David replies. "I have heard that conquistadors wield such swords, but have never heard the same said of Frenchmen."

"You are most observant, sir," says Monk, visibly impressed, as he parries one of David's short thrusts. "And I see zat you have some skill of your own. My grandfather, whose sword this was, was Basque. So, ze answer to your question," he says thrusting at David's knees, "is zat, in a sense, ze sword is Spanish *and* French and, at ze same time, neither."

David registers surprise, as Monk scores a touch just above his knee. While the thrust has not pierced the muscle, it has scratched his thigh, which is sure to bleed.

Chester flails his sword at both Bennetts. Although Chester is plainly a better swordsman than either of them, he knows that his energy will eventually flag from fighting them both, especially as he cannot afford to move away from the cannon, for they will surely turn it on David.

Besides, his fighting stance is nearly stationary, providing his adversaries with an easy target. His chief concern is that one of them may have a pistol, which could end the fight quickly, and disastrously for him.

The clanking of steel at the front gate tells him that the little fellow is capable of carrying on the fight against David for some time, despite the disadvantage of his stature.

Chester continues to fight valiantly against the odds for several minutes, thrusting at each of his adversaries as soon as they take a step toward him or the cannon. Sweat soon pours from his brow, but he dares not wipe it away, for fear of presenting them with an opportunity. He's sure he's hit one of them at least once, and has pierced him an inch or two.

At last the dreaded pistol makes its appearance in the hand of one of the Bennetts.

"Drop your sword!" shouts its bearer. The other twin presses a bloody kerchief to his shoulder, wincing in pain.

Delaying only a moment to observe the progress of the fight at the front gate, Chester reluctantly drops his sword.

The small man's voice pierces the morning air. "Idiots!" he shouts in a thick French accent, "the falconet!" Evidently unsatisfied with his henchmen's slowness, he shouts in exasperation: "Ze *cannon*, you idiots!"

"Better tie this one off first, Tobias!" says the wounded one, pointing his chin at a nearby oak. "Tie him to the tree."

Tobias grabs Chester and thrusts him roughly against the oak. Chester offers no resistance, instead keenly observing the pace of fighting before the gate, which has accelerated. Though David bleeds from a scratch on his thigh, strangely, he seems to be conversing amiably with his adversary as they fight.

Tobias runs the rope several times around Chester and the tree, prudently tying it off on the opposite side of the tree, but leaving it so loose that Chester nearly laughs at his adversary's lack of skill. Still, he realizes, the knot will be enough to restrain him for so long as his adversaries remain with him.

Tobias steps around to Chester's side of the tree to view his victim.

"You'll never get away with this," mutters Chester, looking Tobias in the eye, heedless of the restraint.

"The devil, you say," says Tobias menacingly, thrusting his face forward so that it's nearly touching Chester's.

"Forget about him!" shouts Cuthbert as he writhes in pain, evidently finding it difficult to stanch the blood flowing from his shoulder. "He's distracting you," says Cuthbert. *Shoot the blond one!*" he shouts urgently, plainly referring to David. "The dwarf can't hold him off indefinitely."

Although it's a long shot from here, Tobias cocks the hammer and turns toward the combatants at the gate.

"Watch it, sir!" shouts Chester at the top of his lungs, hoping to get David's attention. "He's about to shoot!"

David glances over at Chester, having obviously heard the warning.

For his pains, Tobias turns to Chester and slaps him hard in the face.

"*Forget* him, Tobias!" shouts Cuthbert. "*Shoot the blond one!*"

"Watch it, sir!" comes Chester's voice. "He's about to shoot!"

David can see that one of the Bennetts is about to aim a pistol at him, and that Chester's been tied to a tree.

As David has no pistol of his own, his mind races. *How did this fight begin?* Monk held Barbara hostage. Now there's a different hostage whose peril might dissuade the *Bennetts* from firing.

David suddenly reverses the direction of his circling, defying Monk's expectation, and giving himself an opening for a desperate move. He backs off a step, and when Monk makes a corresponding thrust, he steps back in and strikes Monk's sword downward with all his might, as close to the hilt as ever he can.

David's startling aggressiveness turns the trick, and Monk's sword falls to the ground. David puts his foot on Monk's sword, drops his own, and draws a dagger, placing the point at Monk's throat. Monk throws his hands up in surrender and says, "Surely, sir, a gentleman such as yourself will not slay an unarmed combatant!"

David lifts Monk off the ground, placing the dwarf between himself and the scoundrel with the pistol, shielding his own torso with the dwarf's small body.

The gunman hesitates. "Shoot him!" shouts the other Bennett, nearly mad with anger. "Shoot!"

Monk kicks and struggles to free himself, crimson-faced with humiliation at being used as a human shield. "Let me down, sir! This is an outrage—a violation of every rule of combat!"

"I haven't a clear shot!" shouts the one with the pistol.

Monk struggles mightily to free himself from David's steely grip, but in vain. "Ze cannon, you idiots!" shouts Monk.

The Bennetts look at each other in realization, having evidently forgotten that they hold the superior weapon. To Chester's horror, they roll the falconet past him, evidently intending to place it in front of the gate, seeking their adversaries' surrender by threatening to blow a hole or two in Burghley House.

David, momentarily distracted by this new horror, loosens his grip on Monk, who drops to his feet and smiles smugly as he turns on David with a pistol.

Monk cocks the hammer. "I judged you poorly, sir," he says, red in the face, humiliated beyond endurance, spittle flying from his mouth with every word. "You have no honor! You have deceived me by concealing yourself, by forcing the steward to lie about your presence. And now you violate ze laws of combat by using my diminutive person to shield yourself from an adversary!" He takes a furious step toward David. "Now you shall experience ze wages of sin, sir!" He signals to the Bennetts, who roll the cannon into place some ten yards from the gate, aiming it squarely at the front of Burghley House.

In an act of bravado, which he will later recognize as sheer lunacy, David takes a defiant step towards Monk's pistol.

Monk's fury is now beyond containment. He slavers. "I was going to afford you ze pleasure of watching us destroy your beautiful English manor house, sir, but you have pushed me beyond endurance. Prepare to meet your Maker!"

Just inside the house, Andres frantically finishes loading a pistol he's taken from Lord Burghley's now-smashed armoire, and watches through the open gate, awaiting his moment.

Monk is about to cock his pistol, when there's an unexpected musket report from the woods opposite those where Chester remains tied to a tree. There is a sickening "thuck" as the ball penetrates flesh. The pistol flies from Monk's hand; he staggers backward and falls to the ground motionless.

For a moment nothing happens, as no one appears to know where the shot came from, or what to do about it.

Andres, observing the steward's bewildered face, barks a laugh as he realizes what's happened.

"I know only one man who'd take that shot ... and *make* it," says Andres. Running out the gate, he grabs David from behind and drags him into the house.

"What are you doing?" shouts David in outrage, wriggling free.

"Look!" says Andres, pointing toward the source of the musket report.

A very composed Jonathan, Lord Saint Ives emerges from the woods with a smoking musket in his left hand and an unfired pistol in his right. Immediately behind him, four shiny brass cannon roll out of the woods, manned by two cannoneer apiece, and take up positions a few feet to his fore.

"Ready!" shouts Jonathan, and the four cannon take aim at the Bennetts and their falconet.

"Don't shoot!" shout the Bennetts.

Chester, still tied to his tree, realizes he's in the likely path of any cannonballs to be fired at the Bennetts. Despite the unseemliness of joining with his mortal enemies in a desperate chorus, he chimes in nonetheless, "Don't shoot!"

Four cannon are aimed squarely at him. As he struggles to free himself from the rope, to his astonishment and dismay all at once three of them *fire*. The gut-wrenching concussion smacks his head backward into the hard oak. As he loses consciousness, it seems to him a bit ironic—and more than a bit cruel—that the last, hellish sound he'll ever hear on this earth evokes the heroic and pleasing days of his youth.

The Bennetts abandon their once-proud falconet, which suddenly looks rather shabby and insignificant by comparison to the gleaming battery that has lately taken the field. They race to the prostrate, bloody Monk, and spirit him off to their horses. Before anyone has a hope of reaching them, they lay Monk across one of the two stolen chargers, and bolt away as fast as the horses can carry them.

And so ends the unsung Battle of Burghley House.

# CHAPTER 21

**IN THE QUIET** of the summer afternoon, Noah sits in his study, re-reading a message slipped under the front door early that morning, before anyone else was awake to see it. It's from Nerezza.

"Sir, shouldn't they be back by now?" asks Esther, traipsing into Noah's study before supper, startling him. He discreetly slips the note into the bottom drawer and closes it silently.

"Pardon me, dear," he says, "did you say something?"

"Shouldn't they be back by now?" she repeats, regarding him skeptically.

Noah sits back while his heartbeat returns to its accustomed pace, contemplating how many times he's asked himself the same question. "Please take a seat," he says.

Before she sits, she asks him anxiously, "Have … have you *heard* something?"

"No, dear. Not a thing. I was wondering whether your nightmare of David and the dwarf has recurred."

She shakes her head. "The last time was four nights ago. Shouldn't he be home by now?"

He hesitates before answering. "I suppose, if things went *precisely* according to plan, David would have been home one or possibly two days ago. But he could have been delayed by *anything*—even something as mundane as a summer storm."

"A storm?"

"Certainly, a storm can pose severe hazards," he observes. "Why, Yetta told me many times that my parents were killed by a cart that overturned during a storm." He looks down at his hands. "Of course, those were fibs."

"Fibs?"

"Yes," he says. Then, suddenly realizing the word is unfamiliar to her, he adds, "A fib is a little lie told to avoid hurting someone's feelings. As you've heard, my parents were truly killed in the burning of a synagogue."

Esther nods sympathetically. "Yes, I heard what Yetta told you." For a moment, she seems lost in recollection. "Why didn't Yetta want me to hear the name of the man who did all those bad things for Pappacoda?"

Noah sighs. "Oh, I don't know. Perhaps it was another of her superstitions about names, such as spitting whenever she pronounced a name of the wicked."

Lady Jessica enters the study.

"Come, both of you. Supper is served."

Supper begins with chicken broth, and moves on to a thick brown lamb stew made with potatoes, carrots, and legumes. Although such heavy fare is more common in winter, the cool, damp summer has made it quite welcome now, especially toward evening.

"Cook knows what she's doing," says Noah, drawing agreement all around.

"You should be sure to tell her, Father," says Jessica.

"I shall certainly do so," he replies, pushing his empty plate away.

Esther suddenly rises from her chair and stands in place, looking perplexed. As all eyes follow her curiously, she turns and goes to the window.

"What is it, dear?" says Marie.

Esther turns to Marie and curtsies lightly. "Nothing, mistress." She returns her attention to the window, drawing a piece of the sheer curtain aside for an unobstructed view.

At table, Stephen strikes up a conversation with Jessica about her temporary lodgings in town, eventually shifting topics to the cool, damp weather that's dominated the summer.

Marie seems about to remark upon Esther's oddly unsociable behavior. But, before she can get a word out, she's plainly startled by the clopping of approaching horses. She turns to Noah with raised eyebrow. Evidently, she too recognizes that Esther couldn't possibly have heard the horses' approach when she first rose. Noah can only shrug in return, wondering whether Esther is even aware how often she detects events by means other than the workaday five senses.

"'Tis they!" Esther shouts, and claps her hands. "Cheerful and Lord Saint Ives!"

While the two horsemen pass by the window on their way to the stables, Jessica joins Esther at the window, and they giggle and hug as though truly sisters.

Noah is only partly relieved by the new arrival, however. He's concerned that there's been no mention of Andres, whom he would have expected to return straightaway with David. He decides to wait before asking about Andres, however, for fear of worrying everyone needlessly.

Jonathan enters first, a sheaf of papers in hand. He smiles unreservedly, bows smartly to Noah, and hands him the papers, as if in formal presentation.

"Father, I commend these letters to you, as in gathering them we have exposed ourselves to considerable danger, and the Crown to no small expense." Upon seeing his wife, Jonathan immediately falls to one knee and tenderly kisses her hand. "As promised, m'lady, I have returned to you no worse for wear."

Despite her past misgivings, Jessica beams at her husband.

Jonathan's demonstration of affection seems to please Esther as much as it does Jessica, and she leans around the doorway to watch David enter a moment later.

Noah turns to David as soon as he enters. "Where is Andres?" he asks anxiously, before noticing that David is limping.

David smiles and says, "I'm just fine, Serjeant Ames. And yourself?" bringing laughter from everyone who hears. "You will be pleased to learn that Master Salazar is also in fine health and spirits, sir, as are Arthur Arden and Yeoman Gardner. For the moment, Master Salazar remains at Burghley House, *his* only wound having been inflicted by

Cupid's arrow … the dribbling dart of love of which the poets write."

"What's wrong with your leg?" asks Noah, momentarily relieved.

"I got into a bit of a spat," says David, then adds abashedly, "with a dwarf."

Noah and Esther exchange a meaningful glance at the mention of a dwarf. She brings her hand up over her mouth in astonishment. Unable to contain herself any longer, she embraces David.

"It's really just a scratch," says David. "No need for dramatics. Would have been far worse, had not Lord Saint Ives made certain the dwarf got the worst of it." As David far exceeds Esther in height, he gawkily places one arm lightly about her shoulders, while she clings wholeheartedly to his chest. He grins broadly.

Lady Jessica shakes her head in admonition. "Oh, stop it, David. You are quite full of yourself."

David protests. "Nay, madam. A reformed man am I."

Lady Jessica nods skeptically. "We shall see."

Jonathan and David are fed a fine supper while engaging in small talk with Jessica and Esther, who cluck about them as mother hens their chicks.

"Easy on the wine, boys," says Noah, as he prepares to take the papers into his study. Before he can disappear around the corner, Jonathan blurts out: "I've read those letters, Father."

Noah stops and turns back to him, incredulous. "When did you have time?"

"We stopped two nights," says Jonathan, "and I studied them until my eyes closed of fatigue."

"Care to share your learning with me?" asks Noah.

Jonathan smirks. "That's why I examined them, Father. So I could tell you what I found before you needed to read them yourself. Won't you stay and chat at table for a while? I think you'll find I've saved you considerable time. And you could provide us first with some historical context. I don't suppose the ladies will object to eavesdropping on a history lesson in English politics."

Noah equivocates a moment, as he now holds in his hand letters he thought he might never have, and finds himself reluctant to spare even a moment before delving into them. But his good sense and affection for the boys persuade him to take a glass of wine and resume his seat at table.

"Very well," says Noah, "but first I'd like to hear of your confrontation with Sir Gelly Meyrick and Nicholas Skeres, as well as your unfortunate dwarf."

"Don't forget 'Roley' Poley," says David through a mouthful of stew. "Andres and I stopped at Cambridge Castle for provisions and fresh horses, as instructed by Sir Walter. This was sundown," he searches his memory, "about a week ago, I suppose. When we got there, we found that Chester the jailer had been locked in a cell by his own prisoner, a Cambridge student who'd passed out drunk at the jailer's desk. We freed Chester but, before we could enlist his help, he ran off in pursuit of his wayward scholar, leaving Andres and me alone on the hilltop, temporarily bereft of food, rest, and fresh horses.

"While awaiting Chester's return, we spied a dwarf (the very one who later wounded me in the thigh) entering Cambridge town with five other men on horseback, towing what Chester recognized to be a disguised falconet."

Noah regards him incredulously. "A *cannon?*" he asks.

"Aye, sir."

"And the dwarf?" asks Noah. "What did he look like?"

David looks to Jonathan, who defers to David to continue. "He wore a flamboyant costume that appeared to be assembled from diverse pieces of the uniforms of several armies, although which I cannot guess. I spoke with him briefly while fencing with him, and he seemed a curious mixture of *shamelessness* in his mission to steal Lord Burghley's correspondence, and *honor* in his chivalrous conduct toward the steward and his family."

"His name?" asks Noah, expecting the worst.

"Monk," replies David. "Why? Did you know him?"

Noah nods wistfully. "I met him once." He cringes. "Did you run him through with your sword?"

David shakes his head. "No. We fenced for a while. When his henchmen reached their guns and took aim at me from a distance, I had no choice but to lift Monk off his feet and carry him as a shield to cover my torso. He kicked and wriggled to free himself, but I held him for a time.

"I'm ashamed to admit that, in a moment of distraction, Monk escaped my grasp, regained his footing, drew a pistol that I didn't know he had, and brandished it at me. He berated me rather roundly. Although he purported to take offense at my dishonor in using him as a human shield, I think he was *truly* mortified by how ridiculous he was made to appear, kicking his feet in the air like a child.

"As he threatened to discharge his pistol at me, he was struck by a ball expertly fired from quite a distance, the musket being wielded by one Jonathan, Lord Saint Ives." David turns to Jonathan. "Thank you again, m'lord."

Jonathan bows perfunctorily in his seat and takes another swig of wine, as though toasting David's health. "David fails to mention that he came perilously close to taking the ball himself as, in a fit of pointless bravado, he closed the distance between himself and Monk. Incidentally, Father, Monk's henchmen were apparently the Bennett twins who helped us to escape Lord Essex's grasp some years ago."

Noah is confused. "The Bennetts? *Not* Meyrick, Skeres, and Poley?"

David replies. "No, those three never appeared at Burghley House, though I expect they accompanied Monk as far as Cambridge. Andres and I didn't get a close look at the men who arrived at Cambridge with Monk. They did fit the general description of Meyrick, Skeres, and Poley, but, as they were near a half-mile off, we couldn't swear under oath that it was they. In any event, Cambridge was the last we saw of those three. The only ones to arrive at Burghley House were Monk and the Bennetts."

"As soon as Monk was struck by a ball, Lord Jonathan let go with a three-cannon blast that sent them scurrying. Monk's men never got a shot off," replies David.

"Is Monk dead?" asks Noah apprehensively.

Jonathan looks askance at Noah. "He went down hard, but I expect I merely winged him. At least, that's what I was *trying* to do. The Bennetts carried him away before we could examine him."

Noah's unexplained sympathy for Monk is plain, much to Jonathan's evident annoyance.

"Was it necessary," asks Noah skeptically, "to *shoot* him?"

Jonathan places his glass down onto the table hard enough to cause a few wine drops to splash onto the table, and he sits up indignantly. Jessica touches his arm to calm him down.

"What would you have had me do, Father?" asks Jonathan, simmering. "Should I have allowed your precious Monk to shoot David?" Esther gasps. "Because from where I stood, that's precisely what he had in mind—and presently, too."

Noah shakes his head. "Of *course* not."

"Did it ever occur to *you*," says Jonathan, straightening up from his slouch, "to inform Andres and David that you knew of this dwarf before sending them off into the blue?"

Noah shakes his head. "Never did I suspect that he might be involved in this affair. I suppose I *should* have suspected as much, as he appeared at the Saracen's Head to introduce both the Frenchman and the Italian residing at Drury House who, as you know, are suspect." Noah turns to David. "And Andres was smitten by Cupid's arrow?"

"As surely as the moon rose that night," laughs David, breaking the tension. "The fortunate maid is Barbara Bell, daughter of the steward at Burghley House. Already they're inseparable."

Noah rises. "Gentlemen, let us complete our discussion in the study."

"So, Jonathan," says Noah, adopting his customary informality once he's reasonably certain he's out of Jessica's hearing, "what do these letters say?"

Jonathan reaches his hand out for the letters, and Noah hands him the whole stack.

"It took many hours' tedious work to find this out, but Lord Burghley's public collection, which had not yet been archived, incidentally, held only a few letters from Walsingham during the period about which you inquired." Jonathan removes what must be no more than three or four pages from the stack and hands them to Noah. "You've heard it said that Walsingham was not expecting the Huguenot massacre?"

Noah nods. "I've heard it, but never believed it."

"As well you ought not. Walsingham sensed a massacre coming as soon as it was decided that the wedding between the protestant Prince Henri de Navarre and the king's papist sister Margaret would take place in Paris, a very papist city. Walsingham suspected that what appeared to be a papist olive branch was actually a ruse to inflame the populace of Paris against the protestants who had been induced to attend with all their conspicuous wealth and outward shows of piety. Catherine de Medici, mother of both the bride and her brother the king, was believed by Walsingham to be a ruthless Machiavel. He wrote to Burghley on July 25, 1572, warning of the extraordinary tensions between the warring factions."

Though following the tale with rapt interest, Noah interjects, "The violence in Paris began less than a month later with the attempted assassination of Admiral Coligny, leader of the protestant faction."

"Yes," continues Jonathan. "When that incident occurred and protestants were being slaughtered in the streets till the gutters ran with blood, Walsingham deemed it too dangerous to dispatch a written message. So he had one of his assistants commit his first message to memory and dispatched him to Lord Burghley. I was unable to find more than a brief mention of that report in Burghley's public papers. However"—he leafs purposefully through the sheaf, and draws out a smaller batch—"the steward's daughter found *these* letters between Burghley and Walsingham concealed in an adjacent compartment, which looked to be secret. *These* provide the results of Walsingham's research into the causes and progress of the Huguenot massacre." Jonathan smiles proudly.

Noah ponders the secrecy of the papers in his hand. "I can't help but wonder whether copies of these *secret* papers were stored in the chests at the Tower. If the Tower held copies of only the public papers you just described, from the intruder's point of view it would hardly have seemed worthwhile to break in and steal them."

Jonathan nods. "I thought of that, too. I expect they didn't know *what* they'd find, and were probably relieved to find that the papers they'd stolen contained nothing more incendiary than a record of Walsingham's suspicion that the Parisian wedding was a trap set for the Huguenots."

David chimes in. "Or they suspected there might be a cache of private letters, and that's why they sent Monk to fetch whatever he could from Burghley House—on the off-chance."

Noah agrees. "And that made the success of your mission all the more essential." He can't help but smile at them. "Good job, boys." He turns to Jonathan impatiently. "And now for the real news. Keep me waiting no longer. What do the *secret* letters say?"

Before proceeding, Jonathan rises and checks the adjacent rooms for inquisitive ears. All the rooms are vacant, but for one in which Esther silently reads a primer, no doubt to improve her English proficiency. He resumes his seat.

"Well," says Jonathan quietly, "the whole bloody thing started with the botched assassination of Admiral Coligny, head of the Huguenots. A shot rang out while he was riding through the heart of Paris, passing the home of a long-time functionary of the Duke of Guise, head of the papist faction.

"Investigation showed that the Duke's functionary was away, but that the Parisian fellow running the house had allowed a friend of his to take a room facing the street. After the shooting, the temporary lodger was seen galloping away, leaving behind in his room a discharged musket and a hefty bag of coins."

Noah is perplexed. "If he was a paid assassin, why would he leave his loot behind after the job was done?"

Jonathan smiles. "David came up with a most plausible motive."

"And what was that?" asks Noah.

"The job *wasn't* done," says Jonathan. "The assassin had failed. The admiral was wounded, but not mortally. His elbow had been shattered by the ball, and one of his fingers blown off, but he was very much alive, and was taken to his hotel in the company of a few of his own gentlemen, who were immediately surrounded by a 'guard' comprised of the duke's most fanatical supporters. It was David who suggested that the failed assassin feared he would be found by the duke, that his booty would be taken back, and that he would be killed for good measure, if only to keep him quiet for good and all. Leaving his pay at the scene would give his employer one less reason to track him down."

"Either that," says Noah, "or the failed assassin was himself a papist fanatic, who left the money behind to mislead investigators into believing he'd been working for money."

"Also plausible," David admits.

Jonathan resumes. "But there are two things Walsingham found out by surreptitious means that might be of interest to you. First, he discovered that the failed assassin went by some Italian surname, which name he never learned."

Noah sits up attentively, suppressing a mild annoyance that Jonathan is savoring this moment before presenting his *pièce de résistance.*

Jonathan reaches out his hand for the stack of private papers he handed to Noah a few minutes ago, and Noah returns it to him. "Walsingham's men recovered something from the purse left behind by the assassin … a card of the Tarot deck. It cost them a pretty penny, but they recovered the actual card, and Walsingham sent it to Burghley." Jonathan draws the card from the sheaf of papers. "Here it is, Father," he says, handing it to Noah.

As Noah expected, it's the Wheel of Fortune. The Rota Fortunae. All four human figures are there, precisely as described by Nerezza: the rising young man, the man who reigns, the man who formerly reigned and, at the base of the wheel, the man who simply says, "I am without kingdom." On this particular card, those words have been underscored twice.

Jonathan preens. "Our assumption is that the words have been underscored to signify that the assassin intends to finish a job he knows he's botched." He places the papers in his lap and continues. "The following day, the duke's men shot their way into the admiral's rooms, slaughtered everyone in sight, and thrust a pike through the admiral, finishing the job that had been botched the day before. The Duke of Guise himself, standing on the street below, shouted to the murderers, ordering them to toss the admiral's corpse out through the window, which they did. And then, the murder of the Huguenots, which had been sporadic up to that time, became a general massacre such as had not been seen in modern Christendom."

"Did Walsingham learn the identity of the admiral's murderers?" asks Noah.

"He never learned their names, but they were described as the Frenchman who'd allowed the assassin to stay in the room from which shots were fired at the passing admiral the previous day, and ... an Italian. Walsingham speculated it was the shooter, but could never find out enough about him to prove it."

"Gentlemen," says Noah "you have given me much to read and think on. Please leave me now, and thank you for your excellent work. I shall inform Sir Robert and Her Majesty of your exemplary efforts."

# Chapter 22

**NOAH IS OVERCOME** by a wave of nausea as he listens to Jonathan and David clop away. But *some things must be done alone,* he tells himself.

They'd risked their very lives to bring him vital information, but he'd admitted to neither of them that their efforts had convinced him of the identity of those guilty of the recent attempt on the Queen. He deeply regrets leaving them in the dark, but mostly because he's now cut himself off from everyone who could help him in what he's about to do.

While Jonathan, David, and Andres were away on their quest, Noah had twice revisited the room in the Tower that once contained copies of Walsingham's letters to Lord Burghley.

His first visit was aimless, a feckless attempt to dispel the nagging notion that he was powerless to further the investigation on his own. As the futility of his effort became clear, he resolved not to repeat the folly, but rather to exercise a patience befitting his advancing years.

But he couldn't do it.

During a sleepless night after that first visit, he was pondering France's religious wars when he recalled that the Huguenot massacre of 1572 was not the only tragedy suffered by France's body politic about that time. A year or two after the massacre came the untimely death of King Charles the Ninth, who'd died at the unripe age of twenty-four.

When Charles died, it had been put abroad by the French royals that he'd been driven to madness by guilt for the national slaughter that followed the massacre at Paris, as it was said he might have prevented it with a courageous word.

Although the king had initially been innocent of the massacre, his advisors had quickly prevailed on him to pretend that it had all been done on his authority. If he failed to lead the papist mob, they said, it would surely turn on him. So, the day after the admiral's murder, King Charles had publicly announced before the Parliament of Paris that the atrocities perpetrated thus far had been performed at his direction.

After that public announcement, it had proven impossible to keep the protestant Queen Elizabeth of England from learning of the king's admission of responsibility for the massacre of her co-religionists, or to dissuade her from the belief that the French king had been its author. The resulting suspicion rendered it impossible to continue the intractable negotiation of nuptials between the protestant Elizabeth and the papist Duke of Anjou, Henri Valua, who would eventually succeed Charles on the French throne. An attempt to interest Her Majesty in yet another of the king's brothers died off, as well.

Noah recalled from Sir Henry's letter that Walsingham suspected Dorsay of responsibility in the death of the French King Charles. Noah wondered whether King Charles had not in fact been murdered, and decided to find out what Walsingham might have written Burghley about it at the time of the king's death.

On his second visit to the Tower, after considerable searching in the hot confines of the attic, Noah indeed *found* a letter from Walsingham on the topic of the king's death, and secretly removed it to his private study. He now withdraws it from his desk, and reads it one last time to steel himself for what he must do.

> As I mentioned to your Lordship, I have dispatched sundry assistants to recover such information as might be found in Paris touching the particularities of the unfortunate death of the late King Charles. Although I had returned to London by the time of the king's death, I have retained contacts in France and have paid them while on specific assignment.
>
> Your Lordship will recall that, while on embassage to Paris, I had occasion to meet with his highness several times to seek his assurance for the humane treatment of the Huguenots, and saw no sign of mental infirmity or despondency in his highness on those occasions.
>
> As I have told your Lordship of late, I find incredible the rumor, reputedly of royal origin, that the king was driven mad by guilt for the

national slaughter following the massacre at Paris.

It occurred to me that, although to this day no terms of national scope assuring the Huguenots of the right of public worship have been devised, yet his highness, governed by his own conscience and the laws of God, issued the Edict of Boulogne one year after the massacre, providing Huguenots with the privilege of private and discreet worship in the towns of La Rochelle, Montauban, and Nîmes. Although the edict reinforced the prohibition on Huguenot worship outside those towns, it nevertheless gave rise to a papist uproar over the French crown's having deigned to provide the protestant faith with any royal sanction whatever.

I add that it was only *after* issuance of the edict that his highness was reputedly overcome by a wasting disease culminating in madness and death. As wasting, madness, and death have been known to result from an alternative cause, to wit, poison, I deemed it prudent to instruct the Exchequer to expend the funds necessary to conduct a brief investigation, which has now borne fruit.

This day, I have received from one of my most reliable and clandestine contacts in Paris a peculiar item found in his highness's closet. It was evidently stored with his highness's physic under lock and key in a small ornate box. Rather than to describe the item, as it will no doubt appear familiar to you from our past correspondence, I have enclosed the very item with this present letter.

I send it to you in advance of our next meeting to provide your Lordship with ample time to examine it at length. It has occurred to me that it may be in the best interests of the Crown to keep the matter solely between you and me. Perhaps indefinitely. Looking forward to our next meeting, I most humbly take my leave.

From Windsor Forest, the 25th of Juliet, 1574.

Your Honor's to command,
Fra. Walsingham

Lord Burghley's copyist considerately included with the Tower copy a facsimile of the "peculiar" item, evidently made with great care to resemble the original in every respect. Noah removes the item from the envelope.

It's a card of the Tarot deck. The Wheel of Fortune. He examines it beside the Wheel of Fortune card Jonathan handed him a short while ago that had been left behind by the admiral's aspiring assassin.

The cards are virtually identical. Indeed, they're so similar that they were likely made by the same hand. Noah places Walsingham's letters and both Tarot cards into a pocket of his robe.

He now has little remaining doubt that the Italian resident at Drury House calling himself Nerezza is both the musketeer who shot Admiral Coligny (later running him through with a pike), and the murderer of King Charles the Ninth.

Nerezza is as near a figure of absolute evil as there could ever be. So confident was he of the greatness of his maniacal purpose that he felt no need to conceal from Noah his fascination with the Wheel of Fortune— a fascination he *must* have known could inculpate him in the most heinous political crimes of the past century. Indeed, Nerezza had had the temerity to exult in it openly, at a time when he knew he was being investigated for an attempted regicide of which he was in fact guilty.

And what of the self-proclaimed Frenchman of intrigue, Dorsay? His closeness with Nerezza suggests that he was the steward who'd admitted Nerezza to his master's house to provide him with a clear shot at the admiral. And Dorsay may even be the Frenchman who joined Nerezza in skewering the admiral, thus correcting their mistake of the previous day.

But Noah is experienced enough to know that conjecture is not evidence, and fascination with a superstitious trope, such as the Wheel, is simply too common to prove any one person guilty of a crime, though its facsimile be found at the scene.

*No.* For Noah to obtain evidence at a time so far removed from the crime, he needs a confession of guilt from the culprit himself. And *that* he can obtain only by a second interview.

He reaches down to the bottom drawer in which he placed this morning's invitation from Nerezza. The drawer is still closed, as he left it earlier. For his own safety, he knows he should *leave* it closed now.

But he won't. He *cannot.*

He opens the drawer, which slides silently on its runners, and re-moves the envelope addressed to him. In its upper left corner, inscribed in careful calligraphy, is the name "Nerezza."

He removes the invitation from the envelope and reads it again. It invites him to visit the old man at the Saracen's Head a half hour from now. He puts it back into the envelope and drops it on the desktop.

Before leaving the house, he conceals two more items in his robes: Uncle Avram's dagger, and a snaphaunce pistol borrowed from Andres Salazar long ago, which he's powdered and loaded with ball.

As he steps down to the cobblestone street from his wife's home, the feeble sunlight begins to fade and yield to the damp evening, leaving him with a sinking feeling in the pit of his stomach that he will never see this house again. Nor any of the precious souls within.

But ... *some things must be done alone.*

The kitchen is all put away and ready for next day's breakfast. Esther waves good night to the departing cook through the kitchen window, where daylight is fast fading.

Except for Esther and Serjeant Ames, the house is vacant. Mistress Ames and the young children have taken the Ames's coach to escort Jessica to her temporary quarters, help her pack, and return her with her belongings to her own house, where her husband awaits. Stephen is off with friends, as always.

As Esther contemplates whether to read before retiring, she hears the front door close quietly. Too quietly. Either Serjeant Ames has left surreptitiously or someone has secretly entered the house. As she finds either such prospect disturbing, she makes sure her sheathed dagger is in her pocket and goes to investigate.

By the time she reaches the door, all is quiet. She looks out of the window. As there's no sign of anyone outside, she's about to walk back toward the interior when someone comes into view across the street.

It's the Frenchwoman she's seen several times, kneading her hands more fretfully than ever. As the woman passes by the house, she stops directly across from the front door. Esther withdraws from the window to avoid being seen. Out of the corner of her eye, she sees the woman continue hesitantly on her way, apparently undecided whether the time has come to knock at the Ames's door. Esther has the distinct feeling she'll be back soon ... and next time she *will* knock.

Before checking the house for intruders, Esther holds her breath, listening intently. Though she's sure there's no sound, she draws her dagger nonetheless.

She starts her search in the parlor, which turns out to be vacant, and moves next to Serjeant Ames's study. She checks around every corner and behind each item of furniture, but turns up no one.

About to move on to another room, she spies an envelope atop Serjeant Ames's desk. Though she's acutely aware of her complete dependence upon his good will, and makes it a habit to avoid so much as the appearance of impropriety, this envelope looks suspiciously like the one he quickly tossed into a lower drawer earlier, when she'd entered the study without knocking.

And yet here it is now, atop the desk. What could that mean? Did he leave it here by accident, to his regret once he arrives at his destination? Persuading herself that it's in Serjeant Ames's interest that she examine it, she reads the envelope. It's addressed to Serjeant Ames at this house. In the upper left corner is the lone word "Nerezza," written in an archaic, serpentine hand. The envelope has been slit open, revealing the edge of an enclosed note.

Esther picks up the envelope, and the breath immediately leaves her body, as though a horse has suddenly sat on her chest. She struggles for air, and manages a little, but there's something terrible about this note. It's the most fearsome thing she's ever encountered—far more so than the ghost who appeared to her in Southwark; more so than any of the myriad spirits who've appeared to her since early childhood, when she learned to tell no one what she'd seen, lest she be committed to a horrid asylum.

Others just couldn't see what she could, so they thought her mad. Yet, she knew she was *not* mad. It was rather they who were *blind*.

She knows intuitively that this note is not some relic retaining a thin residue of past evil, but rather evil in itself. As she focuses on the tortuous writing, something happens that she would never have thought possible, even in the strange spiritual world she inhabits. The writing begins to vibrate, then to writhe like a worm, at first almost undetectably, but then increasingly so.

To her horror, the squirming worm falls from the envelope to the desktop and wriggles itself into another name: *Ciemnoci*. Polish, for *the dark one*. The name on the envelope, Nerezza, likewise means *the dark one*, but in Italian. Surely, no coincidence.

She wills her mind back to that moment when Yetta whispered to Noah the name of the man who murdered his family. Noah had leaned over to hear it, while Esther politely turned away. But now, repeating the scene in her mind, she strains to hear what Yetta says. And it comes to her.

*Ciemnoci*, says Yetta, ever so faintly. In Polish, *the dark one*. Esther wonders whether she really heard it then. But, regardless, she's quite certain she's hearing it now, and that means that the man who wrote this note is the very man who murdered Noah's family, indeed his whole village, and the same man of whom the ghost of Serjeant Ames's first wife had tried to warn him.

The worm on the desktop wriggles and—slowly, but perceptibly— begins to *grow*. Esther struggles for breath, as the worm grows larger. In a moment, it's not a worm at all, but rather a serpent that begins to snake an S-shaped course about the desktop. In a few circuits along this course, it grows massive, then stops before her, drawing its head back to strike.

She drops the envelope in terror and takes a sharp step backward, nearly falling. The serpent disappears. She steadies herself and her normal breathing returns.

When she looks at the envelope again, the word "Nerezza" is once again still, comprised of mere ink. She picks it up and removes the note. It's an invitation written in the same serpentine hand as the address on the envelope, seeking the pleasure of Serjeant Ames's company at an inn called the Saracen's Head at an appointed hour. She glances at the clock and realizes that Serjeant Ames has accepted the invitation and, even on foot, is bound to arrive within an hour.

She must find him, and bring strong men to help him.

She pockets the invitation and races to the front door with the intention of going first to the street corner to find out which path he's taken, but as she reaches the window, once again she sees the Frenchwoman standing across the street alone, now weeping.

Something inside tells her that this is the time ... the *one* time .... when she has no choice but to contravene every guarded impulse taught to her by a life of jeopardy and fear. She opens her heart to the weeping woman.

She opens the door, and speaks.

# CHAPTER 23

**AS NOAH SLOWLY TREADS** his way to the Saracen's Head Inn on foot, nearly an hour passes in transit, and the last of the daylight fades away.

A dew has quietly settled in, and fat droplets form on the leaves. He stops on Snow Hill to observe the inn in the gloaming, listening to water drip faintly from the eaves and tick gently onto the street.

He enters through the alehouse door and finds the taproom deserted by all but a few old men nursing their drams of ale. They look up at him eagerly, apparently hoping for something interesting to occur. He nods respectfully to them, as though sorry to disappoint, when in fact he hopes that nothing of interest to them *will* occur.

"Serjeant Ames?" the young tapster guesses as Noah enters.

"That am I," Noah assures him.

The tapster points to a dimly lit private room adjoining the main room, its door ajar. "A gentleman's been waitin' for ye in there, suh."

Noah nods politely and peeks hesitantly through the open doorway. The room is lit by tapers in a pair of sconces affixed to opposing walls.

Set on a table at one end of the long room are a couple of burning tapers and a pair of matching silver chalices. Behind the table, in his accustomed dark robes sits Nerezza in a high-backed wooden chair resplendent with gilded carvings. The image reminds Noah of an ancient woodcut of a sorcerer.

For making an ostentatious first impression, this room is far superior to the one Noah hired for Queen's business at the opposite end of the inn. This one is well appointed, containing not only the ornate chair in which Nerezza is seated, but also dark wood carvings all about the unlit fireplace, and pastoral paintings—nothing ostentatious, yet skillful enough to make the room's occupants feel a bit pampered.

"Ah, Serjeant Ames," says Nerezza, beckoning him with a smile. "Come in, come in."

Making a reciprocal show of amiability, Noah steps into the room. He glances over his shoulder at the end of the room opposite Nerezza, where another open door reveals a circummured garden easily thrice the size of this interior room. Its dimly lit footpath is paved with well-hewn slates, though their sheen threatens treacherous footing on an evening as damp as this.

Noah approaches Nerezza cautiously, feigning confidence all the while.

"Cognac, Serjeant?" asks Nerezza, holding up an old bottle with a stained label worn about the edges, its rustic lettering illegible. Without awaiting a response, Nerezza pours a little into each of the two chalices on the table. He lifts one and sniffs it fondly. "This bottle was found in my grandfather's cellar, which makes it quite old indeed. To frame it in the reckoning of your adoptive country, Serjeant, it would have been bottled during the reign of Henry the Seventh." He hands the other chalice to Noah.

"Ah, Her Majesty's grandfather," beams Noah. Behind the smile, his mind races to recall whether, in their earlier interview, he'd said anything that might have revealed that England is not the country of his birth. *Has the old man been doing research of his own?*

"Yes," says Nerezza, smiling. "The seventh Henry was a good papist, as the schism did not make its way to England until being willfully imported by his son, Henry the Eighth."

Noah smiles at the prospect of courteously trapping Nerezza into toasting an English king. "To Henry Tudor," he says, and brings the chalice to his firmly closed lips, making a show of savoring the cognac while allowing not a single drop to pass into his mouth. He sniffs it as he pretends to drink.

Over the strong scent of the cognac, he detects another scent, not offensive, but out of place. Try though he might, he can't identify it. "Pardon my boldness, sir, but religious differences seem to have a way of seeping into your every conversation."

"Please forgive my dotage," replies the old man. "Repeating oneself is an unavoidable infirmity of old age. I can well recall being a younger man, listening to conversations between older men, wondering why each of them said the same things over and over. I foolishly assumed that they must always have done so even when they were young, or that their age had caused them to forget what they'd recently said." He looks curiously at Noah. "Is the cognac not to your liking?"

"It has an unusual botanical scent," observes Noah equably. "I'd guess it's been barreled several times." He smiles. "I don't suppose any written records survive that might inform us."

Nerezza arches an eyebrow. "I am impressed, Serjeant, by both your precise sense of smell, and your knowledge of cognac."

Noah humbly dismisses the compliment. "I can profess no great knowledge of the vintner's art, I'm afraid." He paces a little, holding the top of the chalice by his fingertips. "Tell me, Master Nerezza, have you seen Dorsay's attendant in the past few days?"

The old man's eyes flash briefly, but his countenance rapidly settles into mild bemusement. "You refer to the homunculus?"

"To the dwarf, yes. 'Monk,' I believe he said his name was."

"Well," replies the old man, "come to think on it, I have not seen him in a week or so. But, then, I haven't seen *Dorsay* in about as long. Are you unable to find them?" He shrugs. "I suppose they may be together somewhere. If you'd care to leave a message with me, I'm certain they'll contact me at some point. They always do."

"You've heard from *neither* of them in a week?" asks Noah skeptically.

The old man sits up imperiously. Evidently, he expected no more than banter. "I didn't say quite that … but now that I think on it, I recall I did see Dorsay … perhaps three or four days ago."

"But not Monk?"

Nerezza sneers. "No," he says with a moue of distaste. "He generally approaches me only when necessary, which is how I prefer it." He gestures toward a nearby chair. "Won't you sit down?"

"I prefer to stand, thank you. As I'm sure you know, most of a barrister's life is spent applying the seat of the robes to the seat of the chair."

Nerezza rises. "Then let us walk together in the garden. Would that be to your liking?"

"Certainly," says Noah. Although he's uneasy at the prospect of being alone in the dark with this man, should things get out of hand he has both a dagger and a pistol.

Nerezza takes one of the tapers with them to illuminate their path. As they walk to the door, he asks. "Tell me, how are you feeling of late?"

"I'm quite well, thank you," says Noah, "though the late attempt on Her Majesty's life has complicated my *own* life a good deal. I'm busier than I would wish to be at this warm time of year—or what is *ordinarily* a warm time of year."

"Oh," says Nerezza, stepping over the threshold into the walled garden, "I was beginning to wonder whether this cool, damp weather is not a typical English summer."

Noah shrugs. "I can't say what a typical English summer is like, they are so variable." He sighs. Even in the presence of this dangerous man, he feels surprisingly at ease, almost relaxed. He reminds himself to remain on guard.

They meander slowly through the dark garden, each being careful to keep to the slate paving stones, to avoid slipping, or soiling boots.

"Have you made progress," asks Nerezza, "in your investigation?"

Noah shakes his head. "Not at all. But tell me more of yourself, my friend. I can't recall from our earlier conversation: Were you in Paris during the massacre of the Huguenots?"

Nerezza's eyes flash involuntarily. "Why, what a strange question!" he asks in apparent amazement. "I don't recall mentioning *where* I was during that horrible time. And, as I stand here this evening, I truly can't recall whether I was in Paris. Why do you ask?"

Noah turns to him and continues conversationally. "Truly?" he asks with a note of skepticism. "It seems to me that if I had been there, I should never forget it. The corpses of slaughtered Huguenots were everywhere, from what I've learned. Do you not recall seeing them?"

Nerezza turns to him with some irritation. "I remember them only too well, as I was *somewhere* in France. Perhaps you do not know, but the massacre spread from Paris like wildfire, running rampant throughout the countryside in the days and weeks that followed. I remember the corpses all too well. I just can't quite recall where in France they were ... or where *I* was."

Noah nods. "Curious. I suppose one's mind rather chooses to forget such things ... I mean horrors such as that." He shivers. "Do you know whether Monsieur Dorsay was in Paris at that time?"

Nerezza shrugs nonchalantly. "I have no idea where the gentleman was."

"Did you know him then?"

"I expect I did," says the old man, "although I can't recall how well."

"I take it," says Noah, "that both you and Monsieur Dorsay disapproved of the marriage between the protestant Henri de Navarre and the papist sister of King Charles?"

"Pshaw!" says the old man. "Every member of the True Faith disapproved. And to think: at this very moment, that erstwhile heathen Henri de Navarre is King of all France." He turns to Noah. "See here. What has the Huguenot massacre to do with the late attempt on the Queen's life? These events are separated by many years and Britain's South Sea."

Noah shrugs. "One can never tell when a dispute will spill over from the Continent into England herself. As I expect you'll recall, the massacre put an end to any possible nuptials between the king's brother and our Queen Elizabeth. And there were so *many* horrors in France about that time." Noah can feel his mental sharpness becoming somehow blunted. He can't quite recall if his sleep was interrupted last night, which might explain it. A few yards away is a tree stump carved into the shape of a chair. He wonders whether it's dry to the touch, so that he might take a brief rest there before continuing. "For instance," he says, "there was the tragic death of King Charles a short time later."

Nerezza waves dismissively. "I'd hardly term that death 'tragic.' The man was a vacillating weakling, first attempting to assuage the Huguenots, then those of the True Faith ... then the Huguenots once again."

"Oh," says Noah, as though straining to recall, "that's right. Didn't King Charles issue an edict of some kind shortly before his death that permitted the Huguenots to practice their faith in private?"

Nerezza scoffs. "In private, *indeed*. Under the Edict of Boulogne, they practiced their whorish religion in the bright light of day, an affront against the True Church and God Himself Who, looking down from heaven, must have felt nothing but contempt for all mankind."

Noah's beginning to feel sluggish and a bit woozy. The prospect of resting in the chair before him seems so inviting. What's more, now that he's so near, he can see another stump carved into the shape of a chair set at right angles from the first. Perhaps they might take a short rest.

Nerezza, evidently noticing Noah's lethargy, places a hand on his shoulder and leads him to one of the chairs. "Here. Sit, my friend. I fear that your recent anxiety has stolen your wind. Take a breath." Nerezza places the taper on a flat-hewn rock beside his chair.

Noah sits warily, though he decides his lethargy cannot be the result of the cognac. *I didn't drink any.* He feels a certain shortness of breath, as well. "I've brought with me a couple of items discovered in the course of my investigation," he says. "I wonder if you might offer your view on them, if you'd be so kind."

Now that Noah has agreed to rest a while, Nerezza seems more amused than offended by his questions. "Why, certainly. What have you found?"

Noah reaches into his pocket and places his hand on one of the Tarot cards. "This item was found very near the place where Admiral Coligny was shot, igniting the massacre of the Huguenots." He draws it from his pocket, and exhibits it to the old man. Nerezza's first reaction is utter shock, from which he quickly recovers.

The old man regards Noah with obvious suspicion, then relaxes into his former posture of bonhomie. "Why, of course," he says, "this is a Tarot card … depicting the Rota Fortunae."

Noah blinks a few times to clear his vision. "It is indeed. Does it seem familiar to you?"

Before replying, Nerezza looks at the card a long time, then equally long at Noah's face.

*He's weighing,* thinks Noah. *But weighing what?*

"Well," says Nerezza, "I have seen many like it—but so have thousands of others. Why would you ask *me* about it?" He feigns a search of his memory. "Oh!" he says. "I mentioned the Rota Fortunae when first we spoke, didn't I? Oh, well … yours is a natural mistake."

Noah glances at the door leading back into the private chamber. The distance seems so much greater now than it could possibly be, given the brevity of the journey here. "But the depiction of the four figures and their captions is precisely as you described to me."

As Nerezza shifts his posture, his movements seem to have become short and quick. Noah wonders whether Nerezza is agitated—or could it be that his own perceptions are somehow slowing down?

"The Wheel of Fortune," says Noah, his words seeming a bit slurred even to himself, "has been depicted in innumerable ways. This particular depiction matches your description perfectly."

"Has it occurred to you," says the old man, "that the room's occupant may have kept a Tarot deck there?"

"*Which* room?" asks Noah, feigning confusion. "I have mentioned no room."

"Well, naturally, I assumed—"

"*Which* room, sir?" repeats Noah impatiently. He wants to get this over with, so he can have this man arrested and go home to sleep.

"I naturally assumed you were speaking of the room from which the admiral was shot."

With effort, Noah arches an eyebrow. "Are you suggesting that the Duke of Guise was obsessed with the Wheel, sir?"

"The duke never occupied that room, Serjeant. It was not his home."

"Ah," says Noah. "So you are familiar with the room from which the admiral was shot, and are also aware that it was not located in the home of the Duke of Guise, as was rumored?"

"By now, *everyone* knows that," Nerezza says with open disdain.

"I have another item to show you, sir," says Noah, removing the other Tarot card from his robes and exhibiting it to Nerezza.

Nerezza jolts with alarm. He becalms himself a second time. "At the scene of which crime was this second card found?" Nerezza asks in open contempt.

Noah ignores the question and shoots back one of his own. "Why would you presume that it was found at the scene of a crime, sir? I've said nothing to suggest it." He blinks deliberately to clear his vision, and points to the card with his chin. "As you can see, the depiction of the Wheel of Fortune is identical." He holds them side by side, so the old man cannot avoid seeing them clearly, even in the candlelight.

Nerezza regards him contemptuously.

Noah points to the second card, his edginess flagging. He realizes that he has been drugged, which spurs him on to resolve this business without further delay. "This was found in the room of one King Charles the Ninth of France," says Noah. "My advisor on such matters informs me—"

The guilt on Nerezza's face is unmistakable. "Let me guess," he says. "Your advisor informs you that the king's symptoms might have been induced by poison?"

When Noah makes no reply, Nerezza smiles and, evidently emboldened by the combination of personal pride in his wicked achievements and the certainty of Noah's impending demise by poison, he becomes suddenly voluble.

"This card was no doubt found in a box with his highness's physic," says the old man, "and you thought it a good idea to speak with me about it, as I informed you at our last meeting that I am an apothecary by training."

Noah's breathing is labored, and he wonders if he's soon to die regardless how this meeting ends. "So you confess to these crimes?"

"Of course," says Nerezza, preening with wicked pride, "though they are no crimes, as they were done for the good of the Holy Church. And I would do the same again, a thousand times, if need be." Instead of running away as Noah would have expected, Nerezza resumes his seat, as though to tell a long tale.

"By now," says the old man, "you must know that you cannot leave this garden alive. As a Jew, you are bound for neither heaven nor hell, so my conscience is clear on that score. Instead, after death, you'll return to this veil of tears for another chance to accept the Christ as your savior before the Second Coming. This is the unique favor granted by our

Heavenly Father to his Chosen People. Nevertheless," he intimates, "if you will sit quietly while the cognac takes its inevitable course, I will do you the favor of satisfying your curiosity. So," he says, sitting up straight, "will you sit and listen patiently? If you do, I will tell you more than you could possibly have learned on your own. If you don't, I will have no choice but to put an end to our conversation, and you, without further ado."

Noah looks to the door to the private room. It seems impossibly far away now. What choice does he have? In his present condition, he cannot outrun even this old man. On the other hand, the old man evidently believes that he drank the poisoned cognac in an amount sufficient to kill him. Although there's a possibility he's right, Noah expects he's wrong. Either way, he wants to hear what this vile old bastard has to reveal to him.

He nods his assent, and the old man begins.

# CHAPTER 24

"I WAS BORN in the year of Our Lord 1525," says Nerezza, "to a drunkard father who beat my mother mercilessly. My father was a timberman who earned very little money, and drank up most of what he made. His occupation had but a single salutary effect on my mother and me, in that he was often required to leave our tiny cottage in the forest for a week or more, and travel from camp to camp to earn a living.

"My mother was a simple woman, virtuous and devoutly religious. She was also literate in Latin, if barely so, having learned her letters from the local nuns. Although, as a papist, she was forbidden to read the Bible, there was no general prohibition against teaching a woman to read. During the respites between my father's beatings, my mother, God rest her soul, had the foresight to pass her literacy on to me. I was quite young at the time, perhaps six or seven.

"One day, when I was eleven years of age, my father returned from the woods piss drunk, as you English might say, and beat my mother to death before my eyes. Even when it was quite obvious she was insensate, he would not stop striking her.

"He'd made the mistake of giving me a hatchet the year before, so that I could pretend to be a woodsman such as he. On this occasion, I imitated him quite closely. I grabbed my hatchet and chopped off his right hand. While he was still roaring over his grievous wound, too overcome with horror to turn his wrath on me as yet, I cut off his other hand, as well, and, as he gaped at me stupidly, I buried my hatchet in his face, which split his skull in two, and he quickly bled out on the floor.

"Our parish priest, who was passing through the woods and overheard the tumult, rushed in when it was all over. He looked at my parents' bodies, and then at me, and recognized at once the sequence of events that had taken place. He was evidently familiar with our family's troubles through my mother's frequent confessions, you see, and took pity on me. Deciding that there was nothing to be gained by an inquiry that would inevitably find me guilty of the horrible crime of patricide, he called in confidence upon two of his parishioners who already knew of my father's abuse, and instructed them to bury the bodies many miles away. Upon their return, we all scrubbed the cottage with vinegar until our arms ached.

"When the priest realized I was literate, he impressed me into service of the Church. I did everything; scrubbing, milking, laundry, every menial task. I worked extremely hard and rarely said a word, as I owed my life to him and to the Church. I'd been there barely a year when he recommended my services to the staff at Queen Bona's town home. There, they impressed upon me the need to keep confidential anything I might learn there, and offered me employment."

Noah, who's been listening impassively to this point, at last makes the connection in his mind. The man seated before him is almost certainly the man who murdered his parents. Suddenly, Admiral Coligny and King Charles the Ninth vanish from his thoughts.

"What does 'Nerezza' mean?" croaks Noah, lacking spittle.

The old man, evidently surprised by the interruption, replies: "It means 'the dark one.' It's a translation of the name that was given me in my youth, 'Ciemnoci.'"

Feeling almost too weak to raise his arms, Noah gapes forlornly at the old man. The most rudimentary knowledge of the Italian and Polish languages might have enabled him to solve this mystery weeks ago. Instead, he's staring death straight in the face—for if the cognac doesn't kill him, the old man certainly must try.

Nerezza laughs softly at his expression. "In case you're wondering, it was your aura that gave you away. Once I made the connection after our first interview, I feared that you would make the connection yourself, based upon what I had told you of my life. But then I remembered. I told you I was *Lithuanian* by birth, making no mention of Poland, and I realized that you, a smug, self-concerned Englishman (if

English is how you fancy yourself) would never have learned that the kingdom from which I came was known as "Lithuania *and Poland*." I realized that I was safe for at least as long as it would take me to confirm that you yourself were born in Poland, which was no great feat. You think yourself so much more worldly than you are. It's pathetic, really."

The old man shrugs and resumes his tale. "I was employed by the queen and was loyal to her, as far as it goes, but my true loyalty was always to Mother Church, the place where I'd found safety and understanding for the first time, excepting only the arms of my blessed mother, of course. I reported to Church officials about various goings-on at Queen Bona's townhouse, but felt no particular misgivings about it, as I knew the queen to be a woman of faith, except for a few points on which she took a stiff-necked position contrary to Church teaching. But there were few such points of disagreement, and they were in any event not doctrinal, and so I maintained my double position for some time without qualm."

Noah despises the old man's easy rationalizations. "And were you *paid* for the information you supplied to the Church?"

Nerezza snarls and shoots back, "Are *you* paid for your barrister's services?"

"I've never betrayed anyone for pay," says Noah with open disgust.

"How fortunate for you that you never needed to," the old man replies sourly. "Will you listen to the rest of the tale, or are you too tired to continue living?"

Noah considers how long it would take him to brandish either the dagger or the pistol in his robes. But he decides the time is not yet ripe. "Pray, continue," he mutters.

"One day—a day I shall never forget—there was a public burning of a woman. But the Act of Faith is not the reason I'll never forget that day. As I looked down on the spectators from the queen's balcony, I saw the most beautiful young woman I'd ever seen in my life, perhaps ever *shall* see. Her aura was unique, clean and burnished. I fell in love with her immediately. But when she saw me looking her way, she ran away in fright."

"So, you were already seeing auras by that time?" asks Noah.

"Since birth," says Nerezza, nodding contemplatively. "And I never forget an aura. Some years later, I accompanied Queen Bona's men on an errand to the Jewish village that occupied a parcel of her land. And when I saw this beautiful woman again, I was again smitten. Her aura was the same, but her face and form had matured and were beyond admiration. She was a goddess—"

Noah looks away in disgust. "Spare me the attempt to dignify your lust," he says.

"I separated from the Queen's men and tried to strike up a conversation with her, but she would have none of it."

"Perhaps she detected *your* aura," mutters Noah despondently.

Nerezza seems deeply offended but, strangely, not angered. "Perhaps it is as you say. I cannot see my own aura."

"*I* can," replies Noah darkly, leaving the insult implied.

"Shortly thereafter, King Philip the Second of Spain married your Queen Mary and became King of England."

"In name only," Noah reminds him.

"We could dispute that, I suppose," says Nerezza, "but perhaps you'd rather I put your mind at ease about something else. You can stop wondering where we obtained the keys to the Tower records room."

"From King Philip?"

Nerezza nods smugly. "His Majesty, as he was known in England, sent copies of all the Tower's keys to the Holy See. We could barely believe our good fortune when we discovered that you English fools had not changed a single lock since King Philip's departure more than forty years ago." He resumes his tale. "Some years later, a dispute arose between Queen Bona and King Philip concerning payments allegedly due from King Philip on a mortgage."

"A dispute?" says Noah incredulously. "You mean he refused to *pay* her."

"Queen Bona also refused to clear King Philip's land of Jews. It would have been deemed unbefitting for a Christian prince to own property occupied by a tribe of Jews, now wouldn't it?"

"Unbefitting?" snorts Noah derisively, even in his perilous and weakened state. "I suppose you deemed it would better befit said prince to authorize you and Pappacoda to poison Queen Bona and burn all the Jews residing on the parcel? Befitting, indeed," he says with contempt. "It was *you* who poisoned Queen Bona, was it not?"

Nerezza grins and bows in place. "At your service. Some months later, I received orders to burn the Jewish village. It was not out of my own religious prejudice, of course. The night before, I even visited the village."

"How very Christian of you," says Noah darkly.

From the inn's first storey comes a woman's wail, a high piercing shriek, followed by a long moan. Though there are words in her cry, Noah cannot make them out from the garden.

Nerezza appears less surprised than unnerved by the wailing, as though he'd dreaded to hear it but expected it might come. "From a hilltop on the way to the village," says the old man, as though he could yet see it in his mind's eye, "I could see a young woman on a horse, pulling a cart with a child hidden under an oilcloth. They were escaping into the woods. I could not see the child, but I could see his aura." He turns to Noah. "I never saw it again until our first interview, and it took a great deal of thought for me to remember it. But you *were* the child who escaped the village. Were you not?"

"Is that all it took for you to realize?"

Nerezza shakes his head. "No. It took one more thing. When I caught a glimpse of the young girl who resides in your home, I nearly fell over. The resemblance between her and your dear mother is uncanny. Never have I seen two people resemble each other so closely, unless they were twins. The girl's *aura* was different, but otherwise she and your dear mother could have been the same person."

Despair begins to seep into Noah's heart. "And the attempt on Queen Elizabeth? That was also you?"

Nerezza snickers. "Our *first* attempt. Give us another chance." He resumes his tale. "As I was about to tell you, your mother arrived a few hours after your escape. At dawn, I visited her in secret and offered to spare her alone in exchange for her hand." He sighs. "But, in one of the great tragedies of my life, she declined. She was simply too proud to leave her husband and her village."

"How *awful* that must have been for you!" says Noah, dripping with sarcasm.

Nerezza ignores the remark. "So, just after sunrise, we forced everyone into the synagogue and burned it, precisely as ordered."

"And burned *them*, you mean," says Noah. "You burned everyone in my world, you bloody bastard."

Nerezza rises from his seat, and stands with his back to the inn to block any hope of escape.

Just as Noah is about to reach for his pistol, he realizes something in the vicinity has changed. His mind races, even in his blunted state, as the moment to act has arrived. But first he needs to recognize what's changed. What is it? *What is it?* Then he realizes that the private room is black, which means that the sconces have been extinguished and the door leading to the taproom has been closed.

As Nerezza appears not to have noticed this new state of affairs, Noah concludes that these are likely to be favorable developments. He wonders if they have anything to do with the earlier wail coming from upstairs, and decides it would be to his advantage to play for time.

"And this is what you invited me to hear?" Noah asks in a tone so calm it frightens him a little.

Nerezza scowls in the taper light, his expression a strange mixture of curiosity and determination.

*I must hold his attention away from the doorway.*

Noah asks, "You haven't the least curiosity about my reaction to what you have said?"

Nerezza equivocates. "Very well," he says suspiciously, "what are your final thoughts?"

Noah makes a show of slowly inhaling and exhaling, as though preparing to deliver a valedictory to his own life. "First," says Noah quietly, "I thank you for your honesty, as it was most important at this perilous moment for me to be absolutely certain you are indeed the man who committed all these crimes, some against humanity, some against others, some against me personally. For those of us with remaining morals, honesty sets the mind right."

Nerezza bows ceremoniously with an expression betraying enough pride to take the compliment seriously.

"Second," Noah continues, "it fulfills a lifelong curiosity of mine to learn that scum-sucking scoundrels such as you are capable of rationalizing the most disgusting violations of the laws of God and man, asserting that your crimes are forgiven—or even *ennobled*—on grounds that God has awarded you some special commission, when in fact you're in it for the *money* as much as any common cutpurse or highwayman ever hanged at the Tower of London." He smirks. "And at least *they* have the courage to be honest with themselves.

"Third—"

"Get to the point!" says Nerezza impatiently, his pleasure having obviously evaporated.

Noah had expected it would goad Nerezza to imply that scoundrels such as he are a penny a dozen, and, which is worse, that they occupy a rung on the moral ladder lower than common thieves. But then a memory from the past year comes to him unbidden, that of an assassin lying in the woods in Dorset, losing the last of his lifeblood through a hole in his gut drilled by Noah's shot.

"Third," Noah repeats, "it relieves me of moral culpability for your imminent death."

His confident effrontery opens Nerezza's eyes wide in terror. The old man draws a long dagger and points it at Noah's torso.

At that moment, Noah reaches his hand into his robe and places it around the stock of his pistol—only to discover that an obstruction behind him prevents him from bringing it to bear. At first he expects that the obstruction is the back of the carved chair he's sitting on, but as he turns to find out, he finds that his hand and his whole body are restrained by a huge arm belonging to a man, a *mountain* of a man, who's silently surprised him from behind. In what Noah expects will be his last act on this earth, he looks to his captor's face and is bewildered to see that he recognizes it.

It's Francis of the Tower Guard. Noah's first thought is that Francis has turned against him, just as the Bennetts have done. But he doubts it almost immediately, for Francis's rapt attention is fixed on a second silent man with his long sword held up high, standing next to Nerezza.

Noah watches in amazement as the second man brings his sword down like an executioner's axe on Nerezza's outstretched dagger hand. With one mighty blow, the sword severs Nerezza's wrist, propelling both hand and blade to the slate with a meaty thump and metallic clatter.

Nerezza opens his eyes and mouth wide with horror, too shocked to utter a sound. His face goes white while blood gushes from his arm, forming rapidly into a gory pool on the dark ground. He falls to his knees.

Remembering that Francis's shoulder was wounded only recently, Noah twists to try to free himself from his grasp. But Francis is simply too strong, and Noah too weakened to break free. Francis mutters his assurance, "No harm will come to you, suh. Don't get involved in this domestic matter."

*Domestic matter?* Noah turns toward Nerezza again and sees that the swordsman has faded into the shadows, replaced by an aging woman in worn but respectable clothing. While Nerezza watches, making the soft noises of a wounded animal facing its end, the woman picks up his dagger and brandishes it in his face.

"He is dead! You have killed him!" the woman shouts in Nerezza's face. She points her chin at Noah. "With the poison you laid for *this* man, whom you hate so much!" Her accent is French. Noah expects that she is the woman who tried to speak with Esther in the rain. *"Je suis sa femme,"* she'd said at the time. *I am his wife.*

Nerezza looks up at her pathetically.

"Gaston is dead?" he grunts.

"Not Gaston, you idiot. *Claude* is dead!" she says.

*"Who?"* asks the maimed old man.

"My son!" she weeps. "The one you call 'homunculus!'"

His face becomes a mask of hate, as he snarls up at her. "Why do you trouble me with this report? Go tell his father Gaston!"

She glowers at him as though he'd spat in her face. "His father is *not* Gaston, you fool! *You* are his father!"

"What?" he cries. "No. It cannot be."

"It is true," she replies firmly. "You have starved him and left him dying of thirst ever since he returned with his wound. He followed you. He saw this man leave the chalice when you went to the garden, and drank its contents down." She grabs the old man by the lapels. "You have killed him! You have murdered your own son!"

This knowledge is apparently too much for the old man to bear. At first, he's immobilized and silent, but his bewilderment soon turns to denial, and he points his stump at her in accusation, as though his hand and index finger were still attached.

"You are a deceiver, like all women. Hence! Away, you whore!"

Overcome with grief, she plunges the dagger deep into his chest. Noah cringes to hear the *chunk* made by the blade as it penetrates the meat of the old man and strikes his ribs.

Instead of succumbing at once, Nerezza opens his eyes even wider, which Noah would have thought impossible.

Noah's given up on Francis, but jerks his head around to see whether the swordsman may yet be present. "Will no one *stop* this woman?" he cries. "Take this man into custody!" But his cries are greeted with silence.

Taking no notice of his plea, the woman withdraws the knife and plunges it into the old man again and again until, at last, out of sheer exhaustion from her spent rage, she draws the knife out for the last time and watches him collapse face first onto the ground.

She voids her rheum and spits it at the corpse.

Then, she turns the dagger on herself.

Noah uses the last of his dwindling store of energy to try to free himself. "Someone, stop her! Can't you see she's mad?"

Even in her fury, the woman has the presence of mind to look him in the eye softly enough to let him know that she appreciates his wish to save her from destruction.

But she plunges the knife into her own chest and collapses in a heap next to the scourge for whom she bore a child so many years before, a son whose benign spirit might have overcome his physical deformity, had it not been crushed by a father's wicked rejection.

# CHAPTER 25

**SHORTLY AFTER DAYBREAK,** Noah is awakened by Francis of the Tower Guard.

"C'mon, suh," says Francis. "Sir Walter's up and wants to see ye straight away."

Momentarily disoriented, Noah glances about. He's in a room in the Yeoman's quarters.

"How'd ye sleep, suh?" asks Francis.

"Not badly, I suppose," replies Noah, rubbing his eyes, "but too short by a long shot." In fact, Noah feels as though he was wrestling with angels all night. Yet, never once did he dream of Nerezza or the horrors of the previous evening. Instead, two figures recurred in his dreams: his nemesis, the Earl of Essex, who's about to be released from custody, and his dearest friend Sir Henry Neville, whom he hasn't seen in more than a year but who's expected home in a matter of days. The two were linked in his dreams, although in some perilous way he can no longer recall.

"Well," says Francis, as he absentmindedly folds a blanket that appears no bigger than a handkerchief in his massive hands, "I'm to accompany you to Sir Walter. *Oh*, and please be careful not to speak to no one, suh. Sir Walter's orders."

As they approach Sir Walter's office, there's a man of friendly demeanor sitting outside, evidently waiting to be called in. Noah is shocked to recognize him as his personal savior, the swordsman who disarmed Nerezza by cutting off his hand. Noah stops to thank him, but Francis ushers him past and into Sir Walter's chamber before a word can be exchanged.

Sir Walter is seated behind his desk, cleaning his tobacco pipe.

When he sees Noah enter with Francis, he tucks it away in a long cloth pouch, and rises as energetically as ever.

"Good morning, Serjeant," he says. He turns to Francis. "Wait outside, please." Francis nods and closes the door behind him.

Sir Walter motions for Noah to be seated. "Bit of bloody work this past evening, eh?" he asks. "I've spoken to Francis and the other fellow sitting outside, and taken a few notes." He shuffles a few papers on his desk. "Evidently you were invited by Monsieur Nerezza to visit him at the Saracen's Head Inn last evening. Is that right? It says he offered you poisoned cognac, which you accepted but did not drink." Sir Walter raises his eyebrows inquiringly.

"Correct," says Noah.

"Nevertheless," says Sir Walter, reading from his paper, "you were nearly overcome by poisonous fumes."

Noah nods. "So says the physician, and I have no reason to doubt it."

"These notes say that Nerezza confessed to you that he and his companion, Monsieur Dorsay, were responsible for the late attempt on Her Majesty's life. Is that so?"

"'Tis," replies Noah.

"And he told you they gained entry to the Tower's records room using a key supplied long ago by the now-deceased King Philip. Correct?"

Noah inhales deeply. "That's basically correct, but—"

Sir Walter holds his hand up. "For present purposes, Serjeant, I'd appreciate it if you'd simply answer my questions as I pose them to you. No need to volunteer anything." He returns to his notes. "According to the two gentlemen outside, you told them Monsieur Nerezza drew a dagger, and that you then drew your sword and cut off his hand. When he continued to resist, you disarmed him and, in a desperate struggle, you used his own dagger to run him through. Then the two gentlemen outside, having been alerted by your lovely niece Esther, found you nearly unconscious in the garden with the dead man at your feet."

Noah is dumbstruck.

Sir Walter reviews his notes. "Yes, that's what my notes say." He smiles and folds his hands on the desk.

Noah leans forward and speaks confidentially. "Sir Walter, I don't know what they told you, but that's not what happened at all. Why, those two gentlemen restrained me while they cut off Nerezza's hand, and allowed the mother of his child to stab him—and then herself—to death."

Sir Walter appears confused. "Allow me to review my notes." His eyes run down his notes and when he's done, he shakes his head emphatically. "No, that's not what it says here. Not at all." Sir Walter raises his forefinger, as though to emphasize a coming point, just as Lord Burghley was wont do while he yet lived. "Please remain quietly seated." He goes to the door and admits the two men from the hallway. "Gentlemen! Please enter."

The door opens smartly and Francis enters, followed by the other fellow, who smiles as though he hadn't a care in the world.

Sir Walter addresses Noah. "Do you know these two men, Serjeant?"

"I know Warder Francis, of course, but I'm sorry to say I haven't been formally introduced to the other gentleman."

"You don't even know his name?" asks Sir Walter incredulously.

"No," replies Noah.

Sir Walter turns to the two men. "Francis, could you repeat what happened between Serjeant Ames and the man Nerezza at the Saracen's Head last evening?"

Francis seems a bit confused. "Well, suh, I *can* tell ye it was a bloody scene when we arrived. But Master Nerezza was already dead, so, in answer to your question, I cannot—of my own eyewitness—tell ye what happened between Serjeant Ames and that Nerezza fella. We found a bottle of cognac that smelled so bad we wouldn't so much as sniff it."

"And the fight?" asks Sir Walter.

Francis shakes his head. "Didn't see it, suh," he sniffs. "Wasn't there."

Sir Walter turns to the normal-sized man. "And *you*, Chester?"

"Beggin' yaw pahdon, Suh Walter," Chester says, bowing to Noah. "My name's Chestuh, suh. I'm—or I *have* been—jailer at Cambridge

Castle. Pleased to make your acquaintance. I wouldn't be here, but for your son-in-law's good sense in firin' off warnin' shots from his cannon."

Oh, so *this* is Chester! Noah nods.

Sir Walter continues. "Chester, what did *you* see of the fight at the Saracen's Head last night?"

"Nothin', suh," he says, wide-eyed. "Didn't get there in time to see anythin' of the fight." He beams at Noah. "But, as for me, suh, I'd take Serjeant Ames's word for it any day. That Nerezza fella was a snake if ever I saw one."

"But this is absurd," says Noah incredulously. "Surely the condition of the corpse would show what truly happened." He turns to Francis and Chester. "Where is Nerezza's corpse? And the corpses of the others?"

Francis replies for the two of them. "*Corpses,* suh?"

Noah is non-plussed. "Yes, the bodies!"

"Oh, the bodies!" says Francis. "No, suh, we don't keep those. Just the heads, usually. You can see 'em on pikes at the near end o' London Bridge."

Noah stares at Francis incredulously. "There's more than one head?"

"*Three,* suh," replies Francis. "Nerezza, Dorsay, and the little fella Monk."

"Dorsay!" exclaims Noah. "How did *he* die?"

"Strangest thing, suh. We found his body in a room he'd taken at the Saracen's Head. Looked as though he'd been knifed to death. Somebody'd taken a violent dislike to 'im, suh. We suspect his wife lost her temper when it turned out their son had died o' poison. Turns out the little fella'd returned to London with a gunshot wound, and he'd apparently been healing fine till he got a hold of the poisoned chalice meant for you. We'll find out for sure if we ever get our hands on the woman."

"Which, of course, you never will," says Noah darkly.

"Thank you, gentlemen," says Sir Walter to Francis and Chester. "You may return to your duties."

As soon as the door closes, Sir Walter turns to Noah with a stern glint in his eye. "So, Serjeant. Now you know what happened. Has it come clear to you yet?"

Noah looks at Sir Walter in exasperation, but he keeps his voice down. "Are you mad? That's not what happened at all. They not only *saw* the whole thing. They *did* the whole thing. I don't understand what you're attempting to cover up with this story."

Sir Walter leans over his desk toward Noah. "If we were to provide a full account of what happened, it would come out that Nerezza murdered your parents forty years ago, and a continent away."

Noah shrugs. "So?"

"So," says Sir Walter as though it should be obvious, "with such knowledge, a skilled prosecutor could prosecute our favorite Serjeant for murder."

"*Murder?* Don't be absurd."

"Well," says Sir Walter, "if you suspected Nerezza of murdering your parents, then *perhaps* you took him up on his invitation just to get him alone, and kill him with the pistol and dagger you'd brought along for just such an occasion."

"I didn't suspect him of *that*, but only of the late attempt on the Queen's life and the long-ago murders of Admiral Coligny and King Charles."

Sir Walter regards him skeptically. "If you didn't so much as suspect him of murdering your parents, perhaps you would have had a single, pure motive." He arches an eyebrow. "But how would you *prove* that?"

"Prove it? I'd have no need to prove anything. I'd be a criminal defendant. The burden of proof would rest with the Crown."

"The Crown would have to prove each element of the crime beyond a reasonable doubt, it's true," replies Sir Walter sagely, "but a jury would be *permitted* to conclude, based upon the evidence, that you *did* suspect Nerezza of your parents' murder. Is this not so?"

Noah is brought up short by Sir Walter's impeccable reasoning. "Sir Walter, did you develop this knowledge all on your own?" When Sir Walter declines to answer, Noah protests. "Sir Walter, I *cannot* swear falsely."

"You needn't. You shall be questioned by Sir Robert, who already knows precisely which questions to ask, and which to avoid."

"How could he *possibly* know that?"

Sir Walter knits his brow, as though incredulous that Noah could be such a simpleton. "How do you *suppose* he'd know that?" Noah studies Sir Walter's expression, which all but cries out *because the cover-up was all his idea.*

"Oh," says Noah. "But, when all is said and done, I shall fail to provide Her Majesty with information she needs to have in order to make such decisions as she must for the sake of the realm."

Sir Walter's patience is evidently nearing exhaustion. He turns on his heel in exasperation. "And why on God's green earth would Her Majesty need to know that that bastard murdered your parents? *Hmm?* Do you suppose she might declare war on Poland for your personal vengeance? Don't be stupid, Noah. This is family business—of *your* family—not the Tudors."

Noah's feeling rather defeated. "Her Majesty is *most* in need of full and accurate information," he mutters uncertainly.

Sir Walter pounds his fist once on the desk, and his face reddens. "Damn you, Noah! More lives than yours depend on this subterfuge, so you have no choice in the matter. Besides, Sir Robert now has the 'information,' as you call it, so your duty's been discharged on that point. But, is correct information on an irrelevant point truly what Her Majesty needs *most*?" He rises and begins pacing. "Do you wish to know what Her Majesty *truly* needs most? She needs attendants who will ferret out those who mean her harm, who will obtain a confession at the risk of their own lives, and slay a suspect who confesses to such an attempt and seeks to escape punishment."

He stands over Noah aggressively, and emphasizes each of his next words with a gentle but firm poke of Noah's chest. "*That's* what Her Majesty needs most," he says, "and that's what she has in you, damn it all! And I'll be damned myself if I allow you to throw it all away, as well as the careers of those two fine men out there who did your dirty work for you."

The chamber is quiet for a good half-minute before Noah ventures another question. "I see your point, Sir Walter, but ... may I ask a question of my own?"

"Certainly."

"Why," whispers Noah, "did Francis restrain me while Chester cut off Nerezza's hand? Why didn't they just *arrest* him?"

Sir Walter rolls his eyes in exasperation, and answers in an intense whisper. "Because they're *men*, Noah, not *gods*! They witnessed Monk's death by poisoning, watched his mother weep inconsolably, and waited outside Dorsay's room while she finished him off in his sleep for sending the dwarf on a dangerous errand with insufficient support. Then, when Chester secretly entered the garden (he was first to arrive there, though you didn't know it), he overheard Nerezza's confession to numerous crimes, including the attempt to murder Her Majesty and the actual murder of your whole village. Francis was even further beyond restraint, of course, as he now had the murderer of his beloved Sally virtually in his grasp. Add to that Nerezza's drawing a dagger on you in order to escape punishment. With all that, it would have been a wonder had they *not* done precisely as they did. You owe them both quite a debt of gratitude!"

Noah stares at his feet. "I do indeed, Sir Walter. And not only them, but you and Sir Robert, as well. I doubt I could ever lie to Her Majesty, but unless she puts me to it, I'll rest with the story you have devised."

Sir Walter breathes a sigh of relief. "Well, there you are, then." He leans toward Noah again. "One final thing. We're fairly certain no one witnessed anything. No one still living, anyhow. Francis and Chester were the only ones to hear your niece's warning, and the only ones to come to her aid. They went unseen into the Saracen's Head and were unseen by anyone in the garden, except for you. But you must ensure that your niece never reports anything other than the agreed-upon tale to anyone, for as long as she lives. I'm in earnest about this, Noah. She holds many lives in her hands."

"And I shall ensure she does not let them slip," Noah assures him. "She's a very good person."

"Indeed. She saved your life. She awaits you now in the Warders' mess."

Noah furrows his brow. "That seems an inappropriate place to keep her so many hours."

Sir Walter smirks. "It's as far from you as we could persuade her to go. She'd been kept from you last night. We allowed her to peek into your room as you slept, just to assure herself that you were in health, but I wouldn't allow her to remain by your side while you slept. I wanted to speak with you first when you awoke, for obvious reasons."

"She's been kept under guard?" asks Noah.

Sir Walter laughs aloud. "Hardly. At least a half-dozen Warders have waited on her hand and foot since she arrived, brought her a soft chair, fetched her a blanket, and kept watch on her as she slept. A girl that comely shall never suffer for lack of male attention."

Noah's feelings are all aswirl. "Sir Walter," he says, "you have shown yourself to be my loving friend for the past year. May I prevail upon you by asking a question that may seem impertinent?"

Sir Walter nods curiously.

Noah sighs. "I have been told that Sir Henry Neville has come under severe criticism at court of late."

Sir Walter seems surprised. "Upon what grounds?"

"The failure of his embassage to obtain repayment of Her Majesty's loan to the King of France."

Sir Walter searches his memory for some time. He shakes his head. "Rubbish," he replies. "Who told you this?"

The image of Henry Cuffe, Essex's secretary, surfaces in Noah's mind. "Someone I'd rather not mention. But why do you ask?"

"Because someone has deliberately planted a false notion in your mind, and it seems the kind of thing one does for a reason, although if you can't tell me who it was, I can't help you to discern his possible motive." Sir Walter collapses into his chair. "Now go and find your niece."

Feeling utterly bedraggled, Noah traverses the hallway to the Warder's mess, drawn by the light banter of young men. Among their youthful voices, he hears the familiar husky voice of his niece.

As he passes through the doorway into the mess, Esther is momentarily stunned to see him, as though she cannot believe he's alive and well. Sitting there, holding her little court, she so resembles Noah's mother now-avenged that he's equally stunned.

The gravity of Nerezza's crime against his parents weighs down upon Noah at precisely the same moment that his spirits are lifted up by the countervailing certainty that Esther's resemblance to his mother is no accident. As he was saved by Esther's second sight (something else she has in common with his mother), it seems undeniable that Esther *is* in some sense his mother, returned to him at the precise moment when she might protect him from the fanatic who killed her and her husband. Although Noah knows he can never express such a thought to another living soul, still he stands amazed by his own certainty.

One by one, Esther's admirers notice her distraction and cease talking, following her gaze to Noah, until silence reigns and all eyes are firmly fixed upon him.

Esther tosses off her blanket, rises from her chair, and runs into Noah's arms, burying her face deep in his chest, weeping tears of relief. Though he's tempted to join her in weeping, the Warders rise as one and cheer his name.

"Hurrah for Serjeant Ames!" they cry. "The Queen's true protector!"

It takes him but a moment to realize that they've been misinformed that he heroically, single-handedly detected and slew the Queen's latest assailant.

At that moment, with his precious cousin nestled protectively in his arms, while he's being cheered for acts of courage he's never performed, it seems to him that such lies have been cheered the world over since time immemorial by countless rooms full of eager young men prepared to sacrifice themselves on the altar of some lie disguised as a higher cause. The madness is not local, then, but universal.

The world is mad. And ever has been. And will be forever and ever. World without end. Amen.

He wonders what malign madness will descend upon them next, and suddenly feels terribly weary.

"Let's go home," he mutters to Esther, and she nods in agreement.

# CHAPTER 26

**A SPONTANEOUS ACCOLADE** erupts among the Warders at the Tower gate as Noah and Esther ride out on horseback. While it's nowhere near the frenzy a gentile would have encountered for slaying the Queen's assailant, still, it's far more than a pair of Jews could have expected.

The morning's mist has begun to thin out, leaving the promise of clear sunshine. Noah rides Bucklebury, his accustomed black steed. He pats the horse's flank as well as he can from the saddle.

Esther's been persuaded by the Warders to ride her mount side-saddle "like a lady," instead of straddling it "like a soldier."

Noah turns to his niece. "Thank you for saving my life, Esther."

"I worried that I'd be too late in bringing the news to the Tower," she says, "but thank God I was just in time." She looks with dismay at her own current posture on horseback. "If I'd ridden to the Tower in this fashion, I would certainly have been too late."

Noah looks out at the road ahead. "Which path shall we take?" he asks, feeling a sense of freedom he thought he'd lost forever. "The choice is yours."

"Let us turn right here," she suggests.

Noah's surprised. "That will take us toward Lothbury, a bit out of our way, but that's fine."

"Why do you say Lothbury is out of our way?" she asks.

He regards her askance. "Well," he says, "it's not the most direct route to Holborn."

"Your good friend lives in Lothbury, no?"

"Sir Henry?" he says. "Why, yes, he does. But he's not home from Paris just yet."

She smiles smugly. "He *is* home now."

He turns to her skeptically. "And you know that … how?"

She shrugs. Evidently, she wishes he'd simply stop asking about such things.

Noah gazes at her incredulously. "We really must have a serious talk about this … skill you have." But he resolves to follow her lead to Lothbury without further inquiry. He knows a few ways to get there, but expects she knows them *all*, in that magical way of hers.

As they turn west on Lothbury at last, she says, "You are sorry the dwarf was killed. No?"

"I am," he says, seeing no reason to deny it, and expecting she'd see right through him anyhow.

"Why?" she asks.

He sighs. "Because he'd had a terrible time of it, being reared by that pack of wolves, never having a proper home or loving parents, being so sorely mistreated by the man who was in fact his father. And, of course, there was his disfigurement, which surely rendered it impossible for him to carve for himself. He seemed a kindhearted soul to me, for the brief time I knew him. And I expect his participation in this foul treason was not done by choice."

"Perhaps he didn't know that's what he was doing," she suggests.

"Indeed," he replies. "He may have simply been sent to seize some papers without much of an explanation."

Up ahead, the mist has cleared entirely, leaving only a few diffuse clouds in the sky. Bright sunshine illuminates several luggage-laden carts drawn to the side of the street before Sir Henry's familiar town home, and an unmistakable figure heaves its substantial girth out of the foremost cart.

It's Sir Henry, who appears only slightly hobbled by his accustomed gout. Noah expects that Sir Henry has been unable to replenish his supply of the curative colchicum prescribed for him years ago by Doctor Lopez.

Noah and Esther pick up the pace and hail Sir Henry.

"Master Ambassador!" cries Noah as he draws up Bucklebury and dismounts. Esther follows suit.

"Serjeant Ames!" comes the reply. "So good to see you!" Sir Henry beams at him broadly.

"Where is the lovely Lady Anne?" asks Noah.

"She's staying with her parents overnight," replies Sir Henry, "while Walker and I open the rest of the house." He turns to Esther. "And who is this vision of Arabian beauty, Ames? I've half a mind to have you arrested."

"On what charge?" laughs Noah.

"Surrounding yourself with women more beautiful than you deserve," says Sir Henry.

"Be careful not to craft your statute so broadly, Sir Henry, or every man in Christendom should wind up in Fleet Prison."

"Especially your humble servant," says Sir Henry jovially. "Still," he says, "your selection of female companionship makes the rest of us quite envious. I should have thought that obvious."

"Oh, it's obvious all right. It's simply not a crime." Noah introduces Esther formally. "Sir Henry Neville, this is my cousin Esther who has recently come from Poland to live with us."

"Charmed," says Sir Henry taking Esther's hand and bowing. He turns to Noah. "Best keep this beauty away from Cheerful, Ames. He's staying here in the Lothbury house, I expect."

"Too late," says Noah. "They already know each other passably well."

Sir Henry regards Noah skeptically. "Well, I suppose we have no choice but to trust in *your* judgment, Serjeant. But my nephew's? Well—"

"I know all about David, Sir Henry. But he's behaved himself as a true gentleman in relation to Esther … in Lady Jessica's rather strict view."

Sir Henry shrugs. "Then, who am I to say nay? I wish them both the best of good fortune." He turns to the house. "I was just about to go inside, Ames, and open some windows upstairs. Gets blasted hot in summer. Care to come inside?"

As they cross the threshold, Sir Henry tosses some letters on a table in the entryway and trots off to relieve himself.

Esther smiles at Noah. "Your friend is … remarkable, as you might say. So much imagination, he is almost … mad!"

Noah wonders how she could possibly detect so much of Sir Henry's character, having known him for no more than a few moments. Thinking that perhaps she got it wrong, he's about to ask her about it when his eye is caught by the papers Sir Henry tossed on the table.

While he durst not touch them, two openly show enough information to excite his curiosity. One is a receipt dated August 4, 1600 (only a few days ago) from the Stationer's Register. Three titles are listed on the receipt: *As You Like It, Henry V,* and *Much Ado About Nothing.* Only one such title is familiar to Noah, that being the play about Henry the Fifth which was mounted just last year, if indeed it's the same play.

Following his gaze, Esther asks, "What is the Stationer's Register?"

He scratches his head. "It's the place where a playwright registers his works so that no company can mount his play without his permission."

Next to the receipt lies a very ordinary-looking envelope addressed to Sir Henry, which wouldn't have caught Noah's eye but that it bears the familiar outline of a bootprint, the very same left by Cuffe on the note dropped on the floor that day at the Saracen's Head. *Curious.*

Noah turns to Esther, whose eye has followed his own to the same envelope. "That message is wicked," whispers Esther. "You must destroy it before your friend opens it."

Noah looks at her in shock. "I cannot do that, young lady," he protests. "Besides, it would be pointless, anyhow. The man who wrote it resides here in London and can contact Sir Henry in many other ways."

Henry's heavy footsteps approach from the rear of the house.

"See here, Ames," he says, "I'd love to spend time with the two of you, but Walker and I have our work cut out for us."

"Sir Henry, would you care to join us for dinner at Holborn?" asks Noah. "I can tell you what's happened while you were away."

Sir Henry smiles. "It would be my distinct pleasure," says Sir Henry. "When shall I appear?"

"About three, I should imagine. Or as near as you can make it. Bring your footman Walker. We'll find something for him. He'll need some relief from the hot day, as well."

"Three it is," replies Sir Henry, patting his ample belly with both hands.

"Just one thing ... before I forget," says Noah. "Someone inquired about you a few days ago."

Sir Henry's eyebrows rise expectantly.

Noah nods, studying Sir Henry's face for a reaction. "It was Henry Cuffe." Noah believes he detects a brief moment of concern on Sir Henry's face.

"*Who?*" asks Sir Henry blankly.

"Surely you know him," says Noah. "He's one of Essex's secretaries." Sir Henry registers no recognition. "Oh, well," says Noah, "I'm sure he'll write you if it's anything of import."

"Very like," says Sir Henry.

As Noah and Esther leave Lothbury, the relief they'd both felt with the death of Nerezza has already been tempered by something neither of them can identify.

When Noah and Esther arrive at home, he's pleased to find Marie waiting for him.

"I came to see you last evening," she says, voice full of concern, "but all they would allow me was a peek as you slept. You seemed comfortable, and Esther promised to send an emissary if there was any cause for concern. How are you feeling now?"

"Now that I look upon your beautiful face, my dear, I know that all is right with the world. I feel much better than I did yesterday at this time, when I thought I might never look upon you again."

She scowls at him. "Perhaps you've learned to trust those who love you, Noah. Promise me you shall never do any such thing alone again."

He beams at her. "I promise," he says, and hopes that the need will never again arise.

She regards him skeptically, and hands him a letter from Lord Saint Ives that arrived in his absence. Noah's pleased to read that, at his lordship's formal request, Her Majesty has ordered Monk's head removed from its pike on London Bridge and laid to rest with all Christian rites.

It's cold comfort, but better than none.

The Ames household spends the remainder of the summer of 1600 in relative peace. But near the end of August, there's a brief bustle of activity, nothing so unruly as to cause disruption of the house or family, but something important enough to portend a threat to both.

Near the end of August, the Lord Keeper Egerton, the Lord High Treasurer, and Lord Robert summon Essex to appear before them at the Lord Keeper's residence. Noah and Sir Henry are among the few invited to witness the event.

Essex stands quietly as the three dignitaries take turns reading aloud from the Queen's edict permitting Essex the freedom to go wherever he wishes, except to the Queen's court, which is the one place he *needs* to go for any hope of fiscal sustenance.

Everyone knows that the Queen's barring Essex from her court may portend the end of the private monopoly on sweet wines passed down to him years before, the revenue from which is the only thing keeping the wolf from his door. But that patent will not come up for renewal until Queen's Day in early September, and some hold out hope that Essex will return to the Queen's favor by then. The coldest cut in the edict is the Queen's advice that Essex "go into Oxfordshire, to one of his uncle's houses." At the completion of the reading, Essex informs the assembled that he will heed the Queen's advice and depart the following morning to spend some months in the country.

Before leaving the Lord Keeper's residence, Sir Henry prevails on Noah to return with him the following day to bid Essex a respectful farewell.

The Lord Keeper's house lies hard by the Thames and, by the following morning, the heat has raised an awful stench from the river.

By the time Noah and Sir Henry arrive, Essex's retinue has assembled on horseback before the Lord Keeper's house in the bright sunshine.

Sir Gelly Meyrick tips his hat familiarly to Sir Henry, and warily to Noah. Evidently, Sir Gelly expects he's escaped prosecution for his early involvement in the attempt to steal the letters from Burghley House, and credits Noah, however groundlessly, for saving his hide yet again.

Noah is dismayed to see that, mixed in among Essex's mounted retinue, are the Bennetts, both of whom avoid Noah's direct gaze. One has an arm in a sling, no doubt to aid in his convalescence from the sword wound inflicted by Chester at Burghley House. Noah wonders silently why the twins chose to switch sides, and resolves to do all in his power to bring them back to the fold.

Essex, a free man in all but the most important ways, stops and turns to Noah and Sir Henry.

"Good morning, gentlemen," says Essex.

"Good morning, your lordship," they intone together.

To Noah, he says, "Tell me, Counselor Hebrew. Do you yet counsel patience and penitence?"

Noah, who finds it unnerving to find himself engaged in conversation with Essex, bows and nods, his eyes downcast.

"Always, your lordship. It is the only way."

"You mean," says Essex, "if there *is* a way."

Noah looks into the earl's eyes and sees a countenance of sheer desperation, the look of a man at the end of his tether whose last hope is fast disappearing.

"I shall look you up when I return to London, Serjeant," says Essex. "Perhaps you will have further counsel then."

Noah bows. "It will be my privilege to confer with your lordship at that time, or at any time of your lordship's choosing."

Essex nods curtly to Sir Henry, mounts, and gallops off.

"He'll be back," says Sir Henry, evidently to reassure himself. He turns to Noah. "I trust the Queen shall renew his patent on sweet wines. What do you think?"

Though Noah is sworn to secrecy concerning deliberations with Her Majesty, he looks into his friend's eyes with such sadness that there can be no doubt of the answer.

Sir Henry, evidently surprised by Noah's tacit reply, says, "Then he has no hope." He shakes his head in dismay. "I wonder what he'll do when he returns."

Noah gazes after Essex's departing retinue.

"That I fear," says Noah.

## THE END

The series *In the Den of the English Lion* is a work of historical fiction, a sort of "what if" winter's tale, written for the reader's amusement. A great deal of research has gone into it, but it should not be relied upon for scholarly purposes, other than to excite further inquiry. Book 1, entitled *A Second Daniel*, contained a lengthy historical note covering the story through the end of the unhappy case of Roderigo Lopez. Book 2, *The Impress of Heaven*, contained no historical note, so this note is intended to cover events in both Book 2 and the present Book 3, *A Dragon in the Ashes*.

Many characters in Books 2 and 3 are fictitious, including all who are portrayed as being (or as having once been) Jews or of Jewish descent. Jonathan Hawking (now Jonathan, Lord Saint Ives) and all other barristers formerly resident at Gray's Inn are likewise fictitious, except for Francis Bacon, whose position is more or less accurately portrayed. Mistress Marie Ames is fictitious, as are the individual Yeoman Warders in the book. David "Cheerful" Killigrew is a fictitious member of the real Killigrew family. Cheerful is putatively a nephew of Lady Anne Neville, born Killigrew, who was a real person married to the equally real Sir Henry Neville.

## Book 2 – *The Impress of Heaven*

Book 2 began and concluded with a historic event, namely, the first trial of Lord Essex. But for the participation at the trial by Noah Ames and his second-chair, Arthur Arden (and but for Lord Essex's penitential costume), it is portrayed as accurately as possible in the book, as are the events that got Essex into such serious trouble.

Many of the lines spoken at the trial in the book, including those of Lord Essex, have been lifted nearly verbatim from secondary sources relying directly upon primary sources. There is disagreement among the sources on a few trivial questions, such as whether or not Lord Essex was required to kneel upon the pillow for the whole trial. It is to be hoped that the reader will defer to the author's privilege to decide such questions for narrative purposes.

The activities of the historical figures are more or less accurately portrayed, for example: Lord Mountjoy was chosen to replace Essex as head of Her Majesty's forces in Ireland. Essex had been corresponding with King James of Scotland for ten years, and the Cecils knew of it. The Act forbidding discussion of the royal Succession was real, and its provisions were much as Noah recites in the book. The Infanta was in fact the daughter of Philip the Second and was a potential contestant for the Throne of England.

Essex's (and Sir William Monson's) seafaring exploits are well documented, and accurately (if incompletely) portrayed in the book. Gelly Meyrick was indeed the functionary of Lord Essex who demanded of Sir Walter Raleigh that he refrain from taking the Port of Faial. Sir Walter nevertheless took the port, and was very nearly hanged for his trouble, his neck having been saved in substantial part by the efforts of Vice Admiral Howard, much as that gentleman reports in the book.

The business of the purloined map was entirely fictitious, as was the villainous le Loup, but they were essential to the budding romance between Jonathan Hawking and Lady Jessica, largely inspired by one of the most romantic adventure films of all time, namely, Alfred Hitchcock's *The 39 Steps*.

Augustine Phillips, the player befriended by Jonathan and Lady Jessica at the Rose & Crown at Bridgwater, was real, although whether he ever visited (or even had) relatives in Falmouth is unknown. Master Phillips will appear again in Book 4 engaging in historically accurate action, namely, cagily explaining to the authorities how it came about that, on the eve of the Essex Rebellion, the Lord Chamberlain's Men performed Shakespeare's *Richard the Second*, an already dated play in which a weak and unpopular King of England is deposed by a popular nobleman.

## Book 3 – *A Dragon in the Ashes*

As depicted in the book, Katarzyna Weiglowa was burned in Krakow for violating the Church's tenets prohibiting "Judaizing." The spoken lines attributed to both her and her inquisitor in the book are as translated and reported by secondary sources. As Noah is fictitious, so are his parents Naomi and David, his protector Yetta, and his cousins Beth and Esther.

Bona Sforza was in fact Queen of Lithuania-Poland, was married to the tolerant King Sigismund the Old, and was mother of that king's successor. Her eventual murder by poison at the hands of her trusted advisor Gian Lorenzo Pappacoda (*pace*, Yetta) after her return to Bari is popularly believed to have been committed on behalf of King Philip the Second of Spain, to dispense with the king's obligation to repay his debts to her.

The conversation in the book about the "Night of Errors" on which *The Comedy of Errors* debuted at Gray's Inn in the absence of its putative author, William Shakespeare, is accurate, except for the embellishment concerning the interference by the ersatz Sovereign in the evening's dramatic performance.

Although the particular attempt to poison Queen Elizabeth depicted in the book is fictitious, in fact such attempts were made, and some came very close to fruition.

Henri Valua is accurately depicted in the book as first ascending to the throne of Lithuania-Poland, then resigning it to take the throne of France as Henri the Third.

Except for the involvement of the fictitious Nerezza and Dorsay, the assassination of the Huguenot Admiral Coligny and the massacre of his co-religionists is accurately set forth in the book. The madness and death of King Charles the Ninth of France are reputed to have occurred on account of a consumptive illness. Even from the remove of several hundred years, however, the explanation is less than satisfying and, at the very least, seems incomplete. Monk and his nameless mother are both fictitious.

As rumors grew of Essex's imminent release from detention at the home of the Lord Keeper, many of his supporters took up residence at Drury House, which was the London residence of Essex's friend, the Earl of Southampton.

Rumors circulated that the Queen's most trusted minister, Sir Robert Cecil, favored the Infanta for the Succession. To the extent such rumors were credited at the time, it could only have been because Sir Robert Cecil was believed to desire an alternative to Essex's choice of King James of Scotland. The Infanta's attenuated claim to the English Throne is accurately explained by Sir Robert in the book.

Francis Walsingham was indeed serving as Her Majesty's Ambassador to France at the time of the Huguenot massacre, and his experience as a known protestant during that horrendous event was even more harrowing than described in the book. Although Mister Walsingham corresponded with Lord Burghley and several other Englishmen around that time, the letters central to the book, referring to the Tarot Cards, the identity of Admiral Coligny's assailants, and the death of King Charles, are fictitious.

The Percy brothers were real knights. Lord Grey, who interrupts Noah's interview of the Percys in the book, had in fact been asked by Southampton during the Islands Voyage to take an oath of loyalty to Essex, which he vehemently declined to take. Later, serving under Essex in the Irish campaign, Lord Grey was locked up for one day on grounds that he'd attacked the rebels without authorization from his superiors, which offended him deeply and resulted in his settled hatred of Essex and Southampton. Both the Percys and Lord Grey will appear engaging in factually accurate activities in Book 4.

Nerezza's discussion of the Wheel of Fortune is accurate. His rather bizarre view of the Chosen People's prospects for an afterlife has been around for centuries.

Burghley House is accurately described in the book, but the Battle of Burghley House is fictitious, as is the Herculean effort made in the book to organize Lord Burghley's papers on a moment's notice.

The following items concerning Sir Walter Raleigh are presented in historically accurate manner in the book: Sir Walter's discussion of archaic techniques of locksmithing, his forbidden marriage to Bess

Throckmorton and the resultant interruption in his tenure as head of
the Yeomen Warders and the imprisonment of husband and wife in the
Tower, and his naval adventure that eventually freed them both. Sir
Walter's (and the other characters') descriptions of the dilapidated
Cambridge Castle are accurate also, albeit somewhat disrespectful.

Henry Cuffe was one of Lord Essex's secretaries, wrote the text
attributed to him in the book, and sent Sir Henry Neville the fateful
letter that awaited him upon his return to England. The Stationer's
Register is accurately described in the book, although the reader will
need to await Book 4 to learn why Sir Henry Neville would have a
receipt for several plays registered with the Stationer's Register a few
days after his return from France.

**Sneak Peek at Upcoming Book 4 of**
*In the Den of the English Lion*

# *ALL THE MEN AS MAD AS HE*

by Neal Roberts

*Hamlet:*     Ay, marry, why was [Hamlet] sent into England?

*Gravedigger:*     Why, because he was mad: he shall recover his wits there; or, if he do not, it's no great matter there.

*Hamlet:*     Why?

*Gravedigger:*     'Twill not be seen in him there; there the men are as mad as he.

# CHAPTER 1

LONDON, ENGLAND
AUGUST 31, 1600

**AFTER MIDNIGHT,** cloaked and cowled all in black, the conspirators quietly converge on the courtyard outside a little church adjoining a cathedral. Though some of the dark figures approach through the stone arch to the west and others from sleepy London town to the east, they assemble single-mindedly, facing each other in a tight circle.

Esther awaits their arrival crouched down in a dark corner at a safe remove. She shudders, looks down at her costume and vaguely wonders how she could be wearing nothing but a thin night rail. She vaguely recalls retiring to her room at the Ames's house, but nothing after that. The chill deepens to the kind of bone-chilling cold that comes just before a ghost appears. And it seems already to have spread to the conspirators.

"God, it's flippin' freezin' out 'ere!" blurts one of the conspirators, chafing his sides. "Didn't anybuddy tell the Good Lord it's summertime? Mebbe He'd send us some heat."

Another conspirator, much taller than the first, snarls at him. "What makes ye think God would do *anythin'* for the likes o' you? Not bloody likely, after tonight," he muses. "Keep it down. We can't afford to be seen or heard out here." He points in Esther's general direction. "Here they come."

Esther nearly gasps aloud, but then realizes that he's pointing to two tardy conspirators approaching together from the east. Both are short. One is plump, the other quite thin.

The tall one quietly addresses those already arrived. "If any o' you gentlemen ain't got the stomach for it, just leave it to me. I'll take care of 'em both meself if I need to. *Christ,* it's cold!"

Esther's shuddering so hard, she wonders that her teeth haven't chattered, and prays they don't start now.

"'Ey," says the tall one, roughly greeting the newcomers as they come close enough to hear. "Took yer sweet time about it."

"We had to await an opportune moment to get away," says the plump newcomer, in a far more cultured voice than that of his inquisitor. "You wouldn't want our new friend here accidentally revealing anything by disappearing out of turn, would you?"

"Nah. He wouldn't reveal anythin' *by accident,*" says another of the early arrivals as the newcomers join in their circle.

"What's *that* s'posed to mean?" asks the thinner of the newcomers. "I got away quick as I could!"

"Word has it," says the tall one, "that the Tower Guard's caught wind of what's goin' on. You two wouldn't know 'ow that 'appened, now, *would* ye?"

The newcomers seem startled and defensive. "Well, they didn't find out from us!" the plump one protests.

The tall one steps toward them menacingly. "'*Course* they didn't," he says sarcastically, glancing about at the other early arrivals, as though to assay his support. "Naaah! Weren't *you!*"

With the word *you,* the other conspirators thrust the newcomers to the center of the black circle, which swallows them whole. Blades flash in the moonlight, and the tall one stabs each of the newcomers in the abdomen. The others quickly join in a murderous frenzy, cutting them all over their bodies: neck, belly, back, legs.

The victims gasp in protest, too surprised to do anything but raise their hands to no avail, and gape in horror at their own butchering. Blood flows freely to the ground.

Esther feels the urgent need to cry out, to call for help, but finds that all she can do is whimper in horror.

"No, no," the victims repeat in disbelief. When the assailants step back into their former circle, the victims look briefly into each other's eyes and collapse to the ground in horror, the thin one motionless.

The plump one squirms in agony a few moments. "You bastards will pay for this!" he grunts. "Wait till my brother—"

"Yer brother'll be *joinin'* ye in just a bit," says the tall one, and stabs him in the throat, silencing him at once. Blood spurts over the pavement. "Give 'im my best wishes for all eternity."

With the mention of eternity, the other assassins recoil in horror from the bloody scene, as though they'd forgotten that their evil will follow them past the grave.

In the blink of an eye, killers and victims disappear.

Though Esther's now standing at precisely the same spot where she'd formerly crouched, it's become an overcast winter's day, and she's dressed in the new cloak Mistress Ames just bought for her. But she's still so very cold—what she's come to think of as *unnaturally* cold.

She's surrounded by pandemonium, a scene filled with armed men loosely organized into two opposing groups, though neither side wears any sort of uniform.

One group, with the little church at its back, appears to be comprised of gentlemen with their swords drawn. At its center, a tall thin man with dark red hair and beard desperately pleads with them to avoid fighting.

The opposing group stands athwart the stone archway, defending it—or perhaps preventing the swordsmen from passing through. It's a poorly armed contingent, with most members lacking so much as a sword, instead wielding pointed sticks and partisans to keep the swordsmen at bay.

Immediately before the arch stands a tall young blond man with his back turned to Esther. As he exhorts the pikemen to avoid bloodshed, an opposing swordsman runs him through from the rear, inflicting a ghastly wound. The blond man's head jerks backward as his torso moves forward with the blow. He falls dead to the ground, his face still out of Esther's view. She whimpers to think it might be David Killigrew, with whom she's fallen so deeply in love.

*"Esther!"*

"*Esther!* Wake *up*, dear!"

The voice of a mature woman comes to her from somewhere outside the bloody scene. She feels herself being shaken. "Wake up, dear." It's the soothing voice of Mistress Ames.

With effort, Esther lets the bloody scene go, and opens her eyes. She's relieved to find herself lying in her own bed. Mistress Ames is seated next to her looking quite worried, while everyone else in the house crowds the doorway of her room, looking anxious and rumpled in their bedclothes. The pale glow of dawn seeps through the windows.

Mistress Ames's only daughter, a raven-haired beauty on the cusp of womanhood, breaks the silence. "Why is it so *cold* in here, Serjeant Ames?"

"Yes," adds her brother of nearly the same age, "one could hang meat in this room with no fear of spoilage."

Serjeant Ames looks to Mistress Ames's eldest son. "Stephen," he says in his most serious voice, "please escort your brother and sister back up to their rooms." He turns to reassure the younger ones before they're led off. "Everything will be made clear to you later. Meanwhile, *don't* mention this—especially the *cold* – to anyone outside the family."

The two youngest moan in complaint, but turn to go. While they'd clearly like an explanation now, they know better than to resist when Noah speaks in his serious voice.

Stephen steals a parting look at Esther, his youthful face etched with concern, and reluctantly escorts his younger siblings upstairs.

Marie places her hand on Esther's forehead. "You feel warmer now." She lifts the blanket to feel Esther's bare feet. "Much better now," she says with relief.

For his part, Noah is also relieved to see that her feet are perfectly clean and unbruised, proving that she hasn't been sleepwalking, as Jessica was wont to do in childhood, much to her father's alarm.

A few minutes later Esther is sitting up in bed. Though the late summer's warmth has quickly returned to the room, she holds a small bowl of hot water in her hands, given her by Mistress Ames. Esther dutifully sips it from time to time while Marie looks on from her perch on the bed.

Noah has dressed hurriedly, and now stands by the bed uncertain what to do. He'd planned on seeking out Sir Walter this morning, but he's concerned about his young cousin's health, although to all appearances it's as robust as ever. He's also troubled by the visions that came to Esther in the dreams that she's now recounted twice.

Both deadly scenes were set at precisely the same location, but Noah struggles to discern anything else they might have in common. They took place at different times of day; one on a summer night, the other in winter's harsh daylight. Perhaps they were just dreams. After all, the girl probably has ordinary dreams sometimes, the same as everyone else. But, even if she does, he doesn't believe these dreams were ordinary, not even for her.

Marie turns to him. "There's no reason for you to remain here, dear. Esther is feeling just fine." She turns to the girl. "Isn't that right, dear?"

Esther, who's taking a sip from her bowl, smiles wanly up at Noah, and turns to Marie. "Yes. Thank you so much for all the care you've given me. Both you and Serjeant Ames." Her pretty face breaks out into a broad smile.

"Yes," says Noah. "I may as well go."

"Serjeant Ames," says Marie hesitantly, "may I speak with you a moment first—in your study?" She takes a parting look at her ward, kisses her on the forehead, and follows Noah to the study, where she leaves the door open a crack, apparently so she can hear if Esther calls.

"I suppose," says Marie once they're alone, "that there are several sites in London fitting Esther's description of the place where she saw those terrible events."

Noah shakes his head confidently. "No." He raises his index finger. "One only."

"Are you quite certain?" she asks skeptically. "It's long been common practice in England to erect a small church adjoining a great cathedral."

"So I've learned," replies Noah. "The little church is run by the parish priest, the cathedral by the bishopric."

Marie nods. "But how can you be sure which church she saw?"

"By the *gate* she mentioned," he says.

"But London has several gates."

Noah shakes his head. "In London, only one little church adjoining a cathedral overlooks a city gate." He hears a horsedrawn cart pull up somewhere nearby, but pays it no mind.

Marie arches an eyebrow quizzically. "Which gate?" she asks.

"Ludgate," he replies. "Saint Gregory's church by Saint Paul's overlooks it. The events in Esther's dreams took place—if *ever* they took place, or ever *shall*—in that little square between Saint Gregory's and Ludgate. I've forgotten its name, if it even has one."

There's a sudden pounding at the door.

"Serjeant Ames!" says an urgent voice outside. "Serjeant Ames! 'Tis I, Arthur Arden. Please come to the door, sir, if you can hear me!"

Startled, Noah races to the door. He opens it, and the chill of early morning sweeps in.

Arthur, clad in barrister's robes, seems overcome with anxiety.

"What is it, Arthur?" asks Noah abruptly. Then, hoping to put the young man at ease, he adds: "Have you time to come inside?"

"Much as I would like to see everyone, sir," says Arthur hesitantly, "I'm afraid we're losing time. I've made a rather grisly discovery which I expect will be of concern to you in your duties at the Tower. Come, sir. Please take a seat up front with me and I'll tell you along the way what I've found."

Noah kisses Marie, who watches as he climbs up to the driver's bench. He turns to Arthur with concern. "What have you found?" he asks.

Arthur takes the reins. "Two corpses, I'm afraid. They appear to have bled out on the pavement before I arrived a short while ago. I'd had trouble sleeping, so I'd risen early to go pray."

"*Where* were you going to pray?" asks Noah.

At first Arthur appears mystified by the question, but then realizes it's not as irrelevant as first it seemed. "I was heading for Saint Gregory by Saint Paul's."

Noah's mind starts to buzz. "Is that where you found the bodies?" asks Noah, mindful not to let his suspicions get the better of him. To avoid the appearance that he had foreknowledge of the crime, he adds, "Were the bodies *inside* the church?"

"No, sir. I hadn't a chance to enter before I found the bodies outside, on Bowyer's Row."

*Bowyer's Row.* "That's the street that leads to Ludgate?"

"Aye, sir," says Arthur, "you've passed through there many times, I'm sure, though—not to pray, of course."

Noah answers quickly to save Arthur from the awkwardness that all Christians seem to feel in referring to Noah's Hebrew faith. "Nor to buy an archer's bow," he says. "Of course I've passed through there many times. I just never learned the street's name. How were the men dressed when they died?"

"All in black, sir, though they're so covered in blood, it was hard to find a clean place on their clothing."

As Bowyer's Row comes into view, they find it deserted, and still covered with a fine icy mist that obscures the ground. The corpses, partly obscured, appear as two heaps of bloody black rags carelessly discarded onto the pavement.

Noah wonders what it all means. Why would Esther have seen this crime, in particular? Does it have some connection to her? He wonders whether the crime or its solution might not affect her in some way. Perhaps if the crime is solved, it will reveal something helpful to her. Perhaps if he *fails* to solve it, she'll somehow suffer injury. Or, conversely, perhaps it's *meant* to go unsolved, and he might injure her by solving it. Either way, he feels precisely the same as he does whenever such questions are raised by Esther's strange gift. Completely befuddled. Fortunately, he has no choice but to plod on.

Noah looks to Arthur. "Have you been here before, I mean so early in the morning?"

"A few times," says Arthur, as he slows the horses down to assure a safe approach to the west end of Saint Gregory's.

"Is there always an icy mist like this?" asks Noah.

"Sometimes in late autumn," replies Arthur, drawing the cart to a halt. He gazes toward the eastern horizon. "As you can see, the rising sun strikes Saint Gregory's, which casts its shadow over this courtyard." He pauses a moment and shakes his head. "But there's usually no icy mist at this time of year. It's just too warm."

Noah silently wonders whether it's so cold now merely because Esther was here. He shakes his head dismissively at his own thoughts. She *wasn't* here physically, as shown by her unsullied feet. In what sense *might* she have been here? Though he tries his best to dismiss such thoughts as mystical nonsense, he can't help but locate the corner where Esther, or her spirit, might have cowered in wait for the conspirators. It shows no sign of her former presence … but for the icy mist.

He clears his head and follows Arthur to the first of the two bodies lying in the square. As they reach the nearer one, Noah observes that it's slight of frame and surrounded by a pool of glistening blood. The face looks familiar.

Arthur's been watching Noah, and evidently discerns the look of recognition. "I've seen him, too," says Arthur. "It took me till I was nearly at your house to remember where I'd seen him."

Noah shrugs. "Where?"

"If I'm right," says Arthur, "he's one of Her Majesty's wardrobe servants."

Noah bends down for a better look. He remembers this man's face only vaguely, as he would that of an actor who's appeared many times upon the stage, always in the guise of someone's page or servant, his few spoken lines always self-effacing, always strictly in keeping with his supposed trade. A face meant to be looked at, but not seen. As for any information to be culled from the grievous wounds, Noah will need to attend the examination to be conducted by the coroner, who'll no doubt show up at any moment.

Arthur has already moved on to the second blood-drenched body, this one a bit stockier than the first. As Noah approaches, he asks Arthur, "Did you recognize this one, as well?"

Arthur responds by mournfully pointing his chin at the man's face, half of which is visible. The other half is pressed firmly onto the pavement, as though the victim, having lain down here for an awkward night's rest, had mistaken the street for a pillow. Noah squats by the victim for a better view of his face.

"Do *you* recognize him?" asks Arthur.

Noah sighs. "How could I forget someone who risked his own life to save mine own, however long ago? This is one of the Bennett twins." As he says those words, he remembers Esther's retelling of the last words heard by this victim, the import of which was that his brother would soon follow him in death. Noah wonders whether there's anything he can do to avoid that prophecy's coming true, as he has no idea where the other Bennett twin might be found. "I saw them together just a few days ago," says Noah, "when they left London as part of Lord Essex's retinue."

"That was short service!" Arthur says bitterly.

Noah points to the knife in the victim's hand. "Let's make sure to recover that, once the coroner's through with it." Arthur nods silently.

On impulse, Noah walks to the corner where he imagines Esther stood as she watched the murders, and turns to take in precisely the perspective she had in her dream.

As a hearse clops up to the scene unbidden, Noah glances toward Ludgate, wondering which blond man will die of the cowardly thrust foreseen by Esther. Or perhaps it already befell some poor bastard on a winter's afternoon long ago. Or perhaps, perhaps … *perhaps*. Such wild conjecture exasperates him. He sighs.

It all seems so much madness.

## END OF THE SNEAK PEEK

Visit www.authornealroberts.com
to find out when this book releases.

# ABOUT THE AUTHOR

Neal Roberts and his wife live on Long Island, New York, where they have two grown children. Neal is a practicing attorney and adjunct law professor, and spends as much time as possible researching his next novel while enhancing his lawyer's pallor. When he's not writing Elizabethan politico-legal novels, practicing law, or teaching, he's an editor of an international peer-reviewed publication in the field of intellectual property law. Neal is also an avid student of Elizabethan literature and politics, which subjects form the basis of his first novel, A Second Daniel. His analysis of Shakespeare's Sonnet 121 has been extensively cited by some of the most important authorities seeking to identify the true author of the poems and plays attributed to William Shakespeare. Connect with Neal at his website (authornealroberts.com) or on Facebook (Facebook.com/authornealroberts) and join his mailing list (bitly.com/FreeHistorical) to know when upcoming books release and to grab your free short.

## ALSO BY NEAL ROBERTS

*A Second Daniel*, In the Den of the English Lion, Book 1 (Historical Mystery): London 1558. An orphan from a far-off land is renamed "Noah Ames," and given every advantage the English Crown can bestow.

London 1592. Now an experienced barrister, Noah witnesses what appears to be a botched robbery outside the Rose Theater, a crime he soon suspects to be part of a plot against Queen Elizabeth herself. Steadfast in his loyalty to the Queen, Noah must use every bit of his knowledge and skill to lure her most disloyal subject onto the only battlefield where Noah has the advantage ... a court of law – though in doing so he risks public exposure of his darkest secret, a secret so shocking that its revelation could cost him everything: the love of the only woman who can offer him happiness, his livelihood ... even his life.

*The Impress of Heaven*, In the Den of the English Lion, Book 2 (Historical Mystery): LONDON 1600. When the Earl of Essex is removed from command and placed under arrest for reaching a forbidden truce with the Irish rebels, Serjeant Noah Ames reluctantly accepts a commission to investigate the earl's fitness for command, and the two are pitted against each other once again. Meanwhile, Noah's beautiful daughter, Lady Jessica, has sought to remarry into the nobility, but events have thus far frustrated her plans. One day, Noah attends a briefing where the Queen's new commander displays maps of English military positions in Ireland. Noah's suspicions are aroused when he sees that one map is missing a watermark appearing on all the others. When he informs his young barrister friend Jonathan of his concern, he inadvertently sets in motion events that throw Jonathan and Lady Jessica together on a journey across England into ever greater peril.

*A Dragon in the Ashes*, In the Den of the English Lion, Book 3 (Historical Mystery): LONDON 1600. When an attempt is made on Queen

Elizabeth's life, Serjeant Noah Ames races to her rescue, then sets out to identify the culprit among a band of foreigners who've newly arrived from the Continent to join with the seditious Lord Essex. In the course of his investigation, Noah uncloaks an unmitigated rein of evil that has resulted in the murders of kings, queens, and religious minorities ... and which now threatens Noah's life for reasons no one would ever suspect. Will Noah pay the ultimate price for forgetting that the past is never past?